A BAD STRAIN

Dana thought the hospital looked eerily empty and quiet given the seriousness of the situation. ICU appeared to be closed and there were no medical personnel or auxiliary people in the corridors. No candy stripers and cleaners, no smell of breakfast cooking, no flower delivery people.

"What's going on?" she asked.

"It's a nightmare," Sam said. "The hospital itself is closed, except for admissions." He fixed his gaze on her. What are you doing here?"

"I came to see Jack Dowel. How many people are sick?"

"We've got six new cases and St. Joseph's has four. The hospital is turning ICU into a quarantine room for people with pneumonic plague. They've cleared out half the patients and sent the non-critical patients home. We've called in all our medical staff. I was due for a four-day break, and now I have to work straight through. We're on day and night." Sam lowered his voice and looked around the deserted hallway. "This is a bad strain." He added in a whisper, "It might be deliberate. . . ."

THE LONE STAR
PLAGUE

KATE BIRCH

LEISURE BOOKS   NEW YORK CITY

*This book is dedicated to all those affected by
the August 1998 bombing of the
American Embassy in Nairobi, Kenya.*

LEISURE BOOKS ®

September 2004

Published by

Dorchester Publishing Co., Inc.
200 Madison Avenue
New York, NY 10016

This book was originally published in hardcover under the title
Spring of Fever.

ISBN 0-8439-5424-8

Printed in the United States of America.

Visit us on the web at www.dorchesterpub.com.

THE LONE STAR
PLAGUE

Friday

Chapter 1

On the last Friday of his life, Dudley Shaw woke up sick. He watched the morning news on CNN and felt worse. During the night, the U.S. bombed Mogadishu and bodies lay like driftwood in the sand. The dawn skies were smoking. Dudley read a warning that the pictures were graphic and could be disturbing. He picked up the remote and turned off the TV.

Beside him on the couch, Bingo stretched and rolled onto his back, feet up in the air. Dudley rubbed the hound's chin. "You ready to go, boy?" On Monday, Dudley was taking the trip he had waited for all of his life.

Bingo wagged his tail, shaking his hind end.

Dudley stretched out, raised his legs and shot a can of Budweiser off the coffee table. He lifted the pizza box lid with his big toe. The last piece was gone. "Bingo, did you eat that?"

Bingo raised a paw and batted the air.

Just as well, Dudley thought, for he had vowed to eat better. Gingerly he touched a lump under his left armpit. Jesus, now it was the size of a pecan nut. It seemed bigger and harder to him this morning than it had last night. Whatever it was, was growing fast. A high rate of growth. That was what the doctors told his father when he had lung cancer. He had been sixty-five, the same age Dudley was now. A month later he was dead.

Dudley rubbed his dog's chest and waited for the uneasiness in his stomach to pass. He wasn't going to think about it. Instead, he checked his lengthy to-do list. In two days he was leaving. Nothing would stop him.

The first thing he had to do was wash the car. He could see her out the living room window, under the pecan tree, his '57 T-bird, gleaming in the slanting sunlight. Last week he'd taken her to the car wash to have her waxed and polished, but since then it had rained and Ladybird was splattered with mud. He would wash her before it got too hot.

Dudley stood up. He felt dizzy and put a hand to the wall to steady himself. He had a bad headache and his skin felt tight. The lump under his arm burned. He took three aspirin and hoped that would suffice.

Then he called Bingo and went outside. He stood for a moment on the porch to acclimatize to the heat. It must have been eighty degrees already, though it was not yet nine, not yet May. Summer had come early to Texas.

The weather patterns were changing. Scientists could argue all they liked, but any dummy who lived any length of time could see that the weather today wasn't what it used to be. This year it was too hot, there was too much rain. Already the fleas were bad. Beside him, Bingo propelled a hind leg, scratched an ear.

"Come on, boy." Dudley went around the side of the house, grabbed a bucket and turned on the faucet. Bingo was heading for the woods. He hated to be bathed.

"Not you—Ladybird," Dudley called out, but Bingo didn't look back.

When the bucket was full, Dudley lugged it across the

mucky lawn. The long arms of the sun stretched across the field and strangled him. The bucket was heavy and his breathing was hard. It was 9:00 A.M. and he felt exhausted and worn out.

He reached the car and dropped the bucket, water slopping over the side. He ran his hand across Ladybird's sleek back fin and felt better. She was lemon yellow and shining with chrome. He rested his cheek on the sun-warmed roof. Her surface was smooth and hot and she felt solid and strong beneath his weight, a beauty aging well. He loved his car. Something Nancy, his ex-wife, never got. You have more feeling for that car than for me, she used to say, and Dudley guessed it was so.

He set to work. Bingo reappeared, but kept his distance. Dudley squeezed the sponge and rubbed Ladybird down. Tracks of mud streaked down her flank. The strong sun reflected off the chrome and hurt his eyes. It was too bright, too hot; no gulf wind blew. His head pounded and his underarm ached.

Dudley dropped the sponge and shrugged off his shirt. Perspiration soaked his skin. He pressed his palms against his forehead to counter the pressure building inside. Before him, Bingo rose and loped toward the woods. He stopped at the verge and stared at the trees, head raised, one ear high, and the fur on the ridge of his back raised. He growled loudly.

"What is it, boy?"

Bingo turned, but would not come.

Dudley shivered. There were no clouds but the sun seemed dimmed and far away. He was cold and too sick to finish the job. He would do it later. He bent down to grab his shirt and his head screamed. When he stood, the ground tilted under his feet. Ahead the house shimmered. Or was it him? His body shook and his teeth chattered. The pecan tree was a hundred feet from the house, but the distance seemed like miles. He took a step, then a rest, then another step, and minute by minute he hauled himself to the house where Bingo stood panting.

Inside, the screen door slammed behind them. Past the kitchen, the hallway leading to his bedroom looked endless. Dudley tottered to the couch, flopped down, and gasped for breath. He felt a choking heat on his face and tried to pry open his eyes but could not. From far away he heard a dog's mournful howl.

Chapter 2

Dana Sparks was finishing a paper for the *Journal of Immunology* when the phone rang. Her new boss needed to see her immediately. Of course he couldn't send her an email or say what he wanted over the phone; he had to waste her time in person.

She left her lab and strolled down the hall, staring out the windows. It was April 24, the last day of the spring semester at Duane University and she could feel the change in the air.

In the main office of the Department of Immunology and Microbiology, Dr. TJ McCoy stood waiting. He was a gray man, with gray eyes, gray skin and gray hair. He wore an olive colored military uniform. "Dr. Sparks, I'm glad you could make it."

As if it had been a request. "I managed to drop what I was doing."

McCoy threw back his shoulders. He was stocky, five-ten—Dana's height—and their eyes were level. He was sixty years old and looked every day of it. He had suffered a heart attack in the fall and was forced from the military, where he had spent forty years planning wars. He beckoned her into his office.

In the room it was winter, dark and cold. The curtains were drawn, a floor fan blew and a window air conditioning unit hummed.

"Sit."

Always the imperative. Commands Dana hated to follow even as she did so. They faced one another across his clean and polished desk.

"I'm reassigning parking spaces," he said.

She blinked. He got her down here for this?

"Any comments?" He tapped his fingers on his desk. His nails were meticulously filed. A silver bracelet engraved with the misspelled word 'Dady' slipped down his thick wrist. His wedding ring was the size and color of a thimble. "I have a new parking space. How do you expect me to respond?"

"Let's just say, you aren't amenable to change."

That left her astonished. It was unreasonable change that she minded. "Where is my new space?"

"At the other end of the lot."

That wasn't so bad. "Okay."

"On the other side of the building."

She raised her eyebrows.

"Near the farm."

"What?" That was a mile away. "I might as well park at home and walk."

"Up to you."

"I can't believe you'd give me a space so remote."

"Look, parking is tight. We need to make room for cars near the veterinary clinic. Everyone has to move. Well, not tenured staff of course."

He raised his eyes but made no eye contact. Instead he looked over her shoulder, past her, as if her chair was empty and she was already gone. She needed tenure by June or she was out.

Was he trying to tell her something? Had he already made up his mind to let her go? Could he do that after tenure had been promised? Though, as he liked to remind her, not by him, but by his predecessor, Brian Boswell, who died on Christmas Eve in a car accident. McCoy had been dragged out of retirement to take his place.

Things had gone badly from the start. McCoy's doctorate was in physics, but he'd been an administrator most of his life. His specialty as far as Dana could tell was war and fiscal efficiency. His post was supposed to be temporary, but since he arrived, McCoy had cut positions, cut research and imposed unreasonable rules. Where his power came from, Dana didn't know.

"Okay, fine," she said now. "If that's all, I have work to do." She glanced at his clean and empty desktop. "I know you're busy, but have you found the time to sign the form for the grant extension?" It was a letter of support for three more years of research. She was finishing a three-year, million-dollar grant and had written a proposal for an extension. A letter of support had been signed by his predecessor, but McCoy was dragging his feet.

"I have a problem with it," he said.

"Excuse me?"

"I'm not sure the research is necessary."

"You're not sure." Who was he to decide that? She sat forward in her chair. "A resurgence of the plague could present enormous problems. There—"

He cut her off. "There are antibiotics against the plague."

"The plague bacteria are becoming resistant. Recently, a sixteen-year-old boy in Madagascar nearly died because the antibiotics didn't work."

"You have your monoclonal vaccine. That should suffice. So long as people aren't guinea pigs."

He smiled thinly at his joke. During the initial testing of the monoclonal vaccine, all species save one had responded well. Guinea pigs had problems with the vaccine.

Dana glossed over that now. "The monoclonal vaccine is passive. We need an active vaccine. Something that endures." She raised her hands for emphasis.

"I think there are more relevant health concerns."

"Dr. McCoy, the research was already approved."

He tapped his fingers on the desk again. "Not by me."

"I've spent three years working on this."

"And you've done well. Perhaps it's time to move on."

Another veiled remark? She knew there was little point in arguing with him and stood up.

McCoy stood too, at ease, hands slung around his back, the shiny brass buttons on his blazer strained. "By the way," he said, as he appraised her with a sweeping glance of his eye. "Where is your lab coat?"

On the last day of the semester she had dressed casually in beige jeans, a button down shirt and cowboy boots. "In the lab," she said.

"According to the compendium, section sixteen, lab coats are mandatory whilst at work." McCoy reached down, opened a desk drawer and retrieved his heavy compendium, which outlined, in excruciating detail, all of his new rules. He flipped through the pages and stopped near the end. Jabbed at a line with his finger. "A lab coat must be worn at all times by all faculty."

"I wear a lab coat in the quarantine facility," Dana said. "Lab coats used there have to stay there. That's a rule too."

McCoy's face tightened and his eyes narrowed. Beads of sweat shone through his buzz cut. He said, "You might leave a lab coat in your quarantine room, keep another in your office."

"Right," Dana said, but why wear a lab coat to sit at a desk. "I'll keep that in mind."

She walked to the door, preempting McCoy's, "Dismissed."

Outside in the hallway, the sunlight was blinding. Hands shoved in the front pockets of her jeans, Dana strode to her lab. It was too much. McCoy had been here three months, yet he could get rid of her. Interim or not, he would chair the tenure committee that would decide her future. A shake of his head and she would be gone. It wasn't fair. She had been in Duane eighteen years, half of her life. She thought she would grow old here, but that was before the coming of McCoy.

She reached the end of the hallway and entered her lab, walked through a shaft of sunlight to her office and sat down. She wouldn't go easily. She would make it as difficult for him as she could. She stared at the van Gogh print above her desk that served in the place of a window. *Starry Night* was the painter's view from an asylum window. When van Gogh stared into the night, he saw light in the darkness. In stationary objects, he caught the suggestion of inherent movement and flow. She liked the print because it was so unscientific. Nothing black and white or pragmatic about it, and more going on than the eye could see. There was magic.

At times, Dana caught sight of it in her life. When she looked back on events and all that happened, she thought there had to be a force of good on her side, a force that watched out for her, protected her and helped her succeed. It was magic, but where was it now?

She sat back in her chair and stared at the stars in the print. If she got her grant, and another million dollars, McCoy wouldn't easily be able to refuse her tenure. If she didn't get the grant, she would have to leave. It would look bad on her record, not getting tenure. What would her mother say? *I told you so. You should have taken Family Studies and learned how to find a man and be a wife*. Her father would say nothing, which was worse than anything he could say.

She wouldn't let it happen. If she had to leave, she'd need leverage to secure another position. If she could show an active vaccine was possible, doors would open. She would get the grant and take it with her. All she needed was preliminary proof and with her technician's help, she'd get it. From her small office fridge, Dana retrieved an ampule labeled *Agent X* that contained clear amber fluid. She sat at her desk, eating an apple and making a calculation that would equate a mouse and a man.

Chapter 3

The phone in McCoy's office rang soon after Dana Sparks left. McCoy picked up and heard the frantic voice of the manager of the Lone Star Heritage Hotel.

"Did you hear about the bombing of Mogadishu?" the manager asked.

"Of course," McCoy said. He rose early to watch the story unfolding on the morning news. It pained him greatly that he was not a part of the response, for he personally knew the four-star general who briefed the press. On TV, McCoy caught a glimpse of his old life, a life that was no longer his.

"Already, there's talk of retaliation," the manager said. "Some Islamic faction issued a decree. It was on CNN. What if they bomb my hotel? I've got two hundred guests on the way."

Including the United States' vice president, Rich Rutherford, who was coming in less than a week to deliver the convocation address. Rutherford was an old friend from West Point and McCoy was heading the team planning his visit. Though he was not in charge of security, it was never far from McCoy's mind. "Did the hotel receive a specific death threat against the vice president?"

"Threats have been made," the manager said, in a high whine. "It's no secret the VP will be here. What if the hotel is a target?"

What if. Hysterical words in McCoy's view. "Look, we'll get together with the FBI and discuss security. I'll set it up." Already an advance team from Virginia was in town and McCoy had been working closely with Barry Ackerman, the FBI agent in charge. Ackerman was young, too young in McCoy's view, to realize the weight of his responsibility. McCoy was holding his hand, guiding him along. If there was a threat, they would get more agents. If Ackerman didn't have the clout to authorize it, McCoy would make some calls and it would be done. He phoned Ackerman and set up a two o'clock meeting.

Only now there was a conflict. At 2:00 P.M. McCoy was scheduled to deliver a lecture on biological warfare to seniors in molecular biology. McCoy wanted new blood in his department and was looking for promising graduates. He wanted anyone interested in war.

Who would give the lecture in his place? McCoy ran down his list. The problem was there was no one in the department capable of it. The Department of Immunology and Microbiology dealt primarily with disease. But that would soon change. Once the university's finances improved, the president of the university had promised McCoy his own department in the College of Biological Science. Called Human Health, McCoy's department would contain a small, specialized unit dedicated to research in biological and chemical warfare. When McCoy left the Veterinary College he would take with him those researchers who could contribute to his vision.

In the meantime, McCoy's mandate was to restore discipline to a department run amok. He was given free reign to turn the department around, get rid of "dead wood" as he saw fit. The department was in economic ruin. The year had begun with a deficit of half a million dollars. The former chairman might have been a pleasant, happy-go-lucky guy, but the department had suffered under his tutelage. Brian Boswell spent money he did not have. He had lived off grants not yet approved. He allowed his staff to run wild.

Dana Sparks was a case in point. She could be good. She had a strong publishing record, many students and a demonstrated ability to secure funding. A lot of funding. By most accounts, she was hard working and well liked. Yet her attitude was insufferable. She refused to recognize his authority. He was the man in charge and there would be no lone wolves on his watch. McCoy had dealt with people like her before. Though he had never lived on a farm, he reckoned it to breaking a horse. You let the beast know who was boss. You didn't do that by being soft or reasonable. You hit and you hit hard, over and over, until the spirit broke and submitted to outside direction. If that didn't work, you shot the horse.

He reached for the phone. Dr. Sparks would give the lecture on his behalf. He called her office and received no answer. After scrawling a short note explaining what he wished, McCoy hand-carried it down to her lab. He was in a full sweat by the time he reached the end of the hallway. Cutting down on air conditioning was a cost-cutting measure McCoy was forced to take that he did not like. He had endured the treeless swamps of Quang Tran, the steaming deserts of Kuwait and now this. He mopped the back of his neck. Texas was too damn hot.

He entered Sparks' lab and was taken aback when he saw her in her office. "Dr. Sparks, did you not hear your phone?" It was sitting on her desk, right in front of her, where she sat eating an apple, though consumption of food in laboratories was strictly forbidden.

He walked into her office, studying her cluttered desk. On the wall above it hung a disturbing picture. Weird buildings. Weird clouds. Margaret, his youngest daughter, had painted better pictures when she was five. He averted his eyes and looked down. Sparks seemed to be working on a dose calculation. For an animal that weighed fifty kilograms! What kind of rodent was that?

"What are you doing?" he said.

She covered the paper with her hand. "A calculation."

"I can see that. What type of animal do you intend to inject?"

"A big rat." She put down the apple, scrunched up the paper and tossed it at the garbage can. She missed, but left the wadded paper where it fell.

Her office was a mess. She was surrounded by chaos. Papers everywhere. Binders stacked on the floor. Reprints towering in a corner. Her screensaver was enough to induce an epileptic fit—rolling dice, tumbling over and over.

McCoy was mystified by her success. She was emotional and reactive, qualities unbecoming to a scientist. She lacked the sober, plodding, reasonable, rational temperament he equated with scientific accomplishment. But successful or not, Dana Sparks would have to toe the line if she wanted tenure.

McCoy picked up a vial from her desk. "What's *Agent X?*"

She stood up and took the vial from him. "Can I help you with something?"

She deliberately kept him in the dark about her activities. He said, "You will give a lecture for me."

"When? School's finished."

"Not quite. The fourth-year molecular biology students expect a lecture this afternoon."

"Today?" Her tone was querulous. Her eyes were too blue and her gaze too direct. It made him uncomfortable. She did not fit his image of a scientific researcher at all. She favored denim shirts, blue jeans and cowboy boots. Heads turned when she clanked down the hall. Her hair was blond and unbrushed, shoulder-length and disheveled. She was thirty-six and never married and McCoy had heard rumors about her personal life that he refused to consider and did his best to ignore.

She was still staring. "The lecture is today," he said. "In the Biology building, in the main hall, from two to five."

"Two till five? Three hours?"

She had an annoying habit of repeating his words. "The subject is biological warfare," McCoy said. "Make it interesting. Our graduate program enrollment is down and we need new blood."

"Biological warfare." She frowned and objected. "Why do we want graduate students with that specialty?"

McCoy ignored her question. "Talk about the plague and your vaccine work. How it was developed to save millions of lives in the event of war."

"There are natural infections," she said. "At the moment prairie dogs are the biggest threat in spreading the plague."

What was this talk of prairie dogs? Sparks had a military grant and military funding; military money would not be used on sick prairie dogs, that was for sure.

McCoy held out an envelope. "When you're finished, hand out these evaluations. Betty will collect them at five."

She stared at the envelope. "Teacher evaluations? On the last day of the semester?" She folded her arms, hiding her hands. "You're joking."

"I don't joke." McCoy leaned toward her and slipped the envelope under her arm. "We need these evaluations for your file, for the consideration of your tenure."

"My teaching was already evaluated this year," she said.

"Not by me. We'll repeat the exercise today." McCoy had been puzzled by her previous evaluation. Her overall rating was too good to believe. Did she discard the negative responses while the previous chairman winked and looked the other way? "Today's process will be strictly supervised," McCoy said.

"As it was last time."

"This is not open for discussion." He wanted to add, it's a god damn order and like it or not, you'll do as I say, but he held himself back.

She clucked her teeth with displeasure, tapped the toe of her boot and glanced at her watch.

McCoy would not be hurried. "By the way, I neglected to mention, next week, we have a visitor."

She raised her eyes to the ceiling. "Yes, I know, your friend, the vice president of the United States."

McCoy realized his mistake. "I'm talking about Michael Smith."

"Who?"

There was a bite to her tone and an angry look in her eyes. She was easily provoked.

"Smith is a bacteriologist," McCoy said. "His specialty is anthrax. Like myself, he is a West Point graduate."

"Why is he coming?" Dana asked.

She questioned everything he said; it was most unpleasant. "Because I invited him."

"Great." She picked up the apple.

"There is no eating in the laboratory."

"This is an office."

"Where is your lab coat?"

"In the quarantine room."

They could go around and around in circles like this indefinitely. If she was intentionally trying to drive him crazy, she was nearly succeeding. Not for the first time, McCoy wondered if he was up to the job. He found the civilian setting bewildering and the total lack of respect for command infuriating.

"Don't forget the evaluations," he said, and left her glaring as he retired to the cool order of his office.

Chapter 4

Dana arrived at Halbourn Hall fifteen minutes before the lecture was due to begin. Usually parking on main campus was a nightmare but today there were many empty slots.

This was the building where she worked before she moved to the vet school, before the university fell on hard fiscal times and the Department of Biology was split in two. The part related to human and animal health was relegated to the Veterinary College, and the remaining half, housed here, became the Department of Environmental Biology. Although Dana was at first unhappy with the mandatory relocation, it had turned out for the best in the end. The experience taught her something: when something happens, it just happens, and it's not until later that the significance is clear.

She went inside the building. It was freezing, and the lecture hall was colder than that. There was a row of high windows that let in bright light, but they could not be opened. Dana wished she had brought a sweater. Texans were nuts about their air conditioning and she could live

without it. Growing up in Buffalo, she'd had enough cold
to last her a lifetime.

She opened her briefcase, pulled out her slides and
arranged them in a carousel. Slides pertaining to biowarfare were not in her collection and the students would have
to listen to that part of the lecture. She hoped she could fire
them up, though it would be hard when she wasn't enthusi-
astic about the topic herself. In regards to her own work,
there would be no problem; it thrilled her.

She opened a binder full of lecture notes. McCoy might
not know it but she could effortlessly give a three-hour lecture. For the last few years she had done little teaching, but
before that she had taught many undergraduate and graduate classes.

She flipped through the binder, removing pertinent
pages. She would talk about biological war, get it out of the
way. Then address the history of the plague, its biology and
the disease that it caused. Once the lecture was over she
could get back to work. She had left her technician a message asking her to wait. Dana couldn't do what she wanted
herself and would need Sheryl's help. Though getting
Sheryl to acquiesce would be a problem.

Dana was ready before the students arrived and stood by
the door waiting for them. The lecture hall was set up like a
movie theater with ascending rows and seats for two hundred. At the front there was a podium and a long counter.
Behind that, a huge blackboard. Above that, a retractable
screen. The floors and chairs were covered in gray carpet.

At five past two, the first student strolled in. A guy of
about twenty with hair dyed white and green. He wore a
razor-blade necklace and a ring through his eyebrow. If
McCoy could see who it was that he was trying to recruit,
he would have another heart attack.

Five minutes later, when twenty students in the class of
thirty-two were present, Dana began the lecture. "I suspect
you don't want to be here and I can't blame you."

The opening did not rouse the graduating seniors.

Dana walked to the podium, cleared her throat and eyed the students scattered throughout the hall. Dressed in shorts and muscle shirts, tank tops and sundresses, the class was dressed for the beach. One guy wore sunglasses. At the far back, a girl rubbed sunblock onto her face. A skinny girl next to her in a halter was eating lettuce. "Don't worry about taking notes," Dana said. There was no point anyway, for they wouldn't be tested on the material presented that day; graduating seniors did not take final exams. Nonetheless, a girl in a flowered dress sitting in the front row took out a pad and a pen. Dana smiled at her gratefully. She picked up the attendance sheet McCoy had thoughtfully provided.

"Not only do you have to be here, you have to sign in." Dana added that it was not her doing, if she had her way she would cancel the class and they could go.

The students woke up.

"Unfortunately, someone is coming at five to hand out teacher evaluation forms so you have to stay."

There were scattered cries of protest.

"I don't like it either," Dana said, but I don't have a choice." She began the lecture while the attendance sheet went around the room. "This afternoon we're going to talk about biological warfare."

The young man with two-toned hair yawned loudly. The girl with the sun-protected skin began to brush her hair. So much for McCoy's theory that students loved war.

For the next thirty minutes, Dana spoke about emulsions, delivery systems, bombs and warheads. On the blackboard she listed the names of invisible organisms and toxins so deadly that one teaspoon could kill ten million people at the cost of one dollar. The students remained unimpressed.

Dana paused and stared up at her class. Was forcing the students to listen to a lecture any different from McCoy forcing her to deliver it? Was taking attendance any different than the threat of a West Point recruit whose specialty was war? No, there was no difference at all.

Dana climbed the stairs, collected the attendance sheet from the girl with the shining skin and gleaming hair. Dana crumpled the attendance sheet into a ball and threw it at the garbage pail in the front corner. She missed. "If you all want to leave, you can."

Now she had the students' attention. The guy with sunglasses lowered them. The girl chewing lettuce froze and the girl at the front taking notes gasped. But no one made a move for the door and Dana returned to the front. When you gave people a choice, they usually chose the right thing. A subtle point McCoy seemed to have missed. Dana smiled warmly at the class.

"For the rest of the time, we're going to be talking about the plague." She recited the nursery rhyme, "Ring Around The Rosy," which was about the disease.

The note-taker smiled and scribbled madly, but the others in the class sent Dana blank stares. It would be a hard crowd to turn.

She started the slide show, turned on the projector, pulled down the screen and turned off the lights. The first slide was of *Yersinia pestis*, a gram-negative, rod-shaped bacterium that caused the plague. The slide showed the bacteria magnified twelve hundred times. With a stretch of the imagination, the bacteria resembled safety pins. They were bipolar: dark at the ends, light in the middle.

That slide didn't wake any one up. Dana advanced to the next one. It was an artist's drawing of a man dressed like a penguin. He wore a black cape, top hat and mask in the shape of a beak. She said, "This is the type of quarantine clothes worn by fourteenth century physicians. They filled the beak with camphor, vinegar and other noxious scents that would ward off the aroma of putrefaction. The smell of death."

The students sat up a little straighter.

She showed another picture, this time of people dying, lying prone on the ground, stacked on top of each other like pick-up sticks. Above, angels with bows rained down poisoned arrows. "In the fourteenth century, people used to blame their misery on a punitive god. Bad things happened when God wasn't happy." She described the flagellates, Christian men who went from town to town whipping themselves in a frenzy trying to buy God's favor. "They were trying to atone for the sins they thought they must have committed to earn God's wrath, but most of them died along with everyone else."

The students were listening. They no longer appeared so restless and the only sound in the room was the hum of the projector. She went on.

"Historians believe that the Black Plague of the thirteen hundreds ushered in the Renaissance. Death seemed to be indiscriminate, the devout and infidels died together. The plague made people reexamine their concept of God. Maybe He didn't play the active role that they had thought."

There were some chuckles. This was Baptist country and as far as Dana could tell, most of the students had little trouble mixing religion and science. They clearly saw the line that science was forbidden to cross and had no problem crossing it.

For Dana, who had forsaken her childhood religion, it wasn't so easy. She was originally attracted to science, which saw no need for a god. But as she went along, she recognized the shortfalls, the questions that science couldn't answer and therefore ignored.

Science was a study of causality. One thing happened that caused another and another, and on and on, ad infinitum. But what about the first cause? And where did life come from and why? Science called it a random accident; molecules bumping into each other in a soupy pond, initiating evolution. But Dana had a problem understanding and accepting accidents. Why did two things come together when they did? Was it just chance? That's what science said, but she thought there was more to it than that.

She went on to the next slide, one that showed a chain reaction: a bacterium, a flea, a rat, a cat and a human. "It wasn't until the end of the nineteenth century that a scientist named Yersin realized the disease was associated with rats. Before any humans were afflicted with the plague, rats would die off in great number. Yersin found the safety-pin shaped objects in the blood of dead patients. He showed that injecting this blood into healthy mice caused mortality within a few days. When he looked in the blood of the dead mice, he found the safety-pin shaped objects there, too. A few years later, another scientist recognized that it wasn't the rat that caused the disease, but rather their fleas.

"Now we know it's not fleas, but bacteria that cause the plague. The flea is the vector and transmits the bacteria from animal to animal. The common host animal is the rat. When the fleas feed on the rat, they inject the bacteria into its blood, about four hundred bacteria with every bite. When the rats die, the fleas abscond."

She walked to the front, picked up a pointer and tapped the cat on the screen. "If an infected flea bites a family pet, the disease moves closer to home." She tapped the human.

She paused and eyed the class. She seemed to have their attention; they were focused and intent. There was no hair combing, no eating, just the girl in the front taking notes.

She put the pointer down and began talking about the disease. "If you had the plague, how would you know?" She went to the next slide. "The bacteria actually cause three different diseases, depending upon how they are acquired. A bite from an infected flea results in bubonic plague, which is an infection of the lymph system. The bacteria proliferate, causing the lymph nodes to swell." She raised her left arm. "The glands under the arm and in the groin can grow to the size of an egg. As with most bacterial infections, there is fever, malaise, headache, fatigue. The symptoms usually appear within two to eight days after infection."

She progressed to the next slide, which showed an artist's drawing of two people coughing. Bacteria were moving in an arc in the air from one mouth to another, which was the way pneumonic plague was transmitted, much like a cold. The result was pneumonia and without treatment, death after two to four days.

The third slide showed the viscera of a rat infected with septicemic plague. There were pinpoints of blood dotting the internal organs, a pool of blood in the abdomen. Septicemic plague was an infection of the blood and was acquired by direct contact with the bacteria. Dana swept her finger along the front counter. "If the bacteria were there, and I had a cut on my finger, or if I put my finger in my mouth, I would internalize the bacteria and likely be dead within a day."

Wide-open eyes were fixed upon her. The girl taking notes turned to a new page. Dana went through a series of slides that showed the pathology of the disease. Particularly disturbing was the slide of the purple hands from a corpse that Dana reproduced from a textbook photo. The fingernails were black, something Dana had never seen in real life.

She explained how the bacteria killed. They put out a toxin that impaired the red blood cells from picking up oxygen. Even though the oxygen was present, the cells couldn't use it. It was similar to dying of dehydration in the ocean. "Deoxygenated blood looks blue," she said. "Look at the veins on the back of your hands." When the students did so, she knew she had them. "With the plague, all the blood vessels turn blue, so blue that the skin looks dark purple or black."

"How can we treat the disease?" She advanced to the next slide, which showed three bottles of antibiotics lined up in a row: tetracycline, streptomycin and chloramphenicol. The plague bacteria had become so hard to kill that it required the use of three antibiotics.

She explained antibiotic resistance. "Bacteria mutate very quickly; they adapt to their environment. One of their adaptations is dealing with poisons, like antibiotics. They also reproduce rapidly and have a quick generation time. A bacterium with a favorable mutation makes many copies of itself. If a mutation allows the bacterium to break down an antibiotic, that bacterium becomes resistant to that antibiotic. Even in the presence of the drug, the bacteria will continue to reproduce."

She turned off the projector, but kept the fan running. She raised the screen and turned on the overhead lights, picked up a piece of chalk. In the next section she would discuss immunology and wanted to go slow, make sure the students heard what she had to say.

"Our immune system is our internal defense against disease. We make antibodies that combine with bacteria." On the blackboard she drew a stick person with a round head, ping-pong paddle hands and big feet. "Like a human, the surface of a bacterium is asymmetrical. We have a head, arms, hands, legs, feet. You can think of antibodies like articles of clothing—a hat, gloves, shoes; they fit certain shapes, certain places. A hat goes on the head, not the feet. My boots fit me, not you."

She put the chalk down and wiped her hands on her jeans. "An antibody globs onto a bacterium like a handle. White blood cells use the handle to get rid of the bacterium. It's like using a pair of tongs to catch a snake."

She described the last three years of her research. "In my lab, we've been working on vaccines. Vaccines boost the immune system, get it primed, ready to fight in the event of an invasion." She explained how she and her graduate students found the passive vaccine. They had used two different strains of mice. One strain was resistant to the plague and the other was sensitive. After many failed attempts, they determined that the basis of resistance was the effect of a particular antibody. When they isolated that antibody and injected it into sensitive mice, the mice didn't get sick. The control mice that didn't get the antibody died. "In the lab, we made a human analogue of the antibody, and this monoclonal antibody formed the basis of the passive vaccine."

She paused until the girl taking notes stopped writing.

"There is a problem," she said.

The class saw immediately what McCoy failed to get.

"Yes," Dana said. "The antibody is a protein and it breaks down. It lasts only about three weeks." She did not mention the complication about the guinea pig and the possibility that the passive vaccine might be lethal. She advanced to the concept of an active vaccine.

"Ideally we want to find the piece of the bacterium that causes the immune system to produce the protective antibody. Then we'll give that piece of the bacterium as a vaccine. One shot and you're done." This was what she would work on next.

In truth, she had been working on it for six months. Her strategy was to do the research first, then write the grant. Once you knew the answer, you knew the right question to ask, and were guaranteed success. You didn't waste money on research that went nowhere. Dana had been there before and didn't want to go back there again.

Out in the audience a watch alarm beeped five times. Dana glanced at her watch. The afternoon, the week, the semester, were finally at a close. She walked to the door and looked out. There was no sign of Betty, McCoy's secretary.

Breaking protocol, Dana handed out the evaluation forms. "Just two more minutes of your time, please."

Five minutes later the class was cleared, except for the girl in the front who was scribbling away. She was taking the evaluation far too seriously. What was she writing?

What was so important she had to go on and on? Dana watched as the girl turned the form over and continued writing on the back.

Dana packed up. Without looking at the filled-in forms or fixing the form that had been folded into an airplane, she put them in the envelope. She replaced her notes in her binder and collected her slides. She erased the chalkboard and picked up the pieces of chalk that had fallen on the floor. She turned off the lights and the projector. The girl finally put down her pen.

"I gave you all excellents," she said, handing Dana the form.

"Well, thank you. And good comments I hope?"

The girl nodded.

Dana took her form. "Don't tell me any more." She closed her eyes and shoved the form in the envelope.

The girl stood before her, waiting. Dana picked up her briefcase. It was late and she had to go if she was going to catch her technician before she left for the weekend. "Have a nice summer."

"I have a question."

Dana thought of her technician and forced herself not to look at her watch.

The studious note-taker introduced herself and said she had a problem. Dana learned that Carol Dupuis was doing a fourth year project and had been trapping rats for DNA analysis. That week she collected twenty rats and four of them died.

Carol wrung her hands. "They were bleeding internally and some had fleas. I wonder if they had the plague."

Was that why she took such careful notes? A personal threat? Still, the combination of rats and fleas did not automatically equal the plague. "The rats were probably poisoned," Dana said. "Warfarin stops the blood from clotting and can cause internal bleeding."

"What if I get sick?" Carol said.

It was natural to worry. It had taken Dana a long time to get used to working with chemicals and bacteria that could kill her a million times over. Considering what she was about to do, she might have overcompensated, become too blasé. She said, "You don't have to worry. Duane is too far south for *Yersinia*. The bacteria can't stand the heat."

"Really?" Carol sounded skeptical.

"I'll test the rats if you want."

Carol smiled, for the first time that afternoon, on the last Friday of her life.

Chapter 5

Dana left campus and drove west along University Drive toward the vet school. The campus was dry and the street was lined with bars and currently overflowing with students who spilled onto the road. Music blared and students drank and danced. She had been there, too many times to remember. Back in better days, not that long ago. Four months, four months to the day since a car crash changed everything. One moment everything was fine and then something happened that defied all reason and set a new course forward. It happened all the time in her research.

Dana remembered a lengthy period of despair, not so long ago, when she could not find the immunological difference to explain why one strain of mice was resistant to the plague and another was sensitive. She thought she had wasted a million dollars and saw her career coming to an end before it ever got started.

Then she had a dream that told her where to look for what she sought: a minor antibody that, when made in large quantities, protected against the plague.

A few months later, there was another crisis. The vaccine killed or seriously injured guinea pigs. She thought it was over, but concomitant trials using dogs and monkeys showed the monoclonal vaccine effective beyond all expectations. After some hesitation, the FDA approved Phase One of the clinical trials; human testing would begin that summer.

Ten minutes later she was back at the Veterinary College. She parked in her old spot, happy to see that McCoy was gone, his parking space empty. She tore upstairs. In the main lab, Sheryl was washing glassware. She wore yellow gloves and was up to her soapy elbows in test tubes. Per McCoy's orders, she was in a lab coat. As always, her brown frizzy hair was pulled back in a tight ponytail.

Sheryl was Dana's age and a single mother of three. They had been roommates during their first year of college and friends ever since. Dana was the maid of honor at Sheryl's wedding, and the godmother of her daughter. Sheryl was an English major, a thesis short of a Master's, and a stay-at-home mom until her husband ran off with his secretary. Despite a hiring freeze, Dana managed to get Sheryl a job.

"Where were you?" Sheryl said, lifting a soapy test tube rack out of the sink. "What do you have there?"

Dana held the biohazard bag in her hand. "Rats." She put them in the Revco freezer in the quarantine room and came back.

Sheryl was shaking excess water out of the test tubes. She turned on the tap and filled the sink. Over the sound of the running water, she said, "What's going on? I heard you saw McCoy earlier."

"He changed my parking space."

"I hope you were nice about it."

"Of course."

"When you say it like that I know you weren't." The sink was full and Sheryl immersed the test tube rack. The tubes tinkled against each other and went glug, glug, glug as they filled with water. Over her shoulder, Sheryl said, "You're never nice to him. I don't know why you can't try harder to get along." She lifted the rack, turned it on its side and drained the water. The tubes would now be heat sterilized in the autoclave to kill any remaining contaminants. Sheryl snapped off the gloves.

"McCoy's unreasonable," Dana said.

Sheryl turned around. She was five-foot-three and the white lab coat went below her knees. She was big-boned and though often dieting, not overweight. "McCoy's the boss. He's in charge," she said.

"Not of me."

Sheryl shook her head and the ponytail swung back and forth. "He can make things difficult for you and he is. Can't you go along with him for a change? Try a different approach for once. Do what he wants."

"No," Dana said, more stridently than she wanted. She didn't know why, but she couldn't.

Sheryl glanced at her watch. "Why did you want me to wait?" Her boys got home from school at 2:30 and Penny had to be picked up at daycare by six. How she managed it all, Dana didn't know.

"I need your help. A favor."

"Of course. Anything. What?" Sheryl said.

"Could you take some blood?"

"From you? Sure. Why?" She looked at Dana suspiciously. "Are you worried you're exposed to *Yersinia?* That you're sick?"

"No. I want to look at my antibodies."

"Why?"

"Check their level."

"But why?" Sheryl's eyes were light brown and in some light they looked red.

"I just want to do it. What's wrong with that?" Dana walked toward her office, Sheryl at her heels.

"What's really going on?"

Dana dropped her briefcase on her desk. "All right. I'm going to try the new vaccine. I need to look at my preexisting antibodies."

"Oh, God." Sheryl put her hand to her forehead. "What really happened with McCoy?"

"He doesn't see the need for the active vaccine. That's how obtuse he is."

"He knows you've found it!"

"Of course not. And he's not going to know. What happens here is none of his business." Dana locked the door. From the fridge she grabbed *Agent X* and inverted the vial three times to mix the solution.

As she had told the class, the ultimate goal in vaccine research was to give a person the ability to produce their own protective antibody—to find an active vaccine. Already she thought she had it. *Agent X* was the part of the cell wall of the bacterium where the protective antibody bound. In mice, this piece induced the protective antibody. The piece had also been injected into four guinea pigs and, unlike their reaction to the passive vaccine, there were no untoward side effects. But how would it work in people?

Different species responded differently. Some strains of mice were resistant to the plague and others were sensitive. Some could make a particular antibody and others could not. What if people were like the sensitive mice and unable to make the protective antibody?

If so, her research was in vain. But Dana couldn't study something in people before she had checked it out in mice. The mice work had to be done first. But people weren't big mice, and what might work in a mouse, might not work in a person. The only way she would know how a person would respond was to try it and see.

"You can't take the vaccine," Sheryl said. "What if you get sick?"

"I'll be fine." Dana hoped, as she opened a drawer and

grabbed a needle and syringe. The syringe was covered in paper and she ripped it off, uncapped the case of the needle and shoved it into the base of the syringe.

"Human testing is the final stage," Sheryl said.

Dana unbuttoned her cuff and rolled up her sleeve. "I don't have a choice." She pierced the ampule with the needle and drew the vaccine into the syringe and offered it to Sheryl.

Sheryl shoved her hands in the pockets of her lab coat. "What really happened with McCoy?"

"This is insurance." Dana held up the syringe and lightly pressed on the plunger to clear the air. A drop beaded the point. "If it works we'll get tenure."

"You'll get tenure if the army renews your grant."

"McCoy is army," Dana said. "He'll block the renewal."

Sheryl sighed. "I don't like it."

"I was there for you when you needed me." Dana had traded all her favors to hire Sheryl and it had not been easy.

Sheryl sighed louder and lifted her hands from her pockets. "All right, if I do this for you, then you owe me."

It was a fair deal, or so Dana thought at the time.

Sheryl took the syringe, squirted Dana's biceps with alcohol and neatly jabbed Dana's muscle, injecting the vaccine. There was a localized burning and Dana rubbed the site. Sheryl threw the empty syringe on the counter.

"How will you explain your results?"

"I'll worry about it later."

It was a philosophy Sheryl didn't espouse. "If you had a license, you'd lose it. You're throwing away everything you worked for. What if McCoy finds out?"

"He won't."

"You always think you're going to get away with things and you never do. When are you going to see that?"

Dana neglected to answer. From another drawer she pulled a tourniquet and a stoppered tube. Sheryl took the tourniquet and wrapped it around Dana's arm, just above the elbow and secured it tightly.

"Make a fist."

Dana did so.

Sheryl fitted together another needle and a syringe. Then she raised Dana's arm and held it close to her eyes. She studied the inner elbow before advancing with the needle. There was a slight prick and blood flowed immediately. Dana closed her eyes while the syringe filled. After all this time, the sight of blood still made her queasy.

"When will we know the results?" Sheryl asked, withdrawing the needle.

"Three days."

Sheryl handed her the tube of blood. "If this gets out. I wasn't here. I know nothing. You did it yourself."

Sheryl went to lock the lab and Dana packed her briefcase. Next week she'd draw more blood and look at each individual antibody made against *Yersinia*. Then she would know if humans could make the protective antibody.

Theoretically it should work, though there was always the possibility that things could go wrong. It was best not to think about it. If there was another way, she would have gone that route, but there wasn't. Sometimes when you were backed up against a wall, you had to take a risk.

Dana turned off her computer, turned off her lights and locked her office. She met Sheryl, waiting at the door with the keys.

They walked down stairs, their footsteps echoing off the walls around them. With classes over, it was unusually quiet. Dana liked the summers in Duane the best; the undergrads went home and the town became calm and laid-back.

They talked about their weekend plans. Dana was going to finish the paper for the *Journal of Immunology* and bathe her dogs.

"That reminds me," Sheryl said, "Tim stopped by." He

was the veterinarian who had the office across the hall from Dana's. "He doesn't want you taking Frank home."

Frank was Dana's black Labrador retriever. "Is there a problem?"

"If there was, he didn't tell me." At the landing, Sheryl stopped. "He seemed really sad."

"Frank?"

"Tim."

"He never looks sad."

"Dana, I don't know why you won't go out with him."

Dana continued down the stairs. "I just don't want to, all right?" She hated how defensive she sounded. Sometimes, talking to Sheryl was like talking to her mother.

Sheryl was coming down behind her. "He said you were great together."

"He was wrong."

"Why? He's good looking, successful, rich, smart. Single." She emphasized the last word. "What's wrong?"

"I don't know. It's just not right."

"He asked me if you were seeing someone."

Dana stopped again. "What did you say?"

"I told him the truth. No."

"Shit." Dana was on the move again.

Sheryl caught up to her. "Give him a chance. That's all he wants. And he's not like you, he's not willing to wait forever."

"I don't want him waiting at all."

They reached the front floor and Dana banged open the door. She heard clearly the rebuke in Sheryl's tone and wished she would mind her own business.

"At least think about it," Sheryl said, and headed for the exit.

Dana watched her leave, thinking she had already made the decision and wouldn't reconsider, in case she changed her mind. She went to get Frank. She wasn't leaving him for the weekend, forget that. She was taking him home. He had been in the clinic all week. He was fourteen years old and suffering from arthritis and lung cancer. The drugs used to treat one disease exacerbated the other. To treat the cancer, he needed an active immune system, but to treat the arthritis, the immune system had to be stopped. She didn't know which disease to treat until he stopped walking. By then his prognosis was so poor that no veterinarian would touch him. Only after great coercion, and as a personal favor, did Tim finally agree. Now she felt she owed him, but had nothing she wanted to give.

In the clinic, Dana was happy to see the hallway was empty. She quickly scanned the chalkboard that listed the names of the veterinarians on duty. Phew, Tim Sweeny had checked out. Breathing easier, Dana headed toward his animal room.

A clipboard dangled from a hook on the door. Dana paused and read Tim's notes. He was the best clinician in the vet school, a troubleshooter, and challenging cases throughout the state came straight to him. He was treating an eight-week-old puppy for parvo, a poodle eviscerated by a cougar, a cat in need of a leg amputation and Frank.

Dana saw Frank had been taken for a lung scan that afternoon. The IV infusion of methotrexate, an anti-arthritic drug, had been discontinued. Was Tim stopping the treatment? Was Frank's cancer back? Dana inhaled sharply, drawing air past her tight heart. What if she put him through a week of hell just to have him die?

Dana took another breath and entered the animal room. A row of cages lined one wall. The young parvo puppy was curled in a ball. There was an orange cat with a stump wrapped in a bloody cloth, where a front paw should be. Frank's cage was at the end of the row and she heard his tail thumping before she saw him.

She reached his cage. His body shook with excitement. She lifted the latch and swung open the door. Panting hard, Frank stiffly pulled himself out, dragging his wagging backside on the ground. He weighed over one hundred pounds.

Dana knelt down and threw her arms around his back. He fell against her, nearly knocking her over. She rubbed his gray fur. His breathing was labored and quick. His nose was dry and he looked at her with cloudy blue eyes. Maybe she should have done nothing. Wasn't a lame dog better than no dog?

Dana grabbed a gurney and with difficulty, heaved Frank up. He lay on his side with his tongue lolling out. His tail slapped the stainless steel surface as she rolled him from the room. They went down the deserted hall, out the automatic doors into the heat and bright sunshine. On the way to the car, Dana stopped short. It appeared she would not escape so easily after all, for the veterinarian she wished to avoid stood by her car.

Chapter 6

Tim Sweeny crossed the parking lot with an easy bow-legged stride. He was lean, six-foot-three and thirty-five years old. His hair was blond and he wore it long. On the road behind him, traffic whizzed past and a horn blared. Dana refused to look, but Tim spun around and waved. The horn honked again and Dana saw a pickup truck filled with laughing girls go barreling by.

Tim reached the curb and hopped up beside her, his blue eyes shining, a giant smile on his tanned face. She broke eye contact and stared over his shoulder at his car. He hadn't lost *his* parking space and his cherry red Corvette with the vanity license plate K9-DOC was still parked in its slot.

Tim lowered his head, craned his neck and blocked her view. "I was going to keep Frank over the weekend. You can't take him."

He was always telling her what to do. Not long ago he had said to her, "I won't let you go." She had been lying in his bed, watching the sun rise after a sleepless night.

"It won't work," she had said when he woke up and reached for her.

"Of course it will. It does. What do you mean?" He tried to arouse her, without success.

She knew she needed to explain, but found it difficult because she didn't understand it herself. When she was with Tim, she felt as if she were betraying someone else who was long gone and had vowed never to come back. She might have been easy to leave, but it hadn't been easy for her to let go. Unable to explain herself, she said, "It just won't work."

"Is it me?" he asked. "Something I did?" His hand was back. "Something I didn't do?"

"It's too much."

His hand was gone. "Too much what?"

Too much you, she wanted to say, too close, too intense, but she said, "Too exclusive."

His body tensed and his face turned rigid; he was instantly pissed off. "Who is it?" He was out of bed, pulling on his clothes.

She wouldn't say. He listed names. He would never get it. The man was gone, had been gone for years.

"Why didn't you tell me this before?"

"I should have. I'm sorry. At least now you know."

"Well, I can handle it if you can." He threw himself on the bed.

"I don't think I can."

"I won't let you go."

But she had left, and now she didn't know if she had done the right thing or not. Maybe she should have given Tim a chance, let things progress, see what happened. Maybe someone else was what she needed to go on. Dana sank her hand into Frank's sun-warmed pelt and looked into Tim's open eyes, his eager face. It was true; they were good together. "I want to keep him," she said.

"He needs to be watched."

"I'll watch him. He'll do better at home."

Frank wagged his tail.

"I took him off the methotrexate," Tim said.

"I know. Why?"

"You can see his respiration is poor." That much was obvious. Frank's chest was heaving, his breathing hard and labored. "I took an X-ray of his lungs and they're cloudy," Tim said. "I didn't see any tumors but there are signs of inflammation. It could be nothing more than a cold. Then again, it could be pneumonia." Tim coughed into a fist.

Dana exhaled and stared up at the sky that was the clear shade of blue that came after a storm. She had hoped this treatment would fix everything, not make things worse. "Now what?"

"I think you should put him down."

And this from a man who said his secret of success was to never give up.

She shook her head. "What about colchicine?"

Tim clicked his teeth. "Is that what you want?"

She nodded her head. When he stared in her eyes, she stared back.

"All right. I'll do it." He raised his hand and brushed a dog hair off her sleeve. "For you."

Dana felt a lump in her throat. Her uncertainty about him was back. Had she acted rashly, made a mistake?

"Bring him in on Monday. I'm off to D.C., but Sheila can handle it."

He insisted on lugging Frank to the car and carried him effortlessly across the tarmac. Dana threw open the door. Tim carefully arranged Frank on the passenger seat and Dana rolled down the window.

The scent of cut grass hung heavy in the air. Nearby, a gardener bounced on a mower. He was indiscriminately mowing down the wildflowers, obliterating the pink prim-roses and yellow coreopsis. Dana never cut her own grass until the wildflowers were dead. She closed the car door. Frank poked his head out the window and licked her hand.

"Call me on the weekend if he gets worse," Tim said. "Any time. Day or night." He thrust his hand through the open window and massaged Frank's head with his long, strong fingers. With a tightening in her chest Dana remembered the touch of those fingers on her skin.

She looked up and found Tim's eyes on hers. She wondered if he would kiss her, and while the sunlight streamed across them and the oak leaves waved, she wondered how she would react if he did.

He did not. Abruptly he stepped away, cleared his throat and rearranged his hair with a shake of his head. "I've got to go. Hate to keep a lady waiting." He yanked sunglasses from his pocket and shoved them on his face. Walking jauntily to his convertible, he vaulted over the side. The tires squealed as he tore out of the parking lot.

Dana watched him go, not wanting to, but wondering, which lady he would not keep waiting. Her heart sank to her stomach. Time was moving too fast. She was tired of being alone and tired of wanting someone who could live without her. Why was it so hard to go on? Why couldn't she cut free of her past and let him go, make do with someone else. McCoy's earlier words haunted her: you aren't amenable to change. Was it accurate?

A few minutes later, Dana was backing out of her parking spot when McCoy roared into the lot and blocked her car. He flung open his door and leaped from his bullet proof Mercedes. Sweat drenched his hair and his cheeks were florid.

"I told you, those parking places are for clinic clients only." Mirrored sunglasses hid his eyes.

She got out of her car. "The clinic is closed."

"That's not the point. If I see your car here again I'll have it towed." He frowned at Frank whose head hung out the window. "And pets are not allowed in the building during office hours."

"He's sick. He's been at the clinic."

He dismissed her explanation with a shake of his head. "I have just come from main campus," he said. "Betty could not monitor the evaluation exercise and I went in her stead. Where were you?"

Only then did Dana remember the envelope she neglected to leave on Betty's desk.

"Where are the evaluations?" McCoy stared across the parking lot at the clinic where a painting crew fashioned a scaffold, embarking on repairs in advance of the VP's visit.

Dana retrieved the envelope from her briefcase and handed it to McCoy.

She willed him to take it and leave, but he opened the flap and pulled out the forms. The one folded into the airplane was on top. As McCoy peered at the paper, his sunglasses slipped down his nose and he stared at her over the rim.

"I didn't touch them," she said. "I didn't look at them."

McCoy crammed the sunglasses on the crown of his head, unfolded the airplane and squinted at the form. "Humph."

Holding the evaluations close to his heart he perused the stack. Brian, the former chairman, always showed them to her, but McCoy did not. Usually the student responses were good and she wondered what had happened to the evaluation conducted in the fall. Did McCoy, not liking the response, toss it out?

He looked up. His gray eyes were cold. He held up a form. "All excellent." He picked up another form. "All excellent. How do you explain this?"

"It was an excellent lecture."

He stared at her. The sun slipped behind a cloud and she felt cold. McCoy lowered his head, licked an index finger and began counting the evaluations. Dana backed up against her car. She could hear Frank's labored breathing and the ticking of her watch.

"Twenty evaluations," he said finally. "Twenty evaluations only, yet there are thirty-two students registered in that class."

"Only twenty students came."

"And the attendance sheet is where?" Shifting the evaluations in his hand, McCoy peered into the envelope.

Dana could see it in her mind, crumpled in a ball in the corner of the lecture hall. "I handed it out," she said. "I must have forgotten it."

McCoy threw her another long hard stare. Balancing the evaluations under his arm, he shoved his hand in his trouser pocket and extracted the balled-up attendance sheet.

Dana opened her mouth to explain, but no words came.

Nonetheless, McCoy raised his hand for silence. "We'll talk about this Monday. I hope you realize this is a serious breach of protocol." With a vivid shake of his head, McCoy stalked back to his Mercedes and disappeared behind the dark, tinted windows. He slowly pulled away.

Dana stood by her car until he disappeared. *A serious breach of protocol.* She didn't know whether to laugh or scream. Was he collecting violations for the tenure committee? Did he think she could be dismissed for forgetting an attendance sheet? For parking in the wrong place? For having a sick dog? She thought not. But why did he always catch her? She couldn't break a rule without him knowing. A malevolent force seemed to be on his side.

The sun came out from behind its cloud and Dana stood for a moment in the light, absorbing the rays. Then she headed home. She lived in the country on the south side of town and took the west bypass. She ran the A.C. for Frank and rolled down the windows. The air was heavy, hot and humid. She liked the sound of the wind and though there was a time she always drove with the radio playing, she preferred the silence now. She put a hand on Frank's back, he hung his head out the window and the wind lifted his ears, blew back his fur.

The bypass curved south and Dana sped past vast flat fields. The forest to the west fringed the right horizon. To the left stood a ranch where cows grazed on emerald colored grass. Dana drove past the tree that her former boss hit on Christmas Eve. The tree was wounded still, the soft pulp splintered and shiny with dark sap or dried blood. After Brian's accident, she bought a four-wheel drive Raider that could mow down a tree.

Why did he have to die? Dana asked herself this question over and over: why, why, why? And she saw a long causal chain that took him to a Christmas Eve on a cold and icy night, to a patch of ice and brakes hit too hard and a skid that slammed him into an impenetrable tree. If only she could go back in time and change what happened, break a link in the chain that delivered Brian to his death. If only the weather had been balmy and there was no ice on the road, no Christ's birth to celebrate, no party to go to, no flimsy fence, no solid tree. Could anything stop what had happened? What were accidents anyway? Random events, or things that had to happen?

It was an accident she was here in Duane at all. In her senior year in high school she won a scholarship to a southern university that was in a town that wasn't on the map. She applied to other universities, but this was the only one offering money and down she came, though Texas was not a place she ever saw herself living.

Originally, she enrolled in pre-med but had lasted only a semester. She found that being with sick people made her feel sick herself. She switched to philosophy and adored it, but her father thought it impractical. Following his footsteps, she went into architecture, but trigonometry killed her. She went to biology and from there to biochemistry, molecular biology and finally immunology. It took her five years to get a degree.

By then the oil boom went bust and the job market crashed and Dana's mother begged her to come home. Her old room was waiting. Dana stayed on for a Master's, a Ph.D., then a post doc. Midway through her post doc, there was a funding crisis and money ran out. Departments were juggled, programs were modified and Dana was relocated to the veterinary school. Her supervisor resigned in fury and Dana begrudgingly accepted a new professor, whom she would ultimately replace. She wouldn't be here now if any one of these events had changed.

The bypass circled east and Dana took the first right that led onto a dirt road. A mile down the shaded road she reached the border of her land. *Her land*, which she paid a fortune for, buying at the hilt of the housing boom before the market fell. No matter, it was worth it; here was where she belonged, though in truth she didn't feel she owned the land, but rather, that it owned her. How could she leave?

She reached her driveway, turned right and bounced down a muddy decline. She had five acres of land and her nearest neighbor was a mile down the road. At night when she turned off the lights she could see only stars. During the day, her dogs ran free.

They were running toward the car now. A small one racing in a blur, the large one loping like a pony. Dana parked the car and jumped out. Anthony had his paws up on her shoulders and swiped her face with his tongue. He was a border collie-Labrador mix with black fur and three white paws. An off-center white stripe ran down his face. Beside him, Judy barked shrilly and leaped into the air. Dana moved to catch her mid-flight. She was a poodle-terrier mix, a shaggy mop. Dana put her down gently. She went around the car and lifted Frank out. In their exuberance, the other dogs knocked him over. He struggled shakily to his feet.

They walked together down the driveway to the house, around the back to the front door. Frank needed help climbing the porch steps, which Anthony cleared in a bound. He shoved the screen door open with his nose.

Although it was over ninety degrees outside, inside it was cool. The house was small and square and bright with sunlight. There was a kitchen-dining room-living room combination, with a bathroom and bedroom at the back. A cross-breeze blew across the house through open windows. The walls were paneled with light pine and underfoot a wall-to-wall turquoise carpet hid the dirt.

Dana grabbed a Lone Star beer from the fridge, sat at the kitchen table and kicked off her boots. Wilted petals lay on the table and she looked up. On the ceiling support beams she pinned all her flower bouquets. There were the dozen red roses Tim sent after she said she couldn't see him. There were sprays of wild flowers, bluebonnets and Indian paintbrushes she had collected in long ago springs. The petals on the table were yellow and came from lilies her Ph.D. student gave her earlier that week. The flower that meant the most would last forever. It was a plastic Remembrance Day poppy pinned to a bandanna Frank once stole and Dana once wore to cover small bites of love on her neck, a long time ago.

The phone rang and Dana's neighbor was on the line. Gunther called once a month to see if she had changed her mind about selling her land. He wanted to fell the trees, level the house, grow cotton. She told him no, never, stop asking. He chuckled as he hung up.

Dana stepped into sandals and called the dogs. She took them for a walk in the woods nearly every day.

Judy and Anthony burst outside, but Frank refused to move. He lay in his bed gazing at the door with his clouded

eyes. The week away had been hard on him and she left
him in bed.

Outside, Anthony and Judy raced across the lawn and
disappeared into the woods. Dana ambled through the long
grass after them. A hundred feet across the field, she
reached the woods that spanned her land to the south and
west for miles. She slipped into soft cedar, the branches
parting for her and closing up behind her. The forest,
pulling her into itself. Down a narrow path she went and
soon the canopy filtered out the sunlight. Underfoot, the
ground was littered with spongy detritus and the air
smelled of pine. She came in all types of weather, quietly
watching the changes and the forest in its many moods.

Today it was quiet, close and suffocating, holding her
tight. It seemed to have burgeoned overnight, a burst of
new leaves and vines that grabbed at her. Smilax cut into
her arm, drawing blood. A mosquito whined in her ear.
Halfway down the path she tripped over a fallen limb and
fell in a bog. She lost a sandal climbing free, then stepped
on a thorn. The forest, bearing down on her, turning against
her. Something felt wrong.

Saturday

Chapter 7

Late Saturday afternoon, McCoy was in the Mercedes explaining to his youngest daughter how to start the car when the front door opened and his wife called out he had a phone call. "I'll be right back," he told Margaret who was ensconced in the driver's seat. "Leave the car in park and don't touch anything."

"Okay, Daddy." She smiled at him and McCoy's heart lurched. The move to Texas had been unspeakably hard for her. He had dragged her away from Virginia in the middle of her senior year of high school and she had cried bitterly for weeks. These driving lessons were a great bridge between them.

Leaving her in the car, he rushed to the house. For McCoy, unexpected phone calls meant an emergency. He had five daughters and ten grandchildren, and often received calls in times of crisis. Was a hundred-and-four fever high enough to take James to the doctor? How did you pop Phillip's dislocated shoulder into place? Did an inch-long cut on Hanna's chin warrant stitches? God, how he missed his children. How he would miss Margaret, who at sixteen was too young to be sitting behind the wheel of the Mercedes, too young to be going to college next year. He wondered why he ever allowed her to skip fifth grade. If he knew then what he knew now, he would never have given his consent.

In the house, Marge said, "Mitchell Marshall is on the line."

What did the university president want now? McCoy wondered. Everything for the vice president's visit was on track. The kink at the Lone Star Heritage Hotel had been ironed out—security would be tightened and additional secret service agents were on their way. He grabbed the receiver.

"We've got a problem," Mitchell Marshall said. "The FBI don't like the security in the stadium. They want to move the graduation ceremony to the auditorium."

"It's too small," McCoy said.

"You don't have to tell me. Brackton Hall has seating for two hundred and we've sent out twelve hundred tickets."

McCoy sighed. Organizing the VP's visit was an endless headache. Glancing through the vestibule window, he saw the car lights blaze. The windshield wipers started and stopped. The emergency flashers flickered.

"I don't see why we can't hold it in the football stadium," Marshall complained. "We'll close Johnson Field Thursday night for the security check. Though there is the rain factor. We're expecting a deluge—did you hear? A tropical storm's building in the Gulf."

McCoy said nothing. Three weeks ago he raised the issue of rain, but the university president dismissed his concerns.

"It won't be very pleasant outdoors if there's a tropical storm," Marshall said.

"We'll get tents," McCoy said.

Outside the horn blared. Margaret's patience had worn thin.

"Don't spend too much money," Marshall said. "We

don't need tents for the whole hundred yards. Just enough to cover the vice president and his entourage."

McCoy said "Yes Sir," and imagined the other guests standing in the pouring rain in the midst of a tropical storm.

The university president hung up and McCoy called FBI agent Barry Ackerman and arranged another emergency meeting. Which presented a new conflict. Not only would McCoy have to postpone Margaret's driving lesson, but he also had to find someone to entertain Michael Smith, his West Point visitor.

McCoy pondered his options as Margaret stormed from the car. Her face was angry, her strong jaw set. She had been so unhappy lately. McCoy had promised himself he'd spend more time with her, but so far he was breaking all his promises.

The front door slammed, and McCoy winced and faced his daughter. "Something's come up. I'm sorry baby. We'll do this . . ."

She didn't give him time to finish. She ran crying up the stairs. McCoy's weak heart tightened. When this week was over, he'd make it up to her. He gripped the bracelet she gave him for Father's Day when she was six years old. It seemed like yesterday. She was growing up too fast.

McCoy sighed again and reached for the phone. Since he couldn't keep his dinner appointment, Dana Sparks would go in his place.

Damn, the line at her house was busy. He tried her lab and heard the department's taped message. The other specialists kept beepers or mobile phones, so if he needed to contact them he could, but Dana Sparks refused to be on call.

He tried her home again. He wondered if she took the phone off the hook. She refused to be at anyone's beck and call. If she behaved like this now, how would she behave with tenure? She set a bad precedent for others in the department who struggled to toe McCoy's line.

McCoy threw down the phone and went upstairs to talk with Margaret. But she was locked in her room and would not answer his pleading knock. He tried bribing her with a driving lesson tomorrow after their barbecue, a shopping trip next Saturday to Houston, a summer trip to Virginia, but his overtures went unanswered. McCoy finally gave up and slumped back to the phone.

Chapter 8

Dana's mother usually called her Sunday morning, but this week she broke her routine and called Saturday afternoon.

"I had a bad dream," she said when Dana asked if there was a problem.

When Dana heard her voice she thought her father might be ill, but learned he was out on the golf course. After a heart attack, he had mellowed and become more easygoing and relaxed. Except when it came to her. Now he had joined forces with her mother and wanted her to marry and settle down. "I worried about you all day and finally decided to call," her mother said.

"I'm fine," Dana said. "Really." Her pat answer, recited week after week. She sat down on the back of the couch, swinging her legs.

"Did you get tenure?"

Another question Dana heard every week. And she knew what would follow. "Not yet."

"Maybe you won't get it. Why don't you just come home?"

This is my home, Dana thought, but said, "I'll know

soon." Anthony lay by her feet and she rubbed his back with her foot. With her mother, everything was predictable. Nothing ever changed. It reminded Dana of a philosophy lecture she heard a long time ago. The Greeks believed events were a mix of causality and chance. They called causality, reason and chance, necessity. Plato considered these the two great cosmic forces. Chance was coincidence: things that *had* to come together and *had* to happen. Chance violated the principle of causality and introduced uncertainty into predictable determinism. It was chance that brought surprise and shook things up. Dana wished some element of chance would happen here and put an end to this line of questions.

"Russell is back. You remember Russell?"

How could Dana forget? She had been hearing about Russell since Christmas. Russell, whose marriage to a tramp had dissolved and was officially annulled, which made him acceptable in her mother's eyes. Dana had met him once, two summers back when she flew home when her father was hospitalized. "Russell was asking about you. If you would be home this summer."

"We'll see," Dana said, as Judy leapt up onto the couch.

"Your old room is ready."

Dana hated her old room, done up in candyfloss pink, with dolls and ruffles. A kid's room. She patted one dog, rubbed another and stared at Frank who lay sleeping in his bed. He had slept all day.

"And Monica had a baby, did you hear?"

Monica was a distant cousin and yes Dana had heard, at least ten times. "I think you told me. How's Dad?"

"Oh you know your father. Can't settle down. He'll go to his grave running."

Dana wondered if that was resentment in her mother's voice. Her mother, the good wife, who stayed home and supported her husband. She had sacrificed any chance at having her own life and seemed determined to have Dana do the same.

"I didn't get an email from him this week." Her father sent her weekly emails, keeping her up-to-date about the latest political intrigues and stupid bureaucratic decisions that were guaranteed to block progress and development. He was a well-respected architect, reputed to be Buffalo's best. He was envied though, and had enemies who tried to bring him down. Since the coming of McCoy, Dana finally understood what her father had been up against and what he was fighting for.

She sent him emails each week too, but was always careful not to reveal too much. She didn't want him to think she was having problems, and couldn't handle her job. He was proud of her and, in part, his pride kept her going. Whenever anyone asked him what his biggest accomplishment was, he would say *my daughter, the doctor*. He wouldn't mention a building, or a museum, or a stadium, but her. How could she fail? Lose her job? Let him down? How—

"Dana, are you there?"

Her mother intruding on her thoughts. "Yes, I'm here."

"I asked you if it was raining."

"No. It was a wet spring, but the rain has stopped."

"In my dream, it was raining a lot. Your house was flooded."

"That happened already," Dana said. There were times her mother had prescient dreams. When Dana was a kid her mother dreamed the school bus hit a patch of ice and skidded off the road. She was so freaked out she kept Dana home from school for a week. The day Dana got back on the bus the accident happened. Her mother also had many dreams that didn't come true, and bad things happened that she never dreamed about. Dana always listened to her dreams with a grain of salt.

"I saw about twenty open umbrellas outside your building. They were all yours. As if it was raining, but just on you. Is anything wrong?"

"No, Ma. It was a dream. Look, I've got to go." She stood up.

"A date?" her mother said, with too much hope. "It is Saturday night after all."

Though she felt guilty about it, Dana lied. "It's a date."

"Who is it this time?" Her mother despaired that Dana was running around, reluctant to settle down.

"A colleague," Dana said, thinking of Tim, whom her mother met and liked.

"Well, I told you, when you go to school too long, you narrow your choices."

"Say hi to Dad for me."

"Stay out of the rain."

"Yes, Mother."

"Well, have a good week."

"You too."

A long silence then, as if they were each waiting for the other to say something more. Dana pushed the disconnect button and dropped the receiver. Talking to her mother always wore her out.

The phone rang immediately. McCoy.

"Dr. Sparks," he said, using her title, as was his way. He never called her Dana and no one ever called him anything but Dr. McCoy or Sir. He said, "I'm afraid there's an emergency."

"Emergency?" Had one of her students died? Did someone break into her lab and steal lethal bacteria? Was there a fire? A car crash?

"Michael Smith and I planned a dinner this evening but something came up and I can't make it. I'm hoping you'll go in my place."

"What's the emergency?"

He wouldn't tell her. "I would not make this request unless it was absolutely necessary. It would be a great favor."

Dana tapped her foot and considered. Dinner out would atone for the lie she told her mother and meeting Michael Smith would give her an opportunity to check out the West Point man first-hand. But she wouldn't make it easy for McCoy. "I have a favor of my own to ask. Retain the latest teacher evaluation."

A long silence. "Dr. Sparks, I won't be blackmailed."

"There's no reason to discard it."

"The exercise was unobserved and therefore invalid."

"Nonetheless it was conducted correctly."

McCoy sighed. "Dr. Smith is at the Motel Eight and expects you at seven."

If there was a bright side to Michael Smith's visit, it was his residency at the cheap motel. In Dana's mind it was an insult to be kept at the Motel Eight. Most visiting scientists stayed at the Lone Star Heritage Hotel or the Tremblant Apartments. It was an added insult that the boss had cancelled at the last minute.

But in the faded dingy lobby, the visitor smiled and refused to appear insulted. Michael Smith was slight with short dark hair. He had dark brown eyes, an olive complexion and a thick, wiry moustache. He was a head shorter than Dana and reeked of aftershave and Scope.

She extended a hand and Michael looked at it a moment, before taking her palm lightly in his. His fingers were soft, his handshake weak. He said hello with a hint of an accent Dana couldn't place.

She said, "McCoy is sorry he couldn't be here. He was doing something else tonight."

Michael Smith seemed unconcerned about the last minute change in plans. He smoothed the wrinkled lapels of his beige blazer and followed her to the car. He wore open toed sandals that slapped on the concrete. He walked in a slouch, with his hands in his pockets, staring up at the sky. His mustache resembled the bristled end of a toothbrush.

They drove along Texas Avenue and Dana recited a brief

history of the town. Located between Houston and Dallas, Duane had a population of fifty thousand. About half the people were associated with the college. There were twenty thousand full-time students. The University of Duane started out as an annex to the state university, but had gone private ten years ago. Its reputation was in the arts, but the university president was trying to change its image. Eight years ago the veterinary college opened and if the president had his way, there would be a medical school soon, as well.

Turning west on University Drive, Dana shot past the row of student bars that were packed early for Saturday night. They whizzed by the University Plaza, the outdoor plaza for one stop shopping. It had a car wash, movie theater, giant supermarket and laundromat.

Past the University Plaza, the Lone Star Heritage Hotel shone like a castle. A fleet of dark limousines lined the forecourt and dark-suited men wearing sunglasses huddled on the steps. FBI agents scoping out the hotel where the VP would stay. Dana turned into the parking lot. They would eat at the Pizza Garden, the outdoor bistro behind the hotel.

A doorman in a tux stood by the front door. The lobby was busy and it seemed many parents had arrived early for the graduation ceremonies a week away. A small crowd of people milled outside Caprice, the hotel's five-star restaurant. There was a line-up at the bar and people gripping drinks stood aimlessly in the lobby.

The Pizza Garden was outside on the lawn and the perimeter was demarcated with a string of gold, red and green hanging lanterns. Every table was taken and they had to wait.

Michael went to wash his hands and Dana read notices pinned to the thorns of a large saguaro cactus planted by the bistro entrance. Someone was looking for a roommate, someone wanted a ride to Austin and someone had lost a cat. There was a color photo of a young boy with red hair and freckles clutching a calico cat that looked bigger than Judy. *Please bring Pumpkin home* read the sign written in a childish scrawl. *Call Travis Trelane.* Dana wondered if the cat had been found, if Travis got his call. Poor kid. She knew what it was like to lose a pet. Anthony ran away soon after she got him and in two days she imagined a thousand horrible deaths—drowning, murder, car accidents, puma attacks, abduction. Then he came home and had not run away again.

A short vivacious waitress with a stack of menus indicated that a table was ready. Dana followed her to the pool and sat down facing Caprice. The enormous glass doors were open and the muslin curtains billowed with the night breeze. Caprice was Dana's favorite restaurant, but she didn't eat there often. This year she had only been once, with Tim. He was extravagant, she remembered, and unbidden, the memory of their dinner returned. They had danced as a violinist played.

Michael was back and shrugging off his wrinkled blazer. "Quite a place," he said. He stared at the pool, complete with underwater stools aside a poolside bar. Two voluptuous women relaxed in a Jacuzzi and Michael averted his eyes. The waitress bounced back, pad in hand. She wore a short skirt and a tight tube-top, showing a band of skin on her midriff. Michael stared at the menu and Dana saw beads of sweat on his forehead.

She recommended a large pizza with everything, but Michael objected to the sausage. Dana wondered if he didn't eat pork. Was he Jewish? "Okay, we'll skip the sausage. What about jalapeños? Do you eat hot food?"

Michael did.

Dana placed the order. She wanted a glass of wine and recommended the house white.

"I don't drink." Michael said.

McCoy would like that, Dana thought. He was almost a teetotaler himself. She ordered a glass of wine and

Michael ordered a Coke. But when the drinks came, he sent his back. He didn't want ice.

Fussy, Dana saw, though he tried to laugh off the incident.

"Most people don't realize warm drinks are more refreshing than cold."

"Is that so," Dana said, drinking cold wine. Trickles of condensation ran down the glass. "Are you from a warm climate?"

He wasn't. He grew up in London.

"I thought I detected an accent," she said.

Michael said nothing. She sipped more wine and watched a crowd of students stream into the bistro. Trying to deter the college crowd, the hotel had jacked up its prices, but to no avail. The loud and boisterous beer-swilling students still came.

The waitress brought Michael a new Coke. He took a long pull and nodded his approval but the waitress was already gone. Then to Dana's happy surprise he pulled a box of Winston cigarettes from his pocket. McCoy detested smokers.

"Mind if I smoke?" Michael asked.

"Mind? Be my guest," Dana said. He struck a match and exhaled a puff of smoke. How could an immunologist smoke? She herself had quit smoking in her sophomore year when she was pre-med.

Michael finished his lukewarm Coke and ordered another. He wiped the sweat from his brow, put down his cigarette and rolled up his sleeves. She noticed three lines of deep scratches trailing from his wrist to his forearm.

"I went for a walk in the woods and was caught in a thorny vine," he said.

"Smilax." She pushed up her sleeve and showed him her scratches. His were deeper, hers more numerous.

He sucked on his cigarette intently. Not a big talker. The silence grew thick.

"I work with *Yersinia*," Dana said.

"I hear you found a vaccine. Is it available?"

"Not yet. The clinical trials won't start until July."

"Did you try it against resistant bacteria?" Michael crushed out his cigarette.

"No. A number of wild type strains."

He was lighting up again. "How effective is it?"

"On mice, ninety-seven percent." She did not mention the dismal response of the guinea pig.

"How long does the vaccine take to be effective?"

"Immediately," she said.

He blew a large round smoke ring that grew larger in the air. "How much money do you have?"

His boundaries were a little loose, Dana thought. Would he ask her next how much *she* made? Still, she answered his question. "I should get a grant for a million."

"What's the grant for?"

"To look for an active vaccine. A one shot deal that will last a lifetime."

"Any chance of success?"

Dana picked up her wine and watched the crowd of students march to an adjacent table. "Oh, definitely."

"TJ said the research might not be funded."

TJ. He called him TJ. She narrowed her eyes. "TJ is wrong."

"Nellie showed me your lab."

"She what?" Dana slammed her glass down on the table so hard that wine slopped over the edge.

"You weren't there. It was Friday afternoon. She said you would not mind. That you usually didn't work Friday afternoons."

Bitch! "I was giving a lecture." Dana wondered why she felt she had to defend herself to him.

"There was no one in the lab. You have no students?"

"I have four. A post doc, Ph.D., Master's and fourth year student. *Plus* a technician. All but the undergrad and technician are out of town. The post doc is in California giving a paper. The Master's student is in Mexico looking at an outbreak of cholera. And the Ph.D. student is in France doing a three week course at the Pasteur Institute." She sounded defensive again and knew there was no reason to go into all these details. What she didn't say was that the students would leave soon and she had no replacements. Until she knew she had tenure she could take on no new people.

"It's a big lab," Michael said. "And you have lots of equipment."

"I've had a lot of money," Dana said. "What about you? TJ said you graduated from West Point."

"I did my undergraduate there. West Point has no graduate school."

If that was a rebuke, she ignored it. "Where are you working now?" She did not recognize his name and if he had written any papers, she had not read them.

"Iowa City."

"What brings you to Texas?"

"A job interview."

She choked on the wine. McCoy had neglected to mention he was interviewing people. "Here?"

"TJ said he may have an opening. He asked me to give a seminar."

"You work with anthrax?"

"That's right."

"What are you researching?" she asked. "Anything to do with the mail anthrax scare after the September 11 attacks?"

He raised his dark eyes and blew smoke at the sky. "No. Problems with the vaccine."

Now they were getting somewhere. In the Gulf War, the anthrax vaccine had been widely used and war vets suspected the Gulf War Syndrome was a side effect of a bad vaccine.

"What problems?" Dana said.

"The research is classified," he said, and smoked on.

God, was he secretive. McCoy would like that.

After a few minutes of silence, Dana asked if he was married. He didn't wear a wedding ring and she hoped he wasn't, for McCoy believed strongly in the sanctity of marriage.

"Yes," Michael said. He worked a photograph out of his wallet and passed it across the table. Dana saw a beaming dark-haired mother cradling two infant babies.

"Twins," Michael said, and was distracted by the din from the nearby table. The students were standing, glasses raised. They chugged their glasses. A guy drinking from a pitcher belched loudly then ran to the bushes.

"Does your wife work?" Dana asked, when the adjacent table settled down.

"No," Michael said. "She is happy being a wife and a mother."

McCoy would love that too, men who had wives who stayed at home and raised the children. Except for his chain-smoking, he was winning on all grounds, Dana thought, as the waitress brought the steaming pizza. Michael ordered his third Coke.

They ate the pizza. The jalapeños brought tears to Dana's eyes and she watched incredulously as Michael shook crushed cayenne pepper over his slice. He chomped loudly as pizza juice dripped down his fingers. His cigarette burned in the ashtray. Unlike McCoy, he had not maintained his table manners after leaving West Point. McCoy's manners were fastidious.

As they ate, Michael asked about her personal life and seemed surprised she wasn't married. "You live with your parents?"

An odd question. "No. I live alone. I have a house just outside town."

"In the country?" Michael said. He wanted to live in the country, thought it might be healthy for the twins. "Might I see your place?"

"Sure. Anytime," Dana said vaguely.

They talked about the weather, the heat in Duane, the snow in Iowa and the twins and their mother who were cooped up all winter long. "Here they'd be cooped up all summer," Dana said. "The sun is a major problem." She mentioned the high incidence of malignant melanoma and childhood leukemia, fire ants and killer bees.

"The world is a dangerous place," Michael said.

They discussed the bombing of Mogadishu. The vice president was coming to Duane at a bad time, for the government was being thrashed after its recent attack. There was no official Somali government, but a warlord was adamant that there were no terrorists of any sort in Mogadishu and no military target had been hit, just a warehouse, hospital and mosque. The American air strike was in vain if you discounted twenty innocent civilians who lost their lives.

Finally the meal was done and the waitress came with the check and left with the plates. Michael went for more cigarettes. Dana paid the bill and asked for a receipt. McCoy would pay for this dinner. She wondered if he had set it up on purpose. Was he more conniving than she thought? Was he sending her a covert message? Did he want her to know he considered her position open and available?

Dana stared across the lawn at Caprice. A couple sat near the window. The woman's blond hair was pulled up in a french twist. Heavy gold dangled from her ears. She looked about twenty-five. The man stared into her eyes. His bronzed skin gleaming, his blond hair trimmed. Tim Sweeny, not waiting at home for Dana to call any time.

Then Michael was back, followed by the waitress and Dana was ready to go. Hoping to evade Tim, she led Michael across the grass toward the parking lot. She stopped short when a woman in the restaurant screamed. Dana watched through the open window as Tim jumped up and hauled a writhing man with a purple face to his feet.

Tim wrapped his arms around the man's back and pulled up hard under his thorax. The Heimlich maneuver, designed to stop choking. It was effective. The man gagged and spluttered and began to cough. The girl with the gold grabbed Tim's arm and kissed his cheek. Tim grabbed her back.

"Let's go," Dana said.

She was quiet on the way home and said nothing until she bid Michael goodbye.

She kept the motor running and he got out. "Will I see you tomorrow?"

"Unlikely," she said.

"At TJ's? For the party?"

A party she wasn't invited to. "No." Dana said tightly.

Sunday

Chapter 9

The garden party began after church. McCoy had hoped the barbecue would ease Margaret's loneliness and help her find new and appropriate friends, but she wouldn't co-operate. As the guests arrived, Margaret sulked upstairs. She had refused to attend church that morning and wouldn't talk to him.

McCoy escorted a blue-haired lady whose name he couldn't recall through the house to the garden. The kitchen smelled sweet, of just-baked biscuits. The counter was filled with smoking baked potatoes and steaming beans. Brass bowls collected in the Middle East brimmed with nachos, cheese dip and corn chips. Standard Texan party food according to the cookbooks.

In the backyard, clumps of people holding cups of fruit punch milled under a striped awning. McCoy sat the old lady down next to the dean of the Veterinary College and his wife, Drake and Nellie Duncan. The doorbell rang and McCoy hastened to the door. Father Bob loomed in the entrance, gripping a crate of Lone Star beer, though McCoy had not planned to serve alcohol at his party. Father Bob dropped the case, opened his arms and suffocated McCoy in a strong embrace.

"A great idea, a fine idea," Father Bob said. He released McCoy, grabbed his beer and headed to the garden.

Michael Smith came next, dressed in white and moving shyly. McCoy apologized for his absence the previous night. "I'm afraid there was an emergency, but I'm sure Dr. Sparks explained that."

"It was no problem," Michael Smith said.

McCoy was happy to hear it. This was the kind of man he needed on his team. One who could take last minute set-backs without having a nervous breakdown. "We'll talk later." McCoy pointed him to the yard as a flock of young girls walked up the drive.

They were Margaret's age and their clean appearance pleased him. They wore long dresses and happy smiles. If only Margaret could make new friends. But how to get her out of her room? McCoy aimed the young ladies at the garden and climbed the stairs.

He reached Margaret's door as the phone began to ring. "Margaret, dear," he said, fingering his bracelet. "Can you get that?"

No answer. God, why did children have to grow up? McCoy grabbed the phone. Someone must be lost and looking for directions.

There was an introduction and a name he didn't catch. Then, "Is this Dr. TJ McCoy, head of the Department of Immunology and Microbiology?"

"Yes, yes," McCoy said, as the doorbell rang.

"This is Greenlee Hospital," said the caller.

"One minute." McCoy called to Margaret. "Baby, get the door. I'm on the phone."

No answer.

"We need help," said the caller.

"What is it?" When McCoy arrived he informed both lo-cal hospitals if they needed assistance, they had only to

5

ask. In McCoy's mind, his future department, dedicated to human health, would provide backup and cutting-edge diagnostics to both hospitals. Downstairs the doorbell clanged again. McCoy stared helplessly at his daughter's closed door.

"A man came in this morning with what looks like a bacterial infection," said the caller. "His white blood cell count is two hundred thousand per ml with a predominance of immature and mature neutrophils. He's got enlarged lymph nodes but so far cultures haven't shown anything. We don't know what he's got and our treatment doesn't appear to work."

"Where is your infectious disease specialist?" McCoy asked, as the doorbell went again.

"Dr. Taversham is away for the weekend. We've been trying to reach him but we can't. We don't know what to do."

"Draw the patient's blood," McCoy said. "Have it waiting at the admissions desk. I'll send someone immediately."

McCoy hung up and called to his daughter again, "Margaret, honey, could you please get the door." Still no answer and he yelled, "Come in," as he reached for the phone.

Chapter 10

The phone call brought Dana running in from the yard where she had been bathing Anthony. He was overrun with fleas and ticks, and she left him soaking in flea lotion and snaking on his side across the grass. She leapt over Frank, who lay in a patch of sunlight by the door. Inside, she grabbed the receiver. She thought it was her mother, calling again, but it was McCoy.

"Dr. Sparks, I'm glad you're there. I've got a problem. A blood sample is waiting for you at the front desk of Greenlee Hospital. Run an ELISA with your bacterial antigens. Get back to me ASAP."

Dana frowned and didn't answer. Over the phone she heard much hoopla and high voices calling hello. A doorbell rang. McCoy, indisposed at his party. Even on Sunday he would tell her what to do. She considered refusing, but curiosity won out. Why couldn't the hospital run the test? Was it an unusual infection? "How do you know it's a bacterial infection?"

"I'm hoping you'll confirm it."

McCoy never gave anything away. He always spoke as if

he was at war and information was restricted. Dana pressed him. "What are the patient's symptoms?"

But McCoy distributed information on a need-to-know basis only. "Let his doctor worry about that. Get the blood sample, take it to the lab and run the test. Call me with the results."

"Aye-aye, Sir." She called him *Sir* when she was angry with him. Not that he noticed; the use of his title usually pacified him.

Dana finished rinsing Anthony, then took a shower and dressed. She was worried about Frank and hated to leave him at home by himself. During the weekend his condition had grown worse and he had acquired a rasping cough. Dana called Tim that morning but there was no answer at his house. She decided to take Frank with her.

Leaving the others dogs, she drove down the east side of the bypass, past the latest housing development, where the houses were new and crammed close to each other on curvilinear streets. The lawns were small and the grass was short. What was it that made some people want to live so close to each other?

In ten minutes she was at the hospital, kitty-corner to the university. Greenlee Hospital catered primarily to the university students and staff, while St. Joseph's Hospital on the north side of town served the general population. Neither hospital was equipped for exotic diagnostics or major emergencies and critically ill patients were flown to Houston for treatment.

Dana headed for the emergency entrance on Texas Avenue. She knew the layout of the hospital because she'd served as Sheryl's labor coach; in one of the Lamaze classes, there had been a hospital tour.

The waiting area in the emergency room was empty except for two doctors dressed in scrub suits playing checkers. A young receptionist with curly red hair sat at the information desk filing her nails. She handed Dana a small plastic vial that contained a half-milliliter of blood. There was no biohazard bag, no written indication that the tube might contain an infectious organism. Despite McCoy's orders, Dana inquired about the patient.

The receptionist consulted her computer. "That belongs to Dudley Shaw, room two-oh-two."

Dana thanked the receptionist and left her to her nails. She rode a brisk elevator to the second floor. Room 202 was across the hall. The patient's chart hung on the back of the door and Dana scanned the report.

Dudley Shaw was sixty-five years old and like her had a post office box address. He had been brought by ambulance at ten that morning. He was dehydrated and confused. His temperature was 104°, his blood pressure 100/60, seriously low. His neutrophil and lymphocyte count were three times higher than normal, indicative of a bacterial infection. Routine antibody tests were negative. Dudley's blood had been cultured for bacteria but the results would not be ready for twenty-four hours. A blood smear showed nothing untoward.

Dana checked Dudley's treatment schedule. He was taking acetaminophen for fever and oxymorphine for pain. He was on three different antibiotics that were effective against a wide spectrum of gram positive and negative bacteria. He was on an IV drip and receiving plasma intravenously to boost his blood volume. The clinical observations did little to shed light on the nature of his infection.

As Dana replaced the chart in the slot in the door, a heavy hand clapped her shoulder. She spun around to find a hulking health care attendant with a face as black as old coffee. "I'm sorry ma'am," he said, "but that's a restricted area." His name tag read Sam.

"Oh." She smiled sheepishly. "That's okay. I'm a doctor." She didn't explain what kind. She groped in her purse for the tube of blood and held it up. "I was sent to assay Dudley Shaw's blood."

"I hope you find out what he's got," Sam said. "The doctor here is stumped. When Shaw came in he looked dead, but he's doing better. We got him on morphine and he's off his rocker."

"Have you talked to him?"

"We're fixing to. He wasn't talking when he came in and now he's so stoned he's not making much sense."

"Do you mind if I ask him a few questions?" Dana asked. Sam thought it would be all right.

She left him in the hall and went into the room. It was dark and the drapes were drawn. Dudley Shaw was sleeping. His hair was white and swept across his scalp to hide a bald spot. He cried out in his troubled sleep and Dana froze, not wanting to disturb him.

She eyed the room, her eyes now accustomed to the dark. The room was decorated in shades of pastel. A pink flowered quilt on the bed and pale yellow curtains on the windows. There was a rocking chair and a colorful throw rug on the floor. But all the comfortable furniture and soothing colors in the world could not camouflage the odor, or muffle the drip, drip, drip of the IV that always sounded to her like a clock winding down.

Dudley stirred, flailing his arms. He blinked his eyes and stared up at her, then struggled to sit.

His eyes were light brown, bleary and washed out, the irises floating in a soupy opaque sea. It had been her father's eyes that had bothered her the most when he was sick. Her father's eyes were so brown they were almost black, but not when he was ill. Then, the color had faded, as if his life and vitality were seeping out of him. When he had recovered, their color and intensity came back. She wished she had his eyes, but she had inherited her mother's.

"Who are you?" Dudley said. His voice was soft, his words coming out on wisps of air. His breathing was raspy and labored.

Dana introduced herself. "I came to check your blood. How are you feeling?" A pat and ridiculous question given the circumstances.

Dudley shook his head. His skin was pale and his five o'clock shadow was white and looked like snow sprinkled on his chin. "Been better." She pulled a chair up beside his bed and they talked. He had worked as a gardener at Duane University and recently retired. He was taking a big trip. Then he snapped his fingers. "Bingo."

Was he talking about the game?

"My dog. He'll be hungry. I've got to go."

"It's all right. I can feed him."

Dudley cast his watery gaze on her. "You would?"

"I have three dogs of my own. I don't mind. Where do you live?"

He gave complicated directions that left her confused and she finally asked him to draw a map. His wallet was on the bedside table and from it he pulled out a stack of Visa receipts. He scribbled on the back of one.

She watched him over his shoulder. He didn't live too far from her house, out by the forest.

He handed her the map; she turned it over and saw the receipt was from the car wash next to campus. Thirty bucks for a wash and wax. Unbelievable. Texans were nuts about their cars. She folded the receipt and crammed it in her back pocket.

"When will they let me out?" Dudley asked.

"Probably tomorrow. It's just a bacterial infection. The antibiotics will make you feel better real soon."

"You're sure? Just a bacterial infection? Nothing more?" He touched the flesh under his left armpit.

He sounded worried. Dana asked if he had a pain under his arm.

He answered too quickly. "No."

"The lymph drains into nodes under the left arm," Dana said. "Not the right, just the left. If you have a bacterial infection, sometimes the nodes can swell and the pressure can cause significant pain."

He seemed to consider this. "Do the lymph nodes feel like a lump?"

"If they're swollen. You mind if I feel?"

"My father died of cancer when he was my age." Dudley held out his hand.

Dana looked at his hand and what she saw made her gasp. The bases of his fingernails were black. A classic sign of the plague. It was something she had only seen in textbooks.

"What's wrong?" he said.

She took his hand. "How long have you been sick?"

"A few days."

"So, not too long."

"No." He sounded hopeful.

She pushed up the sleeve of the hospital gown and felt gingerly under his right armpit. He didn't flinch or react. She let go of his arm, and lifted the other. When she felt under this arm he jumped. The lymph node was hard and solid. The size of a chicken egg.

"What is it?" he said.

A bubo, she wondered? A swollen lymph gland teeming with plague bacteria? The hair on the back of her neck stood on end. "A swollen gland," she said. The attending physician must have missed it.

"Not a tumor?" Dudley said.

She shook her head. "Given your other symptoms, no." She sat back down. If he did have the plague, where was he infected? He couldn't get the plague in Duane, it was too far south. The *Yersinia* bacteria maintained a strict geographical range. "Have you been away?"

"To New Orleans to see my sister."

That was further south than Duane. "When was that?"

"Easter."

Four weeks ago. The incubation for bubonic plague was

three to eight days. He couldn't have been infected there. "Have you had any visitors?"

"No."

"Are you married?"

"No."

"Any rats at your house?"

"Pardon?"

"I meant fleas. Does Bingo have fleas?"

"Sure. He hates water. Whatever you do, don't turn on the faucet when you go out. He'll never come. Why do you ask?"

"I have one of my dogs with me in the car. He's got fleas too."

"It was all the rain in the spring."

"And the mild winter," she said, and stood up, looking at her watch. She wanted to ask him more questions, but didn't want to cause him unnecessary worry. Not until she knew for sure what he had. It might not be the plague. An acute or chronic bacterial infection could explain swollen glands, and there were other explanations for hypoxia. The blue color meant a lack of oxygen. It could be a sign of failing respiration, shock, or poor circulation. As McCoy would be the first to tell her, she shouldn't jump to conclusions.

"I'll go," she said. "Feed Bingo and do the blood work. I'll come back tomorrow to see you."

"Am I really going to be okay?"

"You'll be fine."

"Thank you," he said, as if she had bequeathed him good health. He lay back in his pillow. "Thanks."

She drove out to Dudley's after stopping to buy a bag of Dog Chow. She offered a kibble to Frank, but he looked away. He had stopped eating. She had made bacon and eggs for breakfast and he wouldn't touch any of the leftovers.

He wouldn't get out of the car at Dudley's and was fast asleep when she returned after leaving Bingo his food.

There was no sign of the dog, which was worrisome, given the possible diagnosis and the presence of fleas.

When she reached her office, the phone was ringing. McCoy again. "What have you got?"

"A blood sample," Dana said, watching Frank circle the square under her desk. He lay down carefully, breathing easier in the air conditioning. "I was about to start."

"Start? Yet we talked two hours ago."

"I realize that," she said sharply. "And the sooner I start, the sooner I'll get back to you."

The quarantine room at the back of her lab was claustrophobic and windowless. The walls were white and the fluorescent light was blinding bright. The floor was gray and the room smelled of acetone and Lysol.

Dana washed her hands, pulled on disposable gloves and a lab coat. She opened the freezer and retrieved a biohazard box that contained bacterial standards. She thawed eighteen vials in a beaker of warm water. Then she took the standards and Dudley's blood sample to a laminar flow hood and sat down. She flipped a switch that started a fan that created a negative air pressure that drew air and potential airborne pathogens up and out of the room. The bacterial standards were dead and no longer infectious. It was Dudley's blood that demanded care.

She began the assay and labeled an immunological plate that resembled a miniature egg carton. To each well she added a drop of known bacteria: *Staphylococcus, Streptococcus, Pneumococcus, Neisseria, Erysipelothrix, Bacillus, Listeria, Nocardia, Escherichia, Shigella, Klebsiella, Proteus, Salmonella, Brucella, Francisella, Vibrio, Pseudomonas* and lastly, *Yersinia.* Next, she added a drop of Dudley's blood; the assay required all the hospital had given her.

The ELISA used bacterial standards to fish out complementary antibodies from the blood. If the blood reacted with one of the known bacterial standards, then the identity of the infecting bacteria was known.

The assay took forty minutes to run. In the final step, a marker that fluoresced in UV light and recognized antibodies bound to bacteria was added. Dana added the marker, waited five minutes, then turned on a UV light. There was a glowing spot. A positive match for *Yersinia pestis*. Dudley Shaw had the plague.

Dana sunk onto the stool. There was no mistaking the result of the test but it didn't make sense. Where was he infected? She thought of Bingo lost in the forest and a shiver shot up her spine and she felt afraid. Hold on, she cautioned herself. Back up. Wait one minute. Antibodies alone only confirmed a presumptive diagnosis. To make a positive diagnosis, the infecting bacterium had to be grown and identified. Under a microscope, the bacteria looked like safety pins, and according to the hospital report, no untoward bacteria had been found in Dudley's blood. Though, when it came to the plague, blood work to detect the bacteria was notoriously unreliable. With bubonic plague, they would have better luck aspirating the bubo.

Dana took off her gloves and washed her hands. She went to her office and called McCoy.

"There was a positive response for *Yersinia pestis*."

He was quiet for a moment, then thanked her for the information.

"Should I call the hospital and let them know?" she asked. The U.S. Public Health Service policy was for doctors to report all suspected cases of the plague to the local and state health departments, and the Centers for Disease Control. The CDC would then notify the World Health Organization.

"Don't do anything," McCoy said.

"If Dudley Shaw has the plague, he's on the wrong medication. He should be taking streptomycin, tetracycline and chloramphenicol. If he . . ."

McCoy interrupted her. "I'm well aware of what he should be taking. I'll handle this, Doctor."

"All I'm saying is that the hospital needs to be alerted. His lymph node fluid needs to be tested. Dudley should be in quarantine and he could be contagious and . . ."

"Yes, thank you for that information. It might surprise you to know that I am familiar with infectious disease." There was a long silence and then McCoy added stridently. "Don't say a word about this to anyone."

"But . . ."

"But, I will handle this. With the vice president's visit, this could present a precarious complication. Good day."

Dana heard the dial tone in her ear. McCoy hung up before she could tell him about the dog.

Monday

Chapter 11

After a fitful night, Dana lay in bed waiting for the sun to rise. It was a cool morning; she felt uneasy and on edge and could not pinpoint the reason why. She wondered if she'd had a bad dream she had forgotten. Or perhaps it was Dudley Shaw, left in the hands of McCoy who was going to "handle" things and did not need her advice. Dana had tried last night to call him and tell him about Bingo, but according to his wife, he was out for a drive. McCoy had a strange way of handling things.

Anyhow, she reasoned, if she had found out about Bingo, he could too. After the presumptive diagnosis of the plague, someone with experience would move in and conduct a proper interview. But who was the someone? In the town of Duane, Dana was the plague specialist and there had been no resident epidemiologist for seven years. Even if he didn't know it, McCoy needed her help. And if he thought he would exclude her from investigating this case, he was wrong. She wasn't about to let a physicist run an investigation that should be hers. As soon as it was light, she was going back to the hospital to ask Dudley more questions. The most important thing right now was his dog. She would need a description of him and a means to track him down.

When the sky turned purple Dana rose from bed. She fed the dogs and again Frank refused to eat. He had eaten nothing in twenty-four hours. Dana didn't think it would be possible, but overnight, Frank's condition had deteriorated further. Now he refused to get out bed and she had to pull him up. Then he started coughing and couldn't stop. It was a difficult struggle to get him to the car.

At the hospital, outside Dudley's room there was a bright orange sign that read: QUARANTINE AREA. STRICTLY NO ADMITTANCE. In the hallway, next to the door there was a chair piled high with packages of protective clothing. Dana ripped open a bag and donned a yellow paper suit, gloves and booties. There was a paper toque for her hair and a mask for her face.

She went into the room. The bed was empty. The windows were shut and the drapes were pulled. She heard water running in the bathroom and breathed more easily. If Dudley was up and using the bathroom, his condition had improved.

But when the bathroom door opened, Sam emerged. He too was dressed in protective clothing and all Dana could see were his dark eyes and black skin.

"Where's Dudley?" Dana asked.

"Gone."

"Home?"

Sam lifted his eyes to the ceiling. "You might say that."

"When did he leave?"

Sam walked over to the bed and picked up the pillow. He removed the case and tossed it on the floor, tore the bedspread and sheets off the bed. "Middle of the night. He kept getting worse and worse and the drugs didn't help. At the end he couldn't breathe. His skin was blue. He was convulsing. He couldn't get air. Dr. Taversham kept giving him morphine, but he couldn't stop the convulsions. Electroshock couldn't start his heart."

Dudley was dead. Dana leaned against the wall, needing support. He would not live to take his road trip, to describe or help find his dog. What happened? *What the hell happened?* You could treat bubonic plague with antibiotics. Yet Dudley had died.

She watched in silence as Sam stuffed the pillow, sheets, towels, clothes and comforter in a biohazard bag. Dudley died because he was bitten by a flea. *A flea.* There was something wrong with that. Something very wrong.

Dudley was in the wrong place at the wrong time and had been bitten somewhere, somehow, by a flea infected with the plague. It was an accident, something that happened for no reason. Like a cancer that resulted from a random genetic mistake. Or a car crash that took your life because you liked fast sports cars and didn't have snow tires in a town where it didn't snow—usually.

It was a breakdown of causality, a small inconsequent occurrence that had a far-reaching effect. A tenet of chaos theory; a small initial effect exerting a significant influence. Like a butterfly beating its wings in India causing a typhoon in Madagascar.

She caught Sam looking at her. "Are you all right? he said. "I thought doctors were pretty much used to death."

"Most," she said. It was blood and death that locked Dana out of a career in medicine.

Sam swung the biohazard bag in a circle to seal the open end. He knotted the bag and placed it inside another biohazard bag, then tossed the bundle at a corner. "I heard he had bubonic plague." He straightened and looked at Dana.

She nodded her head. "What antibiotics was he taking?"

Sam listed the three usually used for the plague. At least Dudley had been treated correctly.

"You should take prophylactics," Sam said. "Oral antibiotics. Dr. Taversham said they'd protect anyone in contact with Shaw."

Dana nodded again. The antibiotic tetracycline was used in part for treatment and also provided post-exposure protection against the plague. She didn't need oral antibiotics though; for eight years she had been vaccinated against the disease, as recently, she hoped, as Friday. She rubbed her biceps. Later today she would check the antibodies in her blood.

"I heard agents from the CDC were on their way," Sam said. "The hospital called for help."

The CDC couldn't come unless they were asked and Dana had mixed feelings when she heard they would be involved. Once they arrived, they'd take over and she wanted a chance to prove herself. This was the point of all her research, what made her work and her time spent, meaningful.

Sam picked up a large canister that looked like a fire extinguisher. "You'd better go," he said. "I've got to fumigate the room."

"What should I do with the suit?" Under normal quarantine regulations, after working in a hot zone any person exposed to a highly contagious organism would decontaminate their clothes and body in a sealed room. But the small town hospital had no such room.

Sam pointed to the biohazard bag. "Leave the suit there."

The sight of the orange bag rang an alarm in Dana's head and it took her an instant to remember a heavy orange biohazard bag she held in her hand on Friday afternoon. The bag that Carol Dupuis had given her, with the four dead rats who had died under mysterious circumstances, was sitting in Dana's freezer awaiting testing.

She left the hospital at a jog. The sun had cleared the trees and the air was hot. She should have left the window down for Frank, who was standing in the back seat, panting hard. His nose was dry and salt-stained.

She jumped in and started the car, zoomed out, hitting the buttons for the windows and the air conditioner. "Hold on, Frank," she said. "Hold on."

She reached the vet school and in spite of McCoy's threat, parked near the front so Frank wouldn't have to walk far. She would move her car later. Theoretically, she was a clinic client.

But the clinic wasn't open, and Dana took Frank upstairs in the service elevator. She left him in her office while she went to the quarantine lab to test the rats' blood.

She removed the biohazard bag from the freezer. The Revco maintained a minus 70° Celsius temperature, which preserved biological samples nearly indefinitely. At that temperature there was little molecular movement, little decay. She placed the bag in the microwave and set the machine on thaw. While she waited, she put on a lab coat, gloves and a mask, and prepped for the assay.

In forty-five minutes she had the answer she sought. All four rats were infected with the plague. Possible or not, the fact was the plague bacteria were in Duane. A man had died from bubonic plague, a student was likely exposed and a dog that might be carrying infected fleas was lost. How much of this did McCoy know?

Dana removed her protective gear and though she was already late for the weekly staff meeting that began at eight o'clock sharp, she washed her hands with antibiotic soap for the requisite two minutes. Racing from the quarantine room, past her office, she stopped short when she saw Frank. How could she forget about him? It was as if he were already gone.

She left him heaving and sprinted across the hall and pounded loudly on Tim Sweeny's door. No answer. His resident, Sheila, often used his office, but she wasn't there now. She tried the door and found it locked.

"Tim isn't there."

Dana spun around and saw the last person she wanted to see, Nellie Duncan, wife of the dean of the Veterinary College. She was the unaccredited department histologist who was paid a fortune to prepare slides she never made. By virtue of her marriage she held a position she didn't deserve and had power she didn't earn. When Brian Boswell was alive, he kept her in line, but with the coming of McCoy, Nellie was a rising star. She was using her twenty years of experience and history at the vet school to "help" him find his way in the department.

"I know Tim isn't here," Dana said. She turned and headed for the conference room adjacent to McCoy's office.

Nellie was on her heels. "I hate to be the one to tell you but Tim went out on the weekend with another woman."

"He can go out with whomever he wants."

"Oh." Nellie clicked her teeth. "You broke up. I'm sorry." She spoke in a patronizing tone, drawing out her vowels. "But there is a visitor—Michael Smith. Maybe he's available."

"Don't worry about me, and besides, he's married."

"I didn't think that was a problem for you."

Dana increased her pace.

Beside her Nellie pulled on her lab coat then brushed an invisible fleck off the swell of her breast. She was fifty years old and looked thirty. She dyed her hair an unnatural shade of honey brown and had it cut in a pageboy, flipped under at the ends.

They reached the main office and Dana waved to Betty, who was on the phone. Nellie lowered her voice. "Oh, and there's a case of bubonic plague in town, did you know?"

Dana said nothing; they had reached the conference room.

Nellie wasn't finished. "Of course you wouldn't. It's confidential and McCoy's going to handle it."

Chapter 12

By the time the 8:00 A.M. meeting rolled around, McCoy was already exhausted. He had arrived at work early and found a message to call the dean immediately. McCoy made the call.

Five minutes later he slammed down the receiver and placed a hand over his racing heart. The man infected with the plague had died and CDC agents were on their way. God damn it, Greenlee Hospital had called them for help. The State Health Department had also been notified. They would survey hospitals across Texas in search of patients with symptoms similar to Dudley Shaw's. The State Extension Service would commence trapping wild animals throughout the region. Local health officials would interview the contacts of the infected man and dispense prophylactic antibiotics if necessary. McCoy, who last night told the dean he needed no help handling the problem, was left with nothing to handle. The pieces of the investigation he wished to control had been divided already.

McCoy pounded his fist on the desk.

To make matters worse, the infected man had not been

interviewed. No one knew where he had been, where he acquired the bacteria. It couldn't be Duane. In McCoy's view, the state health officials, the hospital and the CDC were overreacting, and he would have told them as much had they consulted him, but they had not.

At least all parties concerned had agreed to keep the details of the case out of the public eye and all inquiries would be discreet. After the anthrax hysteria, the last thing they needed was an influx of hypochondriacs zapping their energy and muddying their focus.

McCoy made some calls. With the VP coming, he wanted his own expert on the case. He called Washington, but the man he wanted was out on an emergency. Damn it.

McCoy called Dr. Taversham, the man in charge of the case at the hospital. McCoy learned the CDC agents would arrive that morning. Since the hospital had no space to spare, McCoy volunteered an office. Here he could keep his eye on the agents, prod them in the right direction and get them out of town before Friday. If McCoy had his way, the VP would never know what hit Duane the week of his visit.

When McCoy hung up the phone it was almost time for the morning meeting. He went to the conference room, unlocked the door and threw it open. Then he gasped for breath and stepped back. Christ, some lunatic had turned off the air conditioning. Despite McCoy's strict instructions that no one should touch the thermostat but him. He marched to the window, cranked the air conditioner, then went to the table and took the lone seat at its head.

Before he arrived at the university, the conference room had been set up as a lounge and held a couch, stereo, bright lights and a coffee machine. McCoy had cleared out the junk, moved in a long rectangular table and hard-backed chairs. He found a chalkboard and a bookshelf he had filled with the latest scientific annals. The room now resembled a place of serious business.

The door opened and the first researcher clumped in. McCoy noticed the high-strung Charlotte Lane was gaining weight. Was she pregnant? Was it possible? She was forty and had four children already. She wasn't planning to take maternity leave, was she? McCoy had barely enough staff as it was.

Bob Fairway came in next wearing a ridiculous bow tie. He stooped beside McCoy to discuss a jam in the scintillation counter. McCoy was not listening. He watched Michael Smith step into the room and realized he had forgotten all about him. Unable to extricate himself from Fairway, McCoy was relieved to see Smith sit down without much ado.

Next Phillip Becker hobbled in. He had a badly hunched back that grew worse by the day. The man was eighty-five and should have retired, but wouldn't go willingly. Unlike the army, the university lacked the policy to force him out.

At precisely two minutes past eight McCoy stood up, effectively dismissing Bob Fairway still crouched by his chair. Though Nellie Duncan and Dana Sparks were late, McCoy would wait for them no longer. Dr. Sparks was often late. He was well aware of her complaint that the weekly Monday morning meeting was a waste of her precious time. In McCoy's mind, the meeting was the most efficient way to monitor the department's activities. His staff provided services to the veterinary clinic, which in turn provided a small percentage of the department's core funding. The clinic wanted to know what it was getting for its money and McCoy held these weekly meetings to find that out.

Shaking off his fatigue, McCoy welcomed his staff and asked Dr. Charlotte Lane for an update on the veterinary cases that she had handled the previous week. She was in the midst of an arbovirus case when Sparks finally arrived.

McCoy eyed her coldly. He held up his hand to silence Dr. Lane. He said, "Good afternoon. Glad you could join us."

Sparks started to speak but he waved her to silence. "Dr. Lane, you were talking about the arbovirus." McCoy nodded to his virologist.

"I'm finished."

Nellie Duncan arrived and McCoy waited for her to take her seat. He was grateful to the dean's wife for her support and advice. She had been around the department a long time. He smiled at her, then asked the verbose Bob Fairway about his current parasitology cases.

Fairway was fifty, a tenured professor, who liked to toot his own horn. He had an air of self-importance McCoy found unsubstantiated. Incredibly, Fairway spoke about a case of babesiosis he treated six months ago as if it were current. All he had to report was that the cow had recovered, yet it took him twenty minutes to do so.

Next the hunched Phillip Becker had his say. The pathologist spent most of his day huddled over dead bodies and microscopes. The messier, the gorier, the better. As long as there was death, and unless it was Becker's own, it was unlikely the pathologist would ever leave the university of his own accord.

Becker said he was about to autopsy a cat. On Friday, Tim Sweeny had amputated the cat's foreleg. Saturday, the cat fell seriously ill.

"Was the illness a result of surgery?" McCoy asked. The last thing the veterinary school needed was a malpractice lawsuit to tarnish its image.

"I don't know," Becker said. "I haven't started the autopsy. But the cat was a hit-and-run so there's no owner and no fear of a lawsuit."

So why the hell was Becker doing an autopsy? It was flagrant waste of time and money. "Incinerate the cat," McCoy said. He moved on to Nellie Duncan. She asked permission to order microscopic slides she had not budgeted for.

"We'll discuss it later," McCoy said. She would have her

slides, despite his warning that once the budgets were written, they were set.

Then McCoy turned to Sparks. "If you could give us an update on the veterinary cases you handled last week."

"I tested about twenty sera samples and identified a cow infected with *Brucella* and a bird infected with *Chlamydia psittaci*."

McCoy stared at her. "*About* twenty samples? Is it possible to be more specific so when I let the dean know *exactly* the value of our service, *I* know it?"

"The information is in my office. I could get it. This morning I did a *Yersinia* ELISA and . . ."

"*And* if you have nothing else to add of relevance, we'll move on."

McCoy was determined to introduce the current complication his way. As the boss, this was his prerogative. He rose from his chair. Dana Sparks' hand was up and he waved it away. He said, "Though not serious, you should know we have presumptive infection of *Yersinia pestis* in Duane. Of course, given its location, the source can't be here. Nevertheless, two CDC agents are on their way. No doubt they'll complete their investigation in one or two days. To this end, I've assured the dean and Mitchell Marshall we'll provide all the assistance they require."

He began pacing. "From this moment on, you will avail yourselves to the CDC. We'll give them an office down the hall and call it Headquarters. The CDC is in charge and we'll provide laboratory assistance. Our goal is to get them out of here as soon as possible. I don't think that will be a problem."

At the far end of the table, Dana Sparks' hand was waving spastically again. He ignored her. "Because of the sensitivity in the timing of this infection, I insist this information remain in this room. We don't want a panic on our hands, and indeed there is no justification for one. We have an isolated case of bubonic plague and that is it.

There's no doubt the bacteria came from somewhere, but that somewhere is not here."

There was a rap at the door and McCoy marched toward it. He was feeling immensely better. The room was finally cool and McCoy's heart raced no longer. His explanation that the origin of the bacteria was elsewhere was logical, reasonable and satisfying. There was nothing to worry about. The bacteria could not thrive in Duane; it was that simple.

McCoy threw open the door.

One look at his federal assistance and McCoy's heart was racing again. *These were the agents?* Who was Washington hiring these days? The older man wore a ponytail and a clump of moss on his chin. His mouth was wide and his smile too big. The younger man looked like a college kid and wore a diamond in his ear.

God help us all, McCoy thought, as sweat ran down his back and he shook hands with the pony-tailed Karl King and the youthful Jeffrey Tuttle.

"I was in Houston," King said. "You might say this was kind of on my way."

He was smiling broadly, like a lunatic, while McCoy felt faint. In a room that suddenly seemed much smaller and hotter, McCoy introduced the agents to his staff. He pulled two chairs to the front and invited the visitors to share his head of the table. He was about to repeat his overview, when Karl King jumped in.

Not knowing McCoy's proclivity for titles and formality, King made his second mistake. "TJ, Jeff and I appreciate your cooperation and the cooperation of your people. We've verified your suspicion of the plague. Unfortunately, the index case, Dudley Shaw, died this morning. We don't know where he was infected or whom he might have infected in turn. It's only a matter of time before more cases surface."

McCoy frowned as his chest constricted tightly. It hurt

to breathe and his ears were plugged as if there had been an abrupt change in air pressure. This was the last thing he wanted to hear. *More cases?* He said, "This is an isolated incident. The source of the plague is not here."

"Maybe, maybe not," King said. "This is something we will determine."

"Look," McCoy said, aiming to be reasonable. "We're too far south. It's too hot. There's no evidence whatsoever of a wildlife infection that always precedes . . ."

Dr. Sparks interrupted him. She raised her hand and spoke without permission. "It appears rats from this area *are* infected with *Yersinia* and . . ."

"What?" McCoy forced his fists to unclench. He took a deep breath, suggested by his cardiologist as a means to control his blood pressure. What was she talking about?

"Rats?" King said, as he smiled at Dana Sparks much too long.

She ignored McCoy's warning tone. "I received four rats Friday afternoon and just finished an ELISA. The lymph nodes of all four tested positive for *Yersinia*."

"Where did you get these rats?" Karl asked.

It appeared someone had given them to her. *The previous god damn week.* Yet, she was only testing them now. McCoy's deep breathing did little to control his hypertension.

"Where is the student?" Karl asked.

McCoy had a question of his own and preempted her answer. "Where did the rats come from?"

Sparks answered King's question first. She didn't know where the student was. Nor did she know where the rats had been trapped. What she did know was that four of twenty rats trapped had died. "If twenty percent of the rodents near town are infected with the plague that means . . ."

McCoy's hands were fists again and he exhaled loudly with exasperation. He took grave exception to her statistics. "There is no scientific basis for that statement, Doctor.

Maybe only sick rats were trapped. And did you type the bacteria? Can you say with a hundred percent certainty that these rats are diseased? Rats are a reservoir. Some species can host the bacteria and not get sick. Do you know what killed these particular rats?"

She backed down. Of course she didn't have the answers to any of these questions.

Then, just as he was feeling in charge of the situation again, she opened her mouth and nearly sent him into cardiac arrest.

"I'm concerned because Dudley Shaw's dog is missing. He could be carrying infected fleas."

McCoy felt the blood rush to his head. Despite his specific emphatic instructions to retrieve the sample and leave the patient alone, she had not complied with his request. "What do you mean Shaw had a dog? How do you know?"

"I talked to him." She stared at the tabletop.

King was on his feet. "Great. What did he say?"

Sparks spoke directly to Karl. In a few sentences she dashed all McCoy's hopes that Dudley Shaw was infected elsewhere.

"Dudley hasn't been anywhere, except to New Orleans to visit his sister at Easter, one month ago. Given the time frame and the elevation, I don't see how he could have acquired *Yersinia* there. It isn't clear to me how he was exposed. Unless *Yersinia* has moved to a lower latitude and . . ."

McCoy cut her off. He would not tolerate idle speculation outside the realm of rigorous scientific investigation. At this point, all they had were possibilities and hypotheses. "This bacterium has been around for thousands of years. It has never moved to a lower latitude."

King ignored this. "What do you know about the dog?"

"His name is Bingo," Sparks said. "He's not at his house."

"We have to find him. Take a closer look at those rats."

McCoy stepped into the conversation. "Dr. Becker will

do the autopsies on the animals and confirm the cause of death."

Becker shrugged, oddly unenthusiastic.

King looked at McCoy. "Fine. We'll trace this student. Jeff can liaise with your staff and the university registrar to track her down. I'll head out to the field and find this dog. We'll lay trap cages and check the wildlife. See if *Yersinia* has moved south. Find out how and where Shaw was infected. Stop the epidemic cold."

"Any assistance you need is yours," McCoy said.

"I have no doubt we'll have the situation cleared up in one or two weeks," King said.

"One or two weeks?" McCoy almost choked. "I'm afraid we'll have it cleared up before Friday, which is when the vice president of the United States is scheduled to arrive."

Karl King rubbed his goatee. "In light of the possible rodent infection and the fatality, we'll advise the vice president to cancel his trip."

"*What?* That's impossible," McCoy managed to talk slowly though he felt he was about to explode. "Only one person is infected. Surely you can't make that recommendation on the basis of a single isolated case."

Karl surely could. "We will begin our investigation and apprise the Bureau of our progress."

McCoy's face fell. It never failed to amaze him how fast things could spiral out of control. The Feebs now? The town was crawling with special agent Ackerman and the like, stuffed shirts from Washington who completed FBI training and thought they were ready for war. No, no, Ackerman and his men would be apprised of nothing if McCoy had his way. If the CDC agents couldn't handle this on their own, he'd call the army and help would be his before the end of the day.

"Do you really think it's wise at this juncture to call Washington?" McCoy spoke in a tone that made his feelings on the matter clear. "At this early stage, shouldn't we be discreet? Many people are coming to Duane expecting to see the vice president."

"I'm aware of that," Karl said, and added to McCoy's immense relief, "We err on the side of caution. No need to scare the general populace without cause. Mention an infectious disease and before you know it, everyone thinks they're sick." He laughed heartily at an issue that McCoy did not find at all funny.

"Okay, let's get to work," McCoy said. "Let me know when you find that dog. We'll get a veterinarian to examine it."

Karl checked his watch. "I'm awaiting a specialist. He should be here any time. He's a veterinarian and can assist with the dog."

McCoy exhaled his frustration. Karl King was bringing in a veterinarian epidemiologist? When a human was already infected and dead? What kind of joker was this CDC man? "A veterinarian?" McCoy now asked with palpable disbelief.

Karl smiled on. "Besides being a professor of epidemiology, he's also a medical doctor. And he lived here. I don't know if you know him. Nick Biget?"

McCoy finally smiled. His chest relaxed and he felt a weight lift from his heart. This was McCoy's expert who was off on an emergency. Now Nick was coming, McCoy felt better. It was good news, good news indeed. Here was a man who could do a job effectively and quietly. McCoy clasped his hands together and thanked God for sending Nick. For a civilian, McCoy held him in the highest esteem. McCoy was just surprised Nick hadn't informed him he was coming. Dr. Sparks looked surprised too, which reminded McCoy of rumors he'd heard and refused to consider. He stood up. "We'll adjourn for now and meet back here at fourteen hundred hours."

Karl threw him an exaggerated salute.

Chapter 13

The room cleared around her, but Dana sat numbly at the table unable to move. Her heart thumped in her ear as if it had moved into her head. Her body pulsed in and out, as if something inside her was trying to grow. Hope, nearly given up for dead, was blooming.

She stood up and walked to the window, drew back a curtain McCoy always kept closed. The sky looked bluer, the leaves more green, the bluebonnets more purple. The sun and everything under it looked brighter. She caught her reflection in the glass smiling at her. Anticipation, disbelief, hope and desire coursed through her blood. Nick was back. Another coincidence, an accident, that there would be an incident of the plague in Duane and he would be called. Dana felt she'd been granted a wish she could not bear to voice.

Not that in the past, hopes hadn't been raised. She was certain after he left, he would miss her and call, but he never did. Later she envisaged meeting by chance, at an airport, or a scientific meeting, but that didn't happen. Then when Brian died, she looked for Nick at the auditorium during the memorial, and later in the graveyard under a cold December drizzle, and there was no sign of him. Later, Dana heard rumors that Nick would be offered Brian's job but the next thing she knew McCoy was here and Nick's name was no longer mentioned. Until today.

She turned from the window. At the far end of the room in the corner, sat an empty chair, and at the table an empty place, a place saved for a man who was seven years in coming. Nick was back. Dana walked the length of the room and moved the chair to the table.

The next plane from Houston landed at nine. She glanced at her watch. He could be at the vet school in five minutes. Even now. He could be in her lab. *Dana, we have to talk.* No, he was never one for words. She would kiss him. There was nothing to say, no need for conversation; contact was enough. Dana left the conference room. Her boots felt light and her body weightless, as if her feet weren't touching the ground and she was gliding on—

The secretary, Betty, stopped her. "Dana, Sheryl called." Betty spoke in a thick Texan accent, elongating every vowel. She was forty-something, single and not happy about it. She wore a rainbow of blue and mauve eye shadow. Her hair was flouncy though stiff. She favored pastel dresses with stripes that camouflaged her weight. She was good and kindhearted, but too desperate when it came to men. Betty was looking at Dana closely. "Are you okay?"

"I'm fine," Dana said.

"Your face looks red."

Dana's cheeks felt flushed, but there was nothing she could do about it.

Betty gave her the message. Sheryl wouldn't be in because Penny was sick.

"Thanks," Dana said. She collected her mail. With Sheryl out, she'd have to delay checking her blood. She was anxious to know what her antibodies would show, but she couldn't draw her blood by herself. She could wait, at least for a while; her antibody levels would stay high.

McCoy's door opened. "Dr. Sparks. My office. Now."

Inside, he closed the door. Though the room was dark and cold, McCoy was red-faced. Beads of sweat glistened on his forehead. He stood with his arms folded across his chest.

"What the hell were you thinking?" he said, in an abnormally high-pitched voice. "Why didn't you tell me about those rats? Why did you dump the information at the last minute?"

"I just found out myself. I tried to tell you at the start of the meeting."

"You weren't even there at the start of the meeting." McCoy narrowed his beady gray eyes. "And what in God's name were you thinking when you went to interview Dudley Shaw?"

"I saw his black fingertips. I thought he had the plague and wondered where he was infected."

"Why didn't you inform me about the dog?"

"I tried. I called you last night, but you were out for a drive."

McCoy waved away her explanation with a swipe of his arm. "Look, this stops right now. I'm handling the investigation. Anything you think the CDC should know, comes through me." He glared at her.

She tried to argue. "This is *my* specialty. I can type the bacteria. I have the antibodies and monoclonals against it. I'm the one experienced in dealing with plague-infected blood. If anyone can help the CDC, it's me."

"I am in charge. You answer to me. Period." McCoy ran the heel of his hand across his forehead. "One more thing." His high tone dropped and he spoke in a normal voice. "Check your vaccine data and make sure everyone is up-to-date on their shots. If the CDC checks, I want our department in full compliance with federal policy." McCoy threw open the door.

Dana left his office, waved to Betty and strode into the hall. Nellie Duncan's shadow fell across her. "You looked surprised when you heard Nick was coming," Nellie said, dancing by her side. "You mean you didn't know?"

Dana increased her speed. This was a conversation she would not have.

"You don't keep in touch?" Nellie sounded incredulous.

Either way it was a loaded question and one Dana wouldn't answer. Up ahead, on the right was her lab, only three doors away.

Nellie skipped down the hall. "I'm as surprised as you, frankly. After Brian died, the dean offered Nick his position and Nick refused though we offered him a lucrative deal. I thought this place had too many bad memories."

Feeling dizzy and faint, Dana kept going.

"You can't blame him though, can you," Nellie said. "His poor wife. Their dead baby. It's enough to make anyone lose their mind. Do things they wouldn't otherwise do. Things they might later regret." She clucked her teeth and shook her head.

Dana ignored her. She had reached her lab and the refuge that she sought. She entered her office and shut the door, relieved to be alone. Then she saw her abandoned and forgotten dog.

Chapter 14

The pilot announced the descent to Duane and Nick Biget turned off his Discman and silenced the wailing of Lucky Dube, who was returning to his roots. Nick fastened his seatbelt, leaned forward and peered out the small window, watching the tiny houses and tinker-toy cars come into focus, then gradually expand. Square and circular swimming pools sparkled in the morning sun. It was a clear morning, but Nick felt uneasy. A bagel chowed down quickly at the airport sat hard in his stomach. It was a mistake to come. He knew that even as he told Blaze Stodgecraft, the National Security Advisor, he would take the assignment. After the Somali bombing, threats from Islamic extremists were pouring in. There was talk of biological warfare. Then a man died from a rare and deadly disease in a town the VP was going to visit. Nick was supposed to check things out, to serve as the liaison between the CDC and National Security. He had the background and the clearance to do the job and refusing would require a lengthy explanation Nick himself could barely formulate, let alone understand. Even after all this time.

He had left a mess behind. An affair that should have never happened, given his situation. Or perhaps it was his situation that had precipitated what happened. In any case, whatever the reason, he had been out of control; he couldn't stop himself, no matter how hard he tried.

Leaving had been the right thing, though it was unspeakably hard. He hadn't spoken to Dana in seven years. She never called him, probably never thought of him, was probably married by now. It was for the best; Nick would never revisit that past. It had taken a long time to break free, and it was over, he told himself; it was over. A verse from a Robin Wheeler song came to him: *I had to go, I couldn't stay; though it was hell, I went away; but left myself behind.*

He stopped the music playing in his head and shifted in his seat. He was too tall to sit comfortably in the chair and there was nowhere to put his legs or rest his arm. He preferred an aisle seat, but at this late notice had to settle for what was left.

The plane's engine roared louder and Nick gripped his seat. He hated to fly, even more so after the attacks of September 11. Any fool could crash a plane and even though the statistics proved it was safer to fly, Nick liked to drive. In a car he was at the wheel—in control.

The pilot landed smoothly. The wheels touched the ground and the plane sped across the runway, rolling to a stop. A click of seatbelts and passengers jumped up. No stewardess accompanied the short flight and the co-pilot manned the door and bid the passengers farewell.

Nick ducked out the door into a wave of heat. The humidity reminded him of D.C. in August. Nick's hands were sticky and clammy. He heaved his overnight bag onto his shoulder and wiped his hand on his slacks. Sweat rolled down his underarms as he clamored down the metal steps. The sun blazed and Nick slipped on sunglasses. The pilot said the ambient temperature in Duane was seventy-eight, but it seemed hotter than that. Nick guessed it was the shock of leaving snowdrifts at Dulles Airport only hours before.

Karl met him in the terminal. They had known each other for more than twenty years, since medical school. They had each been the other's best man. Karl married at twenty, Nick at twenty-one, both ridiculously young. Now they were forty-two.

"I'm sorry about your wife," Karl said.

"I'm sorry about yours." Nick had been shocked to hear Karl was getting a divorce. He always thought Karl and Helena were happily married. Her life was her marriage and her family. She fussed over Karl like a child, choosing his clothes, nagging him about his hair, his drinking, his weight. Since his divorce, Karl had lost weight and his clothes no longer fit. His hair was long and he wore it tied back in a ponytail. Though in the past he was clean-shaven, he now sported a goatee.

"I'm glad you came," Karl said. "Frankly I'm surprised you agreed. It looked to me like you've been avoiding Texas. When was the last time you were here?"

"A while ago," Nick said vaguely. He had deliberately stayed away. Over the loudspeaker, a departure for Houston was announced. The *Eagle* shuttled back and forth between Duane and Houston all day long.

Karl pressed on. "You haven't made it to one Texas meeting. When there was that hantavirus scare in El Paso, you sent a replacement."

"There was an emergency. I went to Uganda." Nick lifted his sunglasses. The terminal was cool and the artificial light was bright.

"Why did you come now?" Karl asked. He raised an eyebrow and looked at Nick askance. "Anything to do with the vice president's trip?"

Nick nodded, shrugging. His mission was confidential and he could not reveal its real purpose, not even to Karl.

Still, Nick wouldn't lie to his friend. "I can't say much, but Blaze Stodgecraft asked me to come."

"The national security advisor?" Karl asked.

Nick nodded and moved out of the way as an old couple advanced, pulling luggage on wheels. "With the VP's visit, Washington wants to stay apprised of events. I'm here as an observer. Don't worry, the investigation is yours." He changed the subject again. "What do we have? One man dead?"

As they walked to the exit, Karl filled him in. Four rats were also infected. The dead man hadn't left town in almost a month. So far no source of the bacteria had been found.

Nick didn't like it. If the dead man acquired *Yersinia pestis* in Duane, it would be the first time the bacterium was found at sea level. Typically, *Yersinia* was not found at an elevation below 4,500 feet. It had also never been found so far south.

They left the terminal and crossed the parking lot. The sky was a brilliant blue. Nick had forgotten the big Texan sky. Also the thick, heavy heat that Dana adored. He lowered his sunglasses and pushed her from his mind. "Do we know the species of rat infected?"

"Rattus rattus," Karl said.

Nick whistled. The black rat was the worst species for harboring *Yersinia pestis* and spreading bubonic plague. "Any infected fleas?"

"Not yet," Karl said.

Well, at least there were infected rats. It would have been suspicious to have a disease carried by rodents appear in an environment where rodents weren't infected.

They reached the car, a navy Buick with a Hertz sticker on the windshield. "There's a problem," Karl said. "A missing dog. The dead guy's hound took off."

Nick whistled again. Calling that a "problem" was a substantial understatement.

"I thought we'd go to Dudley Shaw's house, search for the beast and secure the site," Karl said.

Nick tossed his overnight bag in the trunk. "It's a pity no one interviewed him before he died."

"Someone did. The plague specialist." Karl slid into the driver's seat and threw open Nick's door. "Dana Sparks. Pretty sharp and looks it too."

"Any idea of the origin?" Nick asked, throwing himself into his seat. He could see his sunglasses reflecting back at him through the windshield.

"She didn't speak with a Texan accent. I would guess from the north."

"I'm talking about the bacteria." Nick slammed his door.

"Oh. No." Karl cranked the key. "She's been around a long time. Do you know her?"

"She developed the plague monoclonal vaccine."

Karl whistled and backed out of the space. "Who did she work with? Nellie said she did her Master's, Ph.D. and post doc research here."

"Robert Jones. Until he retired."

"The molecular immunologist."

"Him. Yes."

"And she took his place?"

"No, she finished her post doc."

"With who?"

"Well, me."

Karl braked the car to a full stop and stared at Nick.

In the side wing mirror, Nick saw a car pull up behind them. Karl was blocking the road. "You've got someone behind you."

Karl started moving again. "You never told me."

"It wasn't long. More on paper than anything else. She knew what she was doing. She was good. She just needed a supervisor and I got the job. I didn't have a choice," Nick said, protesting too much.

"I'm just surprised you didn't mention it." Karl pulled

onto the airport access road and increased his speed. The wind blew through the car as the A.C. hummed and chilled the air.

"I left the year she came," Nick said.

"You left quite suddenly as I recall." Karl glanced at him again.

Nick pointed ahead. "There was a new treatment for Rachel-Anne in D.C."

"Nellie said she's single."

What was Nick supposed to say to that? They reached the bypass and he told Karl to turn left. Nick leaned forward and tuned in the radio. The news was on and once again Somalia was the lead story. The U.S. was adamant that a military target had indeed been struck and a warehouse filled with munitions was successfully bombed. But a French physician who had been in Mogadishu on the evening of the strike maintained that a hospital and mosque had also been hit. There had been an enormous explosion. Twenty people died and twice as many were wounded. Arab communities were united in their call for the formation of a UN team to investigate the tragedy. When the news ended, Nick tuned in the classical music station. Debussy was playing and he leaned back in his seat and watched the trees go by.

They were heading south along the bypass. It was eleven o'clock and traffic was light, though in contrast to D.C., Duane traffic was always light. They passed a six-storey high apartment building, then a new condominium complex, a sign for a coming mall. When Nick lived here, there was nothing in this area but the airport. He was appalled by the development that had turned the fallow land to concrete.

He relaxed when he saw the forest, with its thick post oak, cottonwood and white pine. He had forgotten how flat the land was, how humid the air, how strong the south coastal wind. It swept brutally across the land, flattening the grass and stirring the low leaves of the mulberry, hickory and sweet gum.

Karl turned off the highway and bounced down a pitted road that was more dirt than tarmac. The houses were isolated and far from the road, surrounded by fields or dense trees. Karl got lost. He pulled over to the shoulder and opened a map that showed a series of back roads highlighted in pink marker. "The directions to Dudley's house," Karl said, jabbing his finger at the map. "Do you know where we are?"

Nick knew exactly. They were on a rural road not far from Dana's house. "Take the second right ahead," he said. And when they passed the turnoff to Dana's house, Nick closed his eyes. That was a road he would not travel down.

Beside him, Karl said, "Everything all right?"

Nick looked at him. "Fine. Everything is fine. Just fine. Why do you ask?"

"There's no need to tell me three times you're fine," Karl said.

He had a point.

"McCoy's going to be a problem," Karl said, apropos of nothing. "You can tell he wants this thing swept under the carpet. He was trying to convince me I should be somewhere else. Anywhere but here would suit McCoy fine. All he cares about is keeping the VP's trip on schedule."

Nick had worked with McCoy on a number of occasions and knew he would never jeopardize an investigation or place human lives at unnecessary risk. More than once, McCoy had risked his own life for others. In Vietnam, he carried a wounded colleague for three days. When the man died, McCoy would not leave the body behind. Later, in Iraq, near the end of the Gulf War, when the oil refineries were torched and fires were raging, McCoy shared his gas mask with a soldier whose own mask had melted. In Yugoslavia, he gave his MRE rations to starving refugees fleeing Kosovo. Nick knew there was nothing McCoy's men wouldn't do for him. He wasn't a general because he kissed the right boots or said the right thing. He deserved his four stars, and in the army, was a man of awed distinction.

"McCoy is all right once you get to know him," Nick said. "He probably had an arrhythmia when he saw your ponytail."

Karl patted the back of his head.

They reached Dudley Shaw's house and Karl parked in front of a mailbox labeled with the dead man's name. He had no mail. Dudley lived on a flat corner lot ringed with cedar. The grass was cut short and resembled Astroturf. Rows of white and pink petunias lined the driveway. Near the small bungalow stood a spreading pecan tree, and under the tree, an old car.

"Would you look at that," Karl said, pointing to the vintage yellow Thunderbird. The car had extended tail fins, a nose grill, and headlights that looked like eyes.

It had been years since Nick had seen such a car.

Karl made a beeline across the lawn toward it.

Nick followed him through the grass. Since it was cut short, it would not be a good harbor for fleas. Nick saw no butterflies, no moths, no grasshoppers, and wondered if Dudley used insecticides.

Karl reached the car and ran his hand across a fin. "What a beauty. I wonder if it's for sale."

Nick said nothing. He examined his slacks for fleas and saw none. He whistled for the dog and there was no response, only the sound of the wind in the leaves. He walked toward the house. It was edged with bluebonnets, grown in rows. Here, even the wildflowers didn't grow wild.

Nick had forgotten the wildflowers. The highway dividers were brimming with them. He remembered a ceiling full of them.

Nick shook the image from his mind and surveyed the land. It looked clean. No corn fields, no barn, no seed or grain that might interest *Rattus rattus*. No overt sign of fleas.

He walked around the house. The exterior was freshly painted. While there was no garbage lying around that would attract rats, Nick saw a pile of dog kibble in a bowl on the back porch. The crumbs were infested with fireants. Who was feeding the dog?

The back door was unlocked and they went inside. The house was clean and in good shape, with no evidence of rodent feces. Nick shook out a blanket left on the floor. No jumping fleas.

In the kitchen Nick checked the fridge. From the freezer, he picked up a frozen package of meat. The previous year in New Mexico, a hunter had acquired bubonic plague from a rabbit he had shot and skinned. Nick saw a rifle hanging on the wall in the kitchen above the doorway. Was Shaw a hunter? Had he killed something that had fleas infected with *Yersinia*? Would they find *Yersinia* in the wild around Duane if they looked? But what was the bacterium doing so far south?

On the back of the kitchen door was a calendar turned to April. The squares were mostly blank. Nick thought of his own covered calendar and felt a twinge of envy for the quiet, private, uncomplicated life Dudley seemed to have led. Nick saw at the beginning of the month Dudley had returned from New Orleans. On Monday, April 20, Dudley had written *L'bird bath*. Whatever that meant. On Monday, April 27—today—there was a big star covering the square. A significant day.

The day of his death. Marked in advance? No, Nick didn't buy that.

They finished examining the house, drew the drapes, closed the windows and locked the doors. They taped a notice to the front door stating the house was under quarantine. Using a yellow ribbon inscribed repeatedly with the words DO NOT ENTER in black, they ran the ribbon around the circumference of the house. They draped the tape across the car. Until they knew where Shaw had contracted bubonic plague, everything he had been in recent contact with had to be isolated.

Nick walked to the verge of the forest and called for the dog. "Here, Bingo; here, Bingo; come on boy," he yelled. A crow cawed from the woods but no dog came. Karl clapped his hands loudly, but to no avail. Thick smilax vine covered the trees at the edge of the woods and there was no access to the forest.

Nick frowned at the trees. If the dog was carrying infected fleas, it could spread the disease through the wildlife population. The risk of human exposure was proportional to the exposure of the wildlife. "We have to find that dog."

Karl pointed across the road toward a dilapidated house and a lady who pushed a baby on a cockeyed swing. "Let's talk to her. See what she knows."

They walked down the newly paved driveway, across the dirt road and up a bumpy drive that was littered with trash.

The neighbor's name was Susie and she was frowzy and loud. When asked about Bingo, she said, "I ain't seen him. I'd kill him if I did." She was braless and wore a dirty faded shirt and short shorts that showed white bumpy thighs.

The baby began to cry. Behind the house, a dog barked. Nick craned his neck and saw a thin, mangy beast chained to the back porch.

"Shut up, Dog," Susie yelled. Dog barked louder, leaping at the end of his chain so hard he jerked himself backward with each jump. Dog was a black Labrador, and reminded Nick of Frank, his former dog, who Rachel-Anne tried to drown in the swimming pool. Nick wondered if he was still alive.

Before him, Susie yanked the crying baby from the swing and jostled it on her hip. The baby looked about six months old and wore a filthy pink sleeper with built-in feet. The baby grabbed a hank of Susie's matted hair and shoved it in her mouth. Susie was telling Karl all he ever wanted to know about Dudley Shaw.

He was kind of crotchety, Susie thought. "He never had no kids. He'd go bananas if Marty's ball got in his flowerbed. He terrified poor Terry when she climbed on his precious car. He had a temper, for sure."

"Was he away a lot?" Karl asked.

Susie shook her head.

"Did he have a lot of visitors?" Karl asked.

"Um, nope." As far as Susie was concerned, that was self-evident. "As I was sayin', he wasn't so nice."

There was a loud cry from inside the house. Another child had begun to cry. The dog, which had been quiet, was barking again. "Quit yer yapping," Susie yelled.

Susie shifted the baby to her other hip and continued. It was too much for Nick, who couldn't stand crying children and interrupted Susie's tale about her absent drunken husband. "Excuse me. If you want to get that child, we can wait."

"Coming, Terry," Susie bellowed in an ear-splitting scream that silenced the dog and started the baby crying anew. "Come on in, come on in."

With a sweep of her hand, Susie invited the men into a house that smelled of cats and urine. While Susie padded down the hallway, Nick poked his head in the kitchen. Breakfast dishes remained on the table. A sink overflowed with dishes. The floor was sticky under his shoes. Dust balls and dried Cornflakes spotted the graying linoleum. There were no rodent droppings he could see. He went outside.

Karl stood on the porch, looking up at the sky. He followed Nick around the side of the house. Nick examined Dog. His eyes were too large for his skull. His ears were red and irritated and he had dry scabs on his head. His gums were pale and his teeth were rotting. He was under-nourished and his abdomen was distended with worms. When Nick parted the mangy fur by the dog's tail, he saw running fleas, and collected these in a vial.

He looked around. The grass was long and unkempt. Nick took a few strides through the grass and examined his pants. He attracted burrs and a ladybug.

"Hey—where are you? Where you at?" Susie called, looking for them and happy to see them. She came around the house, carrying the baby and trailed by a toddler wearing a droopy diaper and old tennis shoes many sizes too large. She was tripping over the laces.

Nick said, "Look, this dog is suffering from malnutrition and needs treatment for fleas, ear mites and worms."

Susie blinked and Karl laid a restraining hand on Nick's arm. "Ma'am, we'd like to ask you some more questions if we might. Am I correct in understanding that you did not feed Dudley Shaw's dog?" Karl said.

"Meaner than a snake it was," Susie said. "You couldn't walk on that property if that dog was home or he'd come nipping at you so fast you wouldn't believe. He almost tore Marty's head off."

"I see," Karl said. "Now, Ms . . . um . . . Susie, do you know anyone who might be feeding him?"

"No."

"Would you mind if we took a drop of blood from Dog?"

Susie didn't mind and Nick pulled a lance and a capillary tube from his pocket. He pierced the base of the dog's tail and filled the capillary tube with blood.

The toddler watched him intently, picking at a scab on her arm. Her nose was running and her face was filthy. He bent down before her and tied the laces of her shoes, remembering a night when someone had tied his laces and his stomach up in knots. Nick stood up, momentarily unbalanced.

Karl passed Susie a business card. "If you see Bingo,

call me. The number of my pager and cell phone are on the back."

"What about Dudley? If I see him?"

Karl and Nick looked at each other. Karl said, "He's at the hospital."

Susie's mouth dropped open. "What's wrong with him? Why are you asking all these questions about Bingo? Does Dudley got a dog disease? You thinkin' Dog might have it too? Is that why you want his blood?"

"Dudley had an infection," Karl said vaguely. "We're not sure where he acquired it."

Susie's eyes were suddenly bright. "Is it something like AIDS?" she asked. "I didn't know you could get that from dogs—"

"It's a bacterium, not a virus," Karl explained.

The terms were lost on Susie. "Well, go figure. Who could reckon? And you think he might have given Dog something? Or us?"

"Very, very slim chance of that," Karl said. "We just want to make sure Dog's fine." He pointed to the business card bent in her fist. "If you or anyone in your family gets a fever, call me. Or, if you see Bingo. You can call any time."

Susie said she would, and they said goodbye, and though Nick wanted to reiterate his earlier statement about taking better care of the dog, Karl didn't give him the chance. He grabbed hold of Nick's arm and escorted him down the pitted driveway toward the car.

At the road, Karl said, "Nick, we need that lady's help. Where's your bedside manner?"

Nick knew Karl had a point. Returning to Duane had been more stressful than he imagined. Being out in the country had stirred old memories better left dead. Nick reminded himself what happened was over. He had to be careful, keep in the present. He was here on a case, for work, and Karl was right, he had been less than professional. "It won't happen again," he said. "Let's go see the dogcatcher."

The animal pound was on Texas Avenue. As they drove, a Brahms concerto played.

They reached the dog pound, a small square white building in the middle of a large and empty parking lot. Karl parked and they went inside. A tall blond man with cowboy boots waited on them. Nick thought it would be a simple matter to ask him to find the dog, but Jim the dogcatcher was busy with other things.

"I've already looked for him," Jim said.

"How hard?" Nick asked.

Jim shook his head. "We've been busy." He spoke in a quick southern twang. "The end of the semester is always like this. Students leaving and abandoning their pets. I didn't know it was an emergency."

"It is," Nick said,

Karl immediately contradicted him. "There is no emergency."

It was Nick's error. Officially there was no crisis. He stepped away from the counter, letting Karl take over. Nick ostensibly studied posters of lost pets that were tacked to the whitewashed wall. He saw a poster written in a childish hand begging for the return of Pumpkin, a huge orange cat the kid could hardly hold. There was a lost canary. A lost turtle. A lost diamond ring.

Karl was giving Jim his business card. "If you find the dog, give me a call."

Nick turned around.

Jim frowned at the card. "Why is the CDC looking for a dog?"

"We're not," Karl said. "The next of kin are. The dog's owner is dead, the dog is lost and should be found."

Jim shoved Karl's card in the front pocket of his jeans. "I'll call you if I find him."

"The family is actually quite distressed about losing him," Karl said.

"I'm real sorry," Jim said. "But you know, I've got four calls to make this afternoon and I don't have time to look for a dog that's not causing trouble."

Nick cleared his throat. They weren't getting through to this man and he was out of patience. "If I were you, I would make the time."

Jim folded his arms across his chest. "Is that so."

Karl laid a restraining hand on Nick's arm. "What my friend means, is that we've had a complaint from a neighbor that the dog is vicious."

Jim looked at Karl. "In that case, I'll see what I can do."

"We appreciate it," Karl said. Then he turned around and shepherded Nick out the door.

Outside in the sweltering, muggy air, Karl said, "Well, that went well."

Nick didn't reply. He had handled the situation poorly and was appalled how easily he lost his temper. Usually, no matter how hard he was pushed or provoked, he stayed calm. Growing angry never accomplished anything, and in the past, under the worst circumstances, Nick kept his cool. This morning though, control seemed to elude him.

"We've got time for a burger before a two o'clock meeting," Karl said. "Shall we get a bite to eat?"

"Sure," Nick said, though he had no appetite. "Who's the meeting with?"

"The whole department. Dana Sparks will be there. How long has it been since you've seen her?"

"A while," Nick said, though he was beginning to wonder if it had been long enough.

Chapter 15

Twenty-one people in the Veterinary College were deemed to be at high risk of accidental exposure to *Yersinia* and routinely received experimental vaccines. That included everyone in Dana's lab, some professors in the department, various clinicians in the veterinary school and assorted support staff.

The current experimental vaccine on trial at the university was taken as a series of shots. Six in total were required over a period of two years before the vaccine was effective. There was a shot every other month for six months, then a shot every six months for eighteen months and finally, a booster once a year. With staff and students coming and going, maintaining the correct vaccine status of personnel was a complicated business.

Sitting at her computer, Dana matched people with dates of vaccination and verified correct time intervals. At the end of the morning she decided that everyone, with the exception of Sheryl, who was still breast-feeding and couldn't receive experimental vaccines, was up-to-date.

When Dana was finished, she double-checked the data.

She was having a hard time concentrating. More often than not, the timed activation of the screensaver told her that she was daydreaming again. She couldn't stop looking at her watch, stop listening for footsteps in the hall. When would Nick arrive? Would he come see her when he did? How would it feel to see him again? Why had he come back?

Time seemed to have slowed; the seconds were strolling instead of ticking along. Even the dice tumbling on the screensaver appeared to move slower than usual. There was no second hand on Dana's watch, just a minute hand that looked as if it were stuck. Somehow it managed to keep time with the computer's clock.

The morning dragged on and on. What was taking Nick so long? Where was he? Avoiding her? Over the years, she thought he must have been. Now he was back in Duane, something he swore he would never do. And she never saw him coming. He did not cast a shadow before him.

A coincidence brought him back. What were the odds against a local outbreak of the plague appearing during the week of the VP's visit? She stared up at the van Gogh print and thought of Plato's force of necessity. If there was an invisible force that governed chemical reactions, another that worked across great distances and held the planets and stars in place, why not a force that worked across time? A force that governed chance and made coincidence happen.

Dana heard footsteps in the hall and for the hundredth time that morning, took a deep breath and listened hard. The footsteps drew nearer. Her heart pounded and her stomach tightened. She faced the monitor as the footsteps came closer, into her lab. She bent over the keyboard, peering at the screen and the names and the calendar as if it commanded all her attention. There was a knock on her open office door and she took another deep breath and slowly turned her head.

Phillip Becker. He stood stooped in the doorway holding

a small biohazard bag. "I brought a lymph sample from Dudley Shaw for you to culture."

She stood up, disappointment and relief filling her mind. Her heart was racing and her face was flushed. She didn't want Nick to see her like this. "Great." She took the bag from Phillip.

He seemed to study her from afar, squinting to see her better. He was a widower, eighty-five years old and looked like the pope, but with more hair. He dressed comfortably and favored khaki slacks and brightly colored polo shirts.

"You were right," he said. "The four rats had symptoms compatible with bubonic plague."

"Thanks, Phillip." Phillip had been Brian's mentor and in the department longer than anyone. If she had support in the department, it was from him. Now, and even back then when Nick was around and Dana was still a post doc.

"You did right," he said. "Seize opportunity when you can."

She wondered what he was referring to.

"What kind of specialist goes half way?" he asked. "Deliberately shuts one eye? It was only right you talked to Mr. Shaw."

"Thanks, Phillip." She noticed he was sweating. "Are you okay?"

"I seem to have the flu. I'm going home."

"Sure it's not the plague?" she asked.

"Plain old flu I'm afraid. I already checked my blood. My white blood cell count doesn't support a bacterial infection."

"I don't know how we're going to do this without you," she said. She was referring to herself. He was always there to back her up.

"Perhaps that's the point," he said with a twinkle in his eye. "With me out of the way, you'll have to use other resources." He smiled a holy smile. "Say hello to Nick for me."

And with that he turned and shuffled away.

After he left, Dana took the biohazard bag to the quarantine room. The definitive diagnosis was to grow the bacterium so it could be stained and seen under a light microscope fixed on a slide.

The *Yersinia* bacteria were easy to grow in the lab. All they needed was a little food and the right temperature. Dana prepared agar, which contained the nutrients. She weighed agar powder and dumped it in a flask, added a liter of distilled water. She sat the flask on a stirrer, dropped in a magnetic stir bar and stood watching the liquid swirl round and round.

When the agar was mixed Dana poured the solution onto a round culture plate. The agar began to solidify immediately. She moved to the laminar flow hood and lit a Bunsen burner, sterilized the hooped end of a long thin wand. Using the hoop, she scooped out a sample of Dudley's lymph node, which she smeared lightly across the surface of the agar. She put the top on the plate and placed it in the incubator. Left at 28°C, the bacteria would multiply to fill the plate within twenty-four hours.

She returned to her office. No sign of Nick. She sat down in her chair and couldn't stay seated. She jumped up. She couldn't just hang around and wait for him. It would drive her insane. She grabbed her car keys and headed out to Sheryl's.

Dana turned on the radio. It was tuned to the C&W station and playing some country singer she couldn't name. In the last few years, C&W was the only music she could listen to; it was the only music Nick didn't care for. Nick was a musician, a guitarist, and he preferred folk music. Robin Wheeler was his favorite and Nick knew every lyric, every song, and could play Wheeler for hours. In the early days after Nick left, she listened to Wheeler nonstop, but for years now she could not bear to hear his songs.

Dana reached Sheryl's house and pulled into her driveway, inadvertently knocking over one of the boys' bikes. It crashed into a red wagon with a loud clank. Sheryl flung open the front door.

"Sorry, sorry," Dana raised her hands as if Sheryl held a gun.

Sheryl put a finger to her mouth. "Penny's sleeping. I just got her down."

Dana followed her into the house. In the kitchen Sheryl poured two tall glasses of iced tea and brought them to the living room. "She's cutting a tooth," Sheryl said, putting the glasses on the table. "She's okay. Miserable though. But it shouldn't last."

"No fever?" Dana suddenly saw the plague everywhere.

"No."

Dana sipped the iced tea. Lemony and cold. No sugar, just the way she liked it. "Where are Ricky and Paul?" The boys were usually home for lunch. "You got them gagged and bound somewhere?"

"They're in Houston with my mother. I was supposed to pick them up yesterday, but with Penny sick, I couldn't go. They can stay for the week."

Dana picked up a Dr. Seuss book from the couch and flipped through it. *Green Eggs and Ham.* " 'I do not like them Sam I am.' "

"What is it? What's wrong?" Sheryl asked.

Dana stared at her hands, at a line on her palm. A fortune-teller once told her she had a strong love line. "Nick is here."

"Nick who?" Sheryl nonchalantly sipped iced tea and crossed her legs.

Dana was astounded she didn't get it immediately. "Nick Biget."

Sheryl coughed, spilling iced tea down her chin. She dropped the glass on the table. "My God."

Dana put down the book and stood up. She couldn't stand to be still, and circled Sheryl's living room. "There's a case of the plague in town. A fourth year student collected four infected rats. The CDC is here and asked for Nick's help."

"Have you seen him?"

Dana stopped behind the couch. "No."

"Good."

"I knew he would come back."

"You need to stay away from him."

Sheryl never liked Nick, never approved of the affair, and during its time, Dana and Sheryl had become estranged. Dana accepted what happened, gave in to the inevitable, and Sheryl thought she should fight it. Dana could not. Though a married man was the last person she would choose, what happened with Nick was never a choice. At the beginning she said to herself, this can't be. Her mind kept telling her, leave him alone—anyone but him. But what happened defied all reason, laughed at logic. She had not listened, could not listen. The only good thing about Nick leaving was that her friendship with Sheryl was back on track.

But now Dana regretted coming. She knew Sheryl's advice before she opened her mouth. *Find someone else who's available to you.* Maybe that was the real reason Dana had come. To hear the objection voiced out loud. "I can't stay away from him," she said. "This is my disease."

"You're not an epidemiologist. Let the CDC take care of it. Stay out."

"Who will do the immunological tests?"

"I'll be back tomorrow. I'll do them. You should go away. This is the worst thing that could happen to you."

Dana thought it was the best.

"He's married," Sheryl added. "You can't ignore that."

But Dana could. Had. Rachel-Anne was terminally ill and in an asylum indefinitely. Forever, as far as Dana was concerned.

"Maybe Rachel-Anne is better," Sheryl said. "Maybe he brought her with him."

Dana's heart suddenly felt like it had been punched. She hadn't thought of it. What if it were true? What if she had to see them together?

Sheryl struck again. "Even if he didn't bring her, maybe you should have the mindset that he did. They are the couple. Not you."

Dana could not stand to hear any more. "You're right. I've got to go." She had a two o'clock meeting.

Sheryl walked her to the door. "I have a bad feeling about this, Dana. Leave him alone. For your own good."

In the car, heading back to campus, Dana railed against Sheryl's advice. Staying away wasn't for her own good—maybe it was good for Sheryl and their friendship, but not for her and Nick. Here was the opportunity to settle something that desperately needed to be settled. Hadn't Becker intimated as much?

But Sheryl was right too. This was dangerous territory. Seeing Nick was like opening a floodgate. He did something to her, she didn't know what. He drew her to him and she felt the pull now, as strong as ever. Seven years had done nothing. There was no chance of her staying away. Like a black hole, Nick was drawing her irrevocably toward him and she was helpless to stop herself.

Back at the vet school, Dana grabbed her lab coat and headed for the bathroom. She felt like her mother, getting ready for a big evening out with her father. Staring in the mirror, Dana combed her hair with her fingers and despaired at her looks. Her hair was a mess, frizzled with the humidity. She wetted it down. Yanked out a few strands of gray. She washed her face, which had turned a fiery red. She licked her lips that were chapped from the air conditioning. She didn't wear makeup and wished she had something to shield herself with now.

Why couldn't she have more time to prepare? Time to cut her hair, take up jogging again? How could she wake up in the morning and have no clue that today was the day he would come back. Even her dreams had betrayed her.

Oh, what did it matter, she thought as she washed her hands again. He was still married. Nothing had changed. That was why he had left and why he swore he would never be back. He thought it was best for both of them and she gave her word she wouldn't contact him. She understood his guilt, even if she didn't share it. Rachel-Anne was mentally ill and locked in an asylum. She'd been easy to forget.

She might be better now. Psychiatrists at the National Institute of Mental Health were experts in treating schizophrenia, which was why Nick had moved north. By now Rachel-Anne might be cured. Maybe she had come with Nick to Duane. Maybe they had another child. Anything could have happened in seven years.

Dana pulled on the lab coat and washed her face again. It was no longer so red.

The bathroom door banged open. Nellie swept in, sashayed across the floor and dumped her oversized purse on the ledge over the sink. She studied Dana through the mirror.

"Getting all gussied up?" Nellie grabbed a tube of lipstick from her bag.

"I had to pee." Dana turned off the tap.

Nellie held out her lipstick. "Would you like some?"

"No."

"It would help, if you don't mind me saying so. Put some color in your pallor. You wouldn't look quite so grim or sickly."

Dana looked at her reflection in horror. Did it show? Her face was pale now, as if this sickness was written all over it.

"And that lab coat. All that white. Washes out your color. I can see why you don't wear one." Nellie spritzed perfume on either side of her neck, then offered the bottle to Dana.

Dana shook her head. Nellie smelled like musk, something out of an Indian incense shop.

"Go on and smell like dead rats then."

Dana had to stop herself from lifting her arm and checking her scent.

Nellie grabbed her bag and slung it over her arm. "Shall we go? Isn't it exciting? I just can't wait to see Nick!"

Dana took a breath and steeled herself as she walked across the hall and into the main office. They were five minutes early and Dana thought they would be the first to arrive but they were not. The conference room smelled of barbecued meat and Karl sat at the end of the table in the chair she thought of as Nick's. He was stuffing a burger into his mouth.

Nick had his back to her. She recognized his long torso, broad shoulders, thick, wavy brown hair. He turned his head and she saw her own discomfort and anguish in his face. She caught the brightness of his eyes as if she were seeing past them into his soul and years that had changed nothing. Then Nellie was leaning over him and hugging him, and the connection was gone.

Chapter 16

McCoy arrived flushed, out of breath and unpardonably late for his afternoon meeting. He had hoped to be early, had wished to speak with Nick privately, but it wasn't possible. The dean and the university president kept him late at lunch. They wanted an update on the crisis. McCoy had assured them everything would be fine; the VP's trip would proceed as scheduled. Then they spent an hour discussing the graduation ceremony tents. In the end he was late for his meeting, and had only a moment to greet Nick, to wave sheepishly at Michael Smith, who had graciously accepted another cancelled meal, before getting down to business. He wanted to hear that the CDC had broken the case, that the four rats weren't infected with *Yersinia*, that Dudley Shaw had acquired his infection elsewhere.

McCoy introduced Nick Biget to his staff only to be interrupted by a loud hammering coming from the window. What the hell? McCoy strode to the window and yanked open the curtains. Outside, by the window ledge, on a scaffold, stood a painter hacking at chipped paint with a chisel and hammer.

McCoy slid open a window. Hot wet air assaulted him. "We're in the middle of a meeting here."

"That's all right," the painter said. "You won't disturb me."

Jesus Christ, McCoy thought. "Come back later." He slammed the window closed, thrust the curtains together. He sat down, out of breath, thankful to hand over the floor. He gestured to Nick.

Biget went to the chalkboard. He said the outbreak was not unusual. Over the past two decades, five to ten cases of bubonic plague appeared in the U.S. every year. Isolated cases, such as Dudley Shaw's did not pose a serious epidemiological threat.

McCoy's heart stopped racing. This was common. There was nothing unusual. Nothing to interfere with the VP's trip.

Nick described the progression of plague epidemics. Bubonic plague was spread by fleas and usually appeared first. If an infected person lived long enough, the bacteria could move through the lymph system to the lung and cause pneumonic plague. This was an infection of the lung and was very contagious. "Right now, we're at an early stage and the prognosis looks good," Nick said. "So far we have four infected rats and one person infected with bubonic plague. With early diagnostics and treatment, we should stop the bacteria's spread. Our goal is to keep this from progressing past the bubonic phase."

For the first time all day, McCoy felt at ease. Isolated cases of the plague were annual events; they happened every year; they posed no serious danger. No one had pneumonic plague. The prognosis looked good. The VP's trip could proceed. He was settling back into his chair, a heavy load lifting off his mind, when there was a loud crack and the sound of breaking glass. Pebbles of it fell on the carpet.

McCoy was back at the window. He jerked the curtains apart and saw the workman's stupid grin.

"Guess I missed," the workman said.

McCoy could only stare at the man.

"Not to worry. I'll have it fixed in a jiffy." The painter shoved the hammer through a loop in his overalls and climbed down the scaffold.

Hot air billowed into the room, lifting the curtains and letting in the light. McCoy, out of breath again, returned to his seat.

Nick continued as if interruptions like these were routine. "The question we need to answer is, where did the bacterium originate? The key of course is Mr. Dudley Shaw. How did he get the plague? From where?"

New Mexico, McCoy silently prayed. California.

"Since infected rats were found in Duane, we'll assume for now that bacteria are here," Nick said.

McCoy squeezed his hands together and felt his heart tighten.

Nick unfolded a map of Texas and spread it out on the middle of the table. Heads craned forward. With an index finger, Nick pointed to the southwest side of town where Dudley Shaw lived. "We know that ninety percent of the people infected with *Yersinia* are infected within a mile of their home. Perhaps Dudley was infected in the forest near his house."

McCoy mopped his head. His hair was soaking wet. Despite the air conditioner, with the broken window the room was growing hot. Nick, with a hand in his pocket, looked cool and comfortable as he continued.

"We know the plague is not a disease associated with hot climates. Since outbreaks are correlated with high rainfall, this might explain the appearance of *Yersinia* in Duane. There was a lot of rain this spring. More rain means more plants, more food, more animals. Due to increased population, animals increase their range. They travel where they haven't been before and may bring with them bacteria that haven't been here before."

A reasonable explanation, McCoy thought, and one that would satisfy the FBI, if, God forbid, they ever learned of the infection.

"What about bacterial resistance?" Dana Sparks inquired. "Why did Dudley die?"

Christ, she always said the last thing McCoy wanted to hear.

Nick said, "Bacterial resistance is always a factor."

McCoy groaned out loud. "But it's unlikely to be a factor in this case. Shaw didn't come in for treatment soon enough. He left it too late."

Nick agreed. "Antibiotic treatment has to be started early—within twenty-four hours after infection. There's no telling how long the man was sick before he was admitted to the hospital."

"He said a few days," Sparks said.

Which did not provide much information, McCoy thought, but Sparks could not let it rest.

"*Yersinia* resistance could be a major problem."

Nick returned to his seat. "True. There have been highly resistant strains in the past."

McCoy shot his colleague a pleading glance. "We have no scientific evidence we're dealing with resistance, do we?"

"Dana has a valid point," Karl said. "We should test for it." He nodded at Sparks and she nodded back.

McCoy leaned on the table. Under his jacket, his shirt was soaking. There was a bright patch of light on the wall that hurt his eyes. When he was in the tropics, his pupils had been burned by the sun and he could not tolerate the light. He found it irritating, himself irritated. "Test for resistance then," he said, and turned to Karl King. "Have you examined the dog?"

"Examined it?" King laughed. "We haven't found it."

McCoy felt his heart squeeze tighter. He had assured the dean that problem was solved.

"We're working on it," King added, "and should locate the animal imminently."

McCoy shot Nick a worried glance. The apprehension on Nick's face did little to assuage his unease. They couldn't find the dog. That should have been the least of their problems.

"We can't find Carol Dupuis either," Jeff Tuttle piped in.

McCoy groaned aloud. Here was another simple problem that should have been easily solved.

"Carol is the student who trapped the infected rats," Tuttle continued, as if no one could recall who she was. "She's not answering her home phone and no one from her lab knows where she lives. She was in contact with the infected rats and may be infected herself. She didn't show up at the lab today and wasn't there on the weekend. That isn't unusual, seeing as she's an undergraduate and doesn't keep regular hours. Anyway, her professor just returned from an overseas trip on Saturday. He has no idea where she trapped the rats. No one in the lab knows. But none of the other researchers have had similar problems with rodents dying. Though, no one has collected any rodents recently. Anyway we have to find her."

McCoy could not believe what he was hearing. A lengthy list of negative results and statements of the obvious. "Why don't you go through the university records," he suggested frostily. "Find her local address. If she's not there, try her parents."

Tuttle looked offended. "We're working on it," he said with great affront. "We should have that information soon."

He should have had it hours ago. McCoy glanced at his watch. It was two-thirty. If he was going to get out of this inferno with his sanity, he might as well stop here. He stood up. "Anything else?"

It appeared there was. King felt he had to give a long and detailed explanation of his morning trip to Dudley Shaw's house that turned up absolutely nothing.

"His house was clean and tidy," King said. "There were no obvious signs of a flea or rodent infestation. Shaw lived alone. In any case, his sister's en route and we'll talk with her soon. Perhaps she can shed more light on Shaw's last days. Help with the dog."

"When is she expected?" McCoy asked.

"Three o'clock."

"Good." McCoy would wrap up this meeting and go see her himself. The last thing he needed was a grieving relative blabbing to the press.

King wouldn't stop. "Now, we went through Dudley's refrigerator and freezer and removed samples of what appeared to be wild meat," he said. "We saw a rifle and think Dudley might have been a hunter. Maybe he killed something that was infected with *Yersinia*."

A logical explanation, McCoy thought. Lots of rain, and an increase in wildlife population expanding their territory and moving to Duane. Dudley, a hunter, went out in the woods and shot an infected squirrel or rabbit. "We'll test that meat," McCoy said. "Dr. Sparks, immediately."

"Yes, *Sir*," she said.

Fleas from a dog belonging to Dudley's proximal neighbor had also been collected and Karl wanted her to test those as well.

"No problem," she said.

There was no trace of the sarcasm she reserved for him. "Anything else?" McCoy said.

Charlotte Lane wanted to know if they should try and trap rodents by Dudley's house.

Jeff Tuttle twisted his diamond earring and said he'd set traps that afternoon.

No one else had anything to add and McCoy declared the meeting over. "Dismissed. We'll meet here tomorrow at oh-eight-hundred hours." By then the window would be repaired, the painter would be finished, hopefully the dog would be found, as would Carol Dupuis, and maybe the source of *Yersinia* would be pinpointed in an infected sample of meat. Was it too much to hope for?

Apparently. He could not even close the meeting. King was objecting to the crowd invited to attend.

"I mean, do we need researchers whose specialties are toxicosis and histoplasmosis? Visitors to the department? If we need extra people, we'll ask, but otherwise, we don't want to waste anyone's time. The *Yersinia* specialist should be help enough."

McCoy didn't miss the beaming smile the CDC man shot Dana Sparks. He stared at the grinning lunatic in wonder. The CDC agents couldn't find a dog, they couldn't find a student, and here they were turning away offers of help? The only positive development was that no new people were infected with the plague, but at this rate, how long would that last?

McCoy held up his hand. "You let us worry about wasting our time. I told the university president we'll assist you in every way and we will. Until further notice this whole department is at your disposal. Meeting dismissed."

Chapter 17

At the close of the meeting, people were on their feet as if responding to an unspoken order to move out. Dana got caught behind the lumbering Charlie Lane and the jovial Karl King. Ahead, Nick followed McCoy out the door, flanked by Nellie and Michael.

Karl fell into step with her. "Can you come to Headquarters and get the samples?" He had very white teeth and a wide smile that showed them all. His hair was a white-silver streaked with blond and his eyes were brown, the color of mud. Despite his smile, there was a sadness about him.

They went down the hall. He was walking too close to her, kept bumping her elbow with his arm. She increased her pace. Nick was already out of sight.

"I hear you worked with Nick," Karl said.

She wondered how he knew—if Nick had told him. "For a while."

"Congratulations on your vaccine."

She nodded acknowledgment. He knew about that too.

"He said you were good."

"He did?" Dana slowed down, and forced herself not to ask what else Nick said. Instead, "Have you known him long?"

"Since medical school."

Dana looked at Karl with renewed interest.

"He was the best man at my wedding. Though I'm divorced."

She guessed that explained his sadness.

They reached the end of the hall and Karl lunged ahead, threw open the door, and there was Nick, looming ahead of her, within arm's reach. She was close enough to smell his sweat, a scent she had forgotten. The aroma of fried onions. How could she forget? He nodded hello and took a step backward and turned around.

The small office was crammed with three desks and an oversized fridge that bore an orange biohazard sign. From the fridge door, Karl grabbed a bag. He pulled out a small vial. "Fleas." She saw black flecks floating in fluid. He held up a capillary tube. "Dog's blood." Then a Ziplock. "Meat." He offered her the biohazard bag.

She rolled the top of the bag, looked at Nick. He sat at the desk with his back to her, hammering at a laptop computer. Never far from his music, a Discman and a thick case of CDs lay on the desk.

"If you're busy I could Fed-Ex the samples to Atlanta," Karl said.

"This is a priority. I have my orders."

Karl laughed loudly. "I appreciate the help," he said, and did a little jig with his head as he smiled a large smile, and Nick ignored them.

"I'll have the results of the ELISA in forty-five minutes."

"I can help you if you want," Karl said.

Dana needed time to think; she wanted to be alone. "I can do it." She looked at Nick, enthralled with his screen. He was already gone, focused on his work. "I'll let you know the results."

"I'll be waiting." Karl flicked his eyebrows up and down and beamed at her.

"Bye." She slowly backed toward the door.

Nick lifted his head, a quick nod.

She went to her lab and began the assay, trying to decipher Nick's mood and distance. It signified nothing, she rationalized; this was the way he was at work, focused and obsessed. It was what made him good; she had learned much from him.

At the beginning she didn't want him as her supervisor. She found him aloof and preoccupied. He had no time for her. If she saw him in the hall, he looked the other way. She requested Becker as her supervisor, but he made noises about retiring and wouldn't take her on. He suggested Nick, thought he would be perfect. Nick wasn't happy about it, but didn't refuse. She was his only student and he made it clear from the start she couldn't expect much help. He was busy fine-tuning a computer program that used chaos theory to predict the course of infectious disease. And this from a man who believed that life was a series of random accidents, essentially a mistake.

He did not work much on the bench, he had warned her, and he traveled a lot; she would be on her own. That turned out to be far from the truth. It was Nick who pushed her toward the monoclonal antibody technology, Nick who thought she would only understand the immunology if she broke the whole into its component pieces and looked at each part.

He helped her sacrifice the mice. Dana couldn't kill them; she tried, but never expected the mice to fight back. Even research mice wouldn't die willingly. Nick had no trouble with them; he had a way with animals. They would walk into his hands and he would calmly snap their necks, dislocate their spinal cords. The mice never knew what hit them, never saw him coming. She could have learned a lot from them.

The antibody work got complicated fast. When she was ready to give it up, he pushed on. She learned that every unexpected result had something to teach. When things went awry, Nick didn't turn away, he delved, probing, searching for the answers to what went wrong. What didn't they know? What could they learn? What did they need to change?

He was like that in his personal life too, with his wife and her schizophrenia. Nick hung in there, refusing to give up, always ready to try the latest treatment. There would be a cure; she would get better; he could wait.

Then Rachel-Anne slipped into a coma after she tried to poison herself with carbon monoxide. She would likely have died if the car hadn't run out of gas. Frank, paddling in the pool, near the point of exhaustion, would have died too if Nick hadn't arrived home early. Rachel-Anne was put in an asylum and Nick started to travel. It was only in his absence that Dana realized how she felt; when Nick was gone something big was missing from her life. True, he was married, but that was not hard to overlook. Rachel-Anne was out of the picture.

Four months after they started working together, they went to an immunology meeting in Galveston. Nick was the keynote speaker and they drove down to the coast together. They had planned to stay for the day, but Nick's pickup truck developed mechanical trouble and they had to stay the night.

All the rooms at the Grand Hotel were taken, but two of Nick's colleagues doubled-up to give him a room. He gave her the bed and took the floor.

The curtains were open and there was a full moon that night and the room was not dark. It was quiet with only the hum of the A.C., still running in late October. From the king-sized bed she listened to his breathing and heard no change in rhythm, hours after they went to bed. She willed him to come to her, but he did not move. Finally, she went to him, quietly removing her clothes and creeping beneath the sheet beside him. He wore boxers and she was surprised by the amount of hair on his chest. He gave off a heat and a scent that made her hungry. Tentatively she lay against the length of him and when he didn't flinch, placed an arm around his waist. He stirred and turned to face her on his side, slung his arm across her. And slept on while her heart hammered against him.

He woke before dawn, his body tensing and then he was up and pulling on his pants. He needed coffee. He would be right back.

It was a long drive home. He said he was married and there was nothing left to say after that. It was a gray day, the air full with drizzle that did not fall.

The following day he was traveling again, unexpectedly off to Vancouver for a meeting he had not previously mentioned. A week later he was back, out at her house, red-faced and furious and waving an envelope from the *Journal of Molecular Immunology* in her face. She read the letter, a paper she wrote had been accepted. She had put Nick's name down as second author.

"How could you do it? Without asking? Without my knowledge?" He was angry, his voice breaking. "Just do it?"

"I thought you knew." She had put the article on his desk and when it reappeared in her in-box, she assumed he had seen it and had no comments to make.

"I had no idea."

"I'm sorry."

"Don't do it again."

He stormed out, and Dana wondered if it was really the paper they were talking about.

An hour later he was back and looking sheepish and contrite. He was nervous, pulling at his hair, whistling a tune, unable to meet her eyes. He apologized for losing his temper. "I don't know what came over me." He had the article rolled up, which he slapped against his thigh. "I liked it," he said.

"I thought you would."

"I guess it was the surprise."

"I should have been more straightforward."

"You couldn't have been more so. I wasn't asleep." He blushed when he said this, a red sheen beneath his five o'clock stubble. He just wanted to clear that up, then he was leaving.

"Don't go," she said.

"I'd like to stay, but—" He shrugged his shoulders.

"Then stay."

It was dinnertime and he insisted on cooking. That night she learned that, among other things, he was a good cook. He tuned the stereo to the classical station and made a spaghetti sauce while Beethoven's Fifth Symphony played. He hummed along, in places conducting with a wooden spoon.

After dinner he got a Robin Wheeler CD from his car. They danced and he sang in her ear songs she had never heard before, which she would know by heart when the night was through. Every single song from *Black Waters*.

Later he kept saying he was going, but he never did. The CD played on and on. He spent the night and the next day. They read the paper in bed, took a long walk. In the afternoon they drank more wine and made more love. His knees were badly skinned. It was dark when he was ready to leave. He left her his Wheeler CD, searched for but could not find his bandanna and a sock. He stepped into his shoes, his ankles bare. His laces were untied and she leaned down to tie them up. That night he never left.

He was two people, she saw; that much was clear. The man who went to work was serious and rational, while the other kicked off his shoes and had songs in his heart. He brought music into her life.

The mild winter passed and the spring turned to summer, and the abundant time ran together; endless nights when the music played and the wine ran. Always in excess, as if they both knew it would never last—that their time would run out, as it had. A promising new treatment for schizophrenia in Washington D.C. called him away. It was over; he would not call; he would not be back.

He gave her one tangible thing before he left, a red plastic poppy he picked up in Vancouver, which he wore on his blazer: a Remembrance Day poppy to honor those killed in a war. It would turn out to be a fitting gift.

And then he was gone. He left so much undone, so much unsaid, and now he was here. Why had he come?

The timer rang. The assay was done. The results were negative. There was no *Yersinia* in the meat, fleas, or the neighbor's dog's blood. She washed her hands and left the quarantine room.

Near her office, she stopped short. Nick stood in the doorway of her lab. Her chest pounded with her heart as her stomach tightened. She caught the light in Nick's eye before he looked at the floor.

His same old scent wafted toward her. His familiar bulk before her. He was about half-a-head taller than she, and if she took a few steps forward, the top of her head would fit under his nose, and her mouth would reach the indent of his clavicle.

"It's been forty-five minutes," he said. "Do you have the results?"

"Negative."

He looked at her puzzled. "What?"

She stared away from his eyes. They were blue, but their shade varied with the light. In her lab they looked green. "I mean there's no exposure," Dana said. "The samples are clean."

He took a step backward. "I thought as much."

At work Nick possessed an uncanny intuition he didn't

always apply to his personal affairs. She offered him the printout with the ELISA results.

He looked at the results and she looked at him. His dark hair was turning gray. He still wore it long and it curled at his neck. It was receding on top, but like her father, he took no pains to hide this. His eyebrows were thick, his nose straight and sharp, his lips pale and pink. There was a dimple in his chin and one by his cheek that showed when he smiled. He always cut the dimple on his cheek shaving and it was cut now, a slash surrounded by stubble. Nick's five o'clock shadow came early. He shaved a lot.

"I'll take these to Karl," he said, and took another step for the door.

Don't go, Dana thought but she said, "Where could the *Yersinia* come from?" She was heading straight for Nick's focus of interest. The origin of disease. The sudden appearance of a lethal pathogen out of nowhere. For his work on chaos and his computer models, the situation at time zero was of paramount importance.

He paused. "My guess is the forest."

"Mine too." She pointed to her office. "Would you like a cup of coffee?"

He ran a hand through his hair and hesitated before saying sure. He came into her office. His tie was gone and the collar of his shirt was unbuttoned. She could see his chest hair was going gray. She remembered it dark, her fingers tangled in it. How could she have forgotten the power he had over her? She poured two cups of coffee with a shaky hand and carefully handed him one.

"What now?" she said.

"I'll go to the hospital. Interview Dudley's sister. So far, the state has recorded no other cases. Looks like it's isolated. We might never know where it started. So long as it ends, that's the important thing."

What was he saying? She backed up to her desk and sat

down on top, raising the cup of coffee to her lips. He was staring at a glassware catalogue.

How's your work, she meant to say, but she slipped. "How's Rachel-Anne?"

"Dead."

Coffee flew from Dana's mouth as she choked. The coffee spilled on her hand and ran down her arm to her wrist. She dropped the cup on her desk. *"What?"*

"Last August. She had been on life-support for three years when she died."

"In *August*?"

Nick stared at his coffee cup. "I thought you knew. I was surprised when I didn't hear from you."

"When you left, you said don't call. Now you expected me to?"

He shrugged. "My secretary sent out death notices."

"Not to me."

He shrugged again. "There was an announcement in the *Duane Eagle*. Did you stop getting the paper?"

"I don't read obituaries."

He smoothed down his hair. "I assumed you knew."

She shook her head, marveling again at how one second could change everything.

There were footsteps in her lab and Betty rushed into her office. "Good, you're here. I got a call from Sheila." She saw Nick and patted the sides of her stiff hair, blinked heavily. "Frank is in bad shape. You need to get down to the clinic."

She had forgotten her dog. Dana was out the door with Nick at her heels. He pounded down the stairs beside her. *"Frank?"* he said, "Frank?"

She found her dog alone in Tim Sweeny's animal room, sitting on the cold cement floor, long pink tongue hanging out, body trembling. She bent down and threw her arms around his neck.

Nick knelt beside her, holding out his hand. "Hey, buddy."

Frank's tail began to wag. He rested his head on Dana's shoulder and looked past her, at Nick, his first master; Nick who had left him, had left everything.

Frank strained toward him and Dana let him go. He lurched sideways toward Nick, and licked his face with a sweep of his tongue as he fell. Nick caught him as he went, breaking his fall. Frank's tail wagged again and his trembling stopped. The room went silent as his breath went still. Drops of frothy blood trickled from Frank's mouth leaving crimson drops on the floor.

Chapter 18

Death was an unpleasant consequence of both life and war that could not be avoided, and though McCoy had experience relaying bad news to grieving family members, he never got used to it. Standing in the hospital basement, outside the all-denominational chapel, and peering through a stained glass door, McCoy rehearsed the words of comfort he would say to Dudley Shaw's sister, Tabitha Tott, who sat at the head of the chapel, head bowed in prayer.

McCoy had missed her at the airport. Her flight landed early and she was gone by the time he arrived. He thought she'd go directly to the hospital but she did not and McCoy had been waiting for some time. He was about to leave, honor his promise to Margaret for another driving lesson, when a nurse informed him Tabitha Tott had arrived.

Normally, notification of mortality was a job for the attending physician, but Dr. Taversham was in surgery, as he had been all afternoon, and McCoy could not waste time waiting for him. He was prepared to do what it took to learn where Dudley Shaw had acquired his infection.

There was nothing to gain by delaying further and Mc-

Coy pushed open the stained glass door and entered the chapel. The room was small and comforting. Near the door was a marble stand filled with Holy Water and McCoy blessed himself. He said a small prayer as he walked up the aisle. When he turned down the front pew, Tabitha Tott looked up.

She looked about ninety years old. If Dudley was sixty-five, his sister was considerably older. Her eyes were red and puffy and her white hair was done up in an untidy bun. A pillbox hat on her head tilted to one side. She clutched a rosary in arthritic fingers and a heavy gold cross hung from her neck. Catholic, McCoy thought. At least she had faith to support her. He sat down beside her.

"I'm Dr. McCoy. I'm afraid I have bad news."

The old woman stared straight ahead at an altar over-flowing with bright plastic flowers. "Dudley is dead," she said.

How did she know, McCoy wondered. Who had she been talking to? How much did she know? "I'm sorry for your loss, ma'am."

Mrs. Tott crossed herself. "What did he die from?"

"A bacterial infection," McCoy said. "The hospital is still running tests." Though McCoy did not wish to be less than truthful in the house of the Lord, McCoy and Taversham agreed this was the way they would handle the nature of Dudley's disease. A conclusive diagnosis would not be made for a week.

McCoy moved quickly on. "We can talk outside if you wish."

Mrs. Tott said nothing.

"Or here is fine."

"When can I see him?" she said, as if he hadn't spoken.

McCoy hedged. According to Taversham, Dudley had exhibited classical symptoms of the plague, and his extremities were black. McCoy did not want her to see the body. "You'll have to ask the doctor," McCoy said. He watched the candles flickering in unison at the side of the chapel. Nearly every candle was burning. He tried to steer the conversation to Shaw's last days. "Now, we know your brother visited you at Easter, approximately one month ago. How long did he stay with you? For the weekend or was it longer?"

She sighed, "The weekend."

"Did he come straight back to Duane?"

"Where else would he go?"

She was going to be difficult, McCoy saw, as he persisted in his inquiry. "Do you know if Dudley had recent visitors?"

Mrs. Tott bowed her head. "What did he die from?" Her lip quivered and her voice trembled.

"Ma'am, I'm sorry, he died from a bacterial infection." McCoy spoke looking up at the ceiling. If there was anything worse than a woman who cried, it was a woman who wanted to cry but would not allow it. He heard a sniffle, then another, and dared glance at her. A single tear tracked down her cheek.

McCoy gazed helplessly at the burning candles. He rose and walked toward the altar, pulling coins from his pocket. He tossed them in a small basket, picked up a book of matches and lit the three remaining candles. He returned to the pew.

Tabitha Tott was wiping her eyes with a crumpled Kleenex. "I'll be fine," she said.

McCoy silently applauded her effort at self-control. "When did you talk to your brother last?"

"A week ago, Sunday. I talk to him every Sunday. When he didn't answer yesterday I knew something was wrong and I called the police. I came as soon as I could. He was strong, I didn't think he'd go so fast." She swatted her damp swollen face with the tissue and sniffled loudly. "To think this happened just before his big vacation. What kind of bacteria got him?"

"You'll have to ask his doctor," McCoy reiterated. "We

won't know more until the hospital finishes running their tests. It could take a week."

"A week!" Mrs. Tott cried. "How could you treat him if you didn't know what he had? What about antibiotics? Who dies from a bacterial infection these days?"

"Bacterial infections are more serious in the elderly. And we don't know how long your brother was infected." It seemed Sparks had asked everything but the most important question. "Can you tell me, when you last talked to him, did he mention he was feeling under the weather?"

"Elderly?" She was following her own script. "He was only sixty-five. He shouldn't have died first. I was supposed to go first."

"I'm sorry." McCoy repeated a question she hadn't answered earlier. "Did he have any out-of-town visitors?" McCoy hoped if Shaw hadn't contracted the plague elsewhere, then someone had brought him the bacteria.

But according to Mrs. Tott, Dudley wasn't a visitor sort of man.

McCoy tried to hide his disappointment. "We need to know all we can about your brother's habits. Where he went, what he did. The names of his friends, his doctor, his dentist, where he shopped, where he hunted."

"Oh, Dudley hasn't hunted for years," Tabitha Tott said.

And McCoy's high hopes that Dudley was infected when hunting were immediately dashed.

"The only company he needed was his dog and . . ."

McCoy interrupted her. "Yes, the dog, ma'am. Do you have any idea where we can find the dog?" He thought of the hapless dogcatcher, unable to locate the animal.

"Any idea?" Tabitha straightened her hunched shoulders. "I've got him."

She had the dog? "Ah." McCoy was afraid to ask how she managed to find him, though he found great solace in the fact. Finally—a breakthrough. Neither the CDC nor the dogcatcher could find the animal, but the sister could. One of their biggest problems was finally solved. Things might turn out fine after all. McCoy silently listed the positive developments. The dog was found and could be tested. Thirty-six hours had passed since the disease appeared in Duane and no other victims were identified. No other infected rats or small rodents had been found. It appeared as though Dudley *was* an isolated case. Maybe it was fortunate he wasn't a visitor kind of man. His disease was an aberration, an anomaly, an exception.

"May I see the dog?" McCoy said gently, earnestly, for in truth, the question was not completely forthright. McCoy would have to do more than just see him; he'd have to confiscate him.

"Bingo?" Tabitha said. "You want to see Bingo? What on earth for?"

"There are some infections people get from animals," he said.

"You mean rabies? You think Dudley has rabies?"

"If I could just see the dog, ma'am," McCoy said.

She wouldn't budge. "There's nothing wrong with him. Well, he's nearly blind and lame and old, but take my word for it, he's not foaming at the mouth, he's not vicious, he's fine."

McCoy couldn't take her word for it, but he couldn't tell her that. "There may be symptoms we can't see," he said.

She frowned at him. "What kind of symptoms can't you see?"

McCoy stood up and offered his arm. "Ma'am, if there are any, believe me, I'll point them out to you."

She wound her rosary into a ball and slipped it in an oversized purse. "Point out things you can't see," she muttered, but at least she stood up.

She shrugged off McCoy's offer of assistance. Holding her head high, she marched up the aisle toward the door. McCoy wondered where she had the dog.

Outside in the hallway, the fluorescent tube lights were

blinding. It was the dinner hour and candy stripers were pushing carts laden with food trays toward the elevator. The air smelled of stew and reminded McCoy of his daughter awaiting her driving lesson.

They reached the elevator and McCoy impatiently punched the button. The doors opened and Karl King stepped out. He wore a self-satisfied smirk on his face that matched his tone when he said, "I've found Bingo and notified the dogcatcher."

"You did what?" Tabitha cried. Her voice was shrill and harsh.

Karl scratched the back of his neck and looked at McCoy helplessly. McCoy, who had read somewhere that 90 percent of people weren't fit to hold their jobs, believed at least in the civilian setting, it was so.

"The pound is down the street and I called the dogcatcher on my cell phone." Unbelievably, Karl worked the phone out of his pocket and held it up.

McCoy shot him a furious look. "How do you know you got the right dog?"

"He was in Dudley's car." Karl said. "The one parked at his house is now out in the lot."

McCoy's heart suddenly squeezed tightly in his chest. In this investigation, anything that could possibly go wrong was going that way. The CDC couldn't find a lame, blind dog and now Tabitha Tott had apparently taken her brother's car. "That car is under quarantine," he said.

The sister glared at him. "It's my car. You can't take it."

Karl explained that Tabitha couldn't use the car or the house because of the contagious nature of Dudley's bacterial infection.

"What contagious bacteria?" Tabitha asked.

Karl King stroked his dirty goatee and looked at McCoy for help.

"Until we're absolutely positive the bacterium is not contagious, we have to assume that it is," McCoy said.

Karl mercifully changed the subject and asked if the car was a '55 Thunderbird.

"Fifty-seven," Tabitha said.

"It's a nice car," Karl said. "Would you be interested in selling it?"

McCoy could not believe what he was hearing, and apparently neither could Tabitha Tott. "No," she said, sharply. "It's my car and I want it. I want my dog. I want to stay in my brother's house. I want to know what killed him."

Standing in the close basement, with the heat of the boilers and the stoves, McCoy felt the sweat stream down his body. Tabitha Tott had been in contact with the dog and was now potentially exposed to bubonic plague. She would need prophylactic antibiotics and he didn't think she'd take them easily. What if she brought infected fleas into the hospital? How could an investigation go so wrong?

The elevator doors opened and Dr. Taversham came out. He was thin, balding and appeared exhausted despite a substantial tan. In his late-thirties, he was too young in McCoy's mind to be the hospital specialist of infectious disease. Taversham nodded to McCoy. "I'm glad I caught you. We just got our second case."

"Second case of what?" Tabitha Tott demanded.

Taversham looked at the old woman as though noticing her for the first time. McCoy introduced her.

Over his suntan, Taversham's face went red. He offered Tabitha a slender hand. "I'm sorry to keep you waiting. I'm Dr. Taversham. I was treating your brother."

"I want to see him," Tabitha Tott said. "I want to know what killed him."

"Let's go to my office," Taversham said.

But Tabitha Tott shook her head and insisted on going to the morgue.

Chapter 19

Frank lay stretched out in the backseat swathed in sunlight. He looked peaceful to Dana, as if he had died with a smile on his face. His pain was gone, but she felt the loss of his life was her fault. Would he have lived longer if she had just left him alone? Lived long enough to see Nick, who came back in time for him to die?

He sat beside her in the passenger seat and turned on the radio. Dolly Parton was singing. Nick made a face and changed the station, tuning in KLOL from Houston, a rock n' roll station that played 60s and 70s music. She recognized the Rolling Stones "Can't Get No Satisfaction." Nick leaned back and tapped his shoe in time with the music. He had insisted on helping her bury Frank, said he was too heavy for her and that Frank was his dog too. Now they were heading west and Dana adjusted the rear-view mirror so she could see Frank. The sunlight shone on his gray coat; he could have been sleeping. It was too beautiful a day to die. Why now? She wanted him back, wanted her home as it was, with Frank there, waiting by the porch or lying in his basket, wagging his tail. Now he was gone.

The song ended and the weather report came on. There was a high probability of a tropical storm. Other than that, a beautiful weekend loomed. The weather on Friday and Saturday looked great: highs in the low eighties by Saturday and nineties on Sunday.

"That will save us," Nick said suddenly.

"What will?"

"The heat. Temperatures above eighty-two degrees kill plague epidemics. No one knows why."

"Oh." He was talking about work.

"There were three incidents of the plague last year in New Mexico," Nick said, as he stared out the window. "Five in Arizona the year before that. Your vaccine should help."

He knew about the vaccine, but probably not the reaction in the guinea pig.

"I'm kind of nervous how the human trials will go," she said. Nick was the one person she could talk to about her work. With everyone else she felt she had to put on a front, but with Nick she could be honest. "I'm scared that something will go wrong."

"The initial volunteer will be kept under strict medical supervision," Nick said.

He knew that too. In June, a single volunteer would be injected at Walter Reed Hospital. From the guinea pig response, they knew the allergic response was immediate and apparent within twelve hours. "But what if he gets sick?" Dana said.

"The physicians will take care of it," Nick said lightly, as if there was no possibility of any complications.

"I'll be glad when it's over," she said. On every falling star she saw Dana made a wish that the human volunteer would be fine.

The weather report ended and headline news came on. A Somali warlord warned that there would be repercussions against America if compensation was not made for the dead. We're not the terrorists here, the warlord claimed. But the U.S. was steadfast in its refusal to deal with a country that supported terrorism. Incoming intelligence reports verified the American belief that the intended target was hit, and was in fact a warehouse filled with weapons and munitions. The U.S. conceded that nearby buildings may have been damaged in the blast.

Nick was leaning forward, listening intently to the news, when she turned down the dirt road leading to her house. He sat up straight. "You still live here?"

She glanced at him. "It's my house. I bought it."

"I didn't know," he said.

He would have been able to find her, had he looked. All this time he could have picked up his phone and dialed her number and she would have answered, but the call had never been made.

She drove down the rutted driveway and parked the car beside the house. There was no sign of Anthony or Judy. Dana whistled loudly and caught Nick's puzzled glance.

"I think we're going to have to carry him."

"I have two other dogs."

"Oh." He sounded surprised once more, and she wondered, why. What did he think she'd been doing since he left? Well, yes, among other things, waiting for him.

He got out of the car, retrieved Frank and staggered behind her across the lawn toward the trees and what would be a grave. He lay Frank gently down in the shade and retrieved a shovel from under the porch.

Soon he was digging, bent double, dirt flying. Sweat ran down his face, his shirt was soaked and stuck to his skin. She went and got Frank's red blanket from his bed and covered him with it. Nick refused her offer to help and she sat down in a bed of soft needles against a white pine tree.

Frank lay under his blanket in an unmoving heap. She would never again come home to find him waiting. She would never scoop Alpo into his bowl, or feed him by hand when he wouldn't eat. She would never see him in the car again with his head hanging out the window and the wind blowing back his ears. He was gone, gone for good, poor Frank, left alone for most of the day on the last day of his life. Dana lowered her head. She missed him. Everything was suddenly too big. Frank left behind too many holes. Dana remembered well this overwhelming emptiness. It swamped her when Nick left. Everywhere she turned, she was reminded of him. He had become threaded into her life, woven into the fabric that was ripped to shreds when he left. It had taken a long time to get the pieces back together. Now Nick was here and Frank was gone, leaving a ghost to fill the places he'd left behind forever.

A lump grew in her throat. She wiped her face and hugged her knees. A sudden wind swept down from the north and bent the tall blades of grass. The wildflowers bowed to the grave.

With a start, she realized Nick was looking at her, standing near a too-big hole, leaning on his shovel. His face was streaked with dirt. He'd rolled up his sleeves and another button on his shirt was undone, exposing more graying hair. He had tied his handkerchief around his forehead.

"I think the hole is big enough," he said, staring at the dark earth. With Nick everything was more than it had to be; there was either nothing or excess. He removed the bandanna, wiped his brow.

There came then a noise from the woods and he turned. Branches crackled and snapped as Anthony and Judy sprang from the forest. Anthony ran for the plaid blanket and nosed it to the side, exposing Frank's flank. Judy barked loudly at the heap, then launched into her high pitched whine.

Dana watched as Nick made friends with the dogs. He threw a lump of dirt for Anthony to fetch and found the spot on Judy's belly that always itched. He had a way with animals, with her.

The sun had sunk beneath the trees when he laid Frank in his grave. Dana could not watch as the first shovel of dirt fell on the blanket. She took the dogs up to the porch. She would never have been able to bury Frank alone. Nick was right; she needed help. Somehow he was always there when she needed him, doing whatever task had to be done. He made things too easy for her.

And now Rachel-Anne was dead. The unthinkable was real—what she never dared wish for.

Nick came up to the porch, wiping his hands together and then drawing them across the seat of his slacks.

"Would you like a beer?" she asked, the first item on a long list of things she had to offer.

"No." Then, as an afterthought, "Thanks."

"Is that a yes or a no?"

"No, thank you. I should get to the hospital. Talk to Dudley's sister."

"I'll drive you. Maybe later, we could have dinner."

"Karl will be there. He'll drive me back to the hotel. I have a lot of work to do."

"Oh. Another time then."

"Sure." He looked at his watch. "Karl will wonder what happened to me. I don't even have my pager. It's in your car." He was already heading up the driveway.

He would not be distracted. She turned to the dogs. "Stay." But they followed behind, bouncing at Nick's heels.

She ran after him, wondering why he couldn't stay for a few hours. The investigation would go on without him. He could be here with her; his wife was dead. But he rushed ahead.

Dana fell into step alongside him. It was dusk—the magic time of day. In the twilight, Dana asked the question that was on her mind all day. "Why did you come?"

He reached the car and stopped. His eyes were deep blue

now that the sun was gone. The whites of his eyes were bright. "You really want to know?"

"I do."

She heard him exhale and held her breath. "Between you and me?" he said.

"Of course." She waited for his answer, heard the loud beat of her heart.

"*Yersinia* at this low latitude."

Her heart stopped, her breath stalled, hope died.

"It wasn't my choice," Nick said.

He hadn't come to see her, but because he had no choice. "Is it the VP's visit?" she said.

"Well, that too," Nick said.

"You think there's a connection?"

He opened the car door. "I didn't say that. I'm here to rule that possibility out."

It didn't matter why he came, Dana thought, the important thing was that he was here; the effect mattered, not the cause.

On the dashboard, his pager began to beep. He grabbed it. "Karl." They returned to the house so he could use the phone.

She listened to his end of the conversation: Oh. Okay. Which hospital? Right now? No. Yes. I don't know. No, I can make it. I'm on my way. He talked staring at the ceiling, his eyes seemingly fixed on his old bandanna and the Remembrance Day poppy pinned to it.

Nick put down the receiver. "There's another case of the bubonic plague," he said. "A senior at the university. I've got to meet McCoy at the hospital. He wants to know where you are. The results of the assay." He looked maddeningly contrite. "It was my fault."

She drove to the hospital and he sat as far away from her in the seat as he could. There was no sign of the man who sang in the shower and had rocked her to sleep. The cool detached professional was fully present and reeling off statistics. A second case of bubonic plague in twenty-four hours was not good. And where were the rats and infected fleas? "Something's not right," he said.

She did not disagree.

Chapter 20

The hospital lights were muted at night, but the hallway seemed bright to McCoy. He stood with Karl outside a makeshift quarantine room, waiting for Nick so they might interview the latest patient. McCoy heard the low murmur of a television and imagined a late-breaking news report. A ringing phone made him think of the hungry press. Another case now, a student, a popular football player with many friends, and a room with a phone. Was it lunacy to think he could keep this quiet any longer?

McCoy checked his watch. Where the hell was Nick? Karl had no idea. Nick went to Sparks' lab and never returned. Sparks was gone too and McCoy was furious. How did it look to the CDC to have a plague specialist who couldn't be reached in the middle of a . . . situation? According to Nellie, she left without a word, leaving her lab wide open, and her quarantine room with its contagious material, unlocked. No word on the results of the test she ran that afternoon. Such was his expert! Inside his quarantine gear, McCoy felt rivers of sweat streak down his skin.

He felt better when he saw Nick hurrying down the hall.

Less so, when he saw Sparks in tow. She mumbled something about an emergency.

"This is the only emergency I'm interested in," McCoy said. "What were the results of the assay?"

"Clean."

"I'll be damned." Karl King frowned and tapped a clipboard across his thigh.

A quandary McCoy didn't like. How in the hell was Shaw infected? The *Yersinia* had to come from somewhere. Would the football player know?

Nick and Sparks were suiting up. They were dealing with a Class Three contagion and anyone entering the quarantine facility had to wear scrubs, double gloves, paper boots, hair covering and mask. They weren't his rules; he made this clear.

As they dressed, Karl summarized the case. Jack Dowel was twenty-two years old and a senior at the university. He had driven himself to the hospital late that afternoon and arrived complaining of nausea, headache, high fever and swollen glands, primarily in the groin. Karl had examined him and clinically verified a presumptive diagnosis of bubonic plague. The disease was in the early stage. The patient displayed no signs of hemorrhage, circulatory collapse, respiratory distress, or organ failure. He was being treated with the triple antibiotic cocktail and his prognosis was good. Jack was in good shape and excellent health. He'd been given a sedative but it was wearing off and Taversham said he'd be able to answer questions.

When he was through reciting the medical report, Karl positioned the mask over his face, clicked the end of a pen and opened a door that bore the sign: RESTRICTED AREA. AUTHORIZED PERSONNEL ONLY. CLASS III CONTAGION. They all traipsed into the room.

From his bed, the second victim, Jack Dowel, saw them and screamed. He kicked his food tray and it careened toward them smashing into the wall. "Get out," he yelled.

"Take your god damn masks and suits and get the hell out."
He yanked at his IV line. "Don't tell me I have the fucking
flu. Don't dress like that and tell me lies."

Karl tried to explain. "I'm Karl King, from the CD—"

Jack sprang up and heaved the chair that was next to the
bed. It flew across the room, forcing Karl to leap out of its
path. Even sick, the football player was a powerful man.
Dangerous. McCoy tried to speak gently.

"Mr. Dowel, have you left town recently or had visitors
from—"

Jack Dowel hurled a glass of water at him. McCoy
quickly ducked. The glass hit the wall, bounced off and
rolled on the floor.

King tried again. "It's not exactly the flu you have. It's a
bacterial infection."

"Infection? What kind?" Jack asked.

"A bacterium that has compromised your immune system and—"

Dowel flung the phone at him, but the toss was poor and
the phone clattered to the floor. McCoy thought perhaps
they should abort the interview and sedate the patient.
They were getting nowhere.

Of course Dana Sparks had to give it a go. McCoy
watched her saunter toward the bed. His mouth fell open
when she dropped her mask. McCoy knew her acquies-
cence was too good to last. Straining to stay calm, McCoy
said in a sharp tone, "I will remind you, Doctor, of the
quarantine regulations of this hospital."

She ignored him. Keeping her back to him, she said,
"Hi, Jack. I'm Dana. Could I ask you a few questions?"

"Not dressed like that you don't," McCoy said.

Dana Sparks turned around, her mask dangling at her
neck.

"These are hospital rules that must be adhered to." Mc-
Coy said. Rules were rules and policy was policy and once
people ignored protocol, standards deteriorated, anarchy

and chaos reigned. Under no circumstance would he permit this insubordination to pass. "Either replace that mask or leave this room at once."

"We're not dealing with an aerosol contagion. This gear isn't necessary."

From the bed, Jack said, "Dana and me can talk. Everyone else can leave."

Karl didn't like it. "Jack, I'm from the CDC. My name is Karl and if you don't mind, I'd like to conduct the interview."

Jack minded. "I'll talk to her and no one else."

Chapter 21

The door slammed and Dana was alone with Jack Dowel. His hands were clenched, his body tight, like a spring waiting to snap. She crossed the room, retrieving the things he had thrown. Then she dragged the chair beside his bed and sat down.

There was a sour odor in the room, adrenaline, the scent of fear and rage. An apt reaction Dana thought, of someone who had been lied to. If they wanted information from Jack, they couldn't pretend he had the flu. The suits sent a message of danger that Jack had read correctly. His response was appropriate.

She pulled the mask off her neck. They didn't need the gear; it was ridiculous. They were vaccinated against the plague. Besides, bubonic plague was transmitted by fleas, not people, so the strict quarantine protocol was unnecessary.

"I know you," Jack said.

She looked at him. He had short, white blond hair and delicate features that were at odds with his hulking body. His head seemed disproportionately small, but that might have been because his body was huge. He had round blue eyes and big white teeth. She had never seen him before.

"You gave my class a lecture in the fall. It was good."

"Thanks."

"I'm a football player."

She smiled at him. "I know."

"I don't usually get sick," he said. "Well, last week I had the flu but it was nothing like this." He pushed himself upright and stared in her eye. "What do I have?"

He had the right to know. "We think bubonic plague."

Jack blinked. His eyelashes were long, thick and blond. "The plague?" He shut his eyes.

"It's a bacterial infection. You're taking three antibiotics. You'll feel better soon."

He opened his eyes. "I feel like I'm going to die. Like there's a boiling hot snake crawling through my body."

Dana checked his medical chart. He was on morphine and past due for another shot. "You could have more pain medicine if you wanted."

He did and she rang for the nurse.

In a few minutes, Jack's eyes were glazed and he was staring off into space. Dana wanted him to talk about himself and apparently that wouldn't be a problem. He was a senior and would graduate in August. He had a few courses he had to make up on account of football. He'd been on the team four years and recounted one of his plays. It was a tie game. Bucky, the quarterback, threw him a lateral toss that Jack caught in an underhand dive. He dodged the defensive line and started running. The clock ran out. It was the last play of the game. Jack ran from the sixty-yard line and as he went, the fans screamed out his name. He crossed the end line to win the game. With a satisfied smile on his face, he folded his arms across his huge chest.

Dana tried to look appropriately impressed. "That's very interesting. Do you have any pets?"

"Nope. They don't allow them where I live."

"Where is that?"

"The Tremblant Apartments."

She swallowed her surprise. The Tremblant Apartments had a pool, tennis court and maid service. The building was owned by the university and primarily reserved for honorable guests and visiting scientists on sabbatical. Apparently some football players lived there too.

"Have you seen fleas in the house?"

"No." Jack said the landlord sprayed for cockroaches every four months and he had seen no fleas. He couldn't remember a fleabite, but he had what he called a fire-ant bite on his ankle.

"Can I see it?"

He threw off the sheet.

His ankle was as thick as her thigh. The bite had turned necrotic and black. Around that a raised red swell. She touched the bite. It was hot and hard. She did not think it was an ant bite.

"Have you seen mice or rats at your place?"

"No."

"Do you know any one else who is ill?"

He knew lots of people who were sick but there was a bad flu going around. Last week he was sick with it, but it wasn't like this.

"Can you tell me who you've seen recently?"

Jack shrugged. That would be a problem, for he'd been in contact with lots of people. He was taking five classes; he'd been out drinking with his football buddies, at the movies, out on dates.

Dana copied down the list of his classes. She made a note of his friends and acquaintances, and the girls he dated the previous week—Bobbi-Sue, Candy and Lolita. He didn't know their last names.

"I mean, they're not serious," he said.

"Did you have sex?" Dana returned his stare. It was a question she had to ask. If Jack had the bacteria in his blood, boisterous intercourse could rupture small vessels and facilitate the blood to blood transfer of the bacteria and cause septicemic plague.

"Of course," he said.

"Did you use condoms?"

"Of course."

"Good." The condom would prevent the transfer of bacteria.

"When did you first feel sick?"

"Yesterday," he said.

Sunday. Given the incubation period of bubonic plague, Jack was infected some time between a week ago Saturday and Thursday.

"Do you live alone?" Dana asked.

"With Bucky. The quarterback."

"Is he sick?"

"Not when I saw him last. But he flew to San Antonio last week."

Bucky would have to be found. "Do you know a man named Dudley Shaw?"

"Who's he?" asked Jack.

"Someone . . . well . . . someone else who was sick like you." She wouldn't mention Dudley had died.

"I don't know him."

"Where is your home?" she asked.

"Near Bastrop."

Dana nodded and made a note. There were vast grassy fields that ran between Duane and Bastrop. A reasonable habitat for rats. "Have you been home recently?"

Jack hadn't been home since Christmas. He hadn't been anywhere.

That was the last thing McCoy would want to hear. "Have you had any visitors?"

"My mom came last week," Jack said. "She came through town on her way to Houston."

Here was something. "Is she sick?"

"Not that I've heard."

Dana made a note of her phone number. "Did she leave you anything?"

"Lots of advice. Find a nice girl. Settle down."

"Right," Dana said. "Did she stay with you?"

Jack shook his head. "No. When she comes she stays at The Lone Star Heritage Hotel."

"Does she have any pets?" Dana asked.

"Sure. We've got dogs and cats on the ranch."

"Ranch? What kind of ranch?"

"We raise horses."

And where there were horses, there was feed, and where there was grain, there were rats. It was their first lead. "Do you hunt?" she asked.

"You mean animals?" He raised an eyebrow.

What else would she mean? "Yes, animals."

"Sometimes. Not recently."

"Do you eat wild meat?"

"Wild meat? He smiled rakishly. "What kind of wild meat?"

Dana thought that was enough questions for now. "I'll go and let you rest," she said.

He looked at her with open eyes. "Am I going to be okay?"

You're going to be fine, Dana almost said and then recalled saying the same thing to Dudley.

Chapter 22

Out in the corridor Dana saw no sign of her colleagues. She tore off the protective gear and went to the bathroom and washed her hands. She wondered what connected Jack and Dudley. They were both bitten by fleas infected with *Yersinia*. Yet Jack had no pets. Did his mother bring an infected flea with her from Bastrop? And where was Dudley exposed? He was the first to be affected and likely the first infected. But where? And where had Carol Dupuis trapped those rats? Could Jack, Dudley and the rats be linked to one place? But what place? To stop the spread of the disease, they had to find out.

In the hospital lobby, Dana heard loud and pitiful sobs. In the reception area she saw an elderly woman sitting alone, crying. She stared long enough that the woman looked her way. Dana walked tentatively toward her. "Are you Mrs. Shaw?"

The woman shook her head and Dana was mortified.

"I'm Tabitha Tott. Dudley is my brother. My younger brother. My only brother." She stabbed a stray bobby-pin into a bun.

Dana winced at her use of the present tense and introduced herself. "I'm helping with your brother's case. I'm sorry."

She sat down beside Tabitha on an orange scratchy couch that was hard and uncomfortable. There were plastic flowers in a vase on the scarred coffee table in front of them. Too much artificial light overhead.

Tabitha dabbed a tattered Kleenex at her eyes. She looked twenty years older than Dudley. "What in God's name is going on here?" she said. "Why can't I see my brother? Why do I have to wait until the diagnosis is confirmed? Why will it take so long? A whole week?"

She had a strident tone, much stronger than her brother's, but their eyes were the same: watery, bloodshot and brown.

"I want to bury him now, but I can't do that either. He's got to stay in the morgue, here in the basement; he can't even go down the street to the undertaker. They're talking about cremation, but he wanted to be buried. Who are they to tell me what to do? What kind of bacterial infection did he have? Why can't I stay in his house? Why can't I drive his car?" She stared in Dana's eyes.

Dana felt Tabitha's outrage as if it were her own. *A week to identify the infection?* How could McCoy get away with such a blatant lie? It was preposterous. If he expected her to lie like this, he could forget it. Dana told a small one. "There are some diagnostic tests we have to run to absolutely confirm the identity of the infecting organism."

Tabitha looked at her skeptically and frowned.

She wasn't buying it. Dana lowered her voice. "In confidence, we think it was bubonic plague."

Tabitha closed her eyes.

"It's a disease spread by fleas," Dana said.

Tabitha covered her mouth with an old shriveled hand as tears streaked down her quilted cheeks.

"Which is why we're looking for Bingo," Dana said.

Tabitha opened her eyes. "I found him. They took him."

So, they found the dog. That was something. "Bingo needs to be checked. Then you'll get him back. I know Dudley was worried about him."

"You met Dudley?"

"I saw him yesterday," Dana said. "He was sick, but at peace. He was well-medicated."

Tabitha shifted in her seat and faced Dana. She arranged her floral skirt around her ankles. "It's just so sudden. When I saw Dudley at Easter he was planning his big trip. He was very patriotic, always wanted to see his country. Go off with his dog and his car. It ruined his marriage, you know. Dudley liked the car better than his wife. If you knew Nancy, you'd know why."

"Where is Nancy? Is she around? Could he have seen her?"

"No. She remarried. He hasn't seen her in years."

"She wouldn't want Bingo then?"

"Lord, no. I'll take him."

Dana asked her a few more questions. The name Dowel meant nothing to Tabitha and she didn't think Dudley took aimless drives in the country. Nor did he hunt or take walks in the woods. But Bingo, Bingo was another story.

"Did you see any fleas on him?" Dana asked.

"He was scratching mighty bad and that was one dog who hated to be bathed."

Dana wondered what his fleas would show. Had Bingo been infected in the woods? Had the bacteria moved south? She stood up and got ready to leave, then realized that Tabitha had no car, no place to stay.

"Can I give you a lift anywhere?" Dana asked.

Tabitha pulled a fresh Kleenex from under her sleeve and folded it. "I reckon I'll go to the Lone Star Heritage."

"It's on my way. I'll give you a ride."

They drove through the quiet streets to the hotel. Dana was going to drop her off, but when she saw McCoy's bulletproof Mercedes in the lot, she parked and led Tabitha inside.

Chapter 23

The Starlight Room in the Lone Star Heritage Hotel was named for its domed glass ceiling that showed the sky. Tonight there were no stars, just fast moving clouds and a bloated lopsided moon. Sitting at a crowded table, Nick checked his watch for the third time in as many minutes. Where was the waitress? They would accomplish nothing in this bar.

Twenty minutes had passed and the waitress had yet to come. The room was small and claustrophobic and Nick's party was crammed into a bleak corner. They had grabbed the last table, one meant for four, and six people sat huddled around it. McCoy had seen the dean's Cadillac in the hotel parking lot and had to stop. Now here they were, along with Nellie and Michael Smith, wasting time.

From the opposite corner, a piano player was hammering out a John Denver song on a badly tuned piano. The pianist had a gravelly voice and sang off-key.

Nick sunk deeper into his chair. It was a mistake to come; he saw that now. He thought that time and the trouble with Rachel-Anne had hardened him, wrung him out

and squeezed him dry. He decided long ago it was best to
be on his own—that from here on in, he would forego sex
and focus on work. He enjoyed his job, the challenges, the
travel, making a difference, saving lives, always learning
something new. He had friends and colleagues and his music and it was enough. His life was full. He didn't want any
more. He was happy, though it was a sad Wheeler verse
that came to him: *I stood alone and watched the sea roll
out and knew again, that what I craved was forever gone
from me.*

Nellie's loud complaints caught his attention. "The service in this entire hotel is abysmal. Even at Caprice it was
appalling. We wanted to show Mike the best cuisine this
town could offer. I mean, if Caprice was a dump and if it
was reasonably priced, then you could accept inferior service, but come on."

She sat forward, her lips pursed tight. "They even mixed
up Mike's dinner and gave him pork chops instead of
steak. We waited so long he was loath to return the food
even if it was inedible. I do hope they get their act together
before the VP comes."

Without a word the dean stood up and a minute later returned with a harried waitress, who apologized endlessly
about the delay. They were short-staffed because of exam
week and some staff members were out with the flu. She
took their order. Karl asked for two Coronas, which raised
McCoy's brow.

The waitress looked at Karl. "Two?"

"It's after five isn't it?" Karl said.

McCoy glanced at his watch. He was no drinker.

The waitress left and a cell phone rang. Karl, McCoy
and the dean reached into their pockets. Nick hated talking
on the phone and wouldn't get one. He stuck with his
pager.

"That's me." Karl stood up, holding the phone to his ear.

He headed for the lobby as the pianist started into Simon and Garfunkel's "Sound of Silence," which he sang horrendously loud.

Nellie raised her voice and spoke over the music. "Despite the service, we did have a lovely dinner. Did you know Michael's from West Point?"

Nick said, "No."

"Iowa," Michael said.

"Are you married?" Nellie asked.

For a moment Nick thought Nellie was talking to him. She had a bad habit of interrogating people about their personal lives. But, no, she was addressing Michael who pulled out his wallet and passed a dog-eared photo around the table. Yes, Michael was married and had twin baby daughters.

"Nice," Nick said, then checked his watch again. If the drinks didn't hurry up, he would walk to the vet school on his own and examine the dog. He couldn't stand this inactivity, this sitting around doing nothing. He had to move, get away from his thoughts, get out of his head. He listened to the music. The pianist had finally turned down the volume and sang in an appropriate whisper.

Karl returned before the waitress and came bearing news of Carol Dupuis. The undergraduate trapper of rats was in Methodist Hospital in Houston and infected with bubonic plague. "Her doctor reported the infection to the CDC. I called her physician but she won't discuss Carol's condition with me over the phone. I notified Jeff. He'll take the next flight to Houston. It seems the hospital has received calls from less than scrupulous reporters."

"Reporters," McCoy said. "Oh, God." He placed his hand over his heart. Nick noticed he had broken out in a sweat. His face was cherry red and the veins on his neck looked like cords of rope. His heart attack had aged him. McCoy wasn't well.

The waitress arrived with a drink-laden tray and Karl stopped speaking. Everyone was silent as the drinks were dispensed. In error, Karl was given only one Corona.

"Oh, you wanted two, didn't you." The waitress shifted the empty tray to her hip. "Shall I get it?"

"If it's not too much trouble," Karl said tersely.

The waitress flounced away and the dean said, "What does it mean? Will the VP be able to come? You know we spent a fortune arranging the visit. We need the return."

McCoy looked pained and turned the question over to Nick.

He took a sip of whiskey. Now the pianist was playing Leonard Cohen's "Suzanne." Nick considered his answer, tapping his finger in time with the music. He did not believe in coincidences and was unsettled because they could not trace the origin of the bacteria. Still, that was often the case in these kinds of investigations. You couldn't pinpoint time zero. He gave a guarded response. "At this point, no one has pneumonic plague. If we don't reach the contagious phase, we should be fine. It's not unusual to see one, two, even three cases of bubonic plague in a given area. And sometimes we just can't find the source of the bacteria."

"If there are no sick rodents here, doesn't that mean the bacteria had to come from somewhere else?" McCoy said. "This is too far south for *Yersinia* after all."

Karl opened his mouth, as if to respond, then broke into a smile. He raised his hand in a wave. Nick turned and looked in the direction he was staring. Dana was heading toward the table. She was light on her feet and moved fast. Her hair bounced at her shoulders and heads turned as she passed.

Nick quickly reached for his glass and downed it in a gulp. Despite loud internal objections, he studied her approach. She was tall and slender and wore tight beige chinos that hugged her hips and her ankles. She wore cowboy boots with pointed toes that were rapidly advancing. He raised his eyes. Her nipples pointed at him through her shirt. He lifted his eyes further, but she refused to acknowledge him.

Immediately McCoy was complaining about her behavior at the hospital. "What were you thinking?" he said. "How could you breach quarantine and flagrantly violate hospital policy?"

Nellie's mouth dropped open as she stared at Dana wide-eyed.

"We needed the information," Dana said. "You can't just order someone to talk."

"What did he say?" This from Karl.

"Jack's mother was here last week. She came from a ranch in Bastrop. Maybe she brought the bacteria with her by car."

McCoy liked it and nodded his head violently. Yes, it made sense to him.

Except that it didn't, Nick thought. There was no incidence of the plague in Bastrop. At the moment, the only infected wildlife had been found in Duane. When he mentioned this, McCoy frowned immediately.

"That's not to say there aren't infected rodents elsewhere," Karl said. He thought the State Extension Service should concentrate their animal trapping in the fields between Duane and Bastrop. "Maybe if we look in the right place we'll find infected animals."

And McCoy perked up again.

Dana was still standing beside the table and Karl jumped up. He offered Dana his chair. "Here, sit down, we'll get another chair," he said, and snapped his fingers for the waitress. The pianist began to play David Allan Coe.

Staring at his clasped hands, Nick cursed himself for not taking action. He remembered this was the way it had been when he was around her. He was paralyzed as he weighed the appearance of his actions. Would he give himself away by offering a chair, or by doing nothing? He could never tell. He caught Nellie looking at him quizzically and picked up his drink. Empty. He put it back down.

"I can't stay," Dana said. "I came to give you Jack's contacts." She pulled a crinkled sheet of paper from her pocket and passed it to Karl. "Here are the names of Jack's many friends."

"We'll give that to the local health department." Karl folded the questionnaire in half. "Are you sure you have to go?"

She did. "I was just giving Tabitha Tott a ride to the hotel," she said, and turned to McCoy. "Tabitha would like to know when she can get her car back." Her tone was angry and accusing.

McCoy was on his feet. "Look, I've got the vice president of the United States on his way to a town contaminated with *Yersinia* and Tott is the least of my worries. She took that car without authorization and she's lucky she's not in jail. She shouldn't have gone out to that house. A person commits an offense if they refuse to comply with federal quarantine, Doctor."

Dana stared at him and McCoy stared back.

"If that's all," McCoy said to Dana, "dismissed." He sat down.

Dana did not move. She could not stand people telling her what to do.

Karl was still trying to get her to stay and insisting she take his beer, his chair.

Now Dana was leaving. "No, I can't. I've got to go." She backed away from the table, swiveled around, a pirouette. She walked with her back straight, her head high, past the pianist, who had reached his crescendo, forearms bouncing, fingers pounding, voice crooning David Allan Coe, but Nick was stuck on Wheeler: *Into the space you leave behind, I am emptied.* Nick wrung his hands. Despite her emotional volatility, she was dedicated and professional. Yes, she was too passionate, too sensitive, too stubborn, but he admired these things about her too, the depth of her emotion, her compassion, her warmth. Despite his promise to stay detached, he found himself drawn to her still, and longed to go after her. But that would be madness, and he did not move. Instead he raised his hand and ordered another drink.

Tuesday

Chapter 24

On Tuesday morning Dana awoke to the sound of an alarm. She thought it was a clock, but she didn't have one. It took her a moment to realize it was the phone. Lying in bed, she reached on the desk for the receiver and picked up to hear Sheryl's hysterical voice.

"Penny's sick. I don't know what to do. She's got a fever of one hundred and four. She's coughing so hard she can't breathe."

In the morning gloom, goose bumps broke out on Dana's skin. "Take her to the hospital."

"I'm there," Sheryl shrieked.

"I'm on my way."

Ten minutes later Dana was at the hospital and roared into a parking space next to a low-slung sports car with the license plate FB JOCK. Sheryl streaked across the tarmac toward her. She looked a mess. Her face was swollen and her long curly hair was loose and in tangles. She wore dirty jeans and her husband's old Duane University sweatshirt. She smelled of vomit.

"I waited too long," Sheryl wailed. "I should have

brought her in earlier. All night long her fever kept getting higher and higher and the Tylenol did nothing." Sheryl clasped the sides of her head with her hands. "She held her head like this and was rolling back and forth in her crib. Then she started coughing and couldn't stop. As soon as I got her here they whisked her away. They won't let me see her."

Dana grabbed Sheryl's arm and pulled her toward the building.

"What if she needs a transfusion?" Sheryl said. "Her blood type is rare. Richard is the only person I know who is AB negative. How are we going to find him? What if he has to donate blood? What if he won't? It would be just like him."

Dana was thinking along other lines. *Don't let Penny have the plague. Don't let her have the plague. Let it be tonsillitis, an ear infection, please not the plague.*

Leaving Sheryl in the ER waiting room, Dana barged through a door that read Medical Personnel Only. She tore through the area, yanking open curtains that covered examining rooms. There was no one. She went to reception and found the same woman who gave her Dudley's blood on Sunday.

"I'm Dr. Sparks, working with the CDC and looking for Penny Farr."

The redheaded woman with nicely filed pink nails tapped on her keyboard. "Room one-oh-four," she said pleasantly. "Down the hall, just before ICU. It's a quarantine room."

Outside the door stood a cart laden with plastic bags containing protective suits. These were yellow cloth and came with hoods. They suited up and went in. A man hunched over an examining table said they had to leave. He turned around and Dana saw through the face panel of the hood, a round black face. "Sam, is that you?"

It was. He smiled at Dana, and glanced suspiciously at Sheryl. "Who's that?"

"My assistant," Dana walked to the examining table. "How is the baby?"

"Not good," Sam said, and Sheryl sobbed into her gloves. "We can't bring down her temperature and she's badly dehydrated. Her respiration is poor."

Dana felt weak and could barely bring herself to look at Penny. The baby was naked. Three IV lines fed her body, a line to each wrist, one to her ankle. A cannula in her nose fed her oxygen. She coughed constantly. Her lips were blue, her small body so pale it looked green. Her eyes were closed and blue veins snaked across her body. Sam was icing her down with a sponge, trying to bring down her fever.

"Is it the plague?" Dana said.

Behind her, Sheryl choked.

Sam nodded. "Only the more contagious form. Pneumonic plague. Hear that hacking cough?"

Sheryl gasped. "Oh god, no."

"We won't know for sure until we run the tests," Sam said, looking at Sheryl askance. He dropped the sponge into a bucket of ice water and wrung it out, swabbed Penny's chest.

"What are you treating her with?" Dana asked.

"Acetaminophen for fever, the standard antibiotic cocktail for *Yersinia*, plasma for fluid replacement and gamma globulin as a shot in the dark."

Dana reached down and stroked Penny's cheek with her glove. Suddenly, she too had trouble breathing. She had been in the delivery room when Penny was born, had seen Penny fight for her life, saw her fighting now. *Hold on, Penny. Hold on.*

Sheryl was crying louder, and when Sam threw her a questioning look, Dana pulled her into the bathroom. In the tub there was a biohazard bag filled with discarded yellow suits. Dana pulled off her gloves and her hood, then the suit.

Sheryl turned on the faucet and washed her hands as if she would never get them clean. "How did it happen?' she cried. "How could Penny get pneumonic plague?"

"We'll find out."

Sheryl rinsed her hands under the tap. She threw water at her face and it slopped down her shirt. "Was it me? Did I infect her? Did I bring something home?"

Dana had wondered the same thing, but she said, "How could it be you? You're not sick."

"I've been vaccinated."

"No," Dana said. "You're not up to date. You only took one shot and you need six. You should start taking prophylactic antibiotics."

"I might still be protected. I could give it to Penny and not be infected myself."

"I doubt that. What about the boys?"

"As far as I know, they're fine. What about the lab? What if Penny was infected in the lab?"

"She picked this up two or three days ago," Dana said. "Saturday or Sunday. Was she in the lab?"

"No."

"Is anyone at her day care sick?" Dana asked.

Not that Sheryl knew.

"What did you do on the weekend?"

Sheryl had done a lot. Her mother came first thing. Saturday morning and took Ricky and Paul to Houston for the weekend. Sheryl took Penny shopping at the Giant supermarket, then out to the Pizza Garden for lunch. They played in High Park. She got a flat tire going home. Tim had seen her on the side of the road and helped her change the tire. On Sunday they went to church. Then out to the mall. Sunday night Penny was fussy and Sheryl thought it was her tooth. At midnight last night, Penny's fever spiked.

"What if I left it too late?" Sheryl said. "I should have brought her in earlier."

"She's healthy, she'll be fine," Dana said, but she was worried herself. Who had exposed Penny and whom had Penny exposed? Treatment had to start within twenty-four hours after the symptoms appeared or there was no cure. When had Penny been exposed?

Since they had entered the pneumonic phase of the disease, time was critical. Exposed people had to be found and found fast, for without treatment, mortality from pneumonic plague was close to one hundred percent. They had to retrace Sheryl's steps, go everywhere she went, talk to everyone she saw. Dana also wanted to check on Jack and did not want to be late to McCoy's eight o'clock meeting.

She left Sheryl in the hallway and ran upstairs. Jack was sleeping. Dana peered in the room from the doorway. He lay on his back, eyes closed, rolling his head side to side as he moaned. Dana grabbed his chart, went into the room and shut the door. His condition had deteriorated during the night. His fever had soared to 105° and he had been delirious. Acetaminophen and morphine reduced his fever and calmed him down, but his condition was grave.

Grave. Dana flipped the chart closed. *Grave.* How could his situation be grave? He was in good shape, a strong, healthy football player. He should have been better by now, only he was worse. What strain of *Yersinia* was this? Why had Dudley died? What did it mean for Jack and Penny?

Chapter 25

After a long and sleepless night, McCoy arrived early to work Tuesday morning. Sitting at his desk, he unraveled the *Houston Chronicle*. The day's headline featured the Somali bombing and the UN team formed to examine the incident. There was no mention of Carol Dupuis. McCoy opened the *Duane Eagle*. On the front page there was a spread about the VP's visit, but nothing on the plague. Reporters had not picked up the story.

Keeping this quiet was critical. After the anthrax outbreak in the wake of the September 11 attacks, the terrified population's mass hysteria had preoccupied law enforcement agents and seriously hindered any investigation. It was imperative at this point to keep the press out.

McCoy scanned the article about Rich Rutherford's visit. The fund-raising dinner alone would raise one million dollars for the university. Additional pledges and money were expected from alumni and the business elite.

McCoy tapped his finger on the paper. If nothing else happened, if the outbreak was contained in the bubonic phase and the origin of the bacteria identified, the VP could come. McCoy would do everything in his power to see that was so.

He turned the newspaper over and studied the weather map on the back page. A tropical storm was swirling in the gulf. That morning McCoy noticed a vicious breeze. At six-thirty in the morning it was eighty degrees. Heat that early could only mean trouble. While the heat might stop the advance of the bacteria, there were other ways too.

McCoy had a contingency plan. Last night, after leaving the bar, he had called his former superior at the Pentagon and requested help in procuring a potent pesticide. The chemical he had in mind required a special dispensation from the EPA and this had been requested. While DDT was primarily an insecticide, it was also an effective rodenticide and in the past had been used successfully to kill house mice, and thus limit the urban host population. If the *Yersinia* blew up in their faces, one aerial spray of DDT and the fleas and rats in town would be history. One way or another the problem would be solved. But it would not happen with this wind.

McCoy bowed his head and prayed for good weather. He reassured himself that things weren't so bad and indeed, could be worse. There could be dead rats with fleeing fleas everywhere. The FBI could be on the case, and the VP scared away. They could be hit with the more contagious pneumonic plague and have tens or hundreds of people sick. Under the circumstances, McCoy thought things were going well.

Then he remembered Dr. Sparks. McCoy had spent a great deal of his night formulating a battle plan to deal with her. Yes, she might be a good researcher but she had to learn to take orders and behave professionally. There would be no more temperamental outbursts like the one last night. Was it McCoy's fault that Shaw's sister had placed herself at risk? He had to consider the populace and could not concern himself with the comfort of one individual. As a scientist, Dana Sparks should know that.

He saw the line and he was going to draw it. He wanted her at departmental meetings on time and he wanted her in a lab coat. She would comply with all regulations whether they offended her or not. She would increase the security in her lab. She would keep her door locked at all times. Last evening her laboratory had been left unattended for hours. Who knew where she had gone or why? It would not happen again. There would be no more gallivanting to the hospital. No more interviewing patients. She was confined to her lab where she would run diagnostic tests and stay out of trouble.

He heard his stomach rumble and realized he was hungry. He regretted leaving home without breakfast. He should have listened to his wife and taken the time to sit with his daughter, who was not speaking to him after he missed their latest driving lesson. When this week was over, McCoy would take her to Austin to tour the University of Texas campus. She wished to return to Virginia, but McCoy wanted her here. He put a hand on his heart. He didn't know if he was up to the task of letting her go.

Just before eight, McCoy headed for the conference room. Christ Almighty, who had messed with his room? The air conditioner was off; the curtains were open, as were all of the windows. God damn it! McCoy cranked the air conditioner. He slammed each and every window, the repaired glass vibrating in its frame. He drew the curtains to blot out the sun. He turned around, wiping his hands together as a young woman carrying a paint can burst into the room.

"I'm here to paint the place," she said sprightly. "Got to get ready for the VP's visit you know. Orders from General TJ McCoy."

The former and familiar use of his title brought him

comfort. McCoy told the painter they were having a meeting and to come back in an hour.

"Yes, Sir."

She left and McCoy wiped his brow and went to his chair. If only his other problems could be solved so easily.

At eight sharp, McCoy began his meeting. Becker was absent and Sparks had not arrived, but he wasn't going to wait. Charlotte Lane was already watching the clock. Nellie Duncan doodled on a notepad. Bob Fairway examined his fingernails. Karl King appeared to be asleep and Nick rubbed his eyes. Only Michael Smith, McCoy's forgotten visitor, sat with rapt attention.

McCoy began by warning his staff to stay clear of the media. If any reporters came poking around, he would deal with them. No one was to make a comment. He asked Nick for a report on Shaw's dog.

"After a gross examination, the dog appears healthy and not infected with *Yersinia*. But we need the blood work to confirm."

"Dr. Sparks will do that." When she comes. Her absence couldn't deflate McCoy's good mood. The dog wasn't infected, wasn't out spreading *Yersinia* through wildlife populations. He turned to King. "Did you catch anything in the traps out by Shaw's house?"

"Three mice and a rat. They look healthy. But rodents aren't our biggest problem now."

McCoy hated indirect ways of coming to a point. "And what might that be?"

King exhaled dramatically. "We've got our first case of pneumonic plague."

McCoy's chest hurt immediately. *Good god—not pneumonic plague. Not the contagious form.* McCoy thumped his chest to catch his breath. "Who is sick?"

"An eighteen-month-old baby. Penny Farr. She was hospitalized early this morning and Russ Taversham just confirmed *Yersinia*."

McCoy gripped the sides of the chair. Penny Farr was the daughter of Dana Sparks' technician. Had the mother infected the child? It was the worst case scenario. Lethal bacteria maintained in a lab under his jurisdiction escaping to infect the town.

Just then Dana Sparks came in, hurrying to her seat. McCoy stood up and faced her across the table. "Penny Farr has pneumonic plague," he said.

"I know," she said quietly, as she pulled out a chair and sat down.

"Is your lab the source of this?" He could see it now. An accidental spill of *Yersinia*. The bacteria picked up by one of the dogs she was always bringing to the lab. Somehow the fleas were infected and now a baby was stricken with pneumonic plague.

Dana Sparks shook her head. "Sheryl isn't sick, and since she's breast-feeding she can't work with the bacteria. She couldn't have infected Penny. Besides, the timing isn't right. The rats, Dudley, Jack and Carol were all infected before Penny, which indicates another source of bacteria."

McCoy glanced at King. "Do we know where Carol Dupuis trapped her rats?"

"We know," Karl said. "But it's not good."

McCoy waited. His heart thumped so loudly he wondered if everyone in the room could hear it.

"It would have been nice if the rats came from the woods near Dudley Shaw's house, but they didn't," Karl said.

McCoy groaned loudly. Why all the theatrics? Why not just state where they were found? "Where?" he said in a high voice he hated.

"Down the street. In High Park. Across from campus."

McCoy loosened his collar. It was coming closer. Dudley Shaw lived far from campus, but High Park was right here, across from the university and the Lone Star Heritage Hotel, in the heart of town.

"Penny Farr's daycare is close to the park," Dana Sparks said. "And she was in the park on Saturday."

"Was she in your lab?"

"No."

McCoy wiped his forehead and his hand came away soaking wet. This new outbreak changed everything, introduced a new urgency. He listed what had to be done and who would do what. Each of Penny Farr's recent contacts had to be notified, and he assigned Karl and Nick to the job. Doctors Lane and Fairway would fan out in town and assist with the trapped animals, retrieve the blood samples and bring them to Dana Sparks to test. She would remain in the lab and assay samples, beginning with Bingo's fleas and blood. Becker would autopsy the rodents collected out at Dudley's.

But McCoy had forgotten Becker was out with the flu as Nellie now reminded him.

"Dr. Sparks will do the autopsies."

Her hand was raised and waving. "Since we don't know the source of the bacteria, shouldn't we advise people to bathe their pets and get rid of fleas?"

"We'll advise nothing," McCoy said. "We have a campaign to control the local population of both fleas and rodents. This meeting is adjourned." He rose from his seat.

Sparks was still objecting. "What campaign? What controls both fleas and rodents? Only DDT, and you can't use that, it's banned."

"It can be used in an emergency," McCoy said.

"DDT?" Sparks was up out of her seat. Did McCoy know it had a half-life of fifteen years? That it got into the soil, the water and the food chain? That it mimicked estrogen, thinned eggshells and killed fish? "DDT is banned and for good reason."

"You can use it in an emergency," McCoy said, clenching his fists. He could hear every single one of his loud, strained breaths. "And whether you realize it or not, this is an emergency." His voice was high and vibrating with anger. His actions did not require her approval. He was the boss. He was in charge. It was his call and he had made it. He would take the responsibility for the act. The risk was his and his alone. "I said, dismissed."

Then McCoy stalked to the door. He had to call his cardiologist. His face was purple and he knew his blood pressure was off the charts. He needed stronger medicine for his heart, something for his nerves. He needed the wind to stop so he could spray.

Chapter 26

After the meeting, Dana raced after Nick. Despite Penny's illness and Jack's decline, she was equally upset about McCoy's decision to spray DDT. It was nonspecific, untargeted lunacy. Where was he going to spray? The rooftops and the trees? Why not have a flea dip? Go after the vector, not the host.

She caught up to Nick in his office. "I can't believe you went along with McCoy's plan to spray DDT."

Nick stopped rifling through his briefcase and turned around. His face was already darkened with stubble, which meant he had been up early. He said, "It's not my decision."

"Or your city? And you don't care where he sprays. In the park. The woods. My house?"

Nick loosened his tie and shook his head, disapproving. "McCoy's no fool. He'll take appropriate precautions."

"He shouldn't use it at all. If you objected, he'd listen to you."

Nick ran his hand through his hair. "McCoy is in charge of the investigation. I'm here as an observer."

"And unable to speak?"

Nick exhaled slowly. "We have a serious problem. If we don't act, we'll have a city of corpses. One way or another, we need to stop the bacteria."

"There are other ways." Dana stared out the window. The wind that had been raging that morning was raging still. "This is like amputating your foot when you stub your toe."

"This isn't a toe. It's a deadly disease. Instead of going off half-cocked, focus on the disease."

"Half-cocked? What does that mean?"

He returned to his briefcase. "Nothing."

He meant emotional. "I am focused on the disease. On saving lives. But there are other lives to consider here too. DDT lasts for fifteen years. A warmonger shouldn't be making biological decisions."

Nick made another disparaging noise. "He's not a warmonger. He's trying to stop an epidemic."

"Tell that to the birds."

She left the office, and was in the hallway when he called her. "Dana."

She took a few steps before she turned.

"Maybe test Frank's blood. He could be the source."

She remembered Frank's labored breathing. She had not considered the plague.

"And perhaps talk to Becker. Confirm the flu."

She nodded. Nick knew how to talk to her; he offered suggestions, never orders.

He said, "With this wind, McCoy can't spray."

She nodded again, feeling better. Even nature was against the general.

She left Nick and continued on down the hall, stopping at Tim's lab. Sheila was there and Dana asked for a tube of Frank's blood.

"Why?"

Did the gag on truth extend to her too? Dana assumed so. "I'm thinking of cloning him." .

Sheila lifted an eyebrow, but went to the fridge and got a tube of blood from a box in the door.

"Just kidding," Dana said. "Have you heard from Tim?"

"No. He'll be back tomorrow. Sorry about Frank."

Dana returned to her lab. Next to the sink, she found a biohazard bag containing a rack filled with tubes of blood. Seventy-five samples had been drawn from rodents trapped overnight around Duane. She picked up a tube and saw a number. The assay was blind. Each sample identified by number only. Dana did not know what type of animal blood she had, or where the animal had been trapped. Her job was to determine if the blood was positive or negative for the bacterial antibodies and pass on the results.

She carried the tubes to the biohazard room and did the assay. There was no color change at all. Nothing. Frank did not have the plague. Nor did any of the animals. Whatever they were and wherever they were trapped, they were not carrying plague antibodies.

Still, the bacteria had to come from somewhere. Four rats were infected, as were four people, which meant the bacteria were in Duane, but where? Every time Dana considered the problem, she hit a dead end. The facts didn't make sense. There wasn't enough information. How did Nick solve epidemiology cases? How did he live with loose ends and uncertainty?

Well, she knew how. He kept himself far removed from the emotional aspect of his work. He refused to let himself feel and could therefore remain objective and rational. Dana wondered if this characteristic had spilled too much into his personal life.

She emptied the tubes of blood into the biohazard waste and then began the disk test to assess antibiotic resistance on the *Yersinia* cultured from Dudley's lymph nodes. *Dudley*. She remembered him jumping when she felt under his arm. The pain from the pressure of the swelling alone must have been enormous, yet he wasn't going to mention it. He didn't want anything to interfere with his trip.

At the hood, she studied the bacteria that killed him. They dotted the culture plate and appeared as little white bumps. The bumps were clumps of bacteria that arose by cell division from a single cell. In the disk test, she would assess the ability of the antibiotics to kill the cells.

She would test the antibiotics that were normally used to treat the plague: streptomycin, chloramphenicol and tetracycline. Dana prepared the antibiotics. She used a pair of straight tweezers to draw a line in the agar to divide the plate in half. On a filter paper the size of a dime, she pipetted a drop of each of the three antibiotics in the standard cocktail. She carefully laid the filter paper in the center of one sector. On another filter paper she dabbed a dot of distilled water, which would serve as the control.

It would take twenty-four hours to see a response. During this time, the antibiotics would diffuse from the filter paper into the agar. If the antibiotics were effective, the bacteria would die and leave a clear area. If the drugs didn't work, the bacteria would continue to grow and there would be no clear zone. Dana returned the plate to the incubator. All she could do now was wait.

Sit in the lab and receive samples, according to McCoy. Forget that. Dana shrugged off her lab coat, washed her hands, grabbed her keys and left the vet school. She went to see Becker. Though he lived within walking distance of campus, Dana drove. Down College Avenue, over the railroad tracks and left on Duane Way to High Street. Phillip lived on the corner, up the street from the park, in a tiny bungalow with a well-kept lawn.

The front door opened as Dana pulled into the drive. Becker stood in the doorway in khaki pants and a lime green polo shirt. He smiled as she crossed the flagstone path, then held up his hand in warning to keep her distance when she reached the porch. His face was shiny, as if it glowed with an inner light. He looked tired, but other than that, healthy for someone his age. "This is a pleasant surprise," he said.

"How are you feeling?"

"Better."

"You're still sure it's the flu?"

"I've been testing my blood every day." He waved her inside. "Come and see."

She followed him into the house. It was immaculate and comfortable. Becker lived alone ever since his wife died ten years before. He had a microscope set up on his dining room table and he flicked a switch that turned on a light. A slide was set on the stage and Becker peered through the eyepiece. "Yep." He got out of the way so Dana could take a look.

It was a blood smear. She looked at the white blood cells. In a bacterial infection, neutrophils were the predominant immune cell in the blood, but these were normal in number.

He was hovering over her. "See?"

She straightened. "I see."

He invited her to stay for a cup of tea and she followed him into the kitchen.

He put a kettle on the stove to boil. "What's going on?" he said. "I wish I was there." He took two flowered china cups and saucers out of a cupboard. He sat on a stool at the kitchen counter and she sat down next to him.

"McCoy's talking about using DDT and no one says a word. When I do, I'm *emotional*." She heard her voice break. "Maybe it's true."

"There is nothing wrong with thinking with your heart."

"Maybe I *am* overreacting. It's been a bad time. Frank died yesterday and Penny is sick. She has pneumonic plague."

He clicked his teeth. "How did she get that?"

"The suspicion is my lab. I don't see how. But I'm the

only one in town who has the bacteria. What if it did come from my lab? Aside from the four rats, there is no natural source." The kettle was boiling and she jumped up, poured the steaming water into the teapot and brought it to the counter.

"The rats weren't lab rats, were they?" Becker said.

"No. Wild rats. *Rattus rattus*."

"The worst carrier. You would think the bacteria would be everywhere. Dead rats dying in the streets."

"I just checked seventy-five samples of blood and there was nothing." Dana poured two cups of tea.

"Weird."

"Nick thought maybe some animals increased their range due to population pressure."

"But the bacteria shouldn't be in this clime. It's strange." Becker lowered his face into the steam and took a loud sip of tea. "Perfect. The peppermint is good for calming the nerves." He put down his cup.

Dana took a sip. She didn't feel calm at all. "Phillip, I feel like I should be doing something. This is my disease, my bacteria, and I'm being shut out. Sidelined. I'm supposed to stay in the lab and be a technician."

"You're a good technician. There are a lot of specialists here. Everyone has a job."

Dana took another sip of tea. "I'm under strict orders not to leave my lab."

Becker stirred his tea with a small spoon. "You make trouble for yourself. You know that, don't you."

"I do what I have to do."

"Yes, sometimes trouble is necessary. And it's good for you. Shakes you up." He put down the spoon. "How is Nick?"

"Ignoring me. His wife died, you know."

"No. I didn't. Why would he ignore you?"

"He doesn't want to be reminded of the past. It's like he's gone."

Becker put a finger to his mouth. He shook his head. "No, he's gone because he's working. He'll be back. Nick is serious. His gift is focus, not heart. It's good that he's here."

"So he can solve this case?"

"No. So he can solve his past."

But from what Dana could see, it was already solved, buried deep and forgotten. She finished her tea. "I should get back."

Becker followed her to the door. "Dana. A piece of advice. Go with what you think is right. If there are decisions made you don't agree with, speak up. Don't allow yourself to be silenced." He pushed open the screen door and she stepped outside.

"Call me if you need anything," he said.

"And you know where to find me."

Chapter 27

Nick rode shotgun, slumping low in his seat, as Karl drove down University Drive toward Penny Farr's daycare. They were moving slowly, traffic was bad and they hit every red light. Nick watched the wind gust across the campus lawn.

He regretted having mentioned to McCoy the spectacular record of DDT in curbing outbreaks of the plague in third world countries. McCoy jumped on the bandwagon and would not hear of newer pesticides that had a lower impact on the environment. McCoy wouldn't use a bullet when a cannon was nearby.

The situation had taken a serious turn. They were now in the pneumonic phase and still did not know the bacteria's origin. This was the strangest outbreak of the plague Nick had ever seen. He felt unsettled and uneasy. Or was that Dana's influence?

He couldn't put her out of his mind. In D.C. when she hovered at the edge of his thoughts, he was able to push her away. Though she came to him in his dreams, usually naked. He banished the image now from his mind. It was madness. He had forgotten how dangerous she was. She could expose herself without warning, bare it all. As soon as this was over, he would leave. Inside his head, he heard Wheeler: *When the blood pooled on the ground, and the moon was gone, I stood on the wasteland with all that I had; just what I knew: there was no other way.*

Beside him, Karl leaned forward and turned on the radio. On the classical station, Nick heard Vivaldi's *Four Seasons*. It was *Winter*. They hit another red light. Students were crossing the street, heading for campus, ignorant of the crisis around them. They had to stop this thing.

In order to contain pneumonic plague, it was imperative to locate Penny's contacts and get them on prophylactics. Anyone she was in contact with during the past three days had to be found.

In Nick's mind, epidemiology was an exercise in collecting and assembling facts. In any investigation, one of the most important pieces of information was identifying the first person to fall ill. That person was the index case, the person to whom all subsequent infections could be traced. Right now, they were dealing with basically two outbreaks of *Yersinia*—bubonic and pneumonic plague. Because fleas spread bubonic plague, identifying the index case was not critical. This was not true for pneumonic plague.

At the moment, Penny Farr appeared to be the index case and they had to know where she was infected. Her daycare was in a private home on Front Street, across the road from High Park. Karl swung into a driveway.

The babysitter, Christine Grey, lived in a small house on a large lot that was surrounded by a chain-link fence. The yard was full of bikes, a Toys-R-Us wagon and a convoluted jungle gym. A determined looking gray-haired lady stalked toward the fence.

"There's no parking here. Move that car."

Karl pulled out his business card and passed it over the fence. "I'm with the CDC." He introduced Nick. "Penny

Farr is ill and we're investigating the source of her infection."

Toddlers followed Christine to the fence. One of the kids raised her hands to be picked up and Christine swung her up on her hip. Another child gripped her leg. His nose was running and when he coughed, Nick winced. A single exhalation and a million bacteria could be released into the air. It only took a single bacterium to infect another person. He reached over the fence and felt the child's forehead. No fever. It couldn't be pneumonic plague, probably just a cold.

"At the moment, Penny is sick with a very bad cough and high fever," Karl said. "Do any of the other children have similar symptoms?"

"Petey has a cold," Chris said, patting the head of the boy wound around her leg. "He's getting better. Everyone else is fine."

"Then Penny Farr wasn't ill last week?" Nick said. It was essential they pinpoint precisely the day she was infected. Given her mother's vaccination, albeit incomplete, and because Penny was still breast-feeding, her course of infection could be skewed from the norm.

"Penny was fine," Christine said.

"How many kids do you watch?" Karl asked.

Chris had five kids, which was all she would take. She gave them breakfast, lunch and wholesome snacks. She abided by the food groups and watched the kids' nutrition. In a few minutes there'd be snacks, and then naps. Later on in the day, when the sun was past its peak, they'd go to the park. Take a nature hike, pick leaves, or look for bugs for their collection.

"And feed the squirrels and chipmunks?" Karl asked.

Chris looked offended. "Of course not. Squirrels and chipmunks can bite."

The girl on Christine's hip jammed her thumb in her mouth and stared at Nick. He smiled at her and thought of his son, who was put in daycare when he was a month old. Rachel-Anne, suffering from postpartum depression, could not care for him. Two months later when he died she couldn't forgive herself. She made her first suicide attempt a week after his son was buried.

Another Wheeler tune played in Nick's head: *My only son, I gave the world to you, and it grew valuable to me; I watch well, what is yours.*

On the grass, Petey started to cry and Chris shifted the child she was holding to pick him up.

"Don't worry," Karl said. "If you and the other children were exposed to Penny's infection, you're in no danger."

Across the fence, Chris demanded to know what kind of contagious infection Penny had.

Nick wondered how to reply. On one hand, he didn't want to overreact and terrify people, but on the other hand, he couldn't accept a "wait and see" approach that might leave many dead.

Karl addressed Chris's question. "It's an infection that can be treated if we catch it in time," he said. "We notified the health department and they'll visit with you today, arrange for everyone to begin prophylactic antibiotics."

Two other kids joined the fray and hid behind Christine's skirt.

"Prophy—what?" she said.

"Precautionary, protective, preventive antibiotics," Karl said.

On the grass, another child raised her arms, but both of Chris's hips were taken. She patted the child on the head as she returned to her effort of ascertaining the name of the disease. "I mean, what kind of sickness is this? What will get the Department of Health out here?"

"Between you and me, it's caused by a bacterium called *Yersinia pestis,*" Karl said, in a lowered voice.

"Is that like chicken pox?" Christine asked.

"Not really," Karl said. "Now, we do request you try to

keep this as quiet as possible. Both for your own protection and the protection of those that might panic and try to leave town."

"Panic and try to leave town?" Christine said. "Because of *Yer*—what? I've never even heard of it."

"Don't worry. We're prepared to deal with this problem, but doctors elsewhere might not be so adept."

With a few additional assurances that antibiotics would take care of the problem, Nick and Karl left Christine to her children. It would be up to the discretion of the Department of Health to answer any more questions she had, but Nick didn't like it. He never felt comfortable with evasions and half-truths.

As they drove around the block to the Tremblant Apartments, Karl talked about his ex-wife and his four kids. He thought they would have been happier if Helena had put them in daycare. The four of them were too much for her and by eight in the morning she was wasted. But Karl guessed there was no point worrying about it now, for his kids were grown and the decision not to do daycare was made long ago and couldn't be changed now. Nick couldn't argue with that. At the moment he was more concerned with things he could change.

Jack lived in the Tremblant Apartments, diagonally across the street from High Park. The white clapboard complex had steep red roofs and the elaborate trim reminded Nick of a doll's house. Karl parked in a visitor's parking spot.

They interviewed the superintendent and learned Jack had lived in the building for two years. Except for a few loud parties, he was no trouble. He had a two-bedroom apartment he shared with another football player. The apartments were fully serviced. A maid cleaned twice a week, and the complex was sprayed for insects every other month. The building and grounds had been fumigated the previous week. Pets weren't allowed in the building, and fleas and rodents weren't a problem.

The landlord gave Karl a key to the apartment. It was on the second floor, and the apartment looked clean. There was no sign of fleas or rodents. No sign of the roommate who was out of town and would have to be found.

After checking the apartment, they stepped out onto the narrow balcony that faced south. To his right, Nick saw the railroad tracks, and past that, the yellow-brick facade of the veterinary school. Ahead and to the left stood Christine Grey's house, her front yard empty now. Across from her was the busy High Park, adjacent to the back parking lot of the Lone Star Heritage Hotel. Across the street from that was the University Plaza, with the supermarket, movie theater, car wash and coin laundry. Except for Dudley Shaw, everyone else infected could be traced to this area.

In an epidemiological investigation, identifying the epicenter, the source of the bacteria, was as important as establishing the index case. Was this the epicenter? Did the bacteria spread from here? But how did it get here?

Nick watched students hurry away from campus. An exam must have just ended. The park was busy. The wading pool was packed with kids and edged with mothers and nannies. A large black dog loped across the grass. The park filled half a city block. There was a playground on one end and a wooded area on the other. At the verge of the trees, he saw two technicians dressed in white coats, laying cage-traps. He watched squirrels leaping in the trees, chipmunks scurrying on the ground. His heart nearly stopped when a young boy held out a crust of bread to a black squirrel. It was close interactions like this that facilitated the movement of fleas from the wild to human populations.

"Would you look at that stupid kid," Karl cried.

Nick's heart nearly froze, but before he could react, a park employee shooed the child away. A mother came running. Nick watched the exchange: the frown on the woman's face, the park official shaking his head, the crying child as the mother dragged him away.

"It could have happened like that," Karl said. "Penny Farr played in the park and got too close to an infected rodent and contracted pneumonic plague."

Nick agreed it was plausible. If Penny was infected here, he did not like what he saw. There were too many people, too many kids in the vicinity of the proposed epicenter. People had to be warned. Nick disagreed with McCoy and Karl's policy to dispense as little information as possible.

In the past, Nick had managed to contain many epidemics with honesty. He preferred to deal with people openly rather than keep them in the dark. He did not like watching kids play in a park, oblivious to the threat around them. He did not like watching students going to school, thinking that the only thing they had to worry about was an exam. Until they could pinpoint the source of the disease, everyone in town was at risk.

"Our policy is wrong," he said. "People have a right to know what's going on."

Karl disagreed. "You were involved in the anthrax investigation. You know what happened there. The hysteria screwed everything. This is a college town; if students catch wind of what's going on, they'll be gone. We make an announcement and Duane will be a ghost town. We could spread the plague throughout the whole of Texas. The whole country."

Nick watched the kids swinging on the swings. "No. Give people the truth and ask them to behave responsibly. Tell them to stay home, and minimize outside contacts. Tell them to call a doctor if they have flu-like symptoms. Let them protect themselves."

Karl leaned against the balcony railing. "Shit, Nick, there's already a flu epidemic in this town. Can you imagine what will happen if everyone with a sniffle runs to their doctor? How many doctors do you think there are here? Imagine the chaos if everyone thinks they have the plague."

Nick flung his hand at the direction of High Park. "Look at those kids. We know four rats collected there were infected with *Yersinia*. How can we keep that park open?"

"Close it and you'll have a lot of explaining to do."

Nick exhaled heavily. "Maybe we need to start explaining. Maybe we should hold a press conference."

"No way," Karl said. "I won't do it. We need these people here so we can trace this thing. We go public and the road out of Duane will be a parking lot."

Nick shook his head. "We keep this quiet and the town will be a morgue."

Chapter 28

That afternoon, Dana began to autopsy the four rodents trapped during the night at Dudley's house. In light of the negative blood tests, she thought the autopsies were unnecessary, but McCoy had ordered them and Nellie delivered the bodies.

At the hood in the quarantine room, Dana opened the biohazard bag and pulled out three mice and a rat. The rodents had been tagged and identified. The mice were *Peromyscus attwateri* and the rat, *Dipodomys ordii*. The names meant nothing to her, except they weren't the typical species that spread the plague.

Starting with the rat, she arranged him on his back on a tray. His body was cold but soft. His fur was brown and smelled of the ether that had been used to kill him. Dana grabbed the loose fur by his stomach and cut into it with a pair of sharp scissors. The intestines began to spill out, a twisted, gray, slimy, gelatinous mass. She pushed them to one side with a finger, then pulled back the skin and peered inside. No bulbous lymph nodes. The liver was a bright reddish-brown and the lobes were firm. She examined the spleen and thymus, two organs of immunity. The tissue was not swollen or enlarged; no sign of an intensive immune assault. She saved the organs for Becker, then dropped the body of the rat into a biohazard bag and grabbed the next victim.

Dana finished the autopsies in an hour and all the animals appeared healthy. One of the mice was pregnant—she carried six tiny comma-shaped babies in her womb. None of the rodents resembled the sick rats Carol gave her Friday afternoon. The rodents out by Dudley's house were clean, just like Bingo's fleas.

Before leaving the quarantine room, Dana checked the progression of the disk test. There was no clear zone. The bacteria plaques still grew flush against the filter paper. There seemed to be more colonies now then there had been earlier. Were the bacteria still dividing? The antibiotics should have stopped that.

Still, it was too early to expect a response. Only four hours had passed. The rest took time and she couldn't expect conclusive results in less than twenty-four hours. Each *Yersinia* strain was different. She often ran disk tests to assay new strains for antibiotic resistance and would never use even a moderately resistant strain. In case of an accident, Dana wanted an effective antidote. Generally, with non-resistant *Yersinia*, a lethal effect of the antibiotic cocktail was visible early. While some strains had a delayed reaction, never had Dana seen a non-resistant strain continue to divide after exposure to antibiotics.

Was this a strain of bacteria resistant to antibiotics?

No, she told herself, it was too early to tell.

But the quiet voice in her brain nagged on about resistance. Over the years, one thing she had learned was to pay attention to that voice. Another thing she had learned was not to underestimate bacteria. Because of rapid cell division, they evolved quickly. Bacteria exhibited many strategies to deal with antibiotics. They might block the entry of antibiotics into the cell, actively pitch them out, or chemically modify them so that they no longer worked. There were some bacteria that used more than one mechanism. The super-bugs. And *Yersinia* was in that category.

In Madagascar, Dana told herself, on an island far off the coast of Africa, not here.

The phone was ringing when she reached her office and she grabbed the receiver. Once more Sheryl was on the line and screaming. "Penny's worse. The antibiotics aren't working. Her temperature is one hundred and five. She's having convulsions. She's dying."

Dana struggled to breathe.

Sheryl's voice turned quiet. "How much of the monoclonal do we have?"

Dana closed her eyes. "We sent the monoclonal to Fort Troy and froze the remaining hybridomas." She wasn't telling Sheryl anything she didn't know already.

"We didn't freeze them all. We're still feeding a few cells. How much do we have?"

"It doesn't matter," Dana said. "Penny can't take it." Morally and ethically it was unthinkable. "Sheryl, give the antibiotics more time."

"Don't you tell me that," Sheryl screamed. "I saw what that monoclonal antibody did to the mice. It saved their lives. But you had to give it to them in time. And there's no time, Dana. Penny can't breathe. She's burning with fever. She's had seizures. And you can do something," Her voice again grew calm. "Dana, you can do something. You can't let her die."

"The guinea pigs. Remember the guinea pigs." Fifty percent of them had allergic lung reactions, thirty percent suffered systemic shock, twelve percent had renal failure and eight percent died.

"The rabbit, dog and monkey responded well," Sheryl said. "It's our only hope. We can't do nothing."

In her mind, Dana ticked off potential side effects. Kidney failure, lung infection, shock, death. It was too big a risk; she couldn't do it.

"You owe me," Sheryl said. "On Friday you said you owed me."

Dana pressed the receiver on her shoulder and stared up at the van Gogh print. Injecting herself with an experimental vaccine was one thing, but injecting someone else was another. She touched her muscle, the site of Friday's injection.

She had taken an antigen, which was different than the monoclonal. The antigen was a piece of a bacterium and the monoclonal was a modified human protein.

As they saw in the guinea pig, a foreign protein could provoke a massive autoimmune response.

Penny was no guinea pig. She was a soft, small baby with four milk teeth and fine hair that was beginning to curl at the ends, who smelled like baby powder and was just starting to talk. She could say Mama, Pau, Wicky, even Nayna, but her favorite word was *Mine*, usually spoken in two determined syllables. What if something went wrong?

The monoclonal antibody might work in humans in ways they could not predict or imagine. It might do more harm than good. What if the monoclonal antibody bound to a cellular protein and caused a widespread allergy? This wasn't a guinea pig, this was a baby—her godchild.

Still, there were no side effects in mice, rats, rabbits, dogs, or monkeys. And what was the alternative if the antibiotics didn't work? Dana looked at her watch. Penny had been on antibiotics for eight hours. Maybe the bacteria were resistant. Maybe the antibiotics would never work.

What about Penny's life? Dana had put on her best clothes and gone to church and swore she would do everything she could to protect the baby. But what if she made things worse? How could she live with herself? What if the antibiotics worked and Dana administered a monoclonal that killed her?

So, better to sit around and wait for Penny to die? Like Dudley? Or for her condition to get worse? Like Jack? If she left it too long, there would be no choice; it would be over. Time was against them. She glanced at her watch again and heard it ticking.

A life without Penny. Dana saw in her mind, a small casket and a gravestone. What clothes did Penny have to be buried in? What would happen to her crib? Her toys? Her books? Her room, which held a life that would end forever. Like Frank, gone and leaving too much space. No, Sheryl was right. Waiting was insane.

She stared up at the print. *Go with what you think is right.* Becker's advice resounding in her head. She raised the receiver to her ear. "Hold on. I'm coming."

Dana got up and went to the cell culture room, trying to empty her mind, blank out the consequences of what she was about to do. She opened the cell-culture incubator and stared at the neatly stacked Petri plates that contained the protective monoclonal antibody.

The technology to produce the monoclonal was simple. Antibodies were made in a specialized immune cell called a plasma cell. One plasma cell made a single type of antibody. Once they knew the antibody they were looking for, they could identify the cell that produced it and isolate that cell from the rest. Then they fused that cell to a tumor cell to create a hybrid. The hybrid divided indefinitely and produced a single type of antibody, a monoclonal antibody.

When the production stage was at its peak, they had a hundred plates and collected a total of one milliliter of the monoclonal antibody a day. For six months Sheryl had done little but mass-produce the monoclonal. A month ago they had shipped enough vaccine to Fort Troy to test sixty thousand people. They had frozen the remaining hybrid cells and had less than a half a milliliter of the monoclonal left.

Using a glass pipette, Dana transferred one-tenth of a milliliter of the monoclonal antibody to a vial, which she slipped inside a protective Styrofoam sleeve. She grabbed a needle and syringe and put them in her briefcase. Though it might be unethical, she thought it more unethical to do nothing and let someone die who might otherwise live. Dana locked her lab and headed out.

Texas Avenue was clotted with pre-rush-hour traffic. The sun was bright, but to the south the clouds were building. The wind was still blowing. It swung the traffic lights and kicked a cereal box along a gutter. It whipped through the open windows of the car, tangling Dana's hair. McCoy would not be able to spray.

On the radio, the four o'clock news came on. A senior state department spokesman defended the U.S. strike against Somalia. Yes, a hospital had been damaged, but not by a U.S. bomb. A warehouse containing munitions was targeted and successfully hit. Collateral damage to the hospital was a result of exploding munitions, for which the U.S. would take no responsibility. A nearby mosque may also have been hit. The spokesman reiterated a plea for overseas citizens to take security precautions. He downplayed the possibility of a terrorist strike on American soil. He was confident that the UN investigative team would exonerate the U.S. from all wrongdoing.

Dana reached the hospital. Outside, the world was going crazy, but inside nothing looked amiss. At the reception desk, the secretary with the pink nails sat reading her magazine. There was no one rushing in the hallway, no alarms beeping. From all outward signs, it was as if nothing was wrong, and life was progressing as usual on a Tuesday afternoon. It seemed impossible that here a baby was dying from the plague.

Dana reached Penny's room and stood in the hall, pulling on quarantine clothes. Sheryl opened the door and yanked her inside. "Hurry, hurry, there's not much time. The nurse just left."

Though Sheryl was wearing a biohazard suit and a hood,

Dana saw her wide, fearful eyes through the plastic face panel. She looked pale and frantic as she pulled Dana across the room toward Penny.

A slant of sunlight shone down on the crib across the naked, still, white baby. Penny's hair was soaked with fever. Beads of sweat dotted her forehead. Her pearly fingernails were black. She lay unmoving, uncrying, unresponsive, except for the shuddering of her chest as she grasped for breath.

She was as blue now as she had been at her birth. After a long and hard delivery, her Apgar score had been zero. The doctor wondered if she had broken Penny's shoulder during the delivery and when she was an hour old, Penny had her first x-ray. It was a bad start, but from then on things got better. Aside from tonsillitis, and a few earaches, Penny was healthy. Dana wasn't prepared for a life without her. How Nick survived the loss of his son, she didn't know. Where was the God Sheryl believed in? How could this happen?

Sheryl clutched her arm. "Come on, come on. Hurry, hurry. The nurse went to finalize arrangements for Penny in ICU. She'll be right back."

With trembling fingers, Dana pulled the Styrofoam sleeve from her pocket. She ripped the paper cover off the syringe and fastened it to the needle. She uncapped the glass vial and pulled back the plunger to draw the monoclonal into the syringe.

"Do you want me to do it?" Sheryl asked.

Dana shook her head; she would take responsibility. She twisted the IV tube from the needle in Penny's foot and stemmed the flow of plasma with her thumb. She had trouble because the gloves were too big and the polyethylene made her hands sweat. Her whole body was sweating. She could barely keep her hands from shaking.

As carefully as she could, she shoved the syringe into the base of the IV needle tapped into Penny's vein and slowly depressed the plunger. She wanted to hurry, was terrified the nurse would return and it was hard to go slow. But if she pushed too hard, there would be a back-flow of liquid and the monoclonal would leak out. She could not hurry. *Slow down, slow down*, she told herself.

The monoclonal was finally in. Dana withdrew the syringe and examined the IV needle in Penny's foot. No liquid dripped down the side. Fitting the tubing back onto the end of the IV needle, the tube slipped and plasma spilled onto the bed, blotting the sheet. Sheryl gasped and Dana grabbed the tube and jammed it back in place.

The door opened and a gargantuan nurse burst in. She looked at Penny and yelled at Sheryl for moving the crib. "I am already telling you to keep her from the sunlight." She spoke in a strong German accent and scowled deeply.

"And there are to be no visitors," she added, frowning at Dana. "This is a quarantine room and she is having to leave. Immediate family only." The nurse walked to the crib and pulled it away from the window.

Dana backed up, listened to her heart slam as the nurse examined the baby. Would she see the blot on the sheet? Would she call Taversham? No, she grabbed the IV bottles off their stands and looped them over the rail of the crib.

"I am moving the baby to ICU," the nurse said. "The mother may enter only." The nurse rolled the crib toward the door, which Dana hastened to open.

When the nurse was gone, Sheryl sagged against the wall, hands pressed against her throat. "Thank you, Dana. Thank you."

But Dana was already wondering if she had made a mistake. This was not some small thing she could take back. It was a step taken that could never be undone and if it was the wrong step to take, Dana had given a lethal injection. A death sentence for an eighteen-month-old baby. Murder. God help me, she thought, a first prayer in twenty years.

Chapter 29

The day had been long and frustrating, McCoy thought as he sat in the conference room awaiting the start of the five o'clock meeting. He had managed to squeeze in a visit to his cardiologist, who had increased his heart medication. Now his heart rate was normal, as was his blood pressure, but McCoy was experiencing side effects he hadn't experienced with his medication before. His ulcer, dormant five years, was active again and his stomach burned. If he stood up too fast he felt faint. He wondered at times if his thinking was clear.

He had spent most of the afternoon out at the airport clearing the pesticide that had arrived from D.C. A spray plane had been loaded and a pilot was on standby. Once the wind let up, the pilot would fly.

Earlier, McCoy had received a call from the *Washington Post*. Some nosy reporter wanted to know what the DDT was for. McCoy, begging an emergency, hung up. He had promised to call back—and he would—perhaps next week. At least there were no queries from local reporters.

McCoy massaged his temples and felt a headache coming on. Whether it was another side effect of his medication, or the paint fumes, he didn't know. He looked across the room at a half-painted wall. The painter gave her word the job would be finished by lunchtime, but by the look of it, the job was barely underway. He could see where the strokes faded as the paint ran out. At lunchtime the painter went to get more paint, but she had not returned.

Not that it mattered. Given the current situation and the case of pneumonic plague, it was doubtful if the VP would keep his commitment and deliver the convocation address. There were too many unanswered questions, too many things that didn't add up. At the moment the only thing they could do was wait and see what happened. There was a sense of helplessness that McCoy could not stomach.

He closed his eyes. He was very tired. At least no additional people were infected with *Yersinia*. McCoy had the results of the blood tests from the small mammals trapped throughout town and all seventy-five animals were *Yersinia*-free. It was good news to tell Barry Ackerman, the FBI agent who at that moment sat in McCoy's office, waiting to speak with him.

Somehow the FBI had learned that Nick Biget was in town on government business and they wanted to know what it was about. McCoy said they would talk after his meeting. It was just about to start.

McCoy's researchers were walking in. He nodded hello to Michael Smith, again just remembering his visitor. Smith's seminar was scheduled for the following morning and McCoy had neglected to post notices of the talk. He would have Betty do that first thing tomorrow. Next, Nick and Karl arrived, each lugging a large carton containing the prophylactic antibiotic, tetracycline, shipped from a Houston factory. Everyone in the department who was not vaccinated against *Yersinia* would begin taking the antibiotic. No one would get sick on his watch. For a change, Dana Sparks was on time and in a lab coat. Becker was still out with the flu and everyone else was accounted for, all except Nellie, who had gone home early to prepare for a dinner she was hosting that evening.

McCoy began his meeting. He stood up, felt faint, and immediately sat back down. He looked at the blackboard, saw an empty space and remembered the painter had cleared it out. Well, he only had a few words to say and he said them. "We've got no new cases. No sign of a rodent infection in Duane."

He thought it was good news, until he saw Nick frown. Sparks raised her hand. Ignoring her, McCoy asked King to bring them up to date.

The CDC man scraped his chair away from the table and stretched out his legs. He had spoken to state extension officials. During the last twenty-four hours, 352 rodents had been trapped. Their blood had been tested in the state lab. Eight animals had *Yersinia* antibodies. Four of the animals were trapped in the Panhandle near Amarillo, the other four near Plains, just east of the New Mexico border.

Here was the first sign the bacteria *were* in Texas. Perhaps the epicenter *was* far away. "Looks like we should shift our focus to West Texas," McCoy said. "Trap more animals there."

Nick objected. He thought they should continue to focus on Duane. "Epidemiologically, the epicenter appears to be close to High Park."

McCoy's stomach burned and he felt exhausted. "But only four rats in town are infected. Seventy-five rodents are not."

"That may be," Nick said. "Except for Dudley Shaw, all infections can be traced to the area near High Park. That's where Carol trapped the rats, where Jack lives and where Penny goes to daycare."

It was too close, McCoy thought, as his heart thumped too loudly in his chest. Too close to home. McCoy wiped his suddenly sweating palms on his slacks.

Nick wouldn't let up. "If we have any suspicion at all that the park *is* the epicenter, it should be closed."

McCoy looked at him. At the moment, that was out of the question. Closing the park would mean going public and McCoy wasn't prepared to do that. For the time being they would take no overt action. "It seems as if the source is far away. If Parks and Rec are monitoring the park it stays open. We won't do anything until we trap and examine rodents in the park." McCoy turned to Karl. "Are we setting traps?"

They were. In fact, they had caught some chipmunks and squirrels and taken blood to assay.

"Give it to Dr. Sparks," McCoy said. He would wait for the results before deciding what to do next. "That's it for now."

No, Sparks had something to say. "Is it possible the bacteria are resistant to antibiotics?"

"I suppose *anything* is possible," McCoy said. "Maybe you can tell me. You're the one doing the disk test."

"It's only been six hours," she said.

"Let's give the antibiotics time to work, shall we?" he said.

"What if we *are* dealing with resistance?" she asked.

But McCoy hated the game of *What If* and wouldn't play. He closed the meeting. When he jumped to his feet, he almost fainted. Orthostatic hypotension. A side effect of his medicine. McCoy took a deep breath and slowly walked toward the door and the waiting FBI agent.

Chapter 30

Dana sat through the meeting worrying about Penny. Under no circumstances were babies ever included in drug testing. Their growing bodies, high metabolism and rapid rate of DNA synthesis made them, in some respects, unusually sensitive to drugs an adult could easily tolerate. And what about the dose? Dana had extrapolated from a mouse to a baby. But what if Penny needed more because her immune system was incompetent? Or what if she needed less because of low body fat? And what about unique developmental proteins with which the antibody could interact? Dana could easily envision a hundred horrifying deaths: shock, cardiac suppression, lung deflation, circulatory impairment, neural intrusion, mental retardation, or a multitude of problems caused by a full-blown allergic reaction. Halfway through McCoy's meeting, Dana decided to seek medical advice. Nick had trained as a physician and might know the drugs used to treat an immune response that was out of control.

If he asked why she needed the information, she thought she would tell him. There was a time when she could tell him anything and he would listen without judgement. True, she had never done anything like this before, but her back was up against a wall and she felt she had no choice. Nick, who lost an infant, would surely sympathize with a dying baby.

When the meeting was through, she followed him to Headquarters. She opened the door as she knocked and caught him stringing on a tie. He looked tired—his five o'clock shadow a rough stubble, the beginning of a beard. She closed the door behind her. "Nick, I have a question."

Looking downwards, he knotted his tie. "Dana, you have to stop this. If you have questions, ask Karl. Not me. He's in charge." He slipped the knot up to his neck. He was cutting off his heart, pushing her away, increasing the distance between them. It didn't matter what steps she took; for every advance she made, Nick retreated until he would be gone and she would be alone.

He exhaled loudly. "Look, I'm sorry. I'm in a rush. I've got to go." He turned his back and collected papers strewn across the desk.

No matter how busy he had been before, he always had time, or would make time for her. She backed up toward the door, then jumped out of the way when it opened. Karl.

"Dana," he said. "Pleasant surprise."

Why couldn't Nick respond like that?

"Everything okay?" Karl studied her face. "You look a little—off."

"Do you have a minute? I have a few questions."

Karl sat on the top of a desk. "Shoot."

"If the kidneys stop functioning, what are the clinical signs?"

Behind her back, Nick's shuffling of papers ceased. Karl said, "A blood test will show the presence of urea."

A blood test? "Isn't there a change in urine output?"

"A decrease. Oh, and if you smell the patient's breath you can smell urea. It's quite distinctive."

Dana paused before asking the next question. If Nick knew the guinea pig response, he would know why she wanted this information. Unlikely he knew though. "Is there a way to tell the difference between pneumonic plague and a pneumonic allergy?" Behind her Nick answered.

"Look at the blood and the level of basophils. Or more specifically, the level of IgE."

She turned around, saw him studying her intently. He said nothing more.

"Impaired breathing caused by a pneumonic allergy can be treated with epinephrine," Karl said.

She turned back to him. "How would you treat a systemic allergy?"

"Dexamethasone," Karl said.

She nodded. Of course. A steroid. She knew that.

"Anything else?" Karl was smiling his wide smile. At the end of the day, strands of hair had slipped from his ponytail. The hair on his goatee looked tangled.

"Do you think the bacteria are resistant?"

"I don't know. We have to wait and see," Karl said.

He had Nick's patience. How did he live with uncertain outcomes? Dana couldn't stand ambiguity. "What are we going to do if it is?"

"Nothing until we know." Karl leaned toward the fridge and opened the door. He grabbed a large biohazard bag. "Here are the rodents from the park."

Dana took the bag. "I don't think Penny was infected in the park."

Nick crossed the room, sat on the edge of Karl's desk and folded his arms across his heart. "The park seems to be the epicenter."

"Penny came too close to an infected animal," Karl added. "She breathed bad air."

Dana shook her head. "I know Penny. She hates animals. She's terrified of my dogs. To her, all animals are different-sized dogs. She wouldn't go near one."

"How do *you* think she was infected?" Nick's voice had softened but there was still an edge to it.

"I think someone infected her. I don't think she's the index case."

"Usually the index case is the first to get sick. So far, Penny is the only one with pneumonic plague."

"What if there are others we don't know about?" she said.

"We'll deal with them when they arise." Nick glanced at his watch.

Karl stood up, as if on cue. "I'm ready," he said. Then to Dana, "You coming?"

"Coming? I don't think so."

Karl hooted his inappropriate laugh. "I meant coming to the dean's for this big dinner."

"Um. No," she said, thinking back to last night in the bar, and tonight the big dinner, to which she wasn't invited. So much for her inclusion in the investigation. *And the Yersinia specialist was largely ineffectual during the outbreak . . .*

"Pity," Karl said.

"We should go." Nick picked up his briefcase and walked toward the door, passing her in a burst of sweat. His footsteps were loud, as if he was carrying a great weight.

She looked down; his shoelace was untied. "Nick," she touched his arm, "your shoelace."

He kept going, not bothering to stop.

Karl followed him out, flashing his white teeth and crinkling his eyes as he bid her a hearty goodnight.

Dana watched them recede down the hall.

Necessity might bring things together, but it didn't make things happen.

Chapter 31

The Duncans lived in the valley on the south side of town, where the roads were winding and wide and the streets were dark. Karl drove while Nick, slouching beside him, gave directions. If he had his way, he'd skip this dinner altogether.

It had been a long and stressful day and Nick was tired and on edge. He had a headache and despite three aspirins, his head throbbed. It was the case—nothing about it made sense. Where were the rodents that were spreading the bacteria? Why were the infected mammals in West Texas? Where were people being exposed? Protecting people against exposure was of paramount importance, but Karl wouldn't go public.

While Nick understood his reasoning, he didn't agree. They had too little information at the moment to predict the outcome of infection. It could either explode in their faces and become a widespread epidemic, or blow over and die out. Either scenario was possible and while Nick anticipated the worst, Karl hoped for the best. In the end, Karl was in charge and the decision of handling the outbreak was his.

In Nick's mind, the most worrying factor, by far, was the inadequacy of the treatment. What if they were dealing with a resistant strain? It had occurred to Dana as well, and she had an accurate sense about some things. She had raised the point in the meeting, then later in her line of questioning to Karl. Renal failure, systemic hypersensitivity and pulmonary depression were the side effects of her monoclonal vaccine in the guinea pig trials. Was she thinking of using the vaccine on people? Nick was appalled at the thought. She was no physician. It was a preposterous idea. They had other, less extreme options.

Beside him, at the wheel, Karl said, "What's wrong? You seem distracted. Is it this case?"

"Of course." Nick combed his hair with his fingers. They were driving down a wide road lined with huge post oaks. The houses were set far from the street and bright with security lights and well-lit windows. They shot past the Sassafras Drive intersection. "You should have turned there," Nick said.

Karl slowed and made a sweeping U-turn. "Is it this dinner?" Karl said, shifting his attention to Nick. "Why isn't Dana coming?"

"I don't know."

"Is it Nellie?" Karl asked, as he maneuvered the corner. "I get the feeling you're trying to avoid her."

Nick chose not to answer. He was wary around Nellie, to be sure. She knew about his indiscretion and he felt guilty about it. Still, she wasn't to blame, what happened was his fault, not hers. Nick thought of Wheeler: *It was me; I take the blame; I pay the price and sacrifice my heart.*

"My wife reminds me of her," Karl said. "Minding everyone else's business."

Nick said nothing. He kept forgetting Karl was divorced. He had always thought Karl's marriage was strong and he guessed you never really knew what was happening in someone else's life. Perhaps his wasn't as transparent as he thought.

They drove down the street, Karl idly running his finger across the steering wheel. "I'm tired of being on my own. I don't like it. It's different for you, you're a widower and you're used to it, but I can tell you, after being with some-one for twenty-two years, it's hard to be on your own."

"I don't mind it," Nick said. In fact, at the moment he longed for it. His own space, with a door he could close and a phone he didn't have to answer. A place where he could be safely alone.

"I think it's time I started dating again," Karl said. "This time I'm not eighteen years old and I know what I want. Someone open and up front, someone who doesn't hide what they think, who isn't afraid to be who they are. I want someone like, well, like Dana."

Nick nearly choked. *No, it was too much.*

"What were you two talking about earlier?" Karl asked. "Your conversations always seem so intense. Why did she want a drug to stop hypersensitivity?"

Nick didn't answer. Instead he pointed to the Duncans' driveway. "Here we are."

Standing in the doorway under a porch supported by thick, circular columns, Nick once more wished he were home. Nellie, in a tight and shimmering sleeveless dress, left the scent of her musk perfume all over him. The dean wore a tux with cowboy boots and a ten-gallon Stetson that all but buried his face. Nick felt underdressed in his blazer and tie with the benzene rings. His face itched and he wished he'd had time to shave.

The dean showed them to the study off of the living room, while Nellie went to check on dinner. In the dark study, an unnecessary fire blazed. A moose head with im-pressive antlers poked out of the mantle. The black marble floor was covered in animal skins. There was a sweeping bar in one corner, burdened with rows of bottles and crystal glasses that sparkled like diamonds in the firelight. The room smelled of woodsmoke and leather.

McCoy was sitting at the end of a low couch. Beside him, in a chrome-frame chair, hulked the university president, Mitchell Marshall. He was a tall, substantial man with white hair and a large ruddy face. A lazy southern accent belied shrewd intelligence. He had been at the university twenty years and had successfully managed the transition from a public to private institution, which he ran as if he owned. There was another man present Nick didn't know and guessed FBI before the dean introduced Special Agent Barry Ackerman.

After drinks were served, McCoy cleared his throat. "I'm glad we could all make it tonight. I asked Barry to be here because there is, I'm afraid, a late-breaking development." He leaned forward and said in a low tone, "There's a possibility this outbreak is deliberate."

The room fell silent.

McCoy deferred to the special agent. Tall and thin, with short dark hair and dark eyes, Ackerman looked young, about thirty. He was too tall for his chair. Leaning forward, his knees nearly hit his chin and his dangling knuckles grazed the fur-tipped fringe of the zebra hide beneath his chair. "Our bureau has received a credible threat against the life of the vice president."

No one spoke. The glass-eyed moose stared. A log in the fire sparked. Karl reached forward and took a large handful of cashews from a bowl resting on a leather-topped table. He munched loudly.

Ackerman folded together his long, spidery fingers. "As you have probably heard, following the strike in Somalia, various militant Arab factions issued another *fatwa* against us."

"It's been on the news," McCoy said.

The dean tipped back his oversized Stetson. "According to the BBC, Islamic fundamentalists plan to extract payment for their dead with American blood."

The FBI agent nodded. "We have reason to believe the current outbreak of the plague is intentional."

"What was the threat?" Nick said.

Ackerman pulled flimsy facsimile paper from the breast pocket of his dark suit. He read, " 'We will strike you down with bugs in your own backyard.' " Ackerman folded the paper in half. "It's translated from Arabic of course."

Nick replayed the words in his mind. He wondered if there might be an error in translation. Perhaps the original message read, strike you down *like* bugs, not *with* bugs. In any case, equating bacteria to bugs was Western slang. "How do you know the threat is serious?" he said. "And not a joke or college prank?"

Karl, with his mouth full of nuts, agreed with him. "I mean, the threat does sound vague."

"And the timing doesn't fit," Nick said. "The rats had to be infected with the plague before Somalia was bombed."

Ackerman's face was set. "The validity of threats to the vice president's life is our jurisdiction, not yours." He smiled thinly. "Here we have an outbreak of the plague in a region of the country which, in my understanding, is too far south and too hot for the bacteria. We have evidence that the epicenter of the outbreak may be near the hotel where the VP is scheduled to stay. These are factors we cannot afford to ignore."

Nick was surprised by the extent of his information and wondered where it was coming from.

"The VP knows the situation, yet insists on coming," Ackerman said.

"That's our boy." Mitchell Marshall raised a fist and nodded to McCoy.

Ackerman stood up, his long arms dangling like sticks by his side. He had said what he came to say and now his presence was required elsewhere. He reminded everyone the information was confidential and not to be repeated. "We will keep in touch as our investigation unfolds. We're giving you a heads-up and hope you will reciprocate. Good night, gentlemen."

The discussion began the instant Ackerman left. Could it be an act of terror? McCoy, who long seemed intent on proving the outbreak was elsewhere, was suddenly ready for a war on his turf.

Karl thought the allegations were outlandish. "What evidence is there?" he asked. "A half-baked confession? The outbreak is too random to be deliberate. How can you dump bacteria and expect to target a specific person who's not even here?"

"It is an abnormally hardy strain of *Yersinia*," Nick said. "And the treatment isn't working as it should. We have one dead and three people responding poorly. We could be dealing with resistance. We know that former USSR researchers genetically engineered a multi-drug-resistant-strain of the plague. We know there's a plant in Kazakhstan that can produce ninety-six pounds of freeze-dried plague bacteria in a week. We also know that the funding was cut and that half the people in the plant lost their jobs. Where are they now? Somalia? Afghanistan? Iraq? We don't know."

McCoy fervently nodded his head. "All along, we've seen abnormalities in this outbreak."

"We need a backup," Nick said. "We should bring in the antibiotic trimethoprim. It was used in Madagascar and exhibited high efficacy against resistant plague bacteria."

Karl agreed that it would be good to have on hand, but McCoy worried about possible publicity surrounding the request.

While a discussion regarding this raged, Nick wondered what to tell Washington when he called to make his report. There was still a paucity of facts. As yet, no clear picture of the epidemic. They needed more information, but a solid epidemiological assessment of *Yersinia* might take days. Nick doubted the information would be complete by Friday.

Nick privately believed the VP's determination to keep his appointment in Duane was insane. The bacteria seemed unusually virulent and while the VP would be placed on prophylactic antibiotics, if this were an act of biological war, Rich Rutherford should stay away.

In the meantime, the most effective way to contain the outbreak was to identify those at risk. Despite McCoy's aversion to publicity and Karl's fear of hysteria, the easiest way to reach people was to go public. Nick pressed again for a news release.

"If the FBI are treating this outbreak as deliberate, and in view of the fact we haven't identified the source of the bacteria, in the aim for human safety, shouldn't we warn people there's an outbreak of contagious bacteria?"

"No," McCoy, Karl and Mitchell Marshall answered in unison.

McCoy added, "Bad press is the last thing we need. If we're dealing with a kook, we don't want to give him publicity."

"Well, if we're clear on that," the dean said, as if the matter had been settled, "let's go eat." He removed his hat and threw open the door.

Nellie stood in the doorway and laughed nervously. "I came to tell you dinner's ready."

"Wonderful." The dean waved the crowd out of the study.

Obediently they all trooped to the dining room and sat down at a long table. Overhead, a heavy crystal chandelier hung low and light sparkled on polished silver and flow-ered china. The food kept coming, but Nick had lost his appetite and could do no more than cut his food and shove it around his plate as Nellie ran a monologue about a myriad of topics that at one point included her regrets about his poor dead wife.

Nick was barely listening. He heard Wheeler singing inside his head: *What's gone never leaves, it stays; in the blood you drink like wine.*

Chapter 32

Dana's stomach was rumbling as she finished testing the blood from the animals trapped in High Park. The results were negative. In the park, only the four rats Carol trapped had the plague. No other rodents were infected. It was bizarre.

She checked the disk test. Still no zone of inhibition, but it looked as if the bacteria had stopped growing and there were no new colonies. Maybe the antibiotic just needed time to work.

From her office, she called the hospital. Her heart was racing and when Sheryl came on the line Dana could hardly speak.

"The doctors don't know if she'll make it." Sheryl was weeping as she spoke.

"I'll be right there."

"You can't come. Visiting hours are over. I don't want to make the nurse more suspicious than she is."

Dana looked up at her van Gogh. One side seemed full of hope, the other malevolence. She was on the bad side now, the side with the incomprehensible dark twisted shape as high as the stars. An impenetrable barrier. A massive block. She felt helpless. *Please let Penny live*, she said to no one.

"I have to get back to her," Sheryl said.

"Wait. Are there any new symptoms? A drop in blood pressure? Shock? Impaired breathing?"

"No." Sheryl sounded horrified.

"Does her breath smell like ammonia?"

"Why would you ask?"

"If there's a change in her symptoms, call me. If she goes into shock, tell the doctor to give her dexamethasone. If her breathing gets worse, give her epinephrine."

"I've got to go," Sheryl said again.

"Wait!" But the phone was dead in Dana's ear.

She left the veterinary school. A three-quarter moon hung in the sky, a malicious eye. The sky was milky and streaked with light clouds. A heavy wind rattled the trees; branches creaked and leaves sighed.

When Dana reached home the phone was ringing. She grabbed it breathless, terrified it was Sheryl. But it was her father, who preferred email to phones. It was highly unusual for him to call. "Dad, is something wrong?"

"Princess, it's your mother."

"What's wrong?"

"*She* thinks something's wrong. I'm supposed to call and find out. She says you never tell her anything. What's going on?"

"What do *you* think is going on?" She wondered if the story had made the national news.

"Nothing. And I told your mother as much, but she insisted I call."

"Everything's fine," Dana said, childishly crossing her fingers behind her back.

"I tried calling earlier. Working late?"

Dana carried the phone to the fridge and pulled out a beer, popped the top. "Just got home now."

"That's how you get to the top. Got tenure yet?"

"Not yet." She closed the fridge door with her foot. She was nearly out of food and would have to go shopping.

"Typical," her father said. "They'll drag it out and make you sweat. Don't let them get to you."

Dana sat down at the dining table, slung her feet up on a chair and took a large slug. Talking to her father always raised her spirits. He knew what it was like. Trying to do what was best while others dragged you down. He let it roll off him. He never took it personally. She could learn something from that. "Thanks, Dad."

"And your mother wants to know if you met a man."

"Lots."

"That's my girl. You hold out." Unlike her parents who conceived her on an early date and married in haste. "Good things come to those who wait. Just don't wait too long and don't settle for mica when there's gold."

"What if you can't get to it?" The thing was, she knew the gold was there, just buried too deep for her to reach. Seven years ago she got there, but now there seemed no way.

"Be there, baby. Hold out your hand. It'll come."

Dana chugged more beer. "I don't think that's how it works."

"You'll be surprised."

They talked for a few minutes and then hung up. Dana finished her beer and made a grilled cheese sandwich. Then she took a shower and went to bed and didn't sleep all night.

Wednesday

Chapter 33

On Wednesday morning, McCoy rose early after a restless night. He was unable to fall back asleep after a midnight phone call from Agent Ackerman, who was eager to dispense free advice. Until they identified the terrorist, McCoy was warned not to trust anyone lest he be led astray, and his inquiry intentionally derailed.

Ackerman would, of course, be referring to Dana Sparks. According to Ackerman, who had done some checking, she had both opportunity and motive. In the previous months she had placed catalogue orders for numerous strains of *Yersinia pestis*. She was under tremendous academic pressure and her contract with the university had nearly expired. She had no tenure and needed a grant that had not yet been approved. If she could show a need for the research, perhaps the grant would come and she would keep her job.

McCoy listened quietly to Ackerman's accusations. Dana Sparks was ignorant of warfare and politics. The possibility she was behind a deliberate outbreak of the plague was absurd. McCoy could not fathom her jockeying with

Islamic fundamentalists in an international scheme of terror and told Ackerman as much.

"It's always the person you suspect the least," the FBI agent said.

When he could lie in bed no longer, McCoy rose and dressed in the dark. He kissed his sleeping wife goodbye and tiptoed down the stairs. He reached the kitchen breathless and faint. He had to sit down and breathe deeply to stop his head from spinning. He stared longingly at the coffeepot. He had given up coffee after his heart attack and could use a cup now. What if he wasn't up to this? What if he failed? Failed his superiors, the university, the country. If this was a terrorist attack, it had transpired on his watch and he bore the responsibility. Would a younger, healthier man do a better job? What if he could not make the grade? McCoy felt a lump in his throat he tried to clear. It began a coughing fit he could barely control. Once again, he was fighting exhaustion though his day had barely begun.

At six in the morning, he called Greenlee Hospital for an update on admissions. The shift was changing and he had to wait to speak to Dr. Taversham, who came on the line sounding irritable and whiny.

"I just arrived," Taversham said. "Call me later."

"That won't be necessary if there are no new admissions."

But it seemed there were.

"We've got an eleven-year-old boy with bubonic plague," Taversham said. "And five people from the Lone Star Heritage Hotel have pneumonic plague."

So, the hotel was hit after all, and perhaps the intended target. The strike was less random than the pony-tailed Karl King surmised. "Anything else?"

"Not here. At the north hospital, your veterinarian, Tim Sweeny, was admitted during the night, as were two high school students and a university sophomore.

McCoy's heart tightened as if held between the pincers of a vise-grip. "What?" he said in a whisper.

"I said your veterinarian Tim Sweeny, has pneumonic plague."

"No, the high school students."

"Two seniors from Duane High."

McCoy heard no more. His daughter Margaret was a senior at that school. She could have been in the same classroom with the infected students, *breathing their air*. McCoy's chest was badly constricted. He lost his breath and began coughing so hard he couldn't stop. Something was caught in his throat, clogging his esophagus, blocking his air. He pounded his heart with his fist and the phlegm cleared. Breathing hard he pushed the receiver against his ear.

"Are you there?" Dr. Taversham said. "Are you all right?"

"Yes, yes, fine," McCoy answered sharply, though his voice was high and vibrated as if he needed air.

"Well, if there's nothing else," Taversham said.

"There is," McCoy said, fighting for control and winning. His voice sounded normal when he added, "As a precaution, I would tighten security at the hospital. Restrict visitors and post security guards at the door. Keep out the press."

"If you think it's necessary," Taversham said.

McCoy did. He dropped the receiver and stared out the kitchen window at the back yard. The tent was still there from the garden party that now seemed so long ago. He saw the jungle gym he carted down from Virginia. In his mind McCoy saw a younger Margaret scrabbling across the rungs of the high and horizontal ladder, as her mother, cringing for her safety, begged her to take care.

It was the job of parents to protect their children, to provide a safe environment. Now Margaret's health was in danger. He'd keep her home and out of harm's way, leave antibiotics for her and his wife. But what about the people in town? Was it ethical to deny other parents a chance to make a similar choice?

Yet that would mean calling the press and going public. In all likelihood the university would be closed. Rich Rutherford wouldn't come and the expected and much needed revenue would be lost. McCoy's biowarfare unit would remain a distant dream. But Margaret's school was hit!

McCoy always believed that the sacrifice to one's country was the greatest, noblest sacrifice one might make, but what about his family? The VP's trip could be put on hold, postponed, rescheduled. Margaret was only sixteen; she had a long life ahead of her. She had to be protected; the town had to be closed.

McCoy called the university president and voiced words he never thought he'd say. "I think we should go public."

"Excuse me?" said Marshall.

"It appears the hotel may be a target after all, Mitch. We'd better call a news conference."

"I got it the first time. I thought I was dreaming. TJ, you can't be serious."

Keeping his eye fixed on the jungle gym, McCoy said that he was. "We need to warn people there's a contagious bacterium in town and ask everyone to stay home."

"What do you mean, stay home? In two days time we have parents and alumni who make sizeable donations to our institute on their way to convocation. We've got political heavyweights coming—senators, congressmen and the governor of Texas, not to mention the vice president. We can't close the university."

"We'll just go a little public," McCoy said. "If we close the school, close the town, for maybe only a day, minimize exposure, we might still contain this." He took a deep breath and stared out the window where the wind was still blowing. "As soon as weather permits, we'll spray DDT. That should stop it. In the meantime we have to minimize casualties."

He paused, but there was no response, so he went on.

"If we do nothing, if we pretend all is well, and if more and more people fall ill, then this thing will escalate and an outside quarantine will be imposed on us. No one will come."

The university president exhaled heavily. "I hope you know what you're doing."

God, McCoy hoped so too.

He hung up the phone and rose from his stool slowly, like an old man with a heavy burden strapped to his back. He couldn't recall a morning when he felt so weak, so impotent, so uncertain of victory. He paused a moment, and looked up and prayed to God for help.

Skipping breakfast, but remembering his vitamin, McCoy left the cool air-conditioned comfort of his house. Christ Almighty, the wind was blowing hard and the air was wet and heavy. Across a sweep of manicured lawn, McCoy saw the orange sleeve wrapping of the Houston newspaper. Tangled in the branches of a prize rose bush was the blue-sleeved *Eagle*. McCoy retrieved his newspapers and went to his car.

Sitting in the Mercedes, with the engine running and the air conditioner cranked, McCoy unraveled the sleeve from the local paper. There, taking up the whole front page was a picture of the vice president and a reminder of his visit.

McCoy threw down the paper and opened the *Houston Chronicle*. The lead story was the result of a UN investigation of the strike against Somalia. The UN confirmed that a hospital, mosque and warehouse had been hit and suffered serious bomb damage. The U.S. was protesting, adamant that bombs alone could not have caused the extensive damage that ensued.

Taking up a bottom corner of the front page was the warning of a tropical storm. It was expected to land that morning. McCoy peered up through the windshield. Thick clouds skipped across the sky, blown by the virulent wind. He pounded his fist on the steering wheel. They were fighting even the weather. It reminded him of his last days in Vietnam, of typhoons and endless rain, of a time when the deck was stacked against him, and he led his troop to a battle that had already been lost.

Chapter 34

A pale sun climbed in a bruised and purple sky and Dana felt the chill from the air in her bones as she raced to the hospital. Had Penny made it through the night? A couple of times she had tried to call the hospital, but all she got was a taped recording and no news from Sheryl.

This morning, a tall gaunt policeman blocked the entrance to the hospital. "I'm sorry ma'am," the cop said. "There are no visiting hours today."

"Why not?" Dana peered through the glass of the automatic doors into the hallway and saw no bustle of activity that would explain the barring of visitors.

"Temporary hospital regulations, ma'am. However the phone lines are open."

What was going on? Why the security? Did the hospital know she injected Penny? But wouldn't Sheryl have called her? Dana gazed across the parking lot at the dew-soaked grass and the mist rising from it. Should she press on or go to the lab? No, she had to see Penny for herself. Smell her breath. Take her pulse. Touch her warm skin.

"Excuse me," she said, in her nicest voice. "I'm working

with the CDC on a current case. I need to follow up on some patients."

The policeman wanted to see ID and she produced a laminated badge that bore a bad picture and a university ID number. The cop checked the picture, copied down her ID number and let her pass.

A few moments later Dana stood outside ICU staring in the window. The room was vacant. The crib was empty. There was no sign of Sheryl. No nurse, no other patients. Dana banged hard on the door. No answer. She tried the knob. Locked. She jogged down the hallway to the reception desk. No one was there. Where was the lady with the nice nails? She went to the lobby. Empty. Then the bathroom, where she found Sheryl.

She was hanging over a sink, splashing water at her face. Through the mirror Dana saw her eyes lined with dark rings. Her face was pale and tight. She smelled of sweat and vomit. "Where's Penny?" Dana asked, and Sheryl looked up. Dana gripped her arm. "Where's Penny?"

"Upstairs. She's fine."

"She's fine? Fine?" Dana released Sheryl's arm and hugged her tightly, spinning her around in a circle. "When I saw you, I thought . . . I thought . . . I thought . . ."

"No, she's fine."

She was going to live, she would live, Dana could have danced on, but Sheryl was in no shape for it. "What's wrong?"

"I think I got it." Sheryl looked at her through blank, red-tinged eyes.

"How long have you been sick?"

"Since last night. I've been taking antibiotics to no avail."

"And Penny is fine. No side effects. No shock. No organ failure. No allergic reaction? Nothing?"

"The doctors are amazed."

"And Jack?"

"He might not make it," Sheryl said.

That was it then. All the proof Dana needed to know that the human response would not mimic the response of the guinea pig. She told Sheryl to wait, she would go to the lab, get the monoclonal and come back.

Twenty minutes later Sheryl was injected.

Then Dana went to see Jack. He lay in bed, twisting and turning, his fever rising in waves off his body. He was puffy and his cheeks were swollen, his skin marbled with purple. There were IV drips feeding both of his wrists and he had a cannula in his nose that delivered a steady supply of oxygen. Dana did not try to wake him up to ask if he wanted the experimental antibody. As she had with Penny, she injected the monoclonal directly into an IV line.

She was leaving the hospital when she saw Sam, looking exhausted and worn. "I have no time to talk," he said, slowing down nonetheless.

Dana thought the hospital looked eerily empty and quiet given the seriousness of the situation. ICU appeared to be closed and there were no medical personnel or auxiliary people in the corridors. No candy stripers and cleaners, no smell of breakfast cooking, no flower delivery people. "What's going on?" she asked.

"It's a nightmare," Sam said. "The hospital itself is closed, except for admissions." He fixed his gaze on her. "What are you doing here?"

"I came to see Jack Dowel. How many people are sick?"

"We've got six new cases and St. Joseph's has four. The hospital is turning ICU into a quarantine room for people with pneumonic plague. They've cleared out half the patients and sent the non-critical patients home. We've called in all our medical staff. I was due for a four-day break, and now I have to work straight through. We're on day and night." Sam lowered his voice and looked around the deserted hallway. "This is a bad strain." He added in a whisper. "It might be deliberate."

"That's impossible."

"Off the record, there's a terrorist on the loose or something. That's why cops are at the door." He looked over his shoulder. "Federal agents were here last night asking questions. The vice president is due Friday and this has something to do with his visit. It may be an extremist Muslim from Somalia, Afghanistan or Iraq. Take it from me—stay away from crowds, watch where you go. Watch who you trust."

When he left a few minutes later, Dana mulled over what he said. He was mistaken; he must have confused the CDC with the FBI. Karl and Jeff were the only federal agents around. And the policeman at the door was there to keep visitors away, not terrorists out. They couldn't take any chances with pneumonic plague and closing the hospital was a step she thought should have been taken yesterday. Now, there were fourteen cases of the plague. Fourteen people infected in three days. One person was dead. At least Penny was better.

Saved by the antibiotics or the experimental antibody?

Back at the lab, Dana examined the culture plate and the result of the disk test that had been running for nearly twenty hours. There was no clear zone. But no new growth. Perhaps adjacent to the disk, there were fewer colonies than there had been yesterday. She had not counted the colonies though, and did not know for sure if there were fewer cells.

With some strains there was a late, though dramatic response. On the outside, it might look as if nothing was happening, while on the inside the antibiotics were working, though this wouldn't be evident until the cell wall lost integrity and the bacteria were lysed. They had to wait. Four more hours. In four hours they would see a clearer picture.

But what if the bacteria were resistant? At least now they knew the monoclonal worked, though how could Dana admit that? And how would Penny's recovery be interpreted?

Chapter 35

The painter was hard at work when McCoy arrived at the conference room Wednesday morning. To his horror, once again the room was an oven and the air conditioner sat on the floor strangled by its own wires. The windows were shut. The curtains were gone and the room was bright. The paint fumes were suffocating, almost as bad as the hot, humid air that choked him.

Lacking the energy to be pleasant, McCoy roared at the painter. "God damn it, you were supposed to be done yesterday."

The fool of a painter smiled vacuously and removed her paint-splattered cap. "I just got the paint."

"What's wrong with the air conditioner?"

"Nothing. I had to move it so I could paint."

McCoy marched to the end of the room and began opening windows.

"I had strict orders not to open them, Sir."

McCoy shook his head and opened the last window. "When the air conditioner is on, the windows are closed."

He returned to his seat, he had to sit down. "I've got a meeting. Come back later."

"Another meeting." She looked at him in dazed wonderment. "When should I come back?"

"When we're through. Just make sure when you're finished, you leave the air conditioner running. And bring back my blackboard."

"I could get that now."

"Perfect."

After she left, McCoy held his head in his hands. He was sweating profusely. His shirt was soaking wet. Behind his scalp, his head was tightening. McCoy had not felt this weak since his heart attack. Here was a potential terrorist threat, an attack against his country and what he wanted more than anything was sleep.

He closed his eyes, and must have fallen asleep sitting up. He woke up when the painter came back for her purse. He looked at the clock, the meeting was about to start.

When all were present, he began with an announcement. "I'm afraid we have a situation on our hands." He was appalled by the indolence in his tone but his energy was gone and he could not revive himself. To surprised faces, he announced the closing of the university and the town. "The mayor will make an announcement shortly."

At the table, Nellie gasped.

"We will help staff three information centers." He held up three fingers. "At St. Joe's, Greenlee and the campus health clinic. I drew up a timetable." He passed it around the room, caught sight of Michael Smith.

"I'm afraid we will have to reschedule your lecture."

"That is no problem," Michael said.

McCoy smiled at him. "Fine. Now I want you to remember, when dealing with the public, discretion is the word." To his own ears, McCoy sounded like a record stuck on a slow speed, but there was nothing he could do about it. "The goal is to alleviate fear and promote early detection.

You may speak in vague or scientific terms only. No one will mention aloud the word "plague." Call it an infection if you will, a bacterial infection if you must. You may talk about *Yersinia*, lung infections, prophylactic antibiotics, excellent chance of recovery, et cetera, et cetera. You will appeal to people's reason and convince them to stay in town. Doctors here in Duane are prepared for the outbreak, while doctors in distal locations won't know what to do. Assure everyone all is well." McCoy ended his monologue and slumped in his seat. Just speaking wore him out. He could not in his life remember ever being this tired and wondered for a moment if he had been drugged.

Beside him, Karl asked if he was all right.

"Fine. Fine. What have you trapped?"

"We snared thirty rodents in and around Duane last night. I'm afraid we didn't collect any rats or mice in the park."

Of course he would miss the target.

"But we did catch a few more squirrels and a chipmunk. They appear healthy, but we'll have to confirm that with blood work."

McCoy looked at Dr. Sparks. "Did you test the samples from the park yesterday?"

She did and the results were negative.

Karl stretched out his legs. "I don't know if you heard, but five people from the Lone Star Heritage Hotel are ill. Also, Tim Sweeny from here. Two high school seniors. A sophomore who worked at the car wash. And an elementary school boy. A total of fourteen, if you count Dudley Shaw."

McCoy didn't count dead people. Nor did he count people in Houston. "We have twelve infected."

"I spoke to the kid, Travis Trelane, last night," Karl said. "He has bubonic plague and for an eleven-year-old, he's quite lucid. He said he's been to High Park and the Lone Star Heritage Hotel. He also had a cat that's been missing for over a week. All he talked about was the cat."

"I saw Travis this morning," Nick said, "and he wasn't good. Not lucid at all. His doctor said during the night his condition deteriorated rapidly. They're pumping him full of antibiotics, but his prognosis is not good."

Dr. Sparks raised her hand and said, "Could the bacteria be resistant to antibiotics? It's been twenty hours and as yet, there is no clear zone."

McCoy shook his head. "You must have made a mistake. We have clinical evidence the antibiotic cocktail works. Penny Farr recovered. Repeat the test. Michael, lend her a hand."

"I don't need a hand," she said. "There is no mistake. The antibiotics aren't working. This eleven-year-old boy got worse over night. And Jack almost died."

"Jack's fine," Karl countered. "I just spoke to the hospital. Frankly, they're astounded. They didn't expect him to make it. So, we know the antibiotics are working." McCoy did not miss the blatant smile he threw Dr. Sparks.

"Carol isn't responding," Nick said. "I talked to her doctor and she is critical."

"The antibiotics work," McCoy said. "People are recovering. It takes time."

"It's the monoclonal antibody," Dana said.

McCoy heard a sudden, insistent pounding in his head. No, it was the door. The painter was back with the blackboard. McCoy waved her away. What did Sparks just say? "Excuse me?"

From far away, McCoy heard her say, "The antibiotics aren't working. The monoclonal is."

He couldn't have heard her correctly. McCoy stood up, leaned forward and braced himself on the table. "What?" he said, in a desperately small voice. Had she tried her monoclonal on people? Was she out of her mind? It had only been used on lab animals. There were regulations to follow, rules, procedures. Experimental vaccines were used only after the most rigorous of tests. It required FDA approval. You couldn't inject people with an experimental vaccine. It was insane. Especially after the guinea pigs' response. McCoy breathed deeply and placed his hand on his solar plexus.

The room began to spin. He blinked his eyes to clear his sight and prayed to God his ears would stop ringing. He wondered if he would faint. He pressed hard on his chest to make his heart stop racing. The room felt close around him. He turned to the window and the fresh air that could not reach him. There was no air and McCoy staggered, trying to keep his balance when a blackness fell upon him. He tried to call for help, but he had no breath. A vice had clamped his lungs together and an unbearable force pushed his body to the floor . . .

Chapter 36

Dana heard a clunk as McCoy's head smacked the table, then a thud as his body slammed the floor. Karl leapt out of his seat and was on his knees loosening McCoy's tie and yelling for an ambulance. Nellie pulled a cell phone from her purse. Nick straddled McCoy's chest and administered CPR. Dana, hovering over them, covered her mouth to hold back her screams.

Fairway was pushing people back, herding them to the door, trying to make room. Dana couldn't move. What if McCoy didn't recover? What if she killed him? Why couldn't she have kept quiet? What if she was wrong? What if the antibiotics worked and she didn't have to use the monoclonal?

The shrill sound of a siren drew near. Footsteps pounded in the hall and attendants in white rushed in. McCoy was lifted to a stretcher. A respirator placed over his mouth. Dana turned away from his ashen face and sweat-soaked skin. Bile rose in her throat and she staggered against a wall. She bowed her head as McCoy was rushed from the room with Nick in pursuit.

Would McCoy die? Dana pressed her hand over her mouth. She thought she might throw up.

Karl draped a heavy arm across her shoulder "Let's get out of here." He led her out of the conference room, through the head office and into a hall filled with curious veterinary students milling around after the cancellation of their morning exam.

Karl steered her down the hallway. Her feet felt wooden and numb and she was weak and dazed. Her mouth was dry and her throat was sore. She was sweating and her shirt stuck to her skin.

Doubts assailed her. What if the antibiotics worked? What if the plate was contaminated with bacteria other than *Yersinia*? Maybe the antibiotics she used had expired. Maybe she hadn't reformulated them properly. She wasn't absolutely sure the monoclonal explained Penny and Jack's recovery. They were young and healthy, and their infections had been caught early; maybe the antibiotics just took time. Time Dudley didn't have. Maybe she gave the monoclonal without justification, and a man had a heart attack for no reason, and she had sacrificed her reputation, for nothing.

With his hand tight on her shoulder, Karl ushered her into her lab. He closed the office door and poured two cups of coffee. Caffeine was not what she needed. Her hand trembled so badly that coffee slopped over the side of the cup. She put it down. *What if she had made a mistake?* That week she had not been totally focused on her work. *What if she had made a mistake?*

Karl's cell phone rang and he worked it out of his pocket. Nick calling to tell him that McCoy was stable and that the mayor was about to make a statement.

They went into the main lab and Dana switched on the radio, tuned it to the local station. Karl sat down on top of Sheryl's desk. There was a *beep, beep, beep*: the alarm that preceded a severe weather warning and then the mayor came on:

We are afflicted at this time in the city of Duane with a se-
vere form of influenza that is highly contagious and inva-
sive. While there is no need to panic, in an effort to minimize
the spread of disease, we are at this time closing all schools.
Parents are asked to retrieve their children immediately.

Furthermore, any individual who experiences flu-like
symptoms, symptoms which include fever, chills, muscular
aches and pains, lung congestion, or difficulty breathing, is
to proceed to the hospitals.

I repeat, there is nothing to fear, no reason to panic, no
reason to leave town. Local physicians are equipped to deal
with the health emergency and have all the necessary med-
ical and pharmaceutical supplies on hand.

As a precaution, the governor is sending in the National
Guard for reinforcement. They will be in position at all ac-
cess roads leading in and out of town. They will remain on
standby in case of emergency.

As a final note, any individual who may have been in con-
tact with anyone exhibiting these flu-like symptoms may
commence a course of prophylactic antibiotics that may be
collected, free of charge, from either hospital, or the health
center on campus. There are sufficient drugs for all.

I repeat, we are in no danger of running out of medicine.
If you have any questions, any problems, information is
available at any of the three medical centers. I thank you for
your attention and repeat there is no need to panic. Thank
you for your attention.

Karl stood up. "That sounded pretty good."

Dana switched off the radio and stared at him dumb-
founded. The mayor sounded alarmed himself. He was out
of breath and his sentences were choppy. The way he kept
repeating there was no need to panic made it seem as if
people were already panicking. When he assured people
there were enough drugs, she wondered if he was worried
they would run out.

Karl wanted to see the disk test and they went to the quarantine room. At the hood, he lifted the lid and stared at the culture plate, pulling at his chin. There was something different about him today. "Hard to tell isn't it," he said. "Compared to the control, there might be the beginning of a response." He replaced the lid. "I guess we have to wait."

She returned the plate to the incubator.

"I'll give you a hand testing the new blood," Karl said.

"I can do it." Dana wondered if Karl was worried about her mental state and afraid she'd make a mistake.

"It'll go faster if I lend a hand," he said. "I mean, if you don't mind."

She wondered why he thought she'd mind.

They began the blood assay. Karl talked constantly while he worked. Despite everything that had happened, he looked happy and his face was shiny and Dana realized what was different about him. He had shaved off his goatee. He looked better without it.

He invited her to come to Atlanta, to tour the CDC and see the town. It was much more culturally advanced than Duane and if the weather and traffic weren't better, the restaurants and bars were something to see. "L-l-let me know if you want to come and I'll s-s-set it up."

Dana heard the stutter and wondered if he was more nervous than he appeared and trying to hide it. It only increased her anxiety. She couldn't remember a worse morning in her life. Her emotions were pulled in all directions; first her fear of Penny dying, then the euphoria of her recovery, then Jack's decline and McCoy's heart attack, not to mention Tim Sweeny's illness. She was appalled by her disregard for him, had assumed he was in Washington D.C. and forgotten all about him. Her mind had been elsewhere.

She asked Karl how Tim was.

"Last night, unconscious. Not speaking."

"This week he was supposed to go to D.C."

"According to his girlfriend, he got sick and never went."

"His girlfriend?"

"The young lady who brought him in. She was sick too, but he was much worse than her."

"When did he get sick?" she asked. They were beginning the ELISA assay. Sitting elbow to elbow at the bench on high stools. The fan on the hood was making a loud rattle and caused them to talk in raised voices.

"We're not sure," Karl said, shoving a yellow tip on the end of the small Gilson pipette. "Anyway, he was apparently treating himself. He injected himself with gamma globulin and about six different antibiotics."

"Why didn't he go to the hospital?"

Karl shrugged his shoulders, picked up the immunological plate and began dispensing killed bacteria into wells, while Dana diluted animal sera.

"Maybe he was the index case," Dana said. "He could have picked up something from an animal. It's happened in the past."

"Does he come in your lab?"

"You think he was infected here? That he came in and inadvertently picked up the bacteria?"

"Well, something like that."

Dana passed him the rack with the diluted sera. "No, he never came back here," she said.

"And this room is locked all the time?"

She pulled a face. "Not always."

Karl said nothing and Dana wondered if he still believed the origin was her lab.

They finished the assay and the results were negative. Thirty rodents collected in and around Duane the previous evening weren't exposed to *Yersinia*. The squirrels and chipmunks trapped in High Park were healthy.

It was so strange, Dana thought, that there was no wildlife infection. At the moment more people were infected than rodents. It was not a typical picture of the plague. Why weren't more animals infected?

An answer came to her. What if the bacteria were brought in by someone that came and went? They had considered Jack's mother, but their ranch had been checked and was clean. But what if another visitor came to Duane and was just passing through? Someone who stayed at a hotel, say the Lone Star Heritage, where both Penny and Tim had been on the weekend.

"The results don't support an origin at the park," Dana said.

Karl agreed.

"The hotel makes more sense."

Karl looked at her.

"If there's no trail of the bacteria into town, maybe a guest was infected."

Karl nodded his head. "It's looking more and more like it may have been brought in."

Chapter 37

Dana was scheduled to staff the information booth at the health center on campus from ten to one, but she was going to be late. University Drive was clogged with cars. No one was out on the street inhaling contaminated air. Dana drove with the windows closed.

The wind was still gusting, at times from the south, other times from the north. The sky was gray and the air clammy and cool. Five days ago it was in the eighties and now Dana ran the heater. Gone was the heat Nick said would save them.

The car crawled along. On Dana's right stood the deserted campus, on her left, shrouded in gray, the Lone Star Heritage Hotel. Past that, the University Plaza, which was unusually uninhabited. For once there was no line-up at the car wash where another victim of bubonic plague had been employed. Beyond the Plaza was the park, where four diseased rats had been trapped. Why weren't more rats and mice trapped in the park? Where had the traps been laid? Up in the trees? Or were the rats and mice dead and their bodies gone? But gone where and taken by whom?

Dana made an abrupt left turn, pulled into the University Plaza and took a shortcut through the parking lot to the park. Leaving the car idling on the side of the road, she jumped out, rattled the chain on the park's locked gate and roused the attention of a young man carrying two animal cages. He wore overalls and a bandanna tied around his face like a bandit. She called him over.

The man reached the gate. He was young, about twenty, with stringy black hair.

"I'm working with the CDC," Dana said. "Can I speak to the person in charge."

"That would be me." The young man extended his hand. "Howie Dryer, Parks and Rec."

As Dana got older, everyone else seemed to get younger. "Are you in charge of setting the traps?"

Howie admitted he was. "Must have laid out thirty traps last night. Didn't catch much." He stroked the skin over his lips. It looked to Dana as if he was trying to grow a moustache. "I think the bait's no good."

"Why do you say that?"

"We're looking for rats and field mice, and I know they're around, but we're not catching them." Howie shrugged. "I don't think the animals like Ritz crackers and peanut butter."

"Really?" Dana was surprised, for her research mice loved peanut butter.

"When you're used to dining on lobster thermidor and steak Diane, crackers don't cut it," Howie said.

"Lobster?"

Howie pointed to a Dumpster at the edge of the University Plaza. "That's where Caprice throws their leftovers. I think the animals go there to eat."

It made sense, Dana thought. The cage traps used food bait. They weren't enticing the rats and mice with food, because the rodents weren't hungry.

Dana had one more question. According to Sheryl, the

park was notoriously clean of fire ants and most insects. So much so, that the kids in the daycare had trouble finding bugs for their collection. "Do you use pesticides here?"

"Twice a month," Howie said. "Every other Monday. We're due for a repeat next week."

Which meant the park had been sprayed recently. Howie didn't know the name of the chemical, but he thought it was likely effective against fleas.

Dana thanked Howie for his information and headed toward the Dumpster. Did the pesticide explain the anomaly that more rodents in the park weren't infected? If the pesticide killed fleas, it would also kill the bacteria. It was McCoy's thankfully aborted aerial campaign on a smaller scale.

Dana reached the rusted Dumpster and lifted the warped and squeaky lid. There was a rancid smell of rotting trash. The Dumpster had been recently cleaned but it still stank. Flies buzzed loudly. She saw no steak or lobster, but instead, banana peels, smushed strawberries, droopy lettuce rinds and a flattened birthday cake.

What would they get if they laid a trap here? Dana dropped the Dumpster lid and wiped her hands together.

Back in her car, Dana drove around the corner and stopped to see Becker. The front door to the bungalow opened as she pulled into the drive. Becker stood in the doorway in safari pants and a yellow polo shirt. "Come in, come in. Tell me what's happening."

He ushered her into the house, into the living room, where he pointed to a couch, covered in a pink crocheted blanket.

There had been no evidence of his late wife in the kitchen, but her presence filled the living room. She smiled at Dana from a wedding photo; she was there in the doilies on the table, on the petit point pictures hanging on the walls, in the knitted pillows.

Becker sat down beside her.

"Feeling better?" she said.

"Lots. What did I hear on the radio? A cryptic message for people to leave town?"

"Or to start panicking, that we'd run out of drugs," she said.

"Too bad if we do, now the roads in and out of town are sealed and the National Guard is here to make sure everyone stays put."

"I hope it's not too late," she said.

"I hope someone informed the wildlife not to roam."

Dana ran her hand across the blanket and poked her finger through one of the crocheted holes. "That's just it. The wildlife doesn't seem to be infected. The CDC thinks Penny is the index case and was infected in the park, but I don't see how. Nothing makes sense. It's too confusing. I don't get it."

Becker offered tea and she declined. He said, "Hold the confusion in your head. It's like muddy water. Wait for it to clear."

"I don't know how epidemiologists stand this. Too many unanswered questions."

"That's because too many pieces are missing. Or one big one. Just wait."

"But there's no time." She smoothed out the blanket. It had been made by sewing together hundreds of little crocheted circles. Becker's wife had been a patient woman.

"How are you?" Becker asked. "You're not looking well yourself."

Dana came around to the reason she had come. "McCoy had another heart attack."

"Well, he would, wouldn't he. War or not, that man lives in the midst of one."

"It was my fault. I think this strain of *Yersinia* is resistant. I injected Penny with the monoclonal antibody."

"Penny? Penny is sick?"

"Not any more. But I thought she was dying. Still, I used the monoclonal without authorization."

Phillip sat forward in his easy chair, elbows on his knees. "You may have saved her life. You shouldn't feel guilty."

"Phillip, I injected her with an experimental drug."

"After what happened to the guinea pig, that took guts."

"I was desperate."

"Of course you were, if the antibiotics don't work."

"We don't know that for sure. Not absolutely. But so far, the only people who have recovered are the two people who took the monoclonal antibody."

"I fail to see the problem," Phillip said. "You did what you had to do. What's this about authorization? You said no—you don't authorize Penny to die. And I say, good for you. You made a hard choice but it was correct. If you follow your heart, it will show you the way."

Once again, Dana hoped he was right.

She left a few minutes later, and saw him watching through the window as she drove away, heading for campus. As she drove, intermittent drops of rain splashed at her windshield. On the radio she heard a weather update. The tropical storm had hit land south of Houston and was moving fast. People as far north as Dallas were supposed to take precautions. It was the last thing they needed now.

On the main campus, Dana parked her car in the Genetics building lot and went on foot to the health center. She heard the noise before she saw the crowd that swarmed the clinic. There must have been two or three hundred people, more than she could count. They were jostling each other, pushing, shoving, yelling and hitting a hard wall. The clinic was locked, the doors tightly chained.

And there at the front of the clinic, stood Charlie Lane and Michael Smith dispensing boxes of antibiotics. Dana tried to push her way to the front. Her clothes were billowing with the wind, and overhead there was the rumble of thunder, a few drops of rain.

She was midway through the crowd when Michael clambered up on the table. His shoes were white. He was dressed in a three-piece suit, complete with vest and baby blue tie that matched the color of the windbreaker he wore over his blazer. He was dressed for his seminar that had been cancelled. He raised his hands.

"We are out of antibiotics," he yelled.

The roar of the crowd and a loud clap of thunder drowned him out.

"Do not worry," he added. The thunder stopped and the crowd was bellowing again.

Beside him, the eight-month-pregnant Charlie Lane scrambled up on the table and tried to talk to the crowd. "We'll get more antibiotics and come back."

Get down, get down, Dana silently urged her. *Go home.* It wasn't so much of a crowd as a mob. With renewed vigor, Dana pushed forward, enduring the elbows and kicks and jeers of those rightly protesting her progress.

Suddenly the sky turned dark, as if a light had been switched off. There was an abrupt and shocking silence. The wind stopped blowing. A jagged line of lightning cracked the sky and thunder pealed. The rain began to fall and people began to run.

Against her now, pushing her farther back. In a minute she was drenched, rain dumping from the sky, pelting down. She could not see three feet in front of her.

In five minutes she gave up her search for Charlie. The crowd had scattered.

Dana ran to her car, head lowered, back hunched and clothes plastered to her skin. She raced back to the vet school. What did it mean now that the prophylactic antibiotics were gone? Was it just the campus clinic or the whole town? If the roads were closed, did that also mean that no planes were flying in and out of Duane? Could they get more drugs if they ran out?

Dana drove through the pouring rain to the vet school. There were only a few cars in the lot and the main doors were locked. Inside, the building was eerily empty, her footsteps echoing off the walls. Classrooms, offices and labs were locked, the hallway vacant. Her lab was open and she went into her office and found Karl pacing.

"Good, you're here." He too was soaking wet, his ponytail limp at the back of his neck. "We have a problem." There was no trace of a smile, no hint of humor.

"I know," Dana said. "We're out of prophylactics."

"Doesn't matter. The prophylactics don't seem to work. Betty is sick and so is a friend of Jack's who's been taking prophylactics since yesterday."

Dana sunk onto her desk. Tetracycline was used both for treatment and as a prophylactic. If the drug didn't work as a cure, it wouldn't work as a preventative.

Karl wanted to see the disk test and they went to the quarantine room and checked the culture plate. There was no clear zone and by now twenty-four hours had passed. The antibiotics were ineffective. They had no effective treatment for fifty thousand people. No treatment and no preventative. Karl was uncharacteristically quiet as they left the quarantine room. In the lab, there was a loud crack of thunder and rain slogged at the windows.

"The monoclonal antibody," Dana said, "we can use it. But we have to get it back from Fort Troy."

Karl rubbed his chin where the goatee used to be. "*No*. There are other antibiotics that are effective against resistant *Yersinia*. Trimethoprim for example."

"How do you know it will work?"

"It was used successfully in Madagascar."

"Is there enough for everyone?"

"Nick flew in cartons of it this morning." Karl was staring out the window. The wind shook the windowpanes. "Have you seen him?"

"No."

"I'm going to the hospital to alert the doctors about the

antibiotic failure. Look for Nick and ask him to meet me there."

Karl was gone at a jog and Dana understood that if Nick had ordered the trimethoprim that he, too, had been worried about resistance. She was suddenly more worried. They were working blind now, and dealing with a virulent strain of resistant *Yersinia* they knew nothing about. How did they know the trimethoprim would work? They needed time to check its efficacy and time they didn't have.

Chapter 38

The rain caught Nick by surprise. At first his fever had welcomed the cool relief, but now he was freezing and unable to summon the energy to move. Huddled at a rickety picnic bench under a grove of trees, he shivered as icy water ran down his skin and waves of rain swept past him. He lowered his head to the picnic table and hugged his shaking body with his soaking arms. He seldom got sick. He had worked when he had typhoid, malaria and cholera, but he couldn't work through this.

He was vaccinated against *Yersinia* and had been for almost twenty years. He had received the latest vaccines, multiple vaccines, vaccines that were supposed to last a lifetime. Yet, he had the plague. It wasn't possible but it was so.

Three hours ago, he had taken a double dose of trimethoprim and was waiting for it to work. It was a folic acid inhibitor, a bactericide rather than a growth inhibitor. He must have a high titer of bacteria in his body to be this sick. Maybe he should have taken more of the drug. Or perhaps the bacteria were resistant even to this.

Did Dana suspect as much? Is that why she used the monoclonal? She had tried to talk to him about it last night and he had brushed her off. He should have listened to her, tried to talk her out of her foolish plan. Her questions made sense now and he should have paid more attention, tried to stop her.

Nick was simultaneously exasperated and awed by the risks that she took. Still, she demonstrated a lack of foresight, a failure to assess all options. Their backs weren't yet against the wall. They still had choices. There were new antibiotics. If not trimethoprim, then other experimental antibiotics that were at a late stage of human testing. Dana had reacted emotionally, though she had been lucky. What if Penny responded like the guinea pigs? The little girl would have died and Dana would have been responsible.

That morning Nick spoke to the national security advisor, Blaze Stodgecraft, who wanted an update on the situation. Nick said they should seal the town. Do whatever was necessary to contain the bacteria. Close the roads. Suspend air service. Disconnect the water supply. Send in the National Guard. No one should move in or out of the city until the outbreak was contained.

"Is it the work of terrorists?" Blaze asked.

Nick didn't know. He *did* know that the bacterial strain was more virulent than any he had ever seen. Was it genetically engineered to be so? He could not answer, but the general pattern of the outbreak was not right. It could be an act of war.

Nick thought he might throw up and folded his arms around his head. His stomach cramped, his head throbbed and the rain came hard. Wheeler sang to him: *It would never be easy I knew, just didn't think it would be this hard, or feel this bad . . .*

Wheeler must have sung Nick to sleep. Much time passed, one hour became two and still Nick could not move. His head was too heavy to lift from the table. His brain felt like it would explode. His whole body ached. He was either on fire with fever or shaking with cold. He was in the freezing phase now. His teeth chattered. His stomach cramped tighter and he did throw up, a violent spray of frothy, clotted blood. Now he knew what form of the plague he had. Septicemic. The worst form. The bacteria were in his blood. Did this explain the severity of his response? Did the bacteria overwhelm his immune system and render his vaccines ineffective? Was the bacterial load too high for trimethoprim? Or was it this strain of bacteria? Nick knew some strains of *Yersinia* had been bio-engineered specifically for antibiotic resistance. Was this one of those strains?

Nick tried to pry open his eyes and lift his head, but it was impossible. Wheeler sang on: *But through it all I knew, down on my knees, but not dead yet, I would do all I could do.*

The words spurred Nick on. He had to get to a phone, arrange to have the *Yersinia* DNA analyzed. But he had no energy to rouse himself. He gripped his sides with his arms, holding himself as tightly as he could to keep himself together as the rain struck and something hard and cold pressed against his face.

Chapter 39

"Nick, Nick, wake up." Dana leaned down toward him, jarring his arm. She had been searching for him for over an hour, growing more desperate as more time passed. He was not in Headquarters, not in the main office, not in the cafeteria, not at his hotel. He did not answer his beeper. She had nearly given up hope finding him when she saw him sitting facedown at a picnic table out in the rain.

She tried shaking him, calling his name, but there was no response. She sunk onto the bench beside him, slung her arm around his shoulder, lowered her head against the rain. Nick felt limp, wasted, spent. His body burned as he shivered. *He was sick, too*. He had the plague. *And he was vaccinated. He had received vaccinations for years.* He should have been immune.

She felt sick herself. *What if he died?* She began to shiver and could not stop. Beneath them, the rickety bench tottered. Nick groaned and lifted his head off the table, blinking his eyes.

"You have *Yersinia*," she said.

She thought he would deny it, but he did not.

"Septicemic," he said in a thin, weak voice.

Septicemic plague. The most deadly form of all. His blood was infected, which meant all his organs. Even with effective treatment, he could die within twenty-four hours. "You have to get to the hospital. Take trimethoprim."

"Doesn't work," he said. "I took it. Hours ago."

"The monoclonal then. We know it works."

He shook his head and the action made him wince. "There are new antibiotics. Late phase of testing. Fluoro-quinolones."

They were promising, Dana knew. New drugs that altered DNA conformation and its three-dimensional shape. The fluoroquinolone cipruboxin was touted as the new wonder drug. Still, they didn't know that it would work and had no time to test it. Nick had no time. She said, "We have to use something we know is effective."

"No."

How could she convince him to use the monoclonal? They were dealing with a super-resistant strain of *Yersinia*. The monoclonal worked; Penny proved that. The only problem was that the monoclonal was in Fort Troy and if they were going to use it, they had to get it back. With McCoy out, she needed Nick's influence and authority to convince General Shwartzke to ship it down.

"The monoclonal antibody is in Fort Troy," she said. "We need it."

"No."

"We can get it, have it on hand, in case we need it."

"No."

"We don't necessarily have to use it, just have it."

"No."

The wind blew hard across them, like the one-sided conversation. Dana saw the blood on Nick's shirt, on his face. She smelled his sickness. They had no time to argue. Nick had no time. "You need something and you need it now. I have enough monoclonal for one shot."

"No."

"Stop saying no."

It was the wrong thing to say.

As if summoning himself from a deep sleep, Nick shook his head back and forth, spraying rain from his hair. He threw back his shoulders and inhaled as though drawing energy stored deep in his core. He wiped at the dried blood on his face. His voice grew louder and stronger. *"No.* Period. You have no authorization. Do not use the monoclonal antibody. If anything goes wrong, you will be accountable. Even if it goes right, you will lose your job. You will never work in science again. Do you understand?"

He was talking to her as if she was four years old. And more concerned for her future than his own. "You could die," she said.

"And you are out of your field. You are not a physician. You cannot inject people with an experimental drug. All right?" He held her eyes. His were bloodshot and heavily hooded, as though he could barely keep them open.

They were wasting time he did not have. She knew when it came to regulations, whether they were in his best interest or not, he would follow the rules. Only one sector of his life was exempt from this and he was far from that now. "Fine. If you agree to go to the hospital."

Nick argued no further. A few minutes later, in the car on the way to the hospital, he passed out. His head fell forward, cracked on the dash. She pulled over and straightened him. His body was burning, slack and limp.

Outside the hospital, traffic was jammed. A line of ambulances and taxis were parked in the emergency-parking bay. The parking lot was plugged. Dana ditched her car at the side of the road and dashed across a flooded flowerbed. A policeman guarding the emergency door would not let her pass. Two attendants in biohazard suits came for Nick and lumped him on a stretcher as if he were already dead.

Dana was not allowed in the hospital. She returned to work, sliding through streets turned to rivers as the rain stormed down and the wind stole her sobs.

Chapter 40

Back in the lab, Dana called Karl and found him at the hospital with Nick. "How is he?"

"Moving in and out of consciousness," Karl said.

"The trimethoprim may be ineffective," she said.

"Not maybe. Is," Karl said.

She could barely hear him. The line was bad and crackled in her ear.

"Carol Dupuis had been treated with it all along," Karl said. "She fell unconscious this morning. She's not expected to live."

Dana felt a catch in her throat. What if she had remembered the rats earlier? After seeing Dudley, after running the ELISA with the positive result, after being an arm's length away from the freezer, Dana had not given one thought to the dead rats. It was out of character for her to forget, but she had, and now Carol was dying.

"We'll find an effective antibiotic," Karl said, after a long silence.

"Clinically we know the monoclonal antibody works."

Somehow Dana was going to convince someone to listen to her.

"It's not approved. Can't do it."

She wanted to take the receiver and bang it on his head. "It works."

"In two people. But we don't know the intermediate or long term effects. Hell, we don't even know the short-term effects. Imagine the malpractice suits if something went wrong. You'd take the heat."

He was worried about lawsuits? "There'll be no lawsuits if everyone dies."

"We have other experimental drugs. Drugs that the bacteria have never seen. Nick's on cipruboxin. It's close to being approved."

Dana heard a great roar of thunder. The lights blinked off, then came back on. Karl's words were fading in and out, his voice growing louder and softer. She said, "What if it doesn't work? We know the monoclonal does."

"It's out of the question. No physician would ever authorize its use. It's an illegal drug."

"That we know works."

Karl was firm. "We'll go with cipruboxin. This way, there's no personal liability. Not to you, not to anyone. It's the only way."

"The safe way," she said, but did not feel in her heart that it was the right way.

Karl hung up and Dana dropped the receiver and stared at the van Gogh. Karl was wrong. This was not the time to worry about lawsuits, or to try nearly approved antibiotics. Nick needed something and he needed it now.

She remembered a conversation they once had, in which he tried to explain chaos theory. There were points of indetermination, he said, when it appeared the system had a choice to go one way or another, and there was no predicting which direction it would go. At this point, causality broke down and the onward course was decided by some unknown factor.

Dana felt she was near such a branch point, or perhaps past it already. A faulty choice had been made, a wrong fork taken. Without effective treatment, Nick would die. The monoclonal worked, yet she had given her word she wouldn't use it.

Well, what if someone else did?

She looked at the phone. Two hours away, in Fort Troy, there was enough monoclonal for everyone. Could she call the general and ask him to send the monoclonal to Dr. Taversham at the hospital? Then the decision to use it would be his.

Dana picked up the receiver. The line was bad, spitting and buzzing with interference from the storm. General Shwartzke was the man in charge of the biological warfare program at Fort Troy, and was overseeing the vaccine trials. Dana met him once and found him cold and intimidating. He'd been pleased to learn the vaccine was ready ahead of schedule. What would he say when he learned she wanted it back?

It took time for the call to move through the army hierarchy. Finally General Shwartzke came on the line, his voice booming loud above the crackling. Dana said, "I'm calling about the vaccine." Before she could explain what she wanted, he said, "We're on schedule. We do the initial test in late June and if we get a ten-four, we expand in July. Why do you ask? Did you get your letter?"

"Letter?"

"Your grant was approved. As soon as we get the nod from McCoy, Phase Two can commence. The money is available immediately."

Her grant was approved. Dana closed her eyes. A minute ago she had nothing to lose, but now she had her grant. Her excitement was brief. After what happened today with McCoy, the approval might not matter.

"Are you there?" Shwartzke demanded.

Dana opened her eyes. "Yes, I'm here. Thank you. Thank you very much."

"Is there anything else? If that's all . . ."

"It's not all," she said, and there was a long silence. She hadn't figured out a story. She didn't know what to say. She blurted out the first pathetic excuse that came to her mind, something about changing the vaccine buffer.

A long pause. "Is there a problem with the current buffer?"

"A local reaction," she said. "We saw it in mice, but we let it go. The mice were going to be killed anyway." She tried to laugh, but it sounded forced and hollow even to her.

"Doesn't matter," the general snorted. "A local reaction is nothing to my men."

Oh no, she wasn't going to get it back. Resting her forehead in her palm, she tried to think. "It won't take long. It would mean a paper. A comparison between two buffers." Dana closed her eyes and grimaced. She was a terrible liar. Why would he believe her?

"Dr. Sparks, I suggest you confine yourself to your area of research."

"This is my area, Sir."

A long silence.

"Fine," he said. "When the weather clears, we'll ship. Just get it back mid-June."

When the weather clears. No, they couldn't wait that long. "I'd like to start as soon as possible," she said. "What if I come and get it?"

"Sounds like an emergency," Shwartzke said. She heard what sounded like a laugh. "Did McCoy put you up to this? That old dog. Do you really expect me to believe this has nothing to do with the outbreak of the plague in Duane?"

He knew, somehow he knew. She told him the truth. "We've run out of the prophylactic antibiotic and even if we had it, it doesn't matter because it doesn't work. The cocktail antibiotics aren't working either. Trimethoprim has failed as well. So has at least one vaccine."

"Why didn't you explain this earlier." Shwartzke sounded interested.

"Um . . . um . . ." An answer came to her. "It's . . . well . . . you know how discreet Dr. McCoy is. He likes as few people involved as . . ."

"Let me speak to him."

"Uh . . . well he's not here. He's at the hospital."

"Let me speak with the CDC."

"They're not here either."

"Then Nick Biget. Get him."

"Everyone is at the hospital."

Silence, and then, "You have federal permission to use the monoclonal?"

Was that skepticism or wonder she heard in his voice? She took a deep breath. She was in too deep already. "That's correct."

There was a lengthy pause. The sound of air being slowly expelled. "I'll airlift the monoclonal to the Life Flight hospital," Shwartzke said. "But with this weather, the drop won't be tonight. Tomorrow at the earliest."

"But, but . . ."

"That's all I can do."

"Thank you. If you could address the monoclonal to Dr. Taversham—he's the physician in charge at Greenlee."

"I'll send it to McCoy. Over and out."

The phone went dead. Dana dropped the receiver. She leaned her head on her desk. He was going to send it to McCoy. *He was going to send it to McCoy.* And not until tomorrow. She exhaled with difficulty. Well, there was nothing she could do. It was out of her hands now.

Not completely. She had enough of the monoclonal left for one more shot. Nick might not make it to morning. He could die tonight while she waited for the weather to clear.

Still, he said he wouldn't take it. She had given her word. She couldn't force medical treatment on someone who didn't want it.

But he could die.

Because he was worried about her, about the consequences of giving drugs without FDA approval. A medical doctor would lose their license. They would face a malpractice suit, a court of law. He was worried about her career.

But she was no medical doctor and *he could die*.

She stood up and ordered herself to stop thinking. There was no decision to make. Life came first. Before everything. It wasn't a choice.

Nick would hate her for it, though. Probably never forgive her. But at least he would be alive.

Maybe. She went to the cell culture room and picked up the vial with the remaining monoclonal antibody. There was so little left. Was it enough? She had no experience with septicemic plague, a much more serious disease than the other two forms. What if he needed more of the monoclonal antibody?

It didn't matter, there was no more. Another decision that didn't have to be made. She tucked the ampule in her bra. At least this would buy Nick some time.

She shoved a syringe into the pocket of her jeans, and a few minutes later ran splashing through puddles to her car.

With the storm, an early night had fallen. The skies were black and the wind swept waves of water across the flooded road. Thunder roared and lightning pulsed. A loud boom and a scream from the sky made her jump. The town went dark, as the power cut out. The generator roared. She saw the lights of the vet school flicker and then blaze as the emergency generator kicked in.

Dana reached her car soaking wet. She jumped in and

drove off. The windshield fogged immediately and the wipers couldn't keep up with the rain. At first she went slowly, there was tremendous drag on the tires and she left a high spray in her wake.

Out on the main road, hers was the only car. She fiddled with the radio and got static. The university station and local public station were off the air. An Austin station gave a weather update. The tropical storm had moved inland faster than predicted. After the rain of the spring, rivers and lakes were rising quickly and there was a danger of widespread flooding. She heard a reminder that the roads into and out of Duane were closed. The airport was shut. Planes were grounded and all incoming flights were suspended. The National Guard had been deployed to secure the town, and the governor of Texas had declared a state of emergency in the county.

Yes, an emergency. Dana pressed on the accelerator and sped up. She raced alongside the darkened campus, shot through an intersection past streetlights that didn't work. Ahead she saw a blinding light. Another car. Holy shit, in her lane?

She slammed on the brakes. The car careened through water, turning sideways. She let up on the brake and spun the steering wheel as the car slid off the road. There was a hard slam and darkness as the dashboard lights cut out.

Chapter 41

The car was stuck in the ditch. Dana got out and was pummeled by rain. It came like hail, pouring from the sky and sounding like a waterfall. She pushed on the fender as hard as she could and it wouldn't budge. The wind shook the trees, flinging rain, swinging power lines, rattling streetlights. The town was dark, the storm shrouding the buildings in cloud. Rain flowed in icy rivers that gushed along the roads and sidewalks. She was standing in three inches of water. Her boots were soaked through to her socks.

She wanted to be home in her warm house, under a blanket, with a glass of wine in her hand, dogs by her side. But Nick was dying. *Moving in and out of consciousness.* Dana would go to the hospital on foot.

She started walking, head bowed, rain streaming down her hair, under her clothes, into her boots. She could feel the water sloshing by her feet. The wind raged and howled and time slowed. It took longer to cross campus than she expected.

She reached the hospital. The generator lights were blinding, harsh after the darkness. Over the pouring rain the generator screamed. Dana climbed the hospital steps. At the side entrance, a policeman in a mask and suit slumped against the main door. The same emaciated policeman on guard that morning. He groggily stood up and crossed his arms. "The hospital is closed."

She didn't have her identification. "I'm Dr. Sparks," she said. "I was here earlier. I'm working with the CDC."

"Wait here."

He used a key to unlock the door and slid the automatic doors manually to the side. He came back with a clipboard and flipped through its pages. "You're not on the list." He shoved the clipboard her way.

They had a list of people they were admitting? She scanned the names. Between McCoy and Taversham there was nothing. Sparks wasn't there.

"It must be a mistake," she said. "I was here earlier." She smiled her most charming smile. "It was you; you let me in."

The policeman stood unmoved. "Believe me, you don't want to be here."

It was true, but there were times when there was a vast difference between what she wanted and what was required. The policeman sat back down.

She left him, and keeping to the edge of the building, began to circle its perimeter. What about an emergency exit? An open window? She went down the length of the building, counted the closed windows—no door. She reached the corner. Four windows along the building's width. All closed. Another corner and down the other side. Midway, there was a gray emergency door, but no outside handle. The door was flush with the door jamb. She couldn't pry it open.

She kept going, reached the front of the building. What now? She didn't know. She waited, shivering, huddled under the overhang of the roof as the rain streamed down. She waited and waited and time passed and she wondered

what to do, what to do now, when she saw movement in the
street. What looked like an injured animal, crouched low
and lumbering. A dog hit by a car? No, a man.

At the curb he stopped by a row of low bushes and vom-
ited. Dana saw his shoulders heaving, heard him retching.
He wore a baby blue windbreaker, white shoes. *Michael*.

Dana ran toward him, called his name. He wiped his
mouth and stared up.

He had it too. His dark eyes had lost their glitter and he
looked afraid, like a deer caught in the glare of a headlight.
He was shivering, rose shakily, reached out his hand. She
helped him up and together they staggered toward the
emergency entrance and up the stairs. A heavyset policeman guarding this door moved out of the way. They went
inside. The emergency room was crammed full with the
sick. A baby wailed loudly above the coughing. There was
blood on the walls. The floor was covered with patients lying like scattered pickup sticks. Dana remembered her
slide and looked up; there were no archangels hovering
overhead launching poisonous arrows. If there was a force
of good, it was gone from here.

A tired-looking nurse slumped at the desk with her head
encircled in the crook of her arm. Dana woke her up. The
nurse flung an arm at the waiting room. There was a line-
up to see the doctors. It snaked down the hall.

Dana helped Michael to the end, helped lower him to the
floor. How many people were ahead of him? A hundred?
He was shivering and she wished she had something to
cover him with but she did not.

He closed his eyes, fell back against the wall.

She stood up. "I'll be back."

She walked quickly down the hall toward the bathroom
and stopped at the nurses' station. There was no one there.
She ran around the counter and typed Nick's name into the
computer. He was in ICU.

She went down the hall, grabbed a package of quarantine clothes from a pile and went to the bathroom. She took off her clothes, rolled them up in a ball and carefully placed them behind the trashcan. She would come back for them later. Her skin was splattered with mud and she washed her hands, then threw on sunny yellow quarantine clothes and hurried to ICU. Pounded on the door, waited. She inhaled deeply, feeling detached, uninvolved, as if what was happening wasn't real. She'd had dreams that were more real than this.

The door opened. Sam. In this strange dream, it couldn't be, but it was. He pulled off his hood. He was still working, dressed in a dirtied, bloodied yellow suit and holding an unlit cigarette in his hand. "Oh, it's you Doctor."

Dana said hello with enthusiasm she didn't feel and had no idea of its source "I'm here to assess the situation. What do we have?" Would he send her away? Call the cops? Her indifference to the outcome surprised her.

Sam leaned against the door jamb, yawning. A gray gristle of a beard was sprouting on his coffee-colored face. "I thought you guys gave up. That you were too scared to come make your nightly assessment." His voice was flat, like a talking computer. "The antibiotics don't work." He shoved the cigarette in his mouth. "I guess you know that."

Sam lit the cigarette, though Dana knew that the hospital was a smoke-free environment. You couldn't even smoke in the cafeteria. Sam stuffed the match in his pocket and exhaled smoke at the ceiling.

"You're okay?" she said. "You didn't get sick?"

"I appear to be protected." He let smoke drift out his mouth and inhaled it through his nose. "And you?"

"I'm fine, too."

"Have you given blood? We need antiserum from everyone who isn't sick. For the critically ill patients," Sam said.

"I'll go when I'm through here," Dana said. "Can I come in?"

"Karl never asked for permission." Sam dropped the cig-

arette and crushed the burning ember with the tip of his
shoe. He bent down and retrieved the long butt and shoved
it in his pocket, pushed open the door to ICU.

The room was crammed with beds arranged row-by-row
against two walls. It reminded Dana of an orphanage dor-
mitory she had seen on an elementary school trip years
ago. There were no doctors or other nurses in sight. Sam
passed her a clipboard and told her to sign in. "New regulations. Like we need more red tape."

She scribbled her name, a scrawl she hoped no one
would recognize. Then she surveyed the room that was
dark and lit only by the unnatural light of monitors. There
must have been forty beds, forty men, coughing, retching,
sobbing, wailing amidst a background of machines rhyth-
mically pumping and clicking.

Where was Nick? She said, "How is everyone doing?"
Though a moron could see no one was well.

"You came at a bad time," Sam said. "Karl made the
same mistake and I can tell you he didn't make it again.
I'm making rounds and dispensing medication. Useless antibiotics for grins. Morphine for sedation."

"Do you mind if I look around? Peek at a chart or two?"

"Be my guest."

"Are we in danger of losing anyone?"

"Oh yes," Sam said, without hesitation. "Everyone."

"Nick Biget?" Dana could barely speak his name.

"He's not good." Sam pointed to a bed. "He's the epidemiologist on this case. Should have known better than to
let it go so long. He's in trouble." Dana looked at Nick and
drew a sharp breath. He lay on his back, tossing back and
forth, covered in a tangle of wires and cords and tubing.
He was moaning, as he did sometimes in his dreams: ah,
ahh, ahhh.

"I'll give him morphine," Sam said.

"Please."

Dana stood out of the way while Sam grabbed a bottle

from his cart and filled a syringe. He gave Nick an IV injection and then returned to his cart and the next patient.

Dana sank to her knees by Nick's bed. He wore a yellow smock that made his skin look green. She worked off her hood and dropped it on the floor. The morphine worked fast and within two minutes his breathing was slow. Beside the bed, a monitor showed rhythmic snaking blips. Dana leaned her elbows on the bed and studied Nick's face. His eyelids fluttered, his face was white, his lips were pale and pink. He had a round red bump in the middle of his forehead where he had banged his head on the dashboard of her car. The shaving cut on his chin near his dimple had begun to heal. She reached out and ran her finger lightly across his cheek. His skin was soft, no five o'clock shadow. Were his follicular cells too sick to function?

She leaned into him and jumped when he opened his eyes. *Go back to sleep*, she willed him.

He closed his eyes. She breathed with relief, then gasped when he took her hand. He closed his fingers around hers and bent his elbow, curling their hands over his heart. She could feel it beating. He rolled towards her, still cupping her hand, holding it tight. She lay her head beside him on the bed as she had often done a lifetime ago. The wheels on the cart wobbled as Sam pushed ahead. She would wait until he was further away and then give Nick the injec—

She shot up. She didn't have a syringe. She left it in a pocket of her slacks that were in the bathroom. Shit. How could she have forgotten it?

Should she go back for it? Risk being seen, being caught? There must be a syringe here. She looked at Sam. He had a syringe in his hand. She glanced at his cart, saw a row of bottles, each with a syringe. Why not? Everyone was hooked up to IVs and receiving the same drugs. A single syringe could be used for each medication.

She went to the desk at the front of the room. There was a computer, phone, canister filled with pens, a stack of forms, but no syringes. She looked in the trashcan and saw paper—syringes weren't left lying around.

An alarm began to beep. The one by Nick's bed. She ran to him. Scanned the monitor. His blood pressure had fallen. His heart had stopped. A straight line cursed across the screen. She screamed for Sam, already sprinting toward her.

"He's gone." Sam reached down and pulled the sheet up over the man in the bed next to Nick's. Dana had been staring at the wrong monitor. The alarm screeched and a red button flashed. Sam punched the power switch with his fist. There was a loud silence and then Sam tore wires and hoses from the machine. He wheeled the bed with the dead man toward the door.

Sam was gone. The door closed behind him and Dana was down the length of ICU at the medicine cart. She yanked a syringe from a bottle. How much time did she have? Sam wouldn't be gone long. He couldn't leave all these patients unattended. She raced back to Nick, worked the ampule out of her bra.

He was asleep.

She sucked the amber solution into the syringe. Sweat rolled down her underarms. A drop of monoclonal antibody solution remained in the vial. She drew it up. Every drip counted. No time to lose. She pulled back the sheet and lifted Nick's arm.

With her mind screaming to go slow, she worked the syringe onto the IV's free end. She depressed the plunger. Nick did not move. His eyelids fluttered and he dreamed on. His shirt was damp and spotted with mud. Her hair was still dripping with rain. She counted one thousand and one, one thousand and two, one thousand and three. The plunger met resistance. She disengaged the syringe and heard a pop.

No, that was the door. Sam was back, rolling an empty bed.

She hid the syringe in the palm of her hand and waited as Sam made the adjacent bed. He fluffed the pillow, slipped it into a case. Threw open a sheet and smoothed down the corners, making even, precise envelope tucks.

He returned to his cart. Dana tightened her grip on the syringe. She had to get it back. Sam flipped through a chart, reading intently. How would she do it?

She approached the cart. Could she return the syringe without attracting Sam's notice? No. She saw a medical chart perched precariously on an edge of the cart. Dana knocked it with her elbow. The metal chart thunged to the floor. Sam bent down to pick it up and while he was down, Dana thrust the syringe into the vial. Sam stood up and she apologized.

"Sorry about that. Guess I'll make my report."

Wide-eyed, she watched Sam put away one chart and reach for the syringe she returned. She went past him, on her way to the door. She had the handle in her hand when he called her.

She froze, wondering if she would faint. Should she run for it or turn? She swiveled, wondering if at that distance he would notice her distress.

"You forgot to sign out."

"Right." She went to the desk and scribbled on the page.

Chapter 42

The serology lab on the fourth floor of the hospital had been equipped with cots and blood bags and was being serviced by the gigantic German nurse who had moved Penny to ICU. Dana lay prone on a cot, a needle sticking out of her arm, her blood running through a tube to a pint bag. It was running slowly and Dana felt more weak and tired with every lost milliliter. She closed her eyes. How was she going to get home?

"You are coming very late," the nurse said.

Dana opened her eyes; the nurse was staring down at her.

Nurse Herzog was a tall, thick woman with brassy blond hair pulled back in a bun. She wanted to know why Dana hadn't answered the call for blood earlier. "There are many people sick. They will die. Antiserum is all we have." She was taking two pints of Dana's blood, instead of the usual one.

Antiserum was blood plasma that contained antibodies. Presumably, healthy people exposed to bacteria had developed protective antibodies, which were in the blood plasma and could be donated to other people. Dana asked how many people gave antiserum.

"Not enough. With you, there are five. Myself, I have once been ill with *Yersinia enterocolitica*. There seems to be a cross-reaction. Dr. Taversham himself has had the plague. A patient's mother and another nurse are fine. We are not knowing why. And you?"

"I've been vaccinated many years," Dana said.

"As are others who are ill," the nurse said.

"Each person is different." Dana closed her eyes again, hoping her blood would flow quickly and she could leave. It took nearly an hour for the bags to fill and though the nurse wanted her to stay and rest, drink juice or tepid water, Dana bolted.

She went too quickly into the hall and felt faint, had to lean against the wall and rest a moment. To get home, she had to find Sheryl and borrow her car.

After a quick check of an unattended computer at the pediatric nurses' station, Dana found Penny. She was in the Lollipop wing, in a private room. Dana eased open the door and peered inside. There was a crib and a rocking chair where Sheryl slumped snoring. Dana crept into her room and tapped her shoulder.

Sheryl awoke with a start and a gasp that woke Penny. Dana jumped to the crib and scooped Penny up in her arms. Penny wrapped her legs around Dana's waist and laid her head on Dana's shoulder. Penny was warm and soft and smelled of talc and baby shampoo. She shoved her thumb in her mouth and Dana stroked her fine, sparse hair, wound a finger around a curl.

"What are you doing here?" Sheryl asked, yawning as she stretched.

"I need to ask a favor."

"What are you wearing?"

Dana had traded the quarantine clothes for green

scrubs. "My clothes got wet," she said. She would have to remember to pick them up before she left. "I need to borrow your car."

"Why?"

Sheryl already thought Dana was a bad driver and now Dana had to confess she drove her car into the ditch. "A car came into my lane. It wasn't my fault. I swerved out of the way."

"And you want to borrow my car?"

"I'll return it tomorrow. I'll leave the keys under the seat."

Sheryl worked the keys out of her pocket.

Dana hugged Penny tighter. "How is she doing?"

Her mouth was closed in a smile around her thumb.

"She's doing fine, which is great, but a problem," Sheryl said. "Taversham wants to know why she recovered. I said I worked with *Yersinia* and that I'd been vaccinated and because I'm still breast-feeding, Penny was protected."

"McCoy knows," Dana said. "I had to tell him."

Sheryl clasped her hands to her head. "What did he say?"

"Not much, actually." Dana wasn't going to go into it now.

"He didn't tell Taversham then," Sheryl said. "I really got the third degree. He went on and on. He and this other guy, this tall man in a suit. They said the antibiotics failed totally. Every single one they've tested. This strain of *Yersinia* is resistant to every antibiotic and vaccine. And here I was healthy. And my baby recovered. They wanted to know why, Dana. And they asked about you. How come you didn't get sick." Sheryl looked at her closely. "Why didn't you? Did you take the monoclonal?"

"It's the antigen from last Friday. The bacterial fragment works. It has to."

Sheryl frowned despite the good news. "Then you're in trouble, too. You can't say you're testing bacterial fragments on yourself. You'll lose your job."

For more reasons than one, Dana thought, as she hugged Penny again and kissed her soft cheek. Given the same circumstances, she would do what she did again, but whether that made it right or not, Dana didn't know.

Sheryl was studying her through narrowed eyes. "What are you doing here anyway?"

Dana sat down on the nightstand. Penny melded into her and seemed to have fallen asleep. She felt loose and floppy in her arms. "I came to give blood."

"What else?"

Dana hung her head. "I injected Nick. He had septicemic plague. I gave him the last of the monoclonal. It's all gone."

"If he agreed, we're all right. That proves it had to be used."

Dana looked at her feet. "He doesn't know."

"Oh, god." A shrill cry.

"In fact, he said not to use it." Dana spoke quietly.

Sheryl leaped out of the chair and stood before Dana. "What will he do when he finds out?"

"Maybe he won't."

Sheryl stamped her foot. "Of course he will." Penny was stirring. Dana stood up awkwardly and passed her to her mother. She spoke in a whisper. "I had to do it."

Sheryl stroked Penny's head against her shoulder. "Nick will never forgive you."

Dana didn't want to think about it at the moment, or discuss it.

Sheryl went to the crib and laid Penny down, drawing the blanket up over her. Penny's thumb went to her mouth.

"At least she's safe," Sheryl said, and surprised Dana by hugging her tightly.

Dana hugged her back, then left a few minutes later, clutching the car keys and running quietly down the stairs.

She headed for the fire exit marked with a sign that warned of an alarm if the door was inadvertently opened. Dana punched it anyway and ran, an alarm ringing in her ears, but whether it was real or not, she could not say.

Thursday

Chapter 43

During the night, Nick's fever broke; his muscles stopped aching and doubt began to override his certainty that he would die. His immune system was finally functioning and he felt stronger with each breath he took.

He was stoned on morphine, he knew, and was disengaged, disinterested. He was no longer a participant, but an observer and the distance brought relief. He was high.

Around him, machinery buzzed and the labored, troubled breathing of the sick filled the room. The male nurse slept in a chair by the door, feet up on the desk, snoring loudly. Nick alone was awake and alert and aware of the passing night. He glanced at his watch. Five minutes to three.

He lay staring at the ceiling, hands under his head. Funny, when he thought he was dying, he had looked back on his life and the review surprised him. Instead of finding satisfaction in his work and marital sacrifice, Nick thought of what he had missed, what was left undone, the opportunities not taken. He thought of his father and their estrangement and his death that precluded reconciliation. He

thought of his son and the three months they had that
weren't enough. He thought of Dana and what he had
walked away from. He heard Wheeler singing inside his
head: *You had to go, but could barely move, so you made
the loss less, and the ruin seem not as great.*

Nick moved his hands to his lap and clasped them together; studied the arch of his fingers, the mirror-image fit
of his hands. He turned them over, placed his palms together and remembered being in church. A small boy pray-
ing. Never again. Nick unfolded his hands and lay them by
his side. In his brush with death, he had seen no god, no
tunnel, no light at the end.

He checked his watch. Three o'clock now. Soon he'd
lose his morphine high. He was already worried about
coming down. It reminded him of the addiction to Valium
he acquired soon after he moved to D.C. Like Dana, it had
been nearly impossible to quit, but he had done it.

He closed his eyes and drifted. He was in the country,
surrounded by trees, red and white pine dripping with smilax. He was swinging a machete, clearing a path, sticks and
leaves flying above him, and Dana swearing behind him.
Unlike anyone he knew. Completely independent, with no
need of him. Doing well on her own, following some
desultory system that he couldn't fathom and left him
awed. She ignored logic, preferring hunches and signs. He
would have thought it lunacy except that, for her, it
worked.

He had dreamed of her tonight. She was fresh from the
shower, as he liked her best, and slick with water, hair
streaming. She bent over him and the water dripped from
her hair onto his skin. He held her hand and felt the heat of
her by his side.

So real, Nick opened his eyes. No, he was alone, she
wasn't here. Of course not. How could she be? The hospital was closed. Karl told him that, Karl who lay in the bed
beside him, inhaling oxygen as he snored in a troubled

sleep. Nick couldn't recall when he arrived. At some point an old man had occupied that bed.

Nick checked his watch again. Five minutes after three. The drugs slowed time. He closed his eyes and began to drift once more.

Chapter 44

The rain stopped during the night and when Dana awoke, the birds were singing. She jumped from bed when she thought of Nick. Questions came at her. Did he live through the night? Did he know what she did? What about the monoclonal antibody? Did McCoy know about the order he had not made? In the morning light, current events were hard to believe. It did not seem possible that she had done those things.

The electricity was out, as it had been all night and she could make no coffee. She gulped milk that was beginning to sour. She picked up the phone and found it dead. She fed her dogs, remembering again that Frank was gone. Without him, the house seemed too big, too bleak, too cold; something vital and substantial was missing.

The other dogs followed her up to the car. After Anthony peed on every tire, Dana sped off, sliding in the muddy road. In the morning haze, she saw what she had missed the previous night. On the bypass, she maneuvered around cars abandoned in the middle of the road. Electrical poles were down and lines submerged in deep puddles. The trees had been ravaged, branches laden with new leaves plastered to the muddy ground. A cat carrying something in its mouth slunk low, tiptoeing through the soaking grass.

At the hospital, it took her three tries to parallel park Sheryl's car. She tucked the keys under the driver's seat and got out. The air was cool and crisp; the storm had blown off the humidity. Overhead the clouds were breaking and ribbons of blue sky shone through.

And Nick could be dead. When she got to ICU, would he be there? Was his dose high enough? That was her biggest worry. What if the dose wasn't enough? Sometimes there was a threshold, a minimum amount necessary to see an effect. Did he get the minimum, and did he get it in time?

She climbed the steps at the side entrance. There was no policeman at the door. She pushed against one of the automatic doors and it slid sideways, and she entered the hospital without effort. It was too easy.

She walked the length of the hallway. The patients from last night were gone and the floors were vacant, though filthy with blood, dirt and mud. She crossed the long hallway and outside the ICU, suited up in the quarantine clothes. For anonymity, she pulled on the hood, then knocked on the door.

What if Nick was alive? What would she say? How could she cover up what she had done? Would he guess? No, she thought not. He would not expect her to go against him and she would never tell. He would assume all his years of vaccination against the plague had produced results; some fragment, some remnant of a vaccine had worked.

Still, he could be dead.

She knocked louder on the door and there was no answer. She tried peering through the crack in the curtains, but could see nothing. They could all be dead. She tried the knob and it turned in her hand. The door was open and she went in.

Her face panel fogged up with her breath and she could not see in the darkness. She pulled off the hood, and heard air whistling, people moaning and moving, a low voice talking. Nick on the phone.

She blinked her eyes open and shut. It was him, sitting up with his back to her, cell phone by his ear. He had made it. He lived through the night. She walked toward his bed.

He turned, his eyes, glassy and huge. His cheek shadowed with the beginning of a graying beard. He flipped the cell phone closed. The strawberry bruise on his forehead had turned blue.

"You look better," she said.

"I feel good." He laughed out loud. "My vaccine must have kicked in."

She sat down on the rolling stool across from him. He didn't know about last night. *He didn't know.* And he seemed happy to see her, the first time since his return. The feeling seemed to flow from him into her, bringing them together. This was what she had been waiting for, a connection. Here was the old Nick she knew, relaxed, accessible and present, the Nick she remembered. After his long retreat, he had returned.

He gave her an update on the situation and she tried to read between the lines, to learn if the monoclonal had come. Nick had been on the phone with Carol's doctor in Houston. Dr. Frost had no luck with the cipruboxin and was testing new antibiotics. One showed great promise. CK-202 was a drug that Dana had never heard of before.

"It inhibits DNA twisting," Nick said. "If it works, she'll fly it up. We need something." He scratched at his stubble.

The danger was not over and now a night had passed; time was running short. She looked again in Nick's bright eyes. Was he on morphine? It was out of character for him to be so lighthearted in the midst of a crisis.

"When will we know if this C.K.-two-oh-two works?" she asked.

"Soon."

"That's great." She smiled into his eyes.

"It is. I tell you, this disease is hell." He smoothed down the yellow doctor's smock he wore in lieu of pajamas.

She saw the spots of mud on the shirt that looked like fingerprints.

He noticed something too and pulled the shirt away from his chest so he could study the stain. Then he slowly raised his head, an entirely different look now on his face. His eyes narrowed and he frowned at her through dark troubled eyes.

"You were here last night." It was no question.

She closed her eyes, raised her hands to her chin, covered her mouth and mumbled, "I thought you were going to die."

"You injected me." His voice snapping, loud and angry, stirring the man in the bed next to him.

She saw with a start that it was Karl.

"How could you?" Nick said, not waiting for her reply. He slashed the air with his hand. "I told you *no*. What if something went wrong?"

"I thought you would die."

Karl moaned and rolled over onto his back. He had two IVs in his wrists and seemed to be boxing.

Nick went on. "There were other options. We could have a new antibiotic in an hour."

"For you it would have been too late."

Nick pitched the cell phone on the bed. "So you injected me. As if it were up to you to decide. You had no right. You crossed a line you shouldn't cross. You always do that. You throw your life away. It wasn't your decision."

"Sometimes you have to do what's best, even if it's not right."

"You're wrong. Did you ever think what's going to happen? What the repercussions will be?"

The worst thing she could envision was unfolding. "It was your life."

"Now you make me responsible for what you did. And I said no. I tried to stop you. You put your career and who knows what else in jeopardy." Each word truncated, as if spat.

The words hung in the air. A final sentence passed. He stared at the floor; she stared up at the ceiling.

The door to ICU burst open and the German nurse from the blood bank marched into the room, holding a slip of paper aloft. "A Nick Bigg-et. I am looking for a Nick Bigg-et."

Nick identified himself using the nurse's mispronunciation.

She told him a shipment of drugs had arrived. Could Nick receive them?

Nick could. He jumped out of bed, slipped into his shoes and retrieved the note from the nurse.

"A helicopter is on the roof," she said.

The nurse left and Nick turned to Dana. "C.K.-two-oh-two is here." He spread open his palms, as if to tell her what she had done was in vain.

Dana ran after him. In the hallway, to his retreating back, she said, "I think it's the monoclonal antibody."

He turned.

She lowered her voice to a whisper. "I called General Shwartzke last night and asked him to ship it down. He said he would. This morning by helicopter." The final words of the condemned.

Nick ran a hand through his hair. "He wouldn't do it."

"He will. I said McCoy requested it."

Nick looked once more at the note, then at her. "It can't be used." Then he turned, shaking his head, as he walked away, hands raised in defeat.

Chapter 45

The morphine high vanished in an instant and Nick's detachment disappeared. Feeling listless and feeble, he dragged himself up the stairs to the roof. The hospital was filled with sick people who needed treatment immediately or they would die. There was no late-acting vaccine kick. The bacteria's resistance was astounding. Nick's health was Dana's doing. She had not been in his dreams, as he had thought, but at the hospital giving him the monoclonal antibody he explicitly told her he did not want.

Nick reached the rooftop as a green and beige army helicopter lifted in the sky. It was eight o'clock and the sun was rising, reflecting off the revolving gunmetal blades. The noise of the engine filled the air and the blades sent a vast breeze gusting across the rooftop. A policeman stood in its wind holding a small Igloo cooler.

Nick waited for the man to leave, then went inside and down the stairs to the executive staff lounge. He opened the cooler and saw an envelope on top of chunks of dry ice. Chilled air rose and Nick grabbed the envelope, quickly closed the cooler.

He leaned back on the couch and opened the envelope. It was addressed to TJ McCoy from General Shwartzke at Fort Troy: *Here is the monoclonal you requested. Dilute concentrate 1:100. Godspeed. Fred.*

Nick closed his eyes and ran his hand across his face. No songs played in his head now, no timely advice from Wheeler; the words were silent; the chords were gone; there was nothing. After too little sleep and too much morphine, his brain wasn't functioning properly. He was tired and reality seemed distorted. He still had a headache, though not nearly the intensity of the one he had yesterday. Yesterday, when he sat in the rain unable to move and had made a deal with Dana not to use the monoclonal. Not on him, not on anyone—that it was out of the question.

Nick reread the note stupefied. Did she think ahead? Did she consider what would happen if McCoy intercepted the letter? Nick ripped it up, tore it into tiny pieces. He tore up the nurse's letter too and crammed the shreds into his pocket.

The audacity of it. Like removing her clothes and lying with him on the floor of a hotel room. It scared him to death. As she lay warm and soft against him, he wanted to warn her: *Don't leave yourself open; protect yourself.* But she was right; he could have died.

Karl's cell phone rang and Nick pulled it from his pocket.

Diane Frost calling from Houston with the result of the promising CK-202 antibiotic. "It doesn't work," she said. "Something about this strain. The bacteria have mutated. The cell wall contains modified transport proteins, which seem to have acquired enzyme function. As soon as the transport proteins pick up the antibiotics, they're deactivated."

Nick stared at the cooler. Transport proteins did not just acquire enzyme function. He remembered a conversation he had with a Russian dissident who was working at a biological warfare facility in Moscow. The man had been experimenting with membrane proteins, splicing different proteins together. Was this DNA deliberately altered?

"Do you want me to keep trying new antibiotics?" Diane asked. "I can call Paris and see if the Pasteur Institute has something."

They were out of time. If the monoclonal antibody was effective, it had to be used. Nick kicked the cooler and heard the jingle of soft glass. Dana was right, again.

"Go home, Diane," he said. "There's something else we can try."

"Send it down for Carol, then," Diane said.

Nick said he would, then flipped the cell phone closed and went to see McCoy.

He had a private room and was being closely supervised by a nurse who told Nick to come back later. "He just had a sedative and he's sleepy."

She meant McCoy was stoned. "I need to see him now," Nick said. "It's urgent."

The nurse let him into the room.

It was bright with sunshine and hot with light. McCoy lay in bed, gazing out the window, eyes glazed. He wore a pale blue hospital gown and held a respirator over his mouth that he lifted when he spoke.

"The sun is there. Would you look at that color of orange."

"Yes." Nick sank into a chair. "Look, we're in a quandary."

McCoy continued staring out the window. He was inhaling oxygen and lifted the plastic mouthpiece to say, "I don't know when I last watched the sun rise. Have you ever seen that color of orange? It's glowing, don't you think?"

Nick dragged the chair around to the other side of the bed and sat down, blocking McCoy's window view. "We have evidence this strain of *Yersinia* was genetically engineered for resistance. None of the available or experimental antibiotics work. Most of the vaccines have failed. I'm going to call the national security advisor and explain the situation."

McCoy nodded and craned his head around Nick to ogle the climbing sun.

Nick pried the cell phone from his pocket and called Blaze Stodgecraft. When he came on the line, Nick gave him an update as McCoy waxed on about the unusually vibrant color of the sky.

"You're telling me, we have no treatment," Blaze said, when Nick was through explaining.

"No antibiotics," Nick said. "There is, however, an experimental vaccine."

"How experimental?"

"Very. But there's nothing else."

"Use that, if you think it will work."

"I'll let you speak to General McCoy." Nick handed McCoy the phone. "The national security advisor."

McCoy removed the respirator and accepted the phone. He listened intently for a few minutes and then snapped the phone closed. "Call Shwartzke at Fort Troy. Tell him to ship the monoclonal down. This is biological war and all rules are lifted."

Then McCoy fitted the oxygen cup over his mouth and inhaled deeply, gazing out the window. "Here. Right here. A war. Can you believe . . ."

But Nick was on his way out the door.

Chapter 46

Before leaving the hospital, Dana went to the bathroom to retrieve the wet clothes she had forgotten the night before. In her life she had seen Nick angry and upset only a very few times, but never like this. This was more than anger. She had violated his trust; he said it all: she crossed lines she shouldn't cross and she always did. But it wasn't fair. He didn't get it at all, was too stoned to know his life was on the line. Now he blamed her for refusing to honor his request. The injustice of it burned into her.

In the bathroom, Dana caught sight of her reflection in the grainy bathroom mirror. She looked pale and wasted. She washed her hands, the water at a trickle. No paper towels were left in the dispenser. She wiped her hands on her jeans, then bent down to get her clothes. Gone. She moved the trash can. Nothing behind it. She looked inside. It was filled with crumpled paper towels, no clothes. She shrugged her shoulders to no one; she could live without them.

She left the bathroom, heading for the exit. At the side door where previously no policeman stood, now lurked a

very tall man. Dana tried to go around him, but he moved
to block her way.

He must have been seven feet tall and he gripped a
folded shopping bag he transferred to his other hand, so
that they could shake. "Barry Ackerman, FBI. You must be
Dana Sparks."

She looked up at him. He was at least two heads taller
than she, but younger. Maybe in his early thirties. He had
small, beady eyes, thin lips and a skijump nose. He didn't
look like an FBI agent to her.

"Do you have a moment? I'd like a word with you." He
smiled congenially. "I'm investigating the outbreak."

Sam had been right, in addition to the CDC the FBI was
on the case. "Why? Why is the FBI involved?"

As if she had not spoken he said, "I understand you
talked to Dudley Shaw? What was he like?"

"A nice man."

"Would he bear a grudge against the government?"

"Dudley? No. What makes you think that?"

Ackerman shifted the shopping bag to his other hand.
"You spoke with Jack Dowel. Would he know microbiology?"

"He was a football player. What is this?"

"But you knew him."

"No. I didn't. He was in a seminar I taught. Why does it
matter?"

"Carol Dupuis was also in your class."

"How is she?"

"Critical. You also know Penny," Ackerman continued.
"Where could she have been infected?"

Dana didn't like the turn in the conversation. "I don't
know." She looked down the hallway, distracted by a clack-
ety sound and a squeaky wheel. She saw Nick in a white
lab coat followed by the German nurse and Sam, who was
pushing a cart laden with boxes of syringes and needles.

The helicopter must have brought the experimental antibiotic CK-202. The trio disappeared into a room.

"Could it be your lab?" Ackerman said.

"That's absurd."

"You *do* deal with the plague."

"I don't have bacteria like this."

He stared intensely into her eyes. "Yet you have a vaccine against them."

"What the hell is this?"

"We're dealing with virulent bacteria that exhibit outstanding resistance," he said. "We have evidence the resistance is a result of genetic tampering. Yet you had the antidote to a newly mutated bacterium."

"Genetic tampering? Are you also a molecular biologist?" She shook her head. "This is a natural outbreak."

"Hardly. We are, in fact, quite sure it's deliberate."

"That's ridiculous."

He lowered his eyes and studied her carefully. "There have been severe cutbacks in scientific funding recently. It has affected your position, your research and your future. Whether or not you make tenure is dependent upon federal funding from Washington. You seek a military grant. No one could blame you if you begrudged the government or the military for your unpleasant predicament."

"Me?" She returned his stare, but she blinked first. "You think it's me?"

"Why were you here last night? What were you doing? A policeman said you were at the door. You were in ICU. In serology. Why?" His friendly tone was back.

"I gave blood. Explain that."

He considered it. "A red herring." He took the shopping bag in both his hands, unraveled the top and peered inside. Slowly he pulled out her wet clothes. "Would these be yours?"

She didn't answer, but her knees went soft.

He fiddled with her clothes, turning them over in his hands. "The thing that is most strange about this outbreak is that there is no origin of the bacterium. It seemed to come from nowhere."

She said nothing.

He stopped rearranging her clothes and looked at her. "What if the origin was a syringe?"

She knew what he would pull out of her wet clothes and he did so then, holding it high to make his point.

"I work with syringes," she said, and took a step away from him.

"I suspected as much."

"Excuse me." She turned around and walked steadily away from him, her skin burning as if with a fever.

Ackerman did not follow. "This interview is not over," he called out. "I am not finished and this hospital is under quarantine; you are confined to these premises."

But Dana heard no more for she turned a corner and was gone.

Chapter 47

Nick was shaving when he heard a sharp knock on the bathroom door. It flung open and Barry Ackerman burst in.

"That woman is hiding something," Ackerman said. "Sparks is defensive and highly agitated. Something is upsetting her,"

Nick continued shaving and did not reply. He would try to ignore the FBI agent in the hope he would go away. He couldn't have five minutes alone. There was no privacy in this place. Not even in the bathroom. It reminded Nick of a miserable summer camp he attended thirty-five years ago. He had been stuck there like he was stuck here, under quarantine. He thought of Wheeler: *Stand your ground, as they push you around, and tell you what's on your mind.*

Nick cleaned the razor blade with his finger and ran it across his cheek, carefully avoiding the healing cut. His stomach growled and he realized he hadn't eaten in a day. But he wasn't hungry. He was upset, mostly with himself. He had lost it; it wasn't like him; he didn't act like this. Completely out of control. It was Dana's influence. It infuriated him when people did things that affected him without his permission. Dana was especially good at it.

Ackerman studied him through the mirror. "I wonder what would trouble her?"

"Maybe the outbreak. She's a little sensitive around dying people."

"Lucky for her, she had the antidote."

"Lucky for us. All of us." Nick had just finished injecting a hospital full of sick people. Already people were recovering. The monoclonal worked fast. The less sick you were, the faster it worked.

"But why did she have it? *How* could she have it?" Ackerman asked.

"If you remember, she didn't have it. We got it this morning from Fort Troy."

"No thanks to her. If McCoy wasn't on the ball, we'd be in trouble."

Nick lowered his eyes. "Again, we were lucky." He dropped the razor and lathered his hands with antiseptic soap and vigorously washed his face.

Ackerman pulled a syringe out of his pocket. "I found this in the pocket of her slacks. She left them in the bathroom last night."

The syringe was covered in a paper wrapper. "It hasn't been used," Nick said.

"Why did she have it?" Ackerman tucked the syringe back into his pocket. "Were Carol Dupuis' rats deliberately injected with *Yersinia?*"

Nick turned to face the man. "Unlikely. The rats were wild. They would bite." He picked up a can of rose-scented air freshener from the counter. "It would be easier to place the bacteria in a can and spray it as an aerosol. But then the pneumonic infection would be the first to appear." He slammed the can down on the counter.

Ackerman wouldn't give up. Nick turned the cold faucet on full. Just a few drops of water. The hospital was rationing water and electricity. He dunked his head and let the water crawl across his scalp.

"Do you think the epicenter is the hotel where the VP was scheduled to stay?" Ackerman asked.

"That's what Karl seems to think," Nick said. He turned off the faucet and shook his head. Drops flew. Ackerman jumped out of the way, complaining.

"But why no *Yersinia* trail?" Ackerman spoke like Rachel-Anne's psychiatrist with calm but attentive indifference.

Nick straightened and combed his hair with his fingers, then walked to the hand dryer and punched the "on" button. The dryer didn't work. Probably only essential machines were hooked up to the generator. He leaned against the counter. "Maybe an infected guest flew to the hotel. We should check airline reservations. The hotel registration."

"We're checking." Ackerman pointed to the disposable razor. "Can I borrow that?"

"Go ahead."

Staring in the mirror, the special agent foamed his face with soap. "Do you think Dana Sparks is behind this?"

"Unlikely." Nick shook his head. "No."

Ackerman watched Nick through the mirror. "Why do you say that?"

It was Rachel-Anne's psychiatrist's favorite question. "If you knew her, you'd know she wasn't involved," Nick said.

"How well do you know her?"

"We worked together the last year I was here," Nick said. "A long time ago."

The eyes in the mirror stared hard. Nick looked back as if he had nothing to hide.

Ackerman finished shaving and wiped his face with the sleeve of his dark jacket. He leaned against the counter once more. "As a person, what's she like?" he asked. "Political? Left wing? Religious? Any dalliances with mercenary boyfriends?"

"No," Nick said.

Ackerman smiled. "Just no?"

"All right. She's not a terrorist. She couldn't kill a mouse. Her methods might not be sound, but her intent is good." Ackerman was looking at him. The silence was loud and made Nick uncomfortable. He felt he should say something and added, "Do you think she'd put her own life at risk if she were behind this?"

"I really don't know what she's capable of doing," Ackerman said. "I'm learning a lot." He shot Nick a significant look.

"What about your other suspects?" Nick asked. The best defense was offense—he had learned that from the psychiatrists too. "I thought you had your intelligence on this."

Ackerman seemed to deflate. "As a matter of fact, our investigation has been compromised by the storm. The power is still off in town, phone lines are down and email is out. The fact that the hospital is under quarantine doesn't help either."

No it doesn't, Nick thought. He hated the idea of being incarcerated another night.

"And yet, Dana Sparks is always coming and going. She was here this morning and she left. I haven't finished talking to her."

"She's probably at work."

"No she's not. I called there."

"Then at home."

"Where does she live?"

"Off the bypass on a dirt road."

Ackerman pulled out a pen and a notepad and passed it to Nick. "I'd like a map."

Nick picked up the pen and drew hasty scribbles. A circle for the bypass. A spoke for her access road.

"What's this?" Ackerman complained, frowning at the map.

"Her street."

"What's the name?"

A knock on the door preempted Nick's answer.

Michael opened the door and peered in. "I have been waiting so long," he said.

Ackerman waved him to the toilet. Michael came in and stood with his back to them, urinating.

Ackerman said, "Where's the hospital?"

Nick added an X on the map.

"Is her road marked?" Ackerman asked.

"There's a mile marker at the turnoff," Nick said.

Michael was done and zipping up as he stood behind them. "Sir," he said. "I spoke with Karl and he would like you to know that Carol Dupuis died this morning."

"Damn it," Nick said. The helicopter must not have made it in time.

The agent folded his map and closed the notebook. Without a further word, he strode from the room.

"Is it yours?" Michael pointed to the razor.

"Be my guest." Nick left the bathroom. He had handled himself badly with Ackerman, he knew. He was on edge, his nerves were screaming and he was a word away from requesting more morphine. Get a grip, he told himself. He took deep breaths in fast succession and soon felt light-headed. Once again, a man far from control.

Chapter 48

Dana left the hospital using the emergency exit which, despite its warning, issued no alarm. It must not have been wired to the generator. In the parking lot she looked for her car and when she didn't see it, thought for a moment it might have been stolen, along with the little black sports car with the license plate FB JOCK, which was gone as well. Then she remembered the ditch.

She trudged to the veterinary school on foot. The clouds were thinning; the sky was bright. There was water, dirt and silt everywhere. Underfoot, the streets and sidewalks were littered with garbage and debris. Branches torn from trees littered the roads. Windblown newspapers plastered the shrubs. Plastic bags hung on wind-stripped trees. A landscape in ruin. Bluebonnets trampled in the mud. An aborted spring.

Dana crossed campus and saw no one. The curtains on the dorm windows were closed. Not a window or door was open. The houses were shut tight. It was the same on the streets. No moving cars and no people. The stores in town were still closed. Dana imagined that throughout history the reaction to the plague was just like this.

She reached her car and saw it inclined in the ditch; the night rains had not swept it away. She would call AAA when she reached the vet school. She passed the Lone Star Heritage Hotel and saw the front doors were closed, the proud flags gone. No doormen guarded the mirrored entrance. A red and white gingham tablecloth from the Pizza Garden floated in the gutter. An electrical line lay on the ground.

She reached the vet school. The parking lot was empty. The generator roared loudly in the morning silence. Inside the halls were vacant and laboratory doors were locked. In her office, Dana called AAA and got a recording. She needed coffee, but her can was empty; she headed to the main office to pilfer coffee from Betty's private stash.

She reached the office, found Nellie, and her morning turned worse.

"Oh, Dana," Nellie cried. "Great, you're here." She put down the coffeepot. "I'm dying for java. Could you make it? I never get it right."

Dana would have liked to say no, but her need for coffee at the moment was strong and Nellie liked hers weak. If she wanted a decent cup of coffee, she'd have to make it. She filled the pot with water as Nellie sat down and stared at her.

"My, my, aren't we looking hangdog this morning. What's wrong?"

"Nothing." Dana spooned coffee into the filter while Nellie spun around in Betty's chair like a little girl.

She stopped spinning suddenly. "And please, don't make the coffee too strong. I'm not feeling myself this morning." She lifted her bangs with a small hand.

Dana added an extra scoop.

"I hope I'm not sick. Almost everyone is. Except you." Nellie wrinkled her nose and stared at Dana across the desk.

"And you." Dana said.

Nellie changed the subject. "You got a phone call. From an FBI agent. You are to report immediately to the hospital."

"Right." Dana hit the "on" button of the coffeepot. In a few seconds the pot began to hiss.

"I wonder what he wanted?" Nellie said.

Dana watched a stream of coffee shoot into the pot and said nothing.

"You know, don't you, that the agent thinks this is deliberate?"

Dana turned around. "I know." She saw Nellie's face fall. Dana wasn't supposed to know this.

Nellie lowered her voice to a whisper. "I don't know if I should warn you or not, but in confidence, the agent thinks it's you."

Dana walked to the cupboard and got a cup, wiped the inside with her finger.

"As Nick said, you *are* the only one with the bacteria."

Dana stared at the dripping coffee, keeping her back to Nellie.

"I would have thought Nick would have tried to get you out of the fire, not throw you in."

The coffee was still dripping but Dana filled her cup. Dripping coffee sizzled on the hot plate. So, Nick too, not just Ackerman.

"You probably didn't notice, but they were watching you. They think you're out of step with the investigation, being deliberately misleading."

Dana shoved the coffeepot back in place. Was that why Karl insisted on helping her with the assays?

"For what it's worth," Nellie said, "I tried to tell them you weren't capable of it, that it was beyond you."

Dana picked up her cup and left the room.

In her office, she sat at her desk, gulping deep breaths of air. It was a natural phenomenon. Roving wildlife extending their range after a rainy spring and carrying the bacteria farther south than it would otherwise go. It wasn't deliberate. Nellie was wrong and Ackerman was insane.

There were strange things about the outbreak, though. The *Yersinia* was extremely virulent and highly resistant. The rodents around Duane weren't infected and the bacteria appeared to come from nowhere. They appeared in an environment in which they had no business appearing, during a week that the vice president of the United States was coming to town. Ackerman said the bacteria were genetically engineered, but how would he know? This wasn't a deliberate act of terror. The *Yersinia* had to come from somewhere and if it didn't come from her, and if it wasn't purposely introduced, there'd be a trail and she'd find it. Somehow, she'd find it. She got up and threw her coffee in the sink.

Chapter 49

Dana was no epidemiologist but she knew the theory. The first thing to do was identify the correct index case and from there, trace the infection forward to people who caught the disease and back to the rodents that might have carried it. In theory it shouldn't be difficult, especially since only four rodents were infected.

But first she needed her car. She called AAA and heard the recording again. Maybe she could free the car herself. She left the vet school. Outside the sunshine beat down and the air was steamy and hot. The lakes and puddles on the ground were drying. The sky was bright and the leaves on the trees shone.

She reached her car. In the daylight, it didn't seem as badly stuck as it did the night before. The sun was strong and drying the water in the ditch. She studied the car from all angles, then pushed on it and nothing happened. The front right wheel was half covered with water. It was the only wheel that made contact with the ground, the other three wheels were in the air. The car was tilting to the right, the nose down, the belly stuck on the vertical decline.

Dana would not be able to drive forward, which meant she had to drive back, try to shift the angle so that all the tires touched the ground.

She unlocked the car door and climbed inside. The floor carpet was wet and the interior smelled of damp towels. The windshield was steamy and fogged up. Dana lowered the window, wiped the windshield with her hand then cranked the ignition key. The car jumped to life. She eased off the emergency brake and the car remained immobile. She paused for a moment and read the car manual to learn how to engage four-wheel drive. Push a button. She pushed it. Then she thrust the gear into reverse, depressed the accelerator and felt the backward shift of the car. A scraping sound, coming from beneath her, made her close her eyes.

She accelerated backward and heard mud pelt the car. The front right wheel began to slide and a back wheel made contact with the ground. She opened her eyes. The angle was wrong and the car lurched to the right. She leaned left and spun the wheel counterclockwise as the car began to tip. A warning alarm sounded and Dana let go of the steering wheel and slammed her body against the door. The car stalled—rocked back on forth on its wheels. All four wheels. All now in contact with the ground.

Dana straightened and looked out the window, brushing the hair out of her eyes. The car was parallel to the ditch. She cranked the key once more and pressed on the accelerator. The car slid sideways at first, like a boat, then her momentum picked up, and the car moved faster and faster and then she was cutting across the ditch and up the embankment. She bounced over the curb and hit the road. She was out. In her exuberance, she stalled the car.

She exhaled deeply. Now what? Where to begin? She gazed up and down the empty street. She had no idea what to do. Even the proper epidemiologists were stumped. Words of advice from her father came back: *When in doubt, get help*. Dana went to see Phillip Becker.

His neat and tidy house looked as if it had been struck by a tornado. A drainpipe hung from the roof. A shutter was torn from the window. Branches and limbs were strewn across the short soupy grass that was a glowing green. His car, parked at the end of the driveway, sat in a lake. Dana parked behind him, on the slope.

Phillip's ruddy face beamed as he stepped onto the porch. Today he was decked out in green khakis and a pink polo shirt. He stared at her muddy car. "Where have you been?"

"Stuck in a ditch." She got out of the car.

"What's going on? There seems to be a news blackout."

She filled him in on what had happened. Standing on the porch, squinting in the sunlight, she told him everything. Injecting Nick, Ackerman's accusations, Nellie's revelation that she had been watched and suspected all along.

"Hold on, hold on." Phillip said, laughing through her angst. He wanted her to start over and sat down on the stoop. She sat beside him, picked up a twig and broke it in two, began peeling the bark off in long, slimy strips.

"The bacteria are resistant and intentionally so, according to the FBI," she said. "They think the outbreak is deliberate."

Phillip frowned and tapped a wizened finger to his lips.

Dana continued. "I'm a suspect."

Phillip cocked his head, eyeing her sharply.

"I had both motive and opportunity."

He frowned and shook his head. "What motive?"

"I need to show my work is important so I can keep my job."

Phillip burst out laughing. "That's absurd."

Dana laughed too. Spoken out loud, it did sound crazy, hilariously demented and deranged. She held her stomach and laughed until her eyes watered.

"Feel better?" Phillip said when it was out of her.

She wiped tears from her eyes. Phillip believed that humor was the best medicine. No one should take themselves too seriously and a hearty laugh was better than what any doctor could order. Phillip got up and walked along the path at the side of the house. She followed him, retrieving a plastic grocery bag caught on a bush. "I want to prove it was an accident. A natural outbreak."

Phillip picked up a garbage pail that had blown over.

"Find the source," he said. "Go to the source." He lifted the lid of the pail and she tossed in the bag.

"And where might that be?"

"Assume the outbreak is natural and began with the four rats. That puts us where?"

"I think the Dumpster in the parking lot across from the park."

"Start from there."

All of a sudden it seemed easy again. Until she thought of Nick.

Phillip walked across the lawn toward a huge limb that had fallen off a tree. Dana ambled behind him, sinking in his footsteps. The grass was marshy and wet. They stopped at either end of the branch. Phillip bent down and grasped the limb. "What was finally used against the bacteria?"

"An experimental antibiotic. C.K.-two-oh-two, or something. It came this morning."

Phillip motioned for her to get her end.

"Nick is furious that I injected him," Dana said.

"You did what you thought was right. At the time, it probably was best."

She lifted her end, the leafy crown scratching her skin, as they carted the limb to the edge of the lawn.

Phillip headed up the driveway. He stopped by her car and ran a finger across her muddy back windshield. "Don't worry about Nick. Things will work out the way they're supposed to."

Besides humor, Becker made it a point not to worry. He often told her it did no good, it was a waste of energy and time and accomplished nothing, but she wasn't good at not worrying.

"I gave him the monoclonal after he said he didn't want it. He would rather die than jeopardize my career."

"And you don't think he cares." Phillip's eyes crinkled as he smiled. He had drawn the letter D on her windshield. "Give him time. He'll come around. Let him look at the situation from a hundred sides and he'll see you did what you had to do."

"I doubt it."

Phillip drew something else with his finger. "He thinks too much; he's lost his balance. He says no to his heart and the universe says no to his logic. Nick can think all he wants, it won't get him anywhere."

"He doesn't know that."

Phillip threw her a saintly smile. "He may have lost the battle, but he'll win the war." He made a large sweeping circle on the windshield.

Dana walked the length of her car. "I better go, before the FBI arrests me."

Phillip followed her, wiping his hands. "Dana, it's always darkest before the dawn."

She looked up at the sky. "The dawn is past. The sun's up." She got in her car and drove off.

Chapter 50

In the middle of a day he didn't think he'd live to see, Mc-Coy lay in bed, watching a nurse inject morphine into his IV line.

"Well, you'll feel better now," she said, though McCoy had not been feeling bad. The nurse was perky and smiley and reminded him of his wife, who along with his daughter Margaret, were in the north hospital. Except for the fact he was isolated from them, McCoy felt fine. He knew in a minute he'd feel even better. Better than before, even his burned pupils seemed to have healed.

He stared out his window. The sun was high and bright and rays of light beamed down upon the trees. There were no clouds and the sky was a clear bright blue. Limpid. The word was correct, but not apt. Brilliant was more appropriate. The sky reminded McCoy of summers he spent as a child on the Chesapeake Bay. He inhaled deeply and could almost smell the salt air. These were sights and scents he had not expected to experience again in his lifetime. Now he was on the rebound, life felt new.

Was it the morphine? Finally McCoy understood how

the boys in Vietnam became addicted to heroin. He could see how an opium ban in China could precipitate a war. *Papaver* something was the scientific name of the opium poppy. Funny he could remember a genus name and not a conversation with the vice president he apparently had an hour ago. The nurse told McCoy he spoke to his wife earlier, too, and he couldn't remember that, either. A conversation with the national security advisor was another blank. McCoy closed his eyes as a wave of morphine swept him away.

It seemed only a few minutes had passed when the nurse shook him awake and informed him the men had arrived for the meeting. *Meeting*? It was news to McCoy. He fought his IV lines, struggling to sit up, wondering who had called the meeting. It wasn't him, was it? What did he have to say? Nothing he knew of. His brain felt muzzy and pillowy, like a saggy mattress. He was in no condition for a meeting.

But Ackerman, Nick and Karl flounced in anyway and the nurse hurried to arrange chairs around the bed. Then Ackerman sent her out. When the door closed behind her, Ackerman called the meeting to order. Good, so he had ordered it. All McCoy had to do was listen and appear attentive. He stared back out the window. The leaves on the trees looked liked emeralds glinting in the sunlight. Marge had earrings that color. He smiled, until he intercepted the FBI agent's stare.

"And how do *you* feel?" Ackerman asked.

McCoy dragged his sight from the window. "Just fine, just fine. And you?"

He must have already inquired for Ackerman said sharply, "I said I was fine."

McCoy ordered himself to concentrate. Nick got up and closed the curtains. Still, it was hard for McCoy to focus. He fixed his eyes on the FBI agent. Jesus, he really did have long arms. Like a chimpanzee or a gorilla. Was it normal for your arms to reach the floor when you sat on a chair? Nick and Karl's arms were crossed in their laps so he couldn't compare. McCoy extended his arms but he disconnected something that triggered an alarm that brought in the nurse. McCoy closed his eyes as she re-hooked a tube. When the door closed, he had to fight to pry his eyelids apart.

"Okay," Ackerman said, "we've got twenty dead, but everyone else admitted is recovering. We seem to be over the worst."

Karl was in apparent agreement. "We're on the cusp. The National Guard will disband in the morning. The airport reopens tomorrow."

"Admitted patients will be kept overnight," Ackerman added. "The vaccine works as a preventative as well as a treatment, so there's no danger of new infections. Tomorrow we can go."

Great, McCoy thought. He expected the meeting was nearing its conclusion and was sorely disappointed when Ackerman changed the subject.

"Houston confirmed we're dealing with an unusual strain of *Yersinia*. It may have been genetically engineered for resistance."

Nick explained. "Membrane transport proteins have an enzyme function. The change occurred at the level of the DNA. The length of the transport protein gene is double what it should be."

Ackerman stared at McCoy. "That's twice as long."

McCoy, struggling to keep his eyes open, wondered if the FBI agent had just defined the word *double* for him.

Karl began talking about transport proteins, oxidative enzymes and other things McCoy couldn't follow. He wasn't a geneticist, why did he have to listen to this tripe? Why couldn't they go away and leave him alone?

"We're lucky we got through this as well as we did,"

Ackerman said, when Karl stopped to take a breath.
"There could have been devastating repercussions. Order-
ing the antidote from Fort Troy was an astute call."

McCoy started. Ackerman was addressing him. Here
was another call he made he couldn't remember making.
When had he spoken to General Shwartzke? He turned to
his window. Someone had closed the god damn curtain.

"We know the Russians developed resistant *Yersinia*
strains," Ackerman said. "They also developed an antidote."

Now McCoy was listening. He faced the agent.

Ackerman sat back in his chair and folded his impossi-
bly long fingers together. "Perhaps, in bankruptcy, the Russians sold the bacteria for a price."

McCoy waited for him to continue, but Ackerman was
staring at him. Was *he* supposed to say something? "Very
interesting." McCoy tried to look thoughtful.

"To whom, is the correct response," Ackerman said.
"We're looking at suspects now." He was addressing Nick.
"Despite the lack of power, the downed phone lines and the
problem with the satellite, we're progressing."

Karl agreed that the breakdown in communications was
annoying. Cell phone communication was awry. He was
trying to call Atlanta and make a report.

Ackerman said to try the *woof*.

"Woof?" McCoy said. Were they talking about a dog?
The dead guy's dog? What was his name? Puddley? Mud-
dly? Was the conversation jumping around or was it just
him?

"Roof," Ackerman said, shouting loudly. "I said roof."
He rubbed his eyes. "Look. Now that the health concern is
past, we can concentrate on finding the culprit."

He pulled a sheet of paper from his suit pocket and unfolded it. God, his fingers really were long and skinny.
Like tree branches. He had a long list of suspects.

In the manner of a child learning to read, Ackerman
used his finger to follow words on his sheet. McCoy re-

membered reading to Margaret when she was a child. She loved the book *Night Moon*, and before she was two years old, she had the words memorized and used to say them out loud as McCoy read the story. *Night, spoon. Night, moon.* McCoy used to know the whole thing but that was all he could remember now.

Before him, Ackerman listed his suspects. Dana Sparks was still tops on Ackerman's list. But there were others. The old guy with the dog. The violent football player who threw chairs. Tim Sweeny from the vet school. All of the first cases were possibilities. As were people who didn't get sick, which included two nurses, a doctor and three of McCoy's employees.

Ackerman said they were paying special attention to the local hotels. "We're running the guests' names through our computer."

"We think the epicenter may be the Lone Star Heritage Hotel, and not High Park," Karl said.

"The vice president," McCoy said, and saw bobbing heads. It reminded him of a toy Margaret once had, a fishing game of bobbing fish with snapping mouths and . . .

Ackerman was shaking him, his long fingers like talons on his arm. "McCoy, McCoy are you with us?"

McCoy opened his eyes. "I'm here."

Ackerman continued. The investigation was not confined to Duane. No siree, Ackerman's long reach extended across the state. There was a Russian couple in Dallas who once worked in a chemical plant in Vanova and were given political asylum. As for the airlines, Ackerman had information that a well-known Arab terrorist had flown to Houston two weeks before. The FBI was searching for him. Meanwhile, McCoy, Karl and Nick were in the clear. Even the visiting Michael Smith had been ruled out.

Good god, McCoy had forgotten all about him. Where was he? He was supposed to give a seminar on Wednesday. Had he given it? Did McCoy miss it? Had Michael left?

What day is it?" McCoy said, and received horrified looks.

"Thursday," Karl said.

"Maybe we should go," Nick said. He stood up and opened the curtains and the room turned bright.

McCoy tried to argue but felt himself sinking into a vast abyss. A strange distant feeling crept over him and he felt his body shrinking.

The next thing he knew, he heard the sound of a chair scraping across the floor. His wife and daughter were there. Marjorie moved the chair to the head of the bed and sat down next to him. Margaret sat on the bed and as she did when she was a little girl, tested the springs, bouncing up and down. She was looking robust and healthy.

McCoy's heart pulsed in and out as she bounced. His chest felt tight again, but in a good way, as if his heart was too big for him. He held her hand, moved by the softness of her skin.

There were tears in her eyes. "I didn't think you'd make it."

Her tears looked like diamonds and made her eyes sparkle. "It'll take more than a little heart attack and the plague to get rid of me. We've still got driving lessons, a trip to Austin, maybe a trip up north, a vacation?"

Margaret smiled through her tears, the sun shining on her young, fresh face. Only it was dark. McCoy struggled to sit up. He was alone in the room and it was night. It must have been a dream, a lucid morphine dream that seemed real. His wife and daughter were at the north hospital.

Then he noticed the chair pulled close to the bed, up near his head. It had been moved since the afternoon meeting, he was sure of it. They had been here. McCoy urgently pushed the call button to summon the nurse.

Chapter 51

Dana left Phillip Becker and drove around the block to the Dumpster. There was a car parked by the car wash and she hoped the place was open. She pulled up beside a sports car and jumped out. A young man pounding on the front door turned around. He was young, blond and muscular. Handsome, but for a glistening white scar that snaked from his eye down his cheek to his mouth.

"You work here?" he said.

Dana tried hard to look at him without looking at the scar. "I was hoping *you* worked here. Is the place closed?"

The man raised his fist and pounded the door so hard it shook. A rounded biceps popped out beneath the tight sleeve of his T-shirt. "Everything in town is closed," he said, with a kick to the door. "I can't buy beer. I can't get the blood out of the rug. I can't wash my car."

Dana stood there. *Blood out of a rug?*

"Say, you don't have gas to spare do you?"

Dana shook her head. "I'm nearly out myself."

"You take a honeymoon and look what happens." The man sat down on the stoop. His legs were hairy and short running shorts revealed significant thighs. He traced the line of the scar with his finger. "I just got back this morning from San Antonio. Cut my honeymoon short. I heard on the news the town was closed but I didn't believe it. Looks like it's true. What am I going to do about the blood?"

Dana stood unmoving and intrigued.

"It's been there over a week," the man said. "See, we were going to the airport, Kimberly and me. That's my wife. Well, this was last week, Monday, and back then we weren't married. Anyhow, we see a cat hit by a car on the road. Right there."

He paused to point out the spot on North Street, a busy road.

"And Kim says we can't leave the cat. It's a bad omen or something. It's bleeding and mangled and when I get it in the car it bleeds all over my white carpet." He flung an arm at his car.

Dana turned around and saw a black MG. She read the license plate: FB JOCK. It was the car parked at the hospital all week. Dana looked at the man with the scar. "Are you . . . uh . . . uh . . ."

"Yep. Bucky Finch." He held out his hand. "The football star. I see you recognized me. I suppose you want an autograph."

"No, no." Dana shook his hand. "You're Jack Dowel's roommate."

Bucky Finch smiled and flicked his eyebrows up and down. "You a friend of Jack's?"

Dana introduced herself. "I met him at the hospital." Christ, she had forgotten all about him. "How is he?"

"Fine. They sprung him yesterday."

Dana tried to remember the details of Bucky's story. "Jack took you to the airport, you found this cat, and Jack was supposed to get the car washed." Jack had not mentioned anything about a cat.

"No, Jack had a class," Bucky said. "I left the car at the airport and he came and picked it up. I left him a note to get the car washed. On account of the cat that bled all over the rug. It's been there all week. Not the cat, the blood. Jack took it to the car wash, but it never came out."

He went on, but Dana stopped listening. This was it. This was what she had been looking for. The missing piece.

While Bucky talked about his honeymoon, and a play he had seen at an outdoor theatre that sounded remarkably like *Romeo and Juliet*, Dana surveyed the car wash. This was the epicenter—not the dumpster, not the park, not the hotel, but the car wash. Someone with infected fleas had used the car wash. In all her years in Duane, Dana had used the car wash only once. It was automatic and arranged in an assembly line fashion. The vehicle passed through the wash on a motorized track. The washing bay was fitted with high-pressured nozzles that cleaned the car's exterior. Next the body was buffed with mechanized polishers. Then the interior was manually vacuumed with a powerful suction hose.

Dana eyed the vacuuming station. The debris from a car would be sucked into a vacuum bag. And dumped where? She stared at the dumpster. The place where rats went for steak and lobster.

Bucky was looking at her. "So, do you know how to get out a blood stain?"

"If I can borrow the rug, I'll see what I can do."

He furled it from his car and handed it to her.

"Did you take the cat to the vet school?"

"It was closest. We dropped it off. Maybe we should have stayed, but we were late for our flight."

"Do you remember what the cat looked like?"

"It was big."

"Orange?"

"You know it?"

Dana thought she did.

She left Bucky and crossed the parking lot heading for the Pizza Garden. The restaurant was closed and in disarray. Tablecloths torn from the tables lay in dirty puddles on the ground. One floated in the swimming pool, along with petals, leaves and branches. But the saguaro cactus stubbornly held the notices impaled to its thorns.

Dana tore off a flyer. *Please bring Pumpkin home. Call Travis Trelane*. The eleven-year-old with bubonic plague. Dana knew what had happened to his cat.

Chapter 52

The animal clinic was locked and Dana used her key and entered the clinic from the hallway inside the building. On the front counter lay an appointment book and she turned back ten pages, to Monday, April 20. According to the book, a male calico was dumped at the clinic and Tim signed on as the attending veterinarian. The diagnosis was a damaged spine and crushed front leg, as a result of unspecified trauma. Dana remembered the orange cat with the bandaged stump in the animal room. Pumpkin.

On Saturday, Pumpkin developed pneumonia and Tim put him down. On Monday, Becker wanted to do an autopsy and McCoy told him to forget it. The cat didn't die from pneumonia, but *Yersinia* and was the index case. The cat infected Tim, who initiated the human infections.

Dana went upstairs and let herself into Tim's lab. It took her only a minute to find the cat's blood in the door of his fridge. She took the tube to her lab.

In the quarantine room, she retrieved the tube with Frank's blood. Since his blood had tested negative for *Yersinia* antibodies, she had assumed he died from lung cancer. Now, she was no longer so sure. For four days, Frank had been in the room with Pumpkin, inhaling *Yersinia* with each troubled breath that he took. He was taking an immunosuppressant drug that would have inhibited an immune response. If he was exposed, he wouldn't have been able to make antibodies and his ELISA result would have been misleading. He would have had the bacteria in his blood, but no antibodies against them.

Dana began an antigen capture test, which was a modified ELISA used to assay the bacteria directly. She checked Frank's blood, Pumpkin's blood and a blood sample she eluted off the stained bloody carpet from Bucky's MG. In a little over an hour, she had the results. Three positive samples confirming *Yersinia*. Frank had died of the plague. She had taken him to the clinic for treatment and had hastened his death, doing what she thought was right turned out to be wrong.

She cleaned her lab bench and went downstairs. There was still one loose end. Dudley. Except for him, the pieces fit. But where was he infected? She went through the clinic appointment book more carefully. Did Dudley use the vet clinic? Had he brought in Bingo the same time Pumpkin was dropped off?

The answer was no. Dudley's name wasn't listed in the records book. So where was he infected? Did he know Pumpkin's owner, Travis? Had Dudley taken Bingo to High Park? Did he stop to pet Pumpkin? Did the dog and cat fight? Was there a transfer of fleas? Or did Bingo get into garbage that came from the dumpster? Anything was possible, she thought, and it was unlikely that she would ever know.

It wasn't until she was outside, walking toward her muddy car that it hit her. Dudley had used the car wash. She knew that he had, for at the hospital, when he drew a map to his house, he had drawn it on the back of a car wash receipt. The receipt was still in the pocket of the jeans she had worn that day.

Which might explain why there was no trail of bacteria into Duane. Someone had driven the bacteria to town. Someone who used the car wash and drove on, but not before leaving behind infected fleas that began a sequence of events that would kill many and likely cost her her job.

Dana drove off in the gathering gloom. The bright sunshine of the afternoon had faded, giving rise to a cloudy early night. She tuned into an Austin C&W station, looking for music and finding the news. There was no mention of Duane at all, not even a reminder the roads into town were closed. The lead story was the situation in Somalia. UN investigations concluded that the damage inflicted on the mosque and hospital far exceeded that expected from bomblets raining from a cluster bomb. The evidence indisputably supported the U.S. claims that the mosque and hospital had been used to store munitions and the Somalis themselves had put their own people at risk. The Somalis countered with the accusation that if indeed munitions were present in the mosque and hospital, then it was the U.S. that put them there.

Dana switched off the radio. Overseas things might be a mess, but what happened here was nothing more than an innocent outbreak, started at a car wash by a cat. She knew she should probably go to the hospital and tell Ackerman what she had found out, but fuck it, she wasn't in the mood.

At home, Dana found the receipt that Dudley had given her that placed him at the epicenter. He had taken his car to be washed the same day Pumpkin had been hit by a car. They were both in the wrong place at the wrong time, and like Frank, had paid with their lives.

What happened to the force of good that was supposed to protect them? There was no evidence of it at all that week. Maybe that was the true reality—maybe Nick was right—maybe there was no great force: accidents, good or bad, were just accidents. Anything that was, could also be otherwise. Coincidences were random and events were meaningless. There was no magic and shit just happened.

The evidence was there. A flea killed a person. A man died after getting his car washed. A fourteen-year-old dog died of the plague and not pneumonia because his owner made a decision that spring was no time to be a cripple.

Dana crumpled the car wash receipt and took Anthony and Judy for a walk. They stayed by her side, continually underfoot. Many limbs had fallen and the path was overgrown with prickling vines and scratching branches. The ground was soft and mucky, like quicksand. Overhead, birds were screaming and no light shone through. The forest was dark and dank, and Dana felt she was being strangled. Instead of the calm connection she usually experienced, she felt uneasy and alone.

At home, she opened her last beer. She picked up the phone, wanting to call her father, but the line was still dead. The electricity was still off. She went to the porch and sat down watching the darkness fall. She gazed across the gray field to the dark line of trees and felt cold, as if the warmth of the place had leaked away. Maybe it was release, the forest was letting her go. She had lost everything that mattered to her in a week. Once McCoy learned she had impersonated him, tenure would be out of the question. Her life here would be gone. Maybe her career as well. She had tried to save lives and lost everything, as Karl and Nick warned she would.

Nick. He said it all earlier at the hospital. *You cross lines you shouldn't cross. You throw your life away.* That's what she had done, wasted seven years waiting for him. First thing that morning, she thought maybe they had a chance, but that feeling went pretty fast. The man she knew was gone. She didn't much know this one and didn't much like him. And it didn't seem he knew her. If he thought she was behind this, he could keep on walking backward until he was gone.

Night fell, leaving a starless sky and dark shadows. The wind had stopped and the air was still. There was no sweet scent of jasmine, no chirping crickets and the night birds did not sing.

Dana finished her beer. From far away she heard the engine of a car. It seemed to grow louder. She heard the tires on the dirt road, then two headlights shining through the trees. A car door slammed.

She followed the barking dogs up the drive.

Michael. He emerged from a rental car. Dana saw the Hertz sign on the windshield before he cut the lights. By her side, Anthony snarled and Judy barked.

Michael used the door as a shield, crouching behind it. "Dana? Is this you? I have been lost."

"What are you doing here?"

"I was worried. When you did not show up last night."

Dana felt a pang of guilt when she remembered deserting Michael at the hospital and was glad there was no power and he couldn't see her face. She said, "How did you find my house?"

"Nick drew a map. For the FBI agent. Ackerman is convinced this is deliberate."

So Nick really was helping out the FBI.

"That Ackerman. What an ass," Michael said.

Dana's thoughts exactly. "Would you like to come in for a drink?"

He was worried about the dogs, and stood pressed between the door and the car. "Will they bite?"

Dana yelled at Anthony to quit barking. He was growling and looked ready to strike. Judy hid behind Dana's legs, shaking. "I'll put them in the car." Dana shut them in the Raider, where Anthony flung himself at the windshield and Judy yapped shrilly.

They went inside, she lit a candle and offered wine, forgetting he didn't drink. She found a box of apple juice, poured herself red wine and sat with him at the kitchen table.

"You have a nice house," he said. "You live here alone?"

Dana conceded she did.

"It's very secluded. No neighbors nearby?"

"Nope." She picked up her wineglass and took a sip. Red wine was supposed to be served at room temperature, but she liked her drinks cold. The wine left a sour taste in her mouth. She could almost taste the vinegar it would become. She put down the glass.

"And you are fine?" Michael said. "You didn't get sick?" He brushed the end of his moustache with a finger.

Dana shrugged. She wasn't going to give her competition any details. "Lucky I guess."

"There is no luck," Michael said. "God smiled upon you."

Hardly, Dana thought, as she threw back more bad wine.

He patted the breast pocket of his shirt. "Mind if I smoke?"

"Yes. You should quit."

Nevertheless, he took a package of Winstons from his pocket. He also removed a guitar string and a flashlight. The latter was small and purple, the kind given away free with batteries. He turned it over in his hand. "Ackerman is checking everyone. At the hospital, they are saying the strain is new and genetically engineered, that the outbreak is deliberate."

"What makes them think that?"

Michael yanked out a hair from his moustache. "Its resistance to antibiotics. Unbelievable. I should not tell you, but they find it strange you had the antidote."

"I'm not the only one." Dana was thinking of CK-202, the experimental drug from Houston. "Maybe God was smiling after all."

Michael frowned at her response, lifted his glass of apple juice and drank thirstily. His sleeve fell down his arm.

She saw the scratches on his forearm, three deep parallel crimson tracks that had not healed. He tugged at his sleeve, dropped his hand and covered the guitar string. In the silence, Dana heard Anthony howling and Judy's frantic bark. A strong gust of wind rattled the window. The candle flickered and nearly went out. Dana jumped up.

"What is wrong with those dogs?" Michael asked.

Dana went to the door. "I think I heard something." She opened the screen door.

Michael glided to the window. Crouched low, he peered out the glass. "I do not see anything."

Dana stepped onto the porch. She heard the screech of an owl. Her heart began to pound and her ears filled with blood. "Something's out there."

Chapter 53

After dinner Nick accompanied Ackerman to the basement morgue. The agent had received a fax from Quantico, which bore a grainy photograph of the terrorist sighted in Houston two weeks ago. Ackerman wanted the bodies checked. According to his latest theory, the terrorist was likely the first infected and therefore, presumably dead and in the morgue awaiting identification. They were looking for a slight man with dark hair, dark eyes and a mustache.

There weren't enough body bags and the dead were covered with sheets and laid out on the floor in a row. With his nose to his sleeve, Ackerman pulled back the sheets one by one. The air conditioning was functional, but to conserve generator power, the A.C. unit was turned on low and a rotting stench hung in the air. Holding his handkerchief over his nose, Nick examined the faces of the plague-infected dead.

Ackerman went down the row. There were twenty bodies, twenty black and bloated bodies with tight, screaming faces. Nick could have been one of those bodies, he knew.

He came that close. If not for Dana, he would have been in the morgue, on that floor.

Ackerman dropped the last sheet. "See anything?"

Nick shook his head. No face resembled the image in the photograph. And none of the dead men bore a mustache, though this could have, of course, been shaved.

"Shall we go through one more time?" Ackerman asked.

Nick had had enough. As far as he was concerned, if the man was in the morgue, he was no longer a concern. If he was out of the morgue, now they had the antidote, he was also no longer a concern. He told Ackerman as much.

"What's with you?" Ackerman said. "I don't get it. I thought you were supposed to be helping with this outbreak."

"I'm here, aren't I?" Nick said.

A few minutes later though, he was up on the roof, gulping clean, cool air. He stood on the edge of the parapet and looked over the city. The austral wind was blowing and the air was salty and wet. The sky was ridden with cirrocumulus clouds, scuttling fast. Occasionally a sweep of headlights illuminated the roadblock on the street below. Behind him, next to the satellite dish, Karl was talking on his cell phone.

Karl had lost faith in the FBI and was conducting a parallel investigation of his own. The first person he checked was Ackerman. He was disgusted that the FBI agent was trying to pin the outbreak on Dana. Karl thought Ackerman might be trying to take the heat off himself. And FBI agents were always whipping out their badges but who had ever seen Ackerman's badge?

A call to Quantico, however, verified the FBI agent was on staff and currently in Duane on assignment. Karl was now checking out McCoy.

Nick stared at racing clouds. Once again he was out of control. The loss of morphine had put him in withdrawal and his nerves were screaming. He couldn't wait to leave. In the morning he would get on the first plane and go. He was out of control. Earlier with Dana, he had behaved badly and was ashamed. He knew the sacrifice she made on his behalf and didn't want the responsibility of it. In the morning he would thank her for what she had done, apologize for what he had said and tell her goodbye. Then he would get the hell out.

Beside him Karl hung up the phone. "I got someone at the Pentagon. McCoy's a general all right."

Nick had already told Karl he was wasting his time. Nick believed any terrorist would have been long gone. Who would unleash an agent of biological war and wait around to get sick? Especially a bacterium of this virulence. There were only a very few who didn't get sick. A doctor, two nurses, Nellie, Sheryl and Dana. Sheryl must have injected Dana with the monoclonal, for Nick doubted if Dana could have done it herself.

There were a few who got sick but recovered quickly. Himself, Penny, Jack and Michael Smith. Dana had injected them all. *Even Michael Smith*? Would she do that? Why?

"What do we have on Michael?" Nick said. Karl flipped through his notes. "Ackerman called his university in Iowa. Michael Smith is on the faculty, but Ackerman couldn't talk to him. He wasn't there."

"How could he be? He's here."

Karl read on. "Michael's daughter was in a motorbike accident and he was at the hospital." Karl looked up from his notepad. "Ackerman thought it was a story. Michael didn't tell the university he was looking for a job."

Wait a minute. Nick recalled photos of Michael's twins. Weren't they babies? They couldn't ride a motorbike. Though he could have an older daughter. But how old would that make Michael? Nick didn't think he was more than thirty. Then Nick thought of something else that made the hair on the back of his neck stand up.

"Give me the phone," he said.

He punched in Dana's number. Silence. The phone didn't ring. The line was dead. "It's Michael," he said. Michael had been in the bathroom and had seen the map to Dana's house. Nick threw the phone at Karl. "He's at Dana's."

Nick ran for the stairs and heard Wheeler again: *I turned my back, and closed my eyes so not to see, the demons at your door.*

Down four flights of stairs, in the dark parking lot, Karl searched for his car keys, turning his pockets inside out.

"Hurry up," Nick said. "Hurry up."

"The keys are gone." Then Karl pointed to an empty slot in the crowded lot. "So's the car."

Chapter 54

Dana had lied; there was no one outside. She had heard nothing but the howling dogs, trying to warn her of the danger she hadn't seen. She was running from Michael, Michael with the scratches on his arms that were too vicious and deep to be caused by a vine. He had been clawed by poor Pumpkin, killed by a disease that Dana assumed was innocently transmitted. She had envisaged a traveler coming from the Panhandle and stopping in town to have a burger and the car washed before moving on. But in truth there was no hungry traveler. This was no accident. The outbreak *was* intentional, and the man who deliberately started it was here in her house The electricity was out, her phone was dead, and the closest neighbor was a mile down the road. She was alone.

"What is it?" Michael stood next to her. "I do not see anything."

Dana walked to the edge of the porch, staring up the driveway. "I thought I heard something." The bawling of the dogs was louder now. They were her only hope; Michael was terrified of them.

He was beside her. "It is only the animals. Let us go inside." He held the screen door open for her.

A voice in her head screamed: *Run, Run, Run*.

She ran. Leapt across the stairs, up the drive.

The floorboards on the porch creaked behind her.
Michael yelling something in a foreign tongue. *"Bara
nek!"*

A shadow passed overhead and Dana screamed as
Michael took a flying dive from the porch and tackled her
to the ground. He grabbed her arm and yanked her up.
Dragged her up the steps to the porch. The veins in his
forearm bulged like cords. He was stronger than he looked.
He towed her across the porch, kicked open the door,
pulled her in the house, slammed the door, lifted the chain
and locked them inside. "Sit."

She did as he said. Sat at the table, in the eerie orange
candlelight and watched as he lit a cigarette off the flame.
She felt surprisingly calm and was shocked by her reaction. Her heart was barely beating. She was alert, on edge,
not freaked out or frightened. Her thoughts were focused,
loud, distinct and clear.

Car keys. She needed her car keys. She would not get
out without them. Where were they? Briefcase? Jeans? No,
there, in the living room, on top of the TV. She had to get
past Michael to get them and get out.

He was in good shape for someone who smoked so
much and who was recently sick. He was hardly breathing.
And after what he had done, he would be desperate.

She needed her keys. Michael blew smoke at the ceiling.
"What will I do? You know too much. You will tell them
everything." In the candlelight, his eyes glittered brightly.

"Where did you find the cat?" she said.

He sucked on his cigarette, contemplating the smoke. "I
took it. Two weeks ago. Injected it. Bastard scratched the
hell out of me."

That's what he cared about? Little scratches? "You

killed people. You almost killed yourself. I saw you last night. Puking your guts out, hardly able to stand. I should have handed you to the police then."

He threw back his head and laughed at the ceiling.

His response made her angry. "I met the old man you killed first. He worked all his life to take a trip and when the time finally came, he didn't live long enough to take it. Because of you."

Michael stopped laughing long enough to say, "What is the word for it? Bloody heart?"

"I think the word is murder. You almost killed a baby. My godchild. Don't call me a bleeding heart. What if it was one of your kids?"

"Enough." He pounded the table hard. "It is a dangerous world." He got up and from the dish drainer, grabbed a plate and crushed his cigarette into it.

Dana turned in her chair. "Why did you do it?"

"To let you know." He checked his flashlight, turned it on and off, then on again. "We have weapons too. As deadly as yours."

"Where did you get the bacteria?"

"We bought it." He lit another cigarette.

"Are you Russian?"

"No." Michael threw open a cupboard. "I am starving. What do you have to eat?"

"Not much. Tuna?"

"Fish in a can." He made a spitting noise, swung his flashlight through a cupboard. "What else?" He grabbed a can of Alpo from the shelf. "Lamb chunks," Michael said. "Now here is something."

She stared at him. "There's a can opener in the first drawer."

He directed the flashlight in the drawer. She heard the dogs again. She had to get out. Help was her dogs, shut in the car, crying themselves hoarse in a warning she had not heard. Michael might have the light, but this was her place, she knew the terrain. Her dogs were in the car; she'd drive to the hospital. There were police at the door. She just had to get out. All she needed were a few seconds to get to her car. And her keys.

Michael had the can opener. She watched his arm working as he turned the knob on the opener. "Knife?"

She pointed to the utensil drawer. A stupid response. He pulled out her sharpest knife and ran his thumb along the blade. A thin line of blood beaded on his skin. He dropped the knife. Turned on the tap. Dry.

"Water. I need water." He looked at his thumb with horror.

She stood up. "I've got a napkin."

"Sit down," he screamed. He grabbed a towel from the counter and wiped his thumb.

She watched in silence. He was insane, sulking about a drop of blood after he injected a cat with bacteria that could kill thousands. She had to get out.

"Bread?" he asked.

She pointed to the cupboard. "Crackers. They're a little stale."

He carried a box of garlic flavored Triscuits to the table and sat down. With her sharpest knife he speared a chunk of Alpo and shoved it in his mouth. "Mm, great." He chewed with his mouth wide open.

She looked at the table. He was a heavy smoker—in a race, who would win? Was she fast enough to get to the car? Would the dogs protect her? If Michael charged would Anthony attack?

Michael smeared Alpo across a cracker and popped it in his mouth. Brown sludge trickled down his chin. The candlelight flickered on the walls. She would distract him. Get him talking, and somehow get around him. The TV with her keys was just past the door. She could grab the keys, slip the chain. Get out.

"So, *do* you work in Iowa?"

He chewed loudly, like a cow. No West Point manners, no manners at all. "Of course not," he said contemptuously.

"Where did you meet McCoy?"

"At the department. He saw me looking at the job board and asked if he could help me. And he did."

"Why did he think you were a scientist?"

"My C.V."

"*Are* you a scientist?"

Michael sneered and spread another cracker. He didn't answer.

"You injected the cat. Then what?"

Talking with his mouth open, Michael said, "I waited. There was no news. I thought I had failed. Then, the old man got sick and I knew the plan worked. I did not know the cat was hit by a car, that a good Samaritan took it to the doctor. You Americans and your pets. They are treated better than most people in my country. We are bombed and the world turns their back."

Was he from Somalia? A light-skinned Arab? But the timing didn't work. The country had to be bombed after the cat was injected. She asked again. "What is your country?"

"It does not matter."

"And that story about your wife and twins?" she asked. "Did you make that up?"

He pointed the knife at her. "That was true."

He had a wife and babies to live for. A reason to stop now, not go any further. "Where is your family?"

He used the rim of the can to clean the knife blade. "Dead." He reached for his cigarettes.

Dana felt her heart freeze.

Michael leaned into the flickering candle. It was burning down, the wax running out. He inhaled sharply. "Your president blew them up when he bombed my neighborhood. I was at work. My family was killed. Their bodies burned to black tar. My wife's head was identified by her teeth. We never found her body. My daughters had no teeth."

Sweat rolled down Dana's side from under her arms. "I'm sorry."

Michael impassively blew smoke rings. They drifted across the table in front of her. He had Alpo caught in his teeth. He pointed his cigarette at her. "It is over now. What do you say? Do not cry over spoiled milk? It could not be changed. It was fate. It had to be. Same as here."

There was a time Dana believed in coincidences that were meaningful, but not any more. "What happened here wasn't fate. It was *you*."

"It had to happen."

"I don't believe that."

"Whether you believe it or not, makes no difference. It is true." Michael said.

"This wouldn't have happened without you. *You* did it. All those people died—"

He banged his fist on the table. "There was a plan greater than ours. Nothing went the way it was supposed to. We did not know the bacteria were so bad. We did not know it would spread so fast, that the town would close and I would be stuck. That the antidote would not be strong enough and I would be sick. That you would have one better. This was not our plan. There was another plan at work."

We. He wasn't working alone. Who was *"we"*?

Michael tapped his ash on the plate. "It is one thing to watch something happen a long way away, but another to be in the middle. To listen to grown men cry. To hear someone beg for help and realize it is you."

"But you recovered," she said.

"We had the cure of course. It took more than we thought. Much more. You had a cure too. That was not a part of the plan."

The candle flickered and died then and the room went dark. Michael snapped on the flashlight. "Get a candle."

There was a package on top of the fridge. Dana stood up and began pulling out kitchen drawers. "I can't see."

He passed her the flashlight.

Now she had the light. Bad move for him. "I think they're in the living room."

"Go."

She went past the door and held her breath as she walked behind him. He reached up and grabbed her wrist and squeezed it hard. "Quickly."

She passed him, wondering if he could hear her heart knocking against her ribs. The flashlight beam was shaking on the floor. Her breaths were sharp, short gasps. The adrenaline she needed to run had come.

She walked past the door, one, two steps, to the TV. Her car keys were on top. She grabbed them as she affected to peer behind the TV. She could undo the chain, twist the knob on the door, lock him inside. Buy herself a few seconds of time.

But she stood frozen. What if she couldn't make it? What if he caught her? He had her sharpest knife with Alpo stuck between its serrated teeth. He could stab her to death. He had his wire. A guitar string or garrote? What if he had a gun? What if he had more bacteria? What if he tried to inject her? Could her immune system stand such an assault? She suddenly felt weak and couldn't possibly run.

Go. The word rang like an order that could not be denied.

She went. Lifted the chain, opened the door, turned the knob to lock, slammed the door, sailed across the porch.

Inside, the door handle rattled and Michael was screaming in tongues. *"Zub ur omak."*

She tore up the driveway. Anthony was howling, forepaws up on the dashboard. The windshield fogged with his breath. She cut the light.

Behind her thudding footsteps. Michael was out. Ahead the car was tilting. Tires sunk in the mud? She reached the car. Saw the tire. *Flat.* She unlocked the door.

The dogs tumbled out.

Michael came bolting up the slope.

She took off up the driveway with the dogs by her heels. Her only hope now was her neighbor. She hit the dirt road running, nearly tripping over Judy, too close to her feet. Anthony surged ahead, no interest in Michael now.

She sped up, her arms pumping, legs flying. Both dogs ahead, and the house of her neighbor a dark shadow up at the curve of the road. No lights. Small pebbles and stones flew under her feet as she sped across the pitted road.

He was gaining on her, she could feel his advance, hear his loud breathing.

She scanned Gunther's house. No pickup in the drive. Was he home? Out of candles? Or sick? At the hospital? Was the pickup in the garage? If she checked, she'd be trapped. *Run, run, run.* The trees seemed to call her. She would go to the woods, use the darkness to hide.

Michael was coming closer. A kicked pebble ricocheted off the back of her calf. She felt the fall of his hand on her shoulder and cried out, lunged forward in a spurt. She'd never get away, he was too fast, too close. Close enough to smell the garlic on his breath. Hear his words.

"Allah el akbar."

He came again. His hand slapped her shoulder and fell. Now a grasp for her hair. It slipped through his fingers.

Without breaking stride she whistled for Anthony. No air in her lungs for a whistle. "Anthony," she cried, as the hand seized a clump of hair and yanked back her head.

Up ahead, Anthony turned. The white stripe of his nose and whites of his eyes flashed. He galloped toward her.

Michael gasped and Dana jerked her head and broke free. She scrambled forward as the headlights of a car brightened the road to her left. Gunther's pickup? The *"we"* working with Michael?

The car turned on her road. Lights too low for a pickup. She was trapped, with the car in front and Michael behind.

She veered to the right, leaped across a ditch and scrambled across a field, toward the shadows and the trees.

Behind her brakes squealed and headlights lit the night. She ran faster through the field, feet barely touching the ground, heart on fire, air gone from her lungs as she stumbled across the soft marshy ground, dogs by her side.

They were coming. Coming closer, someone new, she could hear easy breathing, water splashing, muck gurgling, branches snapping. She hit the forest, dodging tree trunks and bushes as smilax grabbed at her clothes. Ahead the brambles were thick and the brush blocked the path. Anthony stopped and Judy ran into him, crying as she rolled. Behind her, Dana heard a rush of air and her name and a scream as she went down.

Chapter 55

Dana sank into the mud. A shadow passed over her and she closed her eyes and the world went dark. She heard loud screams that she wished would stop. When she held her breath they did.

"Dana, look at me. Open your eyes. It's me."

She opened one eye. Nick, down in a crouch beside her. Anthony, nose in his groin. Dana opened her other eye.

Nick brushed hair out of her eyes. "It's okay, you're all right." He paused. "Are you?"

She shuddered, gulping air. Her heart was jumping, her throat ached, and her mouth was dry. She hugged Judy to her and tried to catch her breath.

Ahead on the road, two headlights shone. In the bright light, Dana saw Ackerman wrench Michael's hands behind his back and slip on handcuffs.

Dana straightened and stood up, but her legs were weaker than she thought and she lost her footing. Nick steadied her with his hand.

"He stole Karl's car," Nick said, as they walked across the marshy field toward the road.

Ahead, Ackerman helped Michael into the car and slammed the door. Michael disappeared into the darkness. Ackerman, tall and spindly, leaned against the car, arms folded at his chest. Before they reached the road he was already asking questions. "What happened? What did he say? Who is he?"

Last time she had seen him, he was waving a syringe and slinging accusations. What had he done with her clothes? And he expected answers? She made up her mind not to tell him a thing. "Michael Smith."

"No, he's not," Nick said. "The real Michael Smith is in Iowa."

"Who is this guy?" Dana said.

"Hello?" Ackerman stuck his face in hers. "That was my question."

"I don't know," Dana said.

Ackerman threw open the front door of the car. "I need you to make a statement, Ms. Sparks. Come with me, please."

The interior light shone down on Michael, head resting on his knees. She shook her head.

"It's not a request," Ackerman said. "We need to know what happened here." He smiled a crocodile smile. "The man is a cold-blooded assassin. A terrorist."

"I thought that was me."

"Look, I was doing my job." Ackerman reached in his pocket and pulled out the garrote. He snapped it between his fingers, pulled it tight. "You're lucky to be alive. You owe him nothing. He's a killer."

She looked at Michael, hunched over in the car. He never intended to kill her. He had been close enough to strangle her if he wanted.

"He's a victim too. The U.S. bombed his house and killed his babies and his wife."

Ackerman's eyes gleamed and he leaned down, his face

in hers. "Who's he working with? What were his goals? What did he hope to achieve? *Jihad?*"

The rapid fire of questions again. "Ask him," Dana said. "You bomb his town, he bombs yours. When does it stop?"

"Dana, not now." Nick spoke in a low, warning tone. He turned to Ackerman, "Barry, she's tired. Can't we leave this for later?"

"I need a statement."

Nick argued on her behalf. Ackerman had his suspect and it was late. Dana could make a statement in the morning.

Though Ackerman argued stridently for an immediate statement while memories were fresh, she wouldn't budge. "I can force you," he said. But in the end he chose not to. "All right. Tomorrow. First thing." He tossed Nick a set of keys. "Follow me back."

Ackerman jumped in his car and drove off in a burst of flying pebbles.

Dana and Nick stood in the road and watched the headlights disappear. The night closed in around them.

Dana shoved her hands in her pockets. Her heart had finally stopped racing and she felt exhausted, too tired to deal with Nick, ennui settling in like the night.

"I should get the car," Nick said, jingling the car keys in his hand.

They turned and walked quietly down the dirt road toward her driveway. Dana gazed at the stars. The moon was full, winking in and out of the clouds. Judy kept close to her, intermittently bumping her calf. Nick was shuffling, kicking stones that Anthony chased. He was humming softly and Dana held her breath to listen to the tune. She couldn't make out the song, but it wasn't a happy one.

Mercifully, he stopped singing.

A few minutes later Nick broke the silence and said, "The twins gave Michael away. He used details of his own life instead of the real Michael's life."

She slowed down, caught the sweet scent of jasmine and looked for the vine, but couldn't see it. "I should have known. I saw the scars on his forearm a week ago."

"Scars?" Nick looked at her, his pupils large and bright in the moonlight.

She looked away from him. In a bigger reality, he was far away. "He was scratched by a cat that he stole and injected."

Nick stopped walking.

Dana explained. "A cat by the name of Pumpkin, owned by the eleven-year-old you saw at the hospital, whom you described as not so lucid. The cat was hit by a car and Jack's roommate brought it to the vet school. Tim worked on it. At some point the cat developed pneumonic plague and infected Tim. Tim infected Penny and the people at the hotel."

Nick ran his fingers through his hair. "How did you figure it out?"

"I went to the epicenter. The car wash. Jack took his roommate's car to get it washed. The cat must have left behind infected fleas. They bit Jack, the car wash attendant and Dudley. Infected fleas must have been vacuumed and ended up in the dumpster, where they infected Carol's rats."

Nick clucked his teeth. "And me?"

"Frank after all. He had it, too. The antibody test was negative because he was on the immunosuppressant. But his blood tested positive for the bacteria."

Nick rubbed his cheek and his shaving cut. He made congratulatory noises, but she was numb to his praise. Regardless of what really happened, he had blamed her.

They started walking again, reached her drive and turned. The clouds were gone and the puddles on the road were tinged with silver. They reached Karl's car.

Nick looked up at the sky. He opened his mouth and then closed it again. He looked nervous and uncomfortable. "Before I go, I should say thank you. I'm glad you did what you did. I owe you my life."

Dana looked him in the eye. "Did you really think I did this?"

Nick looked down and kicked a pebble on the road. "Of course not. I know you. I know you couldn't do it." His eyes met hers and he stared at her for a moment.

She looked at the forest, fatigue leaving. She felt bad for having doubts, for believing the worst about him, for rejecting what she knew in her heart was real.

He opened the car door. "I should go."

Don't go, she said to herself, but to Nick, nothing.

"Ackerman will be waiting."

"Count on it."

"I should tell Karl what happened."

"He'll want to know. Where is he?"

"He finally got a call through to Atlanta." Nick bent down to get into the car.

Dana felt herself sinking into the mud. Maybe he was already too far away to come back. His heart was gone; his body had only to follow.

Then he straightened again, peering at her car, scouching down a little. "You have a flat."

"I know."

He had to change it. He couldn't leave her in the country without a phone, no electricity and no car.

Her protests were useless.

He cranked the headlights of Karl's car to get more light, then took the jack and the lug wrench from the Raider. He crawled under the car to position the jack. He lay on his back, kicking mud off the flap.

She smelled jasmine again and saw the vine with white flowers entwined on a bush. She picked off a sprig and tucked the stem behind her ear. She inhaled the scent with each breath she took.

Nick was on his feet and jacking up the car. The jack creaked as the car rose. He lifted off the flat and dropped it before her.

Apropos to nothing he said, "Why did you think I thought this was your fault? After all that you did. All the lives that you saved."

"It wasn't so many."

"Hundreds. Thousands."

"Three. You, Jack and Penny."

Nick stubbed the spare with his toe. "Dana, we used your monoclonal antibody. The experimental drug C.K.-two-oh-two turned out to be useless. If it weren't for you, all those people would be dead: Tim, Karl, even McCoy's wife and daughter. I said we'd never use your monoclonal, but we did."

It took a moment for this to sink in. *The vaccine was used after all?* "How did it work? Any side effects? Cross-reactions? Allergic responses? Respiratory infections?"

Nick laughed at her questions, the whites of his eyes bright. "No side effects reported. It was fabulous."

She inhaled jasmine and turned his words over in her mind. All this time she assumed the experimental antibi-otic had been used, but it was her vaccine. Used on hun-dreds, thousands, without ill effect. Humans weren't big guinea pigs after all. *The vaccine was safe; it was safe.* A rush of relief surged through her blood.

Nick bent down and grabbed the spare, positioning it in place. He screwed the nuts on by hand, then tightened them with the spanner. He hummed while he worked and Dana knew the words of the Robin Wheeler song: *Let it go, babe, release me, let it go.*

Nick threw the spanner down. "Done." He collected the tools and tossed them in the back of her car. Once more, he said he should go.

Dana saw a falling star and made a new wish. "Would you like a glass of wine?"

"I really should get back."

Her wish unanswered. "Don't go." This time, the words spoken out loud. "Stay. For a while."

He exhaled loudly. "I'd like to, but I can't."

"Why not?"

"We live in two different places."

"We could figure something out."

"It's better this way."

"It's not."

"I have my work. You have yours."

"It's not enough."

"It has to be."

He was wrong, but what could she say to change his mind? How could she reach him? Her mind was blank, filled with the cloying scent of the flower. She tore it from her hair.

"This is for you. When it dies, you can think of me." She pressed it in his hand.

He made a choking sound in his throat and she could almost feel his indecision, he didn't want to go, but something called him away that was stronger than she.

He slammed the back door closed, then squinted, peering at her windshield. "What does it say?"

She stepped out of the glare of the headlights and saw what Becker had written in the mud: D & N with a heart around the names.

"Did you write that?" Nick said.

"Someone did."

He shook his head. The flower fell from his hand to the mud.

His shoelace was undone, muck on his boat shoes. The last time she pointed out his trailing laces, he had walked away. A long time ago, when she tied them, he had stayed. This was one of those branch points; he could go either way. Dana made another wish and bent down, one knee cold and wet in the sloppy ground. She took the two muddy ends of his laces and made a double knot that would not come undone.

She looked up. He raised his arm, and with a sweep of his hand, drew a line through the heart, as if to negate it. He would tell her later that he considered drawing an X— blotting out the past and leaving as he wanted, as his mind told him to do—but another part of him held sway, and on his line he drew not the cross of the X, but the point of an arrow. Then he held out his hand, helped her stand and pulled her close. His face in hers, his eyes wide open and big enough to let her in.

Around them the night was alive, the branches waving in the woods, a whippoorwill calling. The sky was twinkling, bright with stars. They were low in the sky, reflecting off the puddles pooled in the grass and shining from his eyes, as the moonlight shone down.

Friday

Chapter 56

In the early morning, Dana watched the stars slowly disappear from the sky. Out the window at the horizon, a band of gold lit up the trees. She listened for the first bird to start to sing. It was a happy song. She tried to remember her dreams and could not, but perhaps she was still dreaming. Nick was back in her bed.

He started in his sleep, his eyelids fluttering, breath catching, hold tightening. She kissed his cheek and his lips and, as the night left off, a new day began with a slow making of love as the sun filled the sky.

And later, Nick slept as he would, his length by her side. His sweat shone on her skin; his stubble burned on her cheeks; his heart beat against her breast. The parts, together and whole.

No, more than whole, the pieces didn't equal the sum; there was something else. She felt it last night, in the air, more than the songs and the wine and the moonlight shining down. Nothing she could see, but in her heart she knew the magic was real.

Dana closed her eyes and hummed to herself. She didn't

know the words, but the melody was distinct. This morning everything seemed explicit, the world had changed. Everything was lucid; nothing seemed as it was, though nothing was different. But things seemed sharper, more defined, as if there was something vital in the empty space that made things more clear.

Outside, birds sang; the singer slept. A car door slammed and dogs barked. Nick woke, throwing his arm over his eyes. "Shit."

Dana leapt up, pulled on a sundress and left the room. Through the front picture window she saw McCoy on the porch, standing straight and impeccable in his military uniform. She flung open the door and the dogs roared out. She stepped outside.

"You didn't show up for work and we came to see if all was well," McCoy said. "Ackerman said you had trouble last night."

She stood there staring, as Nick, barefooted, came out.

The men shook hands. Nellie came tottering around the corner, walking carefully in high spiked heels. She climbed the steps. Despite the heat, she wore a three-piece suit and a tie. Her hair was neatly flipped.

"We heard about that horrible, horrible man," she said, cringing at Nick. She shivered outwardly. "What a man. I always knew there was something not quite right about him."

McCoy's bright face clouded. "I should have realized it sooner."

"You stopped him," Nellie said. "That's the important thing."

"We're fortunate the town is open," McCoy said. "The state of emergency is over. And the VP is on his way."

Dana noticed McCoy's face was beaming. "You're kidding," she said.

"I don't kid," McCoy replied with good humor. "The fund-raisers will proceed as planned. Our man won't let us down. He'll stand up to this terrorist attack."

Now that it's over, Dana thought.

McCoy looked at her. "What was that?"

Had she spoken aloud? She caught Nick's frown. "Ah, nothing," she said.

"The VP lands in an hour," McCoy continued undaunted. "Karl will inject him with the monoclonal." McCoy held up his hands, fingers framing an invisible picture. "Do you think the headline, 'VP GETS SHOT' is too sensational?"

Nellie laughed out loud. "Ooh, I like it."

"The caption's misleading," Dana said.

"Yes, Dr. Sparks, perhaps, you are right." McCoy paused. "By the way, I talked to General Shwartzke this morning."

Dana gulped.

"He called to applaud my order to use the experimental monoclonal antibody."

"Sir, you saved numerous lives," Nellie said. "Your timing was impeccable."

McCoy shrugged. "Sometimes I surprise even myself."

Nellie clapped her hands in delight. "The dean is so pleased. It was a brilliant call," she said. "Just brilliant. You diffused an explosive situation. You saved the VP's trip. Sir, might I say, you saved the town."

"I wouldn't go that far." McCoy smoothed down the sleeve of his crisp army jacket and stared at Dana once more. "No guts, no glory, eh, Dr. Sparks?"

She didn't know what to say. Beside her, Nick was humming. Nellie cleared her throat and had a sudden urge to use the bathroom. Hardly able to refuse, Dana pointed to the house. Nellie wobbled inside, the screen door banging behind her. Dana saw her wander into the living room. It was a mess: half-empty wineglasses, candle stubs and various articles of clothing strewn on the floor.

"One thing puzzles me," McCoy said.

Dana turned her attention from the house. McCoy's gray

eyes were fixed upon her. "Dr. Taversham looked at your blood. Something doesn't add up. You have antibodies in your blood that are similar to, but distinct from, the mono-clonal antibody."

"How are they different?"

"The plague antibodies in your blood have a much higher affinity for the bacteria than the monoclonal. How can you explain that?" He stared into her eyes.

"Hmm," she wondered aloud.

"An effect of previous vaccines," Nick offered. "Individual variability, exposure-affinity enhancement, experimental error."

Dana listened to his preposterous explanations, mouth agape.

McCoy rubbed his forehead, furrowed in puzzlement. "Ackerman wanted more of your blood, but it was all gone."

Nick took a step toward McCoy. "It was given to the sickest patients. You, for instance."

McCoy nodded thoughtfully. "Taversham admitted grave doubts about whether I would have made it through the night without the transfusion."

"They took two pints of blood," Nick said. "She shouldn't give more, not any time soon."

Dana smiled despite herself. She appreciated having Nick clearly and unambiguously on her side, present and connected.

"Anyhow, Ackerman is gone," McCoy said. "Called to Washington for consultations. And what's done is done. Some mysteries are best left in the dark." He was smiling again, his easygoing tone restored.

"He said he would be back." Nellie had returned. "He wants to get to the bottom of this." Her eyes twinkled brightly.

McCoy ignored her. "The general informed me the proposal was approved, Dr. Sparks. Phase Two can begin when I send your letter of support. I told him it was in the mail." McCoy held out his hand. "If you were to accept, I am confident that tenure would be yours."

Dana stared at his hand as the morning heat swirled around her. It was over; this was it. He was going to let it go and she would have her promotion and her job. She offered her hand and held it in his.

"I owe you an apology," he said. "We made a critical error in calling the suspect."

"Yes," Dana said.

Beside her, Nick examined his nails and cleared his throat.

She glanced at McCoy. "I'm sorry too. About your heart attack. About everything."

McCoy rocked on the soles of his feet, grinning. Dana had never seen him so easygoing, or happy before. "The past is past and we can't stand here gabbing all day. The VP is coming and we've got to meet his plane. Nick, see you there at oh-nine hundred?"

Nick cleared his throat again, cocked his head at McCoy.

"And Dana, too, of course," McCoy added. "You'll come to the airport, won't you?"

It was not an order, but a request. "I think I can make it. TJ."

They left and Dana and Nick were alone. From the forest, leaves waved. Around them the grass was bright, wild azaleas were blooming and the morning glories were turned to the sun.

ISOLATION
CHRISTOPHER BELTON

It was specially designed to kill. It's a biologically engineered bacterium that at its onset produces symptoms similar to the flu. But this is no flu. This bacterium spreads a form of meningitis that is particularly contagious—and over 80% fatal within four days. Now the disease is spreading like wildfire. There is no known cure. Only death.

Peter Bryant is an American working at the Tokyo-based pharmaceutical company that developed the deadly bacterium. Bryant becomes caught between two governments and enmeshed in a web of secrecy and murder. With the Japanese government teetering on the brink of collapse and the lives of millions hanging in the balance, only Bryant can uncover the truth. But can he do it in time?

THE
CRIMINALIST
WILLIAM RELLING JR.

Detective Rachel Siegel is a twelve-year veteran of the San Patricio Sheriff's Department. But she's never seen anything like the handiwork of the Pied Piper, the vicious serial killer who's been terrifying that part of California for months. Because she's the best at what she does, it's now her job to catch this maniac—but she has very personal reasons, too, for wanting him stopped

Kenneth Bennett works for the Department of Neuropsychiatry at St. Louis's Washington University. There's something special about the Pied Piper case that draws Bennett almost against his will to the west coast. He has no choice but to help Siegel in her frantic search—even if it gets both of them killed in the process.

BODY PARTS
VICKI STIEFEL

They call it the Grief Shop. It's the Office of the Chief Medical Examiner for Massachusetts, and Tally Whyte is the director of its Grief Assistance Program. She lives with death every day, counseling families of homicide victims. But now death is striking close to home. In fact, the next death Tally deals with may be her own.

Boston is in the grip of a serial killer known as the Harvester, due to his fondness for keeping bloody souvenirs of his victims. But many of those victims are people that Tally knew, through her work or as friends. Tally realizes there's a connection, a link that only she can find. But she'd better find it fast. The Harvester is getting closer.

ANDREW HARPER

RED ANGEL

The Darden State Hospital for the Criminally Insane holds hundreds of dangerous criminals. Trey Campbell works in the psych wing of Ward D, home to the most violent murderers, where he finds a young man who is in communication with a serial killer who has just begun terrorizing Southern California—a killer known only as the Red Angel.

Campbell has 24 hours to find the Red Angel and face the terror at the heart of a human monster. To do so, he must trust the only one who can provide information—Michael Scoleri, a psychotic murderer himself, who may be the only link to the elusive and cunning Red Angel. Will it take a killer to catch a killer?

JOEL ROSS
EYE FOR AN EYE

Suzanne "Scorch" Amerce was an honor student before her sister was murdered by a female street gang. Scorch hit the streets on a rampage that almost annihilated the gang, but it got her arrested and sent away. That was eight years ago. Now Scorch has escaped. The leader of the gang is still alive and Scorch wants to change that.

The one man who might be able to find Scorch and stop her bloodthirsty hunt is Eric, her prison therapist. Will he be able to stand by and let Scorch exact her deadly vengeance? Or will he risk his life to side with the detective who needs so badly to bring Scorch back in? Either way, lives hang in the balance. And Eric knows he has to decide soon. . . .